GRAND SLAM FOR MISS MAPP

The first bid to upset Miss Mapp's social position and emotional state came in the disturbingly masculine forms of two very different retired army officers—both of whom were anything but retiring in their conflicting claims upon her heart.

The second menace to Miss Mapp took the elegant and insidiously evil shape of a ravishing Contessa possessed of dazzling charm and diabolical designs.

Tea cups rattled, the whole town trembled, and even Miss Mapp's pulse began to pound as she played her last desperate trumps in the most dangerous game of her life . . .

MAKE WAY FOR LUCIA is—or soon will be—available from Popular Library in six volumes.

* Though the character "Lucia" does not appear in the novel MISS MAPP, nevertheless MISS MAPP has always been known as a "Lucia" novel and is, in fact, volume III in the series. Mapp is furious.

MISS MAPP

MAKE WAY FOR LUCIA · III
MISS MAPP
by E. F. Benson

Foreword by Nancy Mitford

POPULAR LIBRARY • NEW YORK

Published by Popular Library, a unit of CBS Publications,
the Consumer Publishing Division of CBS Inc.,
by arrangement with Thomas Y. Crowell Company, Inc.

April, 1978

Library of Congress Catalog Card Number: 76-783

ISBN: 0-445-04207-9

FOREWORD
by Nancy Mitford

At long last, here she is again, the splendid creature, the great, the wonderful, Lucia. What rejoicing there will be among the Luciaphils! Those of us who lost her chronicles during the war and have never, by Clique, by barrow or by theft, been able to replace them, now find ourselves armed against misfortune once again; when life becomes too much for us we shall be able to take refuge in the *giardino segretto*. The publishers, in reprinting Miss Mapp (and by degrees, the whole saga) have deserved well of all who like to laugh.

Lucia (Mrs. Emmeline Lucas) is a forceful lady who lives in the South of England in two small country towns —that is, when we meet her first, in the late Twenties, she is the Queen of Riseholme, but half way through her story (which ends just before the war) she transfers, presumably so that her creator can pit her against the formidable Miss Mapp, to Tilling. Tilling, I believe, is Rye, where E. F. Benson himself lived in the house formerly occupied by Henry James; this is the very house which Lucia finally worms out of Miss Mapp.

Lucia's neighbours in both towns are almost all, like herself, middle-aged people of comfortable means. Their occupations are housekeeping, at which most of them are skilled (there is a good deal about food in the books, and lobster à la Riseholme plays an important part), gardening, golf, bridge and bickering. None of them could be described as estimable, and they are certainly not very interesting, yet they are fascinated by each other and we are fascinated by them.

All this fascination is generated by Lucia; it is what happens with regard to her that counts; she is the centre and the driving force of her little world. As she is a profoundly irritating person, bossy, horribly energetic and pushing, the others groan beneath her yoke and occasionally try to shake it off: but in their heart of hearts they know it is she who keeps them going and that life without her would be drab indeed.

The art of these books lies in their simplicity. The jokes seem quite obvious and are often repeated: we can never have enough of them. In *Lucia in London*, Daisy gets a ouija board and makes mystical contact with an Egyptian called Abfou. Now Abfou hardly ever says anything but "Lucia is a snob," yet we hang on his lips and are thrilled every time Georgie says, "I am going to Daisy's, to weedj." Georgie is the local bachelor who passes for Lucia's lover. Then there is the Italian with which Lucia and Georgie pepper their conversation: "Tacete un momento, Georgie. Le domestiche." It never, never palls. On at least two occasions an Italian turns up and then we learn that Lucia and Georgino mio don't really know the language at all; the second time is as funny as the first.

I must say I reopened these magic books after some thirty years with misgivings; I feared that they would have worn badly and seem dated. Not at all; they are as fresh as paint. The characters are real and therefore timeless; the surprising few differences between that pre-war world and its equivalent today only add to the interest. Money of course is one of them—the characters speak of £2,000 as we would of £20,000. At least two people have Rolls-Royces; everybody has *domestiche*. When listening-in begins, Lucia refuses to have a wireless until Olga, a prima donna whom she reveres, owns to having one and listens-in to Cortot on it. None of them ever thinks of going abroad. When Lucia and Georgie want to get away from Riseholme for a little change they take houses at Tilling for the summer; that is what leads to them settling there.

But the chief difference is that, in Lucia's words, "that horrid thing which Freud calls sex" is utterly ignored. No writer nowadays could allow Georgie to do his embroidery and dye his hair and wear his little cape and sit for hours chatting with Lucia or playing celestial Mozartino, without hinting at Boys in the background. Quaint Irene, in her fisherman's jersey and knickerbockers, would certainly share her house with another lesbian and this word would be used.

There are no children in the books—"Children are so sticky," says Georgie, "specially after tea."

I was a fellow guest, at Highcliffe, with Mr. E. F. Benson soon after Lucia had become Mayor of Tilling. We talked of her for hours and he said, "What must she do now?" Alas, he died in the first year of the war; can we doubt that if he had lived Lucia would have become a General?

1

MISS ELIZABETH MAPP might have been forty, and she had taken advantage of this opportunity by being just a year or two older. Her face was of high vivid color and corrugated by chronic rage and curiosity; but these vivifying emotions had preserved to her an astonishing activity of mind and body, which fully accounted for the comparative adolescence with which she would have been credited anywhere except in the charming little town which she had inhabited so long. Anger and the gravest suspicions about everybody had kept her young and on the boil.

She sat, on this hot July morning, like a large bird of prey at the very convenient window of her garden room, the ample bow of which formed a strategical point of high value. This garden room, solid and spacious, was built at right angles to the front of her house, and looked straight down the very interesting street which debouched at its lower end into the High Street of Tilling. Exactly opposite her front door, the road turned sharply, so that as she looked out from this projecting window, her own house was at right angles on her left, the street in question plunged steeply downwards in front of her, and to her right she commanded an uninterrupted view of its further course, which terminated in the disused graveyard

surrounding the big Norman church. Anything of interest about the church, however, could be gleaned
from a guidebook, and Miss Mapp did not occupy
herself much with such coldly venerable topics. Far
more to her mind was the fact that between the
church and her strategic window was the cottage in
which her gardener lived, and she could thus see,
when not otherwise engaged, whether he went home
before twelve, or failed to get back to her garden
again by one, for he had to cross the street in front of
her very eyes. Similarly she could observe whether
any of his abandoned family ever came out from her
garden door weighted with suspicious baskets, which
might contain smuggled vegetables. Only yesterday
morning she had hurried forth with a dangerous smile
to intercept a laden urchin, with inquiries as to what
was in "that nice basket." On that occasion that nice
basket had proved to contain a strawberry net which
was being sent for repair to the gardener's wife, so
there was nothing more to be done except verify its
return. This she did from a side window of the
garden room which commanded the strawberry beds;
she could sit quite close to that, for it was screened
by the large-leaved branches of a fig tree and she
could spy unseen.

Otherwise this road to the right leading up to the
church was of no great importance (except on Sunday morning, when she could get a practically complete list of those who attended Divine Service), for
no one of real interest lived in the humble dwellings
which lined it. To the left was the front of her own
house at right angles to the strategic window, and
with regard to that a good many useful observations
might be, and were, made. She could, from behind a
curtain negligently half-drawn across the side of the

window nearest the house, have an eye on her house-maid at work, and notice if she leaned out of a window, or made remarks to a friend passing in the street, or waved salutations with a duster. Swift upon such discoveries, she would execute a flank march across the few steps of garden and steal into the house, noiselessly ascend the stairs, and catch the of-fender red-handed at this public dalliance. But all such domestic espionage to right and left was flavor-less and insipid compared to the tremendous discov-eries which daily and hourly awaited the trained observer of the street that lay directly in front of her window.

There was little that concerned the social move-ments of Tilling that could not be proved, or at least reasonably conjectured, from Miss Mapp's eyrie. Just below her house on the left stood Major Flint's residence, of Georgian red brick like her own, and op-posite was that of Captain Puffin. They were both bachelors, though Major Flint was generally supposed to have been the hero of some amazingly amorous ad-ventures in early life, and always turned the subject with great abruptness when anything connected with duelling was mentioned. It was not, therefore, unrea-sonable to infer that he had had experiences of a bloody sort, and color was added to this romantic conjecture by the fact that in damp, rheumatic weather his left arm was very stiff, and he had been known to say that his wound troubled him. What wound that was no one exactly knew (it might have been anything from a vaccination mark to a saber cut), for having said that his wound troubled him, he would invariably add "Pshaw! That's enough about an old campaigner"; and though he might subsequently talk of nothing else except the old campaigner, he

drew a veil over his old campaigns. That he had seen
service in India was, indeed, probable by his referring
to lunch as tiffin, and calling to his parlormaid with
the ejaculation of "Qui-hi." As her name was Sarah,
this was clearly a reminiscence of days in bungalows.
When not in a rage, his manner to his own sex was
bluff and hearty; but whether in a rage or not, his
manner to the fairies, or lovely women, was gallant
and pompous in the extreme. He certainly had a lock
of hair in a small gold specimen case on his watch
chain, and had been seen to kiss it when, rather carelessly, he thought that he was unobserved.

Miss Mapp's eye, as she took her seat in her window on this sunny July morning, lingered for a moment on the Major's house, before she proceeded to
give a disgusted glance at the pictures on the back
page of her morning illustrated paper, which chiefly
represented young women dancing in rings in the
surf, or lying on the beach in attitudes which Miss
Mapp would have scorned to adjust herself to. Neither the Major nor Captain Puffin were very early
risers, but it was about time that the first signals of
animation might be expected. Indeed, at this moment,
she quite distinctly heard that muffled roar which to
her experienced ear was easily interpreted to be
"Qui-hi!"

"So the Major has just come down to breakfast,"
she mechanically inferred, "and it's close on ten
o'clock. Let me see: Tuesday, Thursday, Saturday—
porridge morning."

Her penetrating glance shifted to the house exactly
opposite to that in which it was porridge morning,
and even as she looked, a hand was thrust out of a
small upper window and deposited a sponge on the
sill. Then, from the inside, the lower sash was thrust

firmly down, so as to prevent the sponge from blowing away and falling into the street. Captain Puffin, it
was therefore clear, was a little later than the Major
that morning. But he always shaved and brushed his
teeth before his bath, so that there was but a few
minutes between them.

General maneuvers in Tilling, the gradual burstings
of fluttering life from the chrysalis of the night, the
emergence of the ladies of the town with their wicker
baskets in their hands for housekeeping purchases,
the exodus of men to catch the 11:20 A.M. steam tram
out to the golf links, and other first steps in the duties
and diversions of the day, did not get into full swing
till half past ten, and Miss Mapp had ample time to
skim the headlines of her paper and indulge in chaste
meditations about the occupants of these two houses,
before she need really make herself alert to miss nothing. Of the two, Major Flint, without doubt, was the
more attractive to the feminine sense; for years Miss
Mapp had tried to cajole him into marrying her, and
had not nearly finished yet. With this record of adventure, with the romantic reek of India (and camphor) in the tiger skin of the rugs that strewed his
hall and surged like a rising tide up the wall, with his
haughty and gallant manner, with his loud pshawings
and sniffs at "nonsense and balderdash," his
thumpings on the table to emphasize an argument,
with his wound and his prodigious swipes at golf, his
intolerance of any who believed in ghosts, microbes
or vegetarianism, there was something dashing and
risky about him; you felt that you were in the
presence of some hot coal straight from the furnace of
creation. Captain Puffin, on the other hand, was of
clay so different that he could hardly be considered to
be made of clay at all. He was lame and short and

meager, with strings of peaceful beads and Papuan
aprons in his hall instead of wild tiger skins, and had
a jerky, inattentive manner and a high-pitched voice.
Yet to Miss Mapp's mind there was something behind
his unimpressiveness that had a mysterious quality—
all the more so, because nothing of it appeared on the
surface. Nobody could call Major Flint, with his
bawlings and his sniffings, the least mysterious. He
laid all his loud cards on the table, great hulking
kings and aces. But Miss Mapp felt far from sure that
Captain Puffin did not hold a joker which would some
time come to light. The idea of being Mrs. Puffin was
not so attractive as the other, but she occasionally
gave it her remote consideration.

Yet there was mystery about them both, in spite of
the fact that most of their movements were so amply
accounted for. As a rule, they played golf together in
the morning, reposed in the afternoon, as could easily
be verified by anyone standing on a still day in the
road between their houses and listening to the loud
and rhythmical breathings that fanned the tranquil
air, certainly went out to tea parties afterwards and
played bridge till dinnertime; or if no such entertain-
ment was proffered them, occupied arm chairs at the
county club, or laboriously amassed a hundred at bil-
liards. Though tea parties were profuse, dining out
was very rare at Tilling; Patience or a jig-saw puzzle
occupied the hour or two that intervened between domestic supper and bedtime; but time and again, Miss
Mapp had seen lights burning in the sitting room of
those two neighbors at an hour when such lights as
were still in evidence at Tilling were strictly confined
to bedrooms, and should, indeed, have been extinguished there. And only last week, being plucked
from slumber by some unaccountable indigestion (for

which she blamed a small green apple), she had seen at no less than twelve thirty in the morning the lights in Captain Puffin's sitting room still shining through the blind. This had excited her so much that at risk of toppling into the street, she had craned her neck from her window, and observed a similar illumination at the house of Major Flint. They were not together then, for in that case any prudent householder (and God knew that they both of them scraped and saved enough, or, if He didn't know, Miss Mapp did) would have quenched his own lights, if he were talking to his friend in his friend's house. The next night, the pangs of indigestion having completely vanished, she set her alarm clock at the same timeless hour, and had observed exactly the same phenomenon. Such late hours, of course, amply accounted for these late breakfasts; but why, so Miss Mapp pithily asked herself, why these late hours? Of course they both kept summer time, whereas most of Tilling utterly refused (except when going by train) to alter their watches because Mr. Lloyd George told them to; but even allowing for that . . . then she perceived that summer time made it later than ever for its adherents, so that was no excuse.

Miss Mapp had a mind that was incapable of believing the improbable, and the current explanation of these late hours was very improbable indeed. Major Flint often told the world in general that he was revising his diaries, and that the only uninterrupted time which he could find in this pleasant whirl of life at Tilling was when he was alone in the evening. Captain Puffin, on his part, confessed to a student's curiosity about the ancient history of Tilling, with regard to which he was preparing a monograph. He could talk, when permitted, by the hour about recla-

mation from the sea of the marsh land south of the
town, and about the old Roman road which was built
on a raised causeway, of which traces remained; but
it argued, so thought Miss Mapp, an unprecedented
egoism on the part of Major Flint, and an equally unprecedented love of antiquities on the part of Captain
Puffin, that they should prosecute their studies (with
gas at the present price) till such hours. No; Miss
Mapp knew better than that, but she had not made
up her mind exactly what it was that she knew. She
mentally rejected the idea that egoism (even in these
days of diaries and autobiographies) and antiquities
accounted for so much study, with the same healthy
intolerance with which a vigorous stomach rejects un-
wholesome food, and did not allow herself to be insidiously poisoned by its retention. But as she took up
her light aluminum opera glasses to make sure
whether it was Isabel Poppit or not who was now
stepping with that high, prancing tread into the stationer's in the High Street, she exclaimed to herself,
for the three hundred and sixty-fifth time after breakfast, "It's very baffling"; for it was precisely a year today since she had first seen those mysterious midnight
squares of illuminated blind. Baffling, in fact, was a
word that constantly made short appearances in Miss
Mapp's vocabulary, though its retention for a whole
year over one subject was unprecedented. But never
yet had "baffled" sullied her wells of pure undefiled
English.

Movement had begun; Mrs. Plaistow, carrying her
wicker basket, came round the corner by the church,
in the direction of Miss Mapp's window, and as there
was a temporary coolness between them (following
violent heat) with regard to some worsted of brilliant
rose-madder hue, which a forgetful draper had sold to

Mrs. Plaistow, having definitely promised it to Miss
Mapp . . . but Miss Mapp's large-mindedness scorned
to recall the sordid details of this paltry appropriation. The heat had quite subsided, and Miss Mapp
was, for her part, quite prepared to let the coolness
regain the normal temperature of cordiality the moment that Mrs. Plaistow returned that worsted. Out-
wardly and publicly, friendly relationships had been
resumed, and as the coolness had lasted six weeks or
so, it was probable that the worsted had already been
incorporated into the ornamental border of Mrs. Plaistow's jumper or winter scarf, and a proper expression
of regret would have to do instead. So the nearer
Mrs. Plaistow approached, the more invisible she became to Miss Mapp's eye, and when she was within
saluting distance had vanished altogether. Simultaneously Miss Poppit came out of the stationer's in the
High Street.

Mrs. Plaistow turned the corner below Miss Mapp's
window, and went bobbing along down the steep hill.
She walked with the motion of those mechanical dolls
sold in the street, which have three legs set as spokes
to a circle, so that their feet emerge from their dress
with Dutch and rigid regularity, and her figure had a
certain squat rotundity that suited her gait. She distinctly looked into Captain Puffin's dining-room window as she passed, and with the misplaced juvenility
so characteristic of her waggled her plump little hand
at it. At the corner beyond Major Flint's house she
hesitated a moment, and turned off down the entry
into the side street where Mr. Wyse lived. The dentist
lived there, too, and as Mr. Wyse was away on the
continent of Europe, Mrs. Plaistow was almost certain
to be visiting the other. Rapidly Miss Mapp remembered that at Mrs. Bartlett's bridge party yesterday

Mrs. Plaistow had selected soft chocolates for consumption instead of those stuffed with nougat or almonds. That furnished additional evidence for the dentist, for generally you could not get a nougat chocolate at all if Godiva Plaistow had been in the room for more than a minute or two. . . . As she crossed the narrow cobbled roadway, with the grass growing luxuriantly between the rounded pebbles, she stumbled and recovered herself with a swift little forward run, and the circular feet twinkled with the rapidity of those of a thrush scudding over the lawn.

By this time Isabel Poppit had advanced as far as the fish shop three doors below the turning down which Mrs. Plaistow had vanished. Her prancing progress paused there for a moment, and she waited with one knee highly elevated, like a statue of a curveting horse, before she finally decided to pass on. But she passed no further than the fruit shop next door, took the three steps that elevated it from the street in a single prance, with her Roman nose high in the air. Presently she emerged, but with no obvious rotundity like that of a melon projecting from her basket, so that Miss Mapp could see exactly what she had purchased, and went back to the fish shop again. Surely she would not put fish on the top of fruit, and even as Miss Mapp's lucid intelligence rejected this supposition, the true solution struck her. "Ice," she said to herself, and, sure enough, projecting from the top of Miss Poppit's basket when she came out was an angular peak, wrapped up in paper already wet.

Miss Poppit came up the street, and Miss Mapp put up her illustrated paper again with the revolting picture of the Brighton sea nymphs turned towards the window. Peeping out behind it, she observed that Miss Poppit's basket was apparently oozing with

bright venous blood, and felt certain that she had
bought red currants. That, coupled with the ice, made
conjecture complete. She had bought red currants
slightly damaged (or they would not have oozed so
speedily), in order to make that iced red-currant fool
of which she had so freely partaken at Miss Mapp's
last bridge party. That was a very scurvy trick, for
iced red-currant fool was an invention of Miss
Mapp's, who when it was praised, said that she inherited the recipe from her grandmother. But Miss Poppit had evidently entered the lists against
Grandmamma Mapp, and, what made this more dis-
concerting, was that she had as evidently guessed that
quite inferior fruit—fruit that was distinctly "off"—was
undetectable when severely iced. Miss Mapp could
only hope that the fruit in the basket now bobbing
past her window was so much off that it had begun to
ferment. Fermented red-currant fruit was nasty to the
taste, and if persevered in, disastrous in its effects.
General unpopularity might be needed to teach Miss
Poppit not to trespass on Grandmamma Mapp's
preserves.

Isabel Poppit lived with a flashy and condescending
mother just round the corner beyond the gardener's
cottage, and opposite the west end of the church.
They were comparatively new inhabitants of Tilling,
having settled here only two or three years ago, and
Tilling had not yet quite ceased to regard them as
rather suspicious characters. Suspicion smouldered,
though it blazed no longer. They were certainly rich,
and Miss Mapp suspected them of being profiteers.
They kept a butler, of whom they were both in considerable awe, who used almost to shrug his shoulders
when Mrs. Poppit gave him an order; they kept a motor car to which Mrs. Poppit was apt to allude more

frequently than would have been natural if she had
always been accustomed to one, and they went to
Switzerland for a month every winter and to Scotland
"for the shooting season," as Mrs. Poppit terribly remarked, every summer. This all looked very black,
and though Isabel conformed to the manners of Tilling in doing household shopping every morning with
her wicker basket, and buying damaged fruit for fool,
and in dressing in the original home-made manner indicated by good breeding and narrow incomes, Miss
Mapp was sadly afraid that these habits were not the
outcome of chaste and instinctive simplicity, but of
the ambition to be received by the old families of Tilling as one of them. But what did a true Tillingite
want with a butler and a motor car? And if these
were not sufficient to cast grave doubts on the sincerity of the inhabitants of Ye Olde House, there was
still very vivid in Miss Mapp's mind that dreadful moment, undimmed by the years that had passed over it,
when Mrs. Poppit broke the silence at an altogether
too sumptuous lunch by asking Mrs. Plaistow if she
did not find the super-tax a grievous burden on "our
little incomes." . . . Miss Mapp had drawn in her
breath sharply, as if in pain, and after a few gasps
turned the conversation. . . . Worst of all, perhaps,
because more recent, was the fact that Mrs. Poppit
had just received the dignity of the M.B.E., or Member of the Order of the British Empire, and put it on
her cards, too, as if to keep the scandal alive. Her
services in connection with the Tilling hospital had
been entirely confined to putting her motor car at its
disposal when she did not want it herself, and not a
single member of the Tilling Working Club, which
had knitted its fingers to the bone and made enough
seven-tailed bandages to reach to the moon, had been

offered a similar decoration. If anyone had, she would
have known what to do; a stinging letter to the Prime
Minister saying that she worked not with hope of dis-
tinction, but from pure patriotism, would have certainly been Miss Mapp's rejoinder. She actually
drafted the letter, when Mrs. Poppit's name appeared,
and diligently waded through column after column of
subsequent lists, to make sure that she, the originator
of the Tilling Working Club, had not been the victim
of a similar insult.

Mrs. Poppit was a climber; that was what she was,
and Miss Mapp was obliged to confess that very
nimble she had been. The butler and the motor car
(so frequently at the disposal of Mrs. Poppit's
friends) and the incessant lunches and teas had done
their work; she had fed rather than starved Tilling
into submission, and Miss Mapp felt that she alone
upheld the dignity of the old families. She was positively the only old family (and a solitary spinster at
that) who had not surrendered to the Poppits.
Naturally she did not carry her staunchness to the extent, so to speak, of a hunger strike, for that would be
singular conduct, only worthy of suffragettes, and she
partook of the Poppits' hospitality to the fullest extent
possible, but (here her principles came in) she never
returned the hospitality of the Member of the British
Empire, though she occasionally asked Isabel to her
house, and abused her soundly on all possible occasions. . . .

This spiteful retrospect passed swiftly and smoothly
through Miss Mapp's mind, and did not in the least
take off from the acuteness with which she observed
the tide in the affairs of Tilling which, after the ebb
of the night, was now flowing again, nor did it, a few
minutes after Isabel's disappearance round the corner,

prevent her from hearing the faint tinkle of the telephone in her own house. At that she started to her feet, but paused again at the door. She had shrewd suspicions about her servants with regard to the telephone: she was convinced (though at present she had not been able to get any evidence on the point) that both her cook and her parlormaid used it for their own base purposes at her expense, and that their friends habitually employed it for conversation with them. And perhaps—who knows?—her housemaid was the worst of the lot, for she affected an almost incredible stupidity with regard to the instrument, and pretended not to be able either to speak through it or to understand its cacklings. All that might very well be assumed in order to divert suspicion, so Miss Mapp paused by the door to let any of these delinquents get deep in conversation with her friend: a soft and stealthy advance towards the room called the morning room (a small apartment opening out of the hall, and used chiefly for the bestowal of hats and cloaks and umbrellas) would then enable her to catch one of them red-mouthed, or at any rate to overhear fragments of conversation which would supply equally direct evidence.

She had got no further than the garden door into her house when Withers, her parlormaid, came out. Miss Mapp thereupon began to smile and hum a tune. Then the smile widened, and the tune stopped.

"Yes, Withers?" she said. "Were you looking for me?"

"Yes, Miss," said Withers. "Miss Poppit has just rung you up—"

Miss Mapp looked much surprised.

"And to think that the telephone should have rung without my hearing it," she said. "I must be growing deaf, Withers, in my old age. What does Miss Poppit want?"

"She hopes you will be able to go to tea this afternoon and play bridge. She expects that a few friends may look in at a quarter to four."

A flood of lurid light poured into Miss Mapp's mind. To expect that a few friends may look in was the orthodox way of announcing a regular party to which she had not been asked, and Miss Mapp knew as if by a special revelation that if she went, she would find that she made the eighth to complete two tables of bridge. When the butler opened the door, he would undoubtedly have in his hand a half sheet of paper on which were written the names of the expected friends, and if the caller's name was not on that list, he would tell her with brazen impudence that neither Mrs. Poppit nor Miss Poppit were at home, while, before the baffled visitor had turned her back, he would admit another caller who duly appeared on his reference paper. So then the Poppits were giving a bridge party to which she had only been bidden at the last moment, clearly to take the place of some expected friend who had developed influenza, lost an aunt or been obliged to go to London: here, too, was the explanation of why (as she had overheard yesterday) Major Flint and Captain Puffin were only intending to play one round of golf today, and to come back by the 2:20 train. And why seek any further for the explanation of the lump of ice and the red currants (probably damaged) which she had observed Isabel purchase? And anyone could see (at least Miss Mapp could) why she had gone to the stationer's in the High Street just before. Packs of cards.

Who the expected friend was who had disappointed Mrs. Poppit could be thought out later: at present, as Miss Mapp smiled at Withers and hummed her tune again, she had to settle whether she was going to be delighted to accept, or obliged to decline. The argument in favor of being obliged to decline was obvious: Mrs. Poppit deserved to be "served out" for not including her among the original guests, and if she declined, it was quite probable that at this late hour her hostess might not be able to get anyone else, and so one of her tables would be completely spoiled. In favor of accepting was the fact that she would get a rubber of bridge and a good tea, and would be able to say something disagreeable about the red-currant fool, which would serve Miss Poppit out for attempting to crib her ancestral dishes. . . .

A bright, a joyous, a diabolical idea struck her, and she went herself to the telephone, and genteelly wiped the place where Withers had probably breathed on it.

"So kind of you, Isabel," she said, "but I am very busy today, and you didn't give me much notice, did you? So I'll try to look in if I can, shall I? I might be able to squeeze it in."

There was a pause, and Miss Mapp knew that she had put Isabel in a hole. If she successfully tried to get somebody else, Miss Mapp might find she could squeeze it in, and there would be nine. If she failed to get someone else, and Miss Mapp couldn't squeeze it in, then there would be seven. . . . Isabel wouldn't have a tranquil moment all day.

"Ah, do squeeze it in," she said in those horrid wheedling tones which for some reason Major Flint found so attractive. That was one of the weak points about him, and there were many, many others. But that was among those which Miss Mapp found it difficult to condone.

"If I possibly can," said Miss Mapp. "But at this late hour—Good-by, dear, or only au reservoir, we hope."

She heard Isabel's polite laugh at this nearly new and delicious malapropism before she rang off. Isabel collected malapropisms and wrote them out in a note-book. If you reversed the notebook and began at the other end, you would find the collection of spooner-isms, which were very amusing, too.

Tea, followed by a bridge party, was, in summer, the chief manifestation of the spirit of hospitality in Tilling. Mrs. Poppit, it is true, had attempted to do something in the way of dinner parties, but though she was at liberty to give as many dinner parties as she pleased, nobody else had followed her ostenta-tious example. Dinner parties entailed a higher scale of living; Miss Mapp, for one, had accurately counted the cost of having three hungry people to dinner, and found that one such dinner party was not nearly com-pensated for, in the way of expense, by being invited to three subsequent dinner parties by your guests. Voluptuous teas were the rule, after which you really wanted no more than little bits of things, a cup of soup, a slice of cold tart, or a dished-up piece of fish and some toasted cheese. Then, after the excitement of bridge (and bridge was very exciting in Tilling) a jig-saw puzzle or Patience cooled your brain and composed your nerves. In winter, however, with its scarcity of daylight, Tilling commonly gave evening bridge parties, and asked the requisite number of friends to drop in after dinner, though everybody knew that everybody else had only partaken of bits of things. Probably the ruinous price of coal had some-thing to do with these evening bridge parties, for the fire that warmed your room when you were alone would warm all your guests as well, and then, when your hospitality was returned, you could let your sitting-room fire go out. But though Miss Mapp was already planning something in connection with winter bridge, winter was a long way off yet. . . .

Before Miss Mapp got back to her window in the garden room Mrs. Poppit's great offensive motor car, which she always alluded to as "the Royce," had come round the corner and, stopping opposite Major Flint's house, was entirely extinguishing all survey of the street beyond. It was clear enough then that she had sent the Royce to take the two out to the golf links, so that they should have time to play their round and catch the 2:20 back to Tilling again, so as to be in good time for the bridge party. Even as she looked, Major Flint came out of his house on one side of the Royce and Captain Puffin on the other. The Royce obstructed their view of each other, and simultaneously each of them shouted across to the house of the other. Captain Puffin emitted a loud "Coo-ee, Major" (an Australian ejaculation, learned on his voyages), while Major Flint bellowed, "Qui-hi, Captain," which, all the world knew, was of Oriental origin. The noise each of them made prevented him from hearing the other, and presently one in a fuming hurry to start ran round in front of the car at the precise moment that the other ran round behind it, and they both banged loudly on each other's knockers. These knocks were not so precisely simultaneous as the shouts had been, and this led to mutual discovery, hailed with peals of falsetto laughter on the part of Captain Puffin and the more manly guffaws of the Major. . . . After that the Royce lumbered down the grass-grown cobbles of the street, and after a great deal of reversing managed to turn the corner.

Miss Mapp set off with her basket to do her shopping. She carried in it the weekly books, which she would leave, with payment but not without argument, at the tradesmen's shops. There was an item for suet which she intended to resist to the last breath in her body, though her butcher would probably surrender long before that. There was an item for eggs at the dairy which she might have to pay, though it was a monstrous overcharge. She had made up her mind about the laundry; she intended to pay that bill with an icy countenance and say "Good morning for ever," or words to that effect, unless the proprietor instantly produced the—the article of clothing which had been lost in the wash (like King John's treasures), or refunded an ample sum for the replacing of it. All these quarrelsome errands were meat and drink to Miss Mapp: Tuesday morning, the day on which she paid and disputed her weekly bills, was as enjoyable as Sunday mornings when, sitting close under the pulpit, she noted the glaring inconsistencies and grammatical errors in the discourse. After the bills were paid and business was done, there was pleasure to follow, for there was a fitting-on at the dressmaker's, the fitting-on of a tea gown, to be worn at winter-evening bridge parties, which, unless Miss Mapp was sadly mistaken, would astound and agonize by its magnificence all who set eyes on it. She had found the description of it, as worn by Mrs. Titus W. Trout, in an American fashion paper; it was of what was described as kingfisher blue, and had lumps and wedges of lace round the edge of the skirt, and orange chiffon round the neck. As she set off with her basket full of tradesmen's books, she pictured to herself with watering mouth the fury, the jealousy, the madness of envy which it would raise in all properly-constituted breasts.

In spite of her malignant curiosity and her cancerous suspicions about all her friends, in spite, too, of her restless activities, Miss Mapp was not, as might have been expected, a lady of lean and emaciated appearance. She was tall and portly, with plump hands, a broad, benignant face and dimpled, well-nourished cheeks. An acute observer might have detected a danger warning in the sidelong glances of her rather bulgy eyes, and in a certain tightness at the corners of her expansive mouth, which boded ill for any who came within snapping distance, but to a more superficial view she was a rollicking good-natured figure of a woman. Her mode of address, too, bore out this misleading impression: nothing, for instance, could have been more genial just now than her telephone voice to Isabel Poppit, or her smile to Withers, even while she so strongly suspected her of using the telephone for her own base purposes, and as she passed along the High Street, she showered little smiles and bows on acquaintances and friends. She markedly drew back her lips in speaking, being in no way ashamed of her long white teeth, and wore a practically perpetual smile when there was the least chance of being under observation. Though at sermon time on Sunday, as has been already remarked, she greedily noted the weaknesses and errors of which those twenty minutes were so rewardingly full, she sat all the time with down-dropped eyes and a pretty sacred smile on her lips, and now, when she spied on the other side of the street the figure of the Vicar, she tripped slantingly across the road to him, as if by the move of a knight at chess, looking everywhere else, and only perceiving him with glad surprise at the very last moment. He was a great frequenter of tea parties and except in Lent an assiduous player of

bridge, for a clergyman's duties, so he very properly
held, were not confined to visiting the poor and ex-
horting the sinner. He should be a man of the world,
and enter into the pleasures of his prosperous parishioners, as well as into the trials of the less interesting.
Being an accomplished card player, he entered not
only into their pleasures but their pockets, and there
was no lady of Tilling who was not pleased to have
Mr. Bartlett for a partner. His winnings, so he said,
he gave annually to charitable objects, though
whether the charities he selected began at home was
a point on which Miss Mapp had quite made up her
mind. "Not a penny of that will the poor ever see,"
was the gist of her reflections when on disastrous days
she paid him seven and ninepence. She always called
him "Padre," and had never actually caught him looking over his adversaries' hands.

"Good morning, Padre," she said as soon as she perceived him. "What a lovely day! The white butterflies
were enjoying themselves so in the sunshine in my
garden. And the swallows!"

Miss Mapp, as every reader will have perceived,
wanted to know whether he was playing bridge this
afternoon at the Poppits. Major Flint and Captain
Puffin certainly were, and it might be taken for
granted that Godiva Plaistow was. With the Poppits
and herself that made six. . . .

Mr. Bartlett was humorously archaic in speech. He
interlarded archaisms with Highland expressions, and
his face was knobby, like a chest of drawers.

"Ha, good morrow, fair dame," he said. "And,
prithee, art not thou even as ye white butterflies?"

"Oh, Mr. Bartlett," said the fair dame with a provocative glance. "Naughty! Comparing me to a delicious butterfly!"

"Nay, prithee, why naughty?" said he. "Yes, indeed, it's a day to make ye little fowles rejoice! Ha! I perceive you are on the errands of the guid wife Martha." And he pointed to the basket.

"Yes; Tuesday morning," said Miss Mapp. "I pay all my household books on Tuesday. Poor but honest, dear Padre. What a rush life is today! I hardly know which way to turn. Little duties in all directions! And you; you're always busy! Such a busy bee!"

"Busy B? Busy Bartlett, quo' she! Yes, I'm a busy B today, Mistress Mapp. Sermon all morning, choir practice at three, a baptism at six. No time for a walk today, let alone a bit turn at the gowf."

Miss Mapp saw her opening, and made a busy beeline for it.

"Oh, but you should get regular exercise, Padre," said she. "You take no care of yourself. After the choir practice now, and before the baptism, you could have a brisk walk. To please me!"

"Yes. I had meant to get a breath of air then," said he. "But ye guid Dame Poppit has insisted that I take a wee hand at the cartes with them, the wifey and I. Prithee, shall we meet there?"

("That makes seven without me," thought Miss Mapp in parenthesis.) Aloud she said:

"If I can squeeze it in, Padre. I have promised dear Isabel to do my best."

"Well, and a lassie can do no mair," said he. "Au reservoir then."

Miss Mapp was partly pleased, partly annoyed by the agility with which the Padre brought out her own particular joke. It was she who had brought it down to Tilling, and she felt she had an option on it at the end of every interview, if she meant (as she had done on this occasion) to bring it out. On the other hand it

was gratifying to see how popular it had become. She
had heard it last month when on a visit to a friend at
that sweet and refined village called Riseholme. It
was rather looked down on there, as not being sufficiently intellectual. But within a week of Miss Mapp's
return, Tilling rang with it, and she let it be understood that she was the original humorist.

Godiva Plaistow came whizzing along the pavement, a short, stout, breathless body who might, so
thought Miss Mapp, have acted up to the full and fell
associations of her Christian name without exciting
the smallest curiosity on the part of the lewd. (Miss
Mapp had much the same sort of figure, but her
height, so she was perfectly satisfied to imagine, converted corpulence into majesty.) The swift alternation
of those Dutch-looking feet gave the impression that
she was going at a prodigious speed, but they could
stop revolving without any warning, and then Mrs.
Plaistow stood still. Just when a collision with Miss
Mapp seemed imminent, she came to a dead halt.

It was as well to be quite certain that she was going to the Poppits, and Miss Mapp forgave and forgot
about the worsted until she had found out. She could
never quite manage the indelicacy of saying
"Godiva," whatever Mrs. Plaistow's figure and age
might happen to be, but always addressed her as
"Diva," very affectionately, whenever they were on
speaking terms.

"What a lovely morning, Diva darling," she said;
and noticing that Mr. Bartlett was well out of earshot,
"The white butterflies were enjoying themselves so in
the sunshine in my garden. And the swallows."

Godiva was telegraphic in speech.

"Lucky birds," she said. "No teeth. Beaks."

Miss Mapp remembered her disappearance round

the dentist's corner half an hour ago, and her own
firm inference on the problem.

"Toothache, darling?" she said. "So sorry."

"Wisdom," said Godiva. "Out at one o'clock. Gas.
Ready for bridge this afternoon. Playing? Poppits."

"If I can squeeze it in, dear," said Miss Mapp.
"Such a hustle today."

Diva put her hand to her face as "wisdom" gave
her an awful twinge. Of course she did not believe in
the "hustle," but her pangs prevented her from caring
much.

"Meet you then," she said. "Shall be all comfortable
then. Au—"

This was more than could be borne, and Miss
Mapp hastily interrupted.

"Au reservoir, Diva dear," she said with extreme
acerbity and opened the sluice gates wide to the monstrous affair of the worsted, as Diva's feet began
swiftly revolving again.

The problem about the bridge party thus seemed to
be solved. The two Poppits, the two Bartletts, the
Major and the Captain with Diva darling and herself
made eight, and Miss Mapp with a sudden recrudes-
cence of indignation against Isabel with regard to the
red-currant fool and the belated invitation, made up
her mind that she would not be able to squeeze it in,
thus leaving the party one short. Even apart from the
red-currant fool it served the Poppits right for not
asking her originally, but only when, as seemed now
perfectly clear, somebody else had disappointed
them. But just as she emerged from the butcher's
shop, having gained a complete victory in the matter
of that suet, without expending the last breath in her
body or anything like it, the whole of the seemingly
solid structure came toppling to the ground. For on

emerging, flushed with triumph, leaving the baffled butcher to try his tricks on somebody else if he chose but not on Miss Mapp, she ran straight into the Disgrace of Tilling and her sex, the suffragette, post-impressionist artist (who painted from the nude, both male and female), the socialist and the Germanophil, all incarnate in one frame. In spite of these execrable antecedents, it was quite in vain that Miss Mapp had tried to poison the collective mind of Tilling against this Creature. If she hated anybody, and she undoubtedly did, she hated Irene Coles. The bitterest part of it all was that if Miss Coles was amused at anybody, and she undoubtedly was, she was amused at Miss Mapp.

Miss Coles was strolling along in the attire to which Tilling generally had got accustomed, but Miss Mapp never. She had an old wide-awake hat jammed down on her head, a tall collar and stock, a large loose coat, knickerbockers and grey stockings. In her mouth was a cigarette; in her hand she swung the orthodox wicker basket. She had certainly been to the other fishmonger's at the end of the High Street, for a lobster, revived perhaps after a sojourn on the ice by this warm sun, which the butterflies and the swallows had been rejoicing in, was clinging with claws and waving legs over the edge of it.

Irene removed her cigarette from her mouth and did something in the gutter which is usually associated with the floor of third-class smoking carriages. Then her handsome, boyish face, more boyish because her hair was closely clipped, broke into a broad grin.

"Hullo, Mapp!" she said. "Been giving the tradesmen what-for on Tuesday morning?"

Miss Mapp found it extremely difficult to bear this

obviously insolent form of address without a spasm of
rage. Irene called her Mapp because she chose to,
and Mapp (more bitterness) felt it wiser not to pro-
voke Coles. She had a dreadful, humorous tongue, an
indecent disregard of public or private opinion, and
her gift of mimicry was as appalling as her opinion
about the Germans. Sometimes Miss Mapp alluded to
her as "quaint Irene," but that was as far as she got in
the way of reprisals.

"Oh, you sweet thing!" she said. "Treasure!"

Irene, in some ghastly way, seemed to take note of
this. Why men like Captain Puffin and Major Flint
found Irene "fetching" and "killing" was more than
Miss Mapp could understand, or wanted to understand.

Quaint Irene looked down at her basket.

"Why, there's my lunch coming over the top like
those beastly British Tommies," she said. "Get back,
love."

Miss Mapp could not quite determine whether
"love" was a sarcastic echo of "Treasure." It seemed
probable.

"Oh, what a dear little lobster," she said. "Look at
his sweet claws."

"I shall do more than look at them soon," said Irene,
poking it into her basket again. "Come and have tiffin,
Qui-hi; I've got to look after myself today."

"What has happened to your devoted Lucy?" asked
Miss Mapp. Irene lived in a very queer way with one
gigantic maid, who, but for her sex, might have been
in the Guards.

"Ill. I suspect scarlet fever," said Irene. "Very infectious, isn't it? I was up nursing her all last night."

Miss Mapp recoiled. She did not share Major Flint's
robust views about microbes.

"But I hope, dear, you've thoroughly disinfected—"

"Oh, yes. Soap and water," said Irene. "By the way, are you Poppiting this afternoon?"

"If I can squeeze it in," said Miss Mapp.

"We'll meet again, then. Oh—"

"Au reservoir," said Miss Mapp instantly.

"No; not that silly old chestnut!" said Irene. "I wasn't going to say that. I was only going to say: 'Oh, do come to tiffin.' You and me and the lobster. Then you and me. But it's a bore about Lucy. I was painting her. Fine figure, gorgeous legs. You wouldn't like to sit for me till she's well again?"

Miss Mapp gave a little squeal and bolted into her dressmaker's. She always felt battered after a conversation with Irene, and needed kingfisher blue to restore her.

2

THERE IS NOT in all England a town so blatantly picturesque as Tilling, nor one, for the lover of level marsh land, of tall reedy dykes, of enormous sunsets and rims of blue sea on the horizon, with so fortunate an environment. The hill on which it is built rises steeply from the level land, and, crowned by the great grave church so conveniently close to Miss Mapp's residence, positively consists of quaint corners, rough-cast and timber cottages, and mellow

Georgian fronts. Corners and quaintnesses, gems, glimpses and bits are an obsession to the artist. In consequence, during the summer months, not only did the majority of its inhabitants turn out into the cobbled ways with sketching blocks, canvases and paintboxes, but every morning brought into the town charabancs from neighboring places loaded with passengers, many of whom joined the artistic residents, and you would have thought (until an inspection of their productions convinced you of the contrary) that some tremendous outburst of Art was rivalling the Italian Renaissance. For those who were capable of tackling straight lines and the intricacies of perspective, there were the steep cobbled streets of charming and irregular architecture, while for those who rightly felt themselves colorists rather than architectural draughtsmen, there was the view from the top of the hill over the marshes. There, but for one straight line to mark the horizon (and that could easily be misty), there were no petty conventionalities in the way of perspective, and the eager practitioner could almost instantly plunge into vivid greens and celestial blues; or, at sunset, into pinks and chromes and rose madder.

Tourists who had no pictorial gifts would pick their way among the sketchers, and search the shops for cracked china and bits of brass. Few if any of them left without purchasing one of the famous Tilling money boxes, made in the shape of a pottery pig, who bore on his back that remarkable legend of his authenticity which ran:

> I won't be druv,
> Though I am willing.

> Good morning my love,
> Said the Pig of Tilling.

Miss Mapp had a long shelf full of these in every color to adorn her dining room. The one which completed her collection, of a pleasant magenta color, had only just been acquired. She called them, "My sweet rainbow of piggies," and often when she came down to breakfast, especially if Withers was in the room, she said, "Good morning, quaint little piggies." When Withers had left the room, she counted them.

The corner where the street took a turn towards the church, just below the window of her garden room, was easily the most popular stance for sketchers. You were bewildered and bowled over by "bits." For the most accomplished of all there was that rarely attempted feat, the view of the steep downward street, which, in spite of all the efforts of the artist, insisted, in the sketch, on going up hill instead. Then, next in difficulty, was the street after it had turned, running by the gardener's cottage up to the churchyard and the church. This, in spite of its difficulty, was a very favorite subject, for it included, on the right of the street, just beyond Miss Mapp's garden wall, the famous crooked chimney, which was continually copied from every point of view. The expert artist would draw it rather more crooked than it really was, in order that there might be no question that he had not drawn it crooked by accident. This sketch was usually negotiated from the three steps in front of Miss Mapp's front door. Opposite the church-and-chimney artists would sit others, drawing the front door itself (difficult), and moistening their pencils at their cherry lips, while a little further down the street was another battalion hard at work at the gabled front of the garden room and its picturesque bow. It was a favorite occupation of Miss Mapp's, when there was a decent gathering of artists outside, to pull a table right into the window of the garden room, in full view of them, and, quite unconscious of their presence, to arrange flowers there with a smiling and pensive countenance. She had other little playful public pastimes: she would get her kitten from the house, and induce it to sit on the table while she diverted it with the tassel of the blind, and she would kiss it on its sweet little sooty head, or she would write letters in the window, or play Patience there, and then suddenly become aware that there was no end of ladies and gentlemen looking at her. Sometimes she would come out of the house, if the steps were very full, with her own sketching paraphernalia in her hands and say, ever so coyly, "May I scriggle through?" or ask the squatters on her own steps if they could find a little corner for her. That was so interesting for them; they would remember afterwards that just while they were engaged on their sketches, the lady of that beautiful house at the corner, who had been playing with her kitten in the window, came out to sketch, too. She addressed gracious and yet humble remarks to them: "I see you are painting my sweet little home. May I look? Oh, what a lovely little sketch!" Once, on a never-to-be-forgotten day, she observed one of them take a camera from his pocket and rapidly focus her as she stood on the top step. She turned full-faced and smiling to the camera just in time to catch the click of the shutter, but then it was too late to hide her face, and perhaps the picture might appear in the *Graphic* or the *Sketch*, or among the posturing nymphs of a neighboring watering place. . . .

This afternoon she was content to "scriggle"

through the sketchers, and humming a little tune, she passed up to the churchyard. ("Scriggle" was one of her own words, highly popular; it connoted squeezing and wriggling.) There she carefully concealed herself under the boughs of the weeping ash tree directly opposite the famous south porch of the church. She had already drawn in the lines of this south porch on her sketching block, transferring them there by means of a tracing from a photograph, so that formed a very promising beginning to her sketch. But she was nicely placed not only with regard to her sketch, for, by peeping through the pretty foliage of the tree, she could command the front door of Mrs. Poppit's (M.B.E.) house.

Miss Mapp's plans for the bridge party had, of course, been completely upset by the encounter with Irene in the High Street. Up till that moment, she had imagined that, with the two ladies of the house and the Bartletts and the Major and the Captain and Godiva and herself, two complete tables of bridge would be formed, and she had, therefore, determined that she would not be able to squeeze the party into her numerous engagements, thereby spoiling the second table. But now everything was changed; there were eight without her, and unless at a quarter to four, she saw reason to suppose, by noting the arrivals at the house, that three bridge tables were in contemplation, she had made up her mind to "squeeze it in," so that there would be nine gamblers, and Isabel or her mother, if they had any sense of hospitality to their guests, would be compelled to sit out for ever and ever. Miss Mapp had been urgently invited; sweet Isabel had made a great point of her squeezing it in, and if sweet Isabel, in order to be certain of a company of eight, had asked quaint Irene as well, it

would serve her right. An additional reason, besides
this piece of good nature in managing to squeeze it
in, for the sake of sweet Isabel, lay in the fact that
she would be able to take some red-currant fool, and
after one spoonful exclaim, "Delicious," and leave the
rest uneaten.

The white butterflies and the swallows were still
enjoying themselves in the sunshine, and so, too, were
the gnats, about whose pleasure, especially when they
settled on her face, Miss Mapp did not care so much.
But soon she quite ceased to regard them, for, before
the quaint little gilded boys on each side of the clock
above the north porch had hammered out the three-
quarters after three on their bells, visitors began to arrive at the Poppits' door, and Miss Mapp was very
active, looking through the boughs of the weeping
ash and sitting down again to smile and ponder over
her sketch with her head a little on one side, if anybody approached. One by one, the expected guests
presented themselves and were admitted: Major Flint
and Captain Puffin, the Padre and his wife, darling
Diva with her head muffled in a "cloud," and finally
Irene, still dressed as she had been in the morning,
and probably reeking with scarlet fever. With the two
Poppits, these made eight players, so as soon as Irene
had gone in, Miss Mapp hastily put her sketching
things away, and holding her admirably accurate
drawing with its wash of sky not quite dry, in her
hand, hurried to the door, for it would never do to arrive after the two tables had started, since in that case
it would be she who would have to sit out.

Boon opened the door to her three staccato little
knocks, and sulkily consulted his list. She duly appeared on it and was admitted. Having banged the
door behind her, he crushed the list up in his hand

and threw it into the fireplace; all those whose presence was desired had arrived, and Boon would turn his bovine eye on any subsequent caller, and say that his mistress was out.

"And may I put my sketching things down here, please, Boon?" said Miss Mapp ingratiatingly. "And will no one touch my drawing? It's a little wet still. The church porch."

Boon made a grunting noise like the Tilling pig, and slouched away in front of her down the passage leading to the garden, sniffing. There they were, with the two bridge tables set out in a shady corner of the lawn, and a buffet vulgarly heaped with all sorts of dainty confections which made Miss Mapp's mouth water, obliging her to swallow rapidly once or twice before she could manage a wide, dry smile. Isabel advanced.

"De-do, dear," said Miss Mapp. "Such a rush! But managed to squeeze it in, as you wouldn't let me off."

"Oh, that was nice of you, Miss Mapp," said Isabel.

A wild and awful surmise seized Miss Mapp.

"And your dear mother?" she said. "Where is Mrs. Poppit?"

"Mamma had to go to town this morning. She won't be back till close on dinnertime."

Miss Mapp's smile closed up like a furled umbrella. The trap had snapped behind her; it was impossible now to scriggle away. She had completed, instead of spoiling, the second table.

"So we're just eight," said Isabel, poking at her, so to speak, through the wires. "Shall we have a rubber first and then some tea? Or tea first. What says everybody?"

Restlessness and hungry murmurs, like those heard at the sea lions' enclosure in the Zoological Gardens when feeding time approaches, seemed to indicate tea first, and with gallant greetings from the Major, and archaistic welcomes from the Padre, Miss Mapp headed the general drifting movement towards the buffet. There may have been tea there, but there was certainly iced coffee and Lager beer and large jugs with dew on the outside and vegetables floating in a bubbling liquid in the inside, and it was all so vulgar and opulent that with one accord everyone set to work in earnest, in order that the garden should present a less gross and greedy appearance. But there was no sign at present of the red-currant fool, which was baffling. . . .

"And have you had a good game of golf, Major?" asked Miss Mapp, making the best of these miserable circumstances. "Such a lovely day! The white butterflies were enjoying—"

She became aware that Diva and the Padre, who had already heard about the white butterflies, were in her immediate neighborhood, and broke off.

"Which of you beat? Or should I say won!" she asked.

Major Flint's long moustache was dripping with Lager beer, and he made a dexterous, sucking movement.

"Well, the Army and the Navy had it out," he said. "And if for once Britain's Navy was not invincible; eh, Puffin?"

Captain Puffin limped away pretending not to hear, and took his heaped plate and brimming glass in the direction of Irene.

"But I'm sure Captain Puffin played quite beautifully, too," said Miss Mapp in the vain attempt to detain him. She liked to collect all the men round her, and then scold them for not talking to the other ladies.

"Well, a game's a game," said the Major. "It gets through the hours, Miss Mapp. Yes; we finished at the fourteenth hole, and hurried back to more congenial society. And what have you done today? Fairy errands, I'll be bound. Titania! Ha!"

Suet errands and errands about a missing article of underclothing were really the most important things that Miss Mapp had done today, now that her bridge party scheme had so miscarried, but naturally she would not allude to these.

"A little gardening," she said. "A little sketching. A little singing. Not time to change my frock and put on something less shabby. But I wouldn't have kept sweet Isabel's bridge party waiting for anything, and so I came straight from my painting here. Padre, I've been trying to draw the lovely south porch. But so difficult! I shall give up trying to draw, and just enjoy myself with looking. And there's your dear Evie! How de do, Evie love?"

Godiva Plaistow had taken off her cloud for purposes of mastication, but wound it tightly round her head again as soon as she had eaten as much as she could manage. This had to be done on one side of her mouth, or with the front teeth in the nibbling manner of a rabbit. Everybody, of course, by now knew that she had had a wisdom tooth out at one P.M. with gas, and she could allude to it without explanation.

"Dreamed I was playing bridge," she said, "and had a hand of aces. As I played the first, it went off in my hand. All over. Blood. Hope it'll come true. Bar the blood."

Miss Mapp found herself soon afterwards partnered with Major Flint and opposed by Irene and the

Padre. They had hardly begun to consider their first hands when Boon staggered out into the garden under the weight of a large wooden bucket, packed with ice, that surrounded an interior cylinder.

"Red-currant fool at last," thought Miss Mapp, adding aloud: "O poor little me, is it, to declare? Shall I say 'no-trumps'?"

"Mustn't consult your partner, Mapp," said Irene, puffing the end of her cigarette out of its holder. Irene was painfully literal.

"I don't, darling," said Miss Mapp, beginning to fizz a little. "No-trumps. Not a trump. Not any sort of trump. There! What are we playing for, by the way?"

"Bob a hundred," said the Padre, forgetting to be either Scotch or archaic.

"Oh, gambler! You want the poor box to be the rich box, Padre," said Miss Mapp, surveying her magnificent hand with the greatest satisfaction. If it had not contained so many court cards, she would have proposed playing for sixpence, not a shilling a hundred.

All semblance of manners was invariably thrown to the winds by the ladies of Tilling when once bridge began; primeval hatred took their place. The winners of any hand were exasperatingly condescending to the losers, and the losers correspondingly bitter and tremulous. Miss Mapp failed to get her contract, as her partner's contribution to success consisted of more twos and threes than were ever seen together before, and when quaint Irene at the end said, "Bad luck, Mapp," Miss Mapp's hands trembled so much with passion that she with difficulty marked the score. But she could command her voice sufficiently to say, "Lovely of you to be sympathetic, dear." Irene in answer gave a short, hoarse laugh and dealt.

By this time, Boon had deposited at the left hand of each player a cup containing a red creamy fluid, on the surface of which bubbles intermittently appeared. Isabel, at this moment being dummy, had strolled across from the other table to see that everybody was comfortable and provided with sustenance in times of stress, and here was clearly the proper opportunity for Miss Mapp to take a spoonful of this attempt at red-currant fool, and with a wry face, hastily (but not too hastily) smothered in her smiles, to push the revolting compound away from her. But the one spoonful that she took was so delicious and exhilarating, that she was positively unable to be good for Isabel. Instead, she drank her cup to the dregs in an absent manner, while considering how many trumps were out. The red-currant fool made a similarly agreeable impression on Major Flint.

" 'Pon my word," he said. "That's amazingly good. Cooling on a hot day like this. Full of champagne."

Miss Mapp, seeing that it was so popular, had, of course, to claim it again as a family invention.

"No, dear Major," she said. "There's no champagne in it. It's my Grandmamma Mapp's famous red-currant fool, with little additions perhaps by me. No champagne; yolk of egg and a little cream. Dear Isabel has got it very nearly right."

The Padre had promised to take more tricks in diamonds than he had the slightest chance of doing. His mental worry communicated itself to his voice.

"And why should there be nary a wee drappie o' champagne in it?" he said, "though your Grandmamma Mapp did invent it. Weel, let's see your hand, partner. Eh, that's a sair sight."

"And there'll be a sair wee score agin us when ye're through with the playin' o' it," said Irene in tones that could not be acquitted of a mocking intent. "Why the hell—hallelujah did you go on when I didn't support you?"

Even that one glass of red-currant fool, though there was no champagne in it, had produced, together with the certainty that her opponent had overbidden his hand, a pleasant exhilaration in Miss Mapp; but yolk of egg, as everybody knew, was a strong stimulant. Suddenly the name red-currant fool seemed very amusing to her.

"Red-currant fool!" she said. "What a quaint, old-fashioned name! I shall invent some others. I shall tell my cook to make some gooseberry idiot, or strawberry donkey. . . . My play, I think. A ducky little ace of spades."

"Haw! Haw! Gooseberry idiot!" said her partner. "Capital! You won't beat that in a hurry! And a two of spades on the top of it."

"You wouldn't expect to find a two of spades at the bottom of it," said the Padre with singular acidity.

The Major was quick to resent this kind of comment from a man, cloth or no cloth.

"Well, by your leave, Bartlett, by your leave, I repeat," he said, "I shall expect to find twos of spades precisely where I please, and when I want your criticism—"

Miss Mapp hastily intervened.

"And after my wee ace, a little king piece," she said. "And if my partner doesn't play the queen to it! Delicious! And I play just one more. . . . Yes . . . lovely partner puts wee trumpy on it! I'm not surprised; it takes more than that to surprise me; and then Padre's got another spade, I ken fine!"

"Hoots!" said the Padre with temperate disgust.

The hand proceeded for a round or two in silence,

during which, by winks and gestures to Boon, the Major got hold of another cupful of red-currant fool. There was already a heavy penalty of tricks against Miss Mapp's opponents, and after a moment's refreshment, the Major led a club, of which, at this period, Miss Mapp seemed to have none. She felt happier than she had been ever since, trying to spoil Isabel's second table, she had only succeeded in completing it.

"Little trumpy again," she said, putting it on with the lightness of one of the white butterflies and turning the trick. "Useful little trumpy—"

She broke off suddenly from the chant of victory which ladies of Tilling were accustomed to indulge in during crossruffs, for she discovered in her hand another more than useless little clubby. . . . The silence that succeeded became tense in quality. Miss Mapp knew she had revoked and squeezed her brains to think how she could possibly dispose of the card, while there was a certain calmness about the Padre, which but too clearly indicated that he was quite content to wait for the inevitable disclosure. This came at the last trick, and though Miss Mapp made one forlorn attempt to thrust the horrible little clubby underneath the other cards and gather them up, the Padre pounced on it.

"What, ho, fair lady!" he said, now completely restored. "Methinks thou art forsworn! Let me have a keek at the last trick but three! Verily I wis that thou didst trump ye club aforetime. I said so; there it is. Eh, that's bonny for us, partner!"

Miss Mapp, of course, denied it all, and a ruthless reconstruction of the tricks took place. The Major, still busy with red-currant fool, was the last to grasp

the disaster, and then instantly deplored the unsports-
manlike greed of his adversaries.

"Well, I should have thought in a friendly game
like this—" he said. "Of course, you're within your
right, Bartlett: might is right, hey? but upon my
word, a pound of flesh, you know. . . . Can't think
what made you do it, partner."

"You never asked me if I had any more clubs," said
Miss Mapp shrilly, giving up for the moment the contention that she had not revoked. "I always ask if my
partner has no more of a suit, and I always maintain
that a revoke is more the partner's fault than the
player's. Of course, if our adversaries claim it—"

"Naturally we do, Mapp," said Irene. "You were
down on me sharp enough the other day."

Miss Mapp wrinkled her face up into the sweetest
and extremest smile of which her mobile features
were capable.

"Darling, you won't mind my telling you that just
at this moment you are being dummy," she said, "and
so you mustn't speak a single word. Otherwise there
is no revoke, even if there was at all, which I consider
far from proved yet."

There was no further proof possible beyond the
clear and final evidence of the cards, and since everybody, including Miss Mapp herself, was perfectly
well aware that she had revoked, their opponents
merely marked up the penalty and the game
proceeded. Miss Mapp, of course, following the rule
of correct behavior after revoking, stiffened into a
state of offended dignity, and was extremely polite
and distant with partner and adversaries alike. This
demeanor became even more majestic when in the
next hand the Major led out of turn. The moment he
had done it, Miss Mapp hurriedly threw a random

card out of her hand on to the table, in the hope that Irene, by some strange aberration, would think she had led first.

"Wait a second," said she. "I call a lead. Give me a trump, please."

Suddenly the awful expression as of some outraged empress faded from Miss Mapp's face, and she gave a little shriek of laughter which sounded like a squeaking slate pencil.

"Haven't got one, dear," she said. "Now may I have your permission to lead what I think best? Thank you."

There now existed between the four players that state of violent animosity which was the usual atmosphere towards the end of a rubber. But it would have been a capital mistake to suppose that they were not all enjoying themselves immensely. Emotion is the salt of life, and here was no end of salt. Everyone was overbidding his hand, and the penalty tricks were a glorious cause of vituperation, scarcely veiled, between the partners who had failed to make good, and caused epidemics of condescending sympathy from the adversaries which produced a passion in the losers far keener than their fury at having lost. What made the concluding stages of this contest the more exciting was that an evening breeze suddenly arising just as a deal was ended made the cards rise in the air like a covey of partridges. They were recaptured, and all the hands were found to be complete with the exception of Miss Mapp's, which had a card missing. This, an ace of hearts, was discovered by the Padre, face upwards, in a bed of mignonette, and he was vehement in claiming a fresh deal, on the grounds that the card was exposed. Miss Mapp could not speak at all in answer to this preposterous claim; she could only

smile at him, and proceed to declare trumps as if
nothing had happened. . . . The Major alone failed
to come up to the full measure of these enjoyments,
for though all the rest of them were as angry with
him as they were with each other, he remained in a
most indecorous state of good humor, drinking thirst-
ily of the red-currant fool, and when he was dummy,
quite failing to mind whether Miss Mapp got her contract or not. Captain Puffin, at the other table, seemed
to be behaving with the same impropriety, for the
sound of his shrill, falsetto laugh was as regular as his
visits to the bucket of red-currant fool. What if there
was champagne in it after all, so Miss Mapp luridly
conjectured! What if this unseemly good humor was
due to incipient intoxication? She took a little more of
that delicious decoction herself.

It was unanimously determined, when the two rub-
bers came to an end almost simultaneously, that as
everything was so pleasant and agreeable, there
should be no fresh sorting of the players. Besides, the
second table was only playing stakes of sixpence a
hundred, and it would be very awkward and unsettling that anyone should play these moderate points
in one rubber and those high ones the next. But at
this point Miss Mapp's table was obliged to endure a
pause, for the Padre had to hurry away just before six
to administer the rite of baptism in the church which
was so conveniently close. The Major afforded a good
deal of amusement, as soon as he was out of hearing,
by hoping that he would not baptize the child the
Knave of Hearts if it was a boy, or if a girl, the
Queen of Spades; but in order to spare the suscepti-
bilities of Mrs. Bartlett, this admirable joke was not
communicated to the next table, but enjoyed privately. The author of it, however, made a note in his

mind to tell it to Captain Puffin, in the hopes that it
would cause him to forget his ruinous half-crown defeat at golf this morning. Quite as agreeable was the
arrival of a fresh supply of red-currant fool, and as
this had been heralded a few minutes before by a
loud pop from the butler's pantry, which looked on to
the lawn, Miss Mapp began to waver in her belief
that there was no champagne in it, particularly as it
would not have suited the theory by which she accounted for the Major's unwonted good humor, and
her suggestion that the pop they had all heard so
clearly was the opening of a bottle of stone ginger-
beer was not delivered with conviction. To make sure,
however, she took one more sip of the new supply
and, irradiated with smiles, made a great concession.

"I believe I was wrong," she said. "There is something in it beyond the yolk of egg and cream. Oh,
there's Boon; he will tell us."

She made a seductive face at Boon, and beckoned
to him.

"Boon, will you think it very inquisitive of me," she
asked archly, "if I ask you whether you have put a
teeny drop of champagne into this delicious red-currant fool?"

"A bottle and a half, Miss," said Boon morosely,
"and half a pint of old brandy. Will you have some
more, Miss?"

Miss Mapp curbed her indignation at this vulgar
squandering of precious liquids, so characteristic of
Poppits. She gave a shrill little laugh.

"Oh, no, thank you, Boon!" she said. "I mustn't
have any more. Delicious, though."

Major Flint let Boon fill up his cup while he was
not looking.

"And we owe this to your grandmother, Miss Mapp?" he asked gallantly. "That's a second debt."

Miss Mapp acknowledged this polite subtlety with a reservation.

"But not the champagne in it, Major," she said. "Grandmamma Nap—"

The Major beat his thigh in ecstasy.

"Ha! There's a good spoonerism for Miss Isabel's book," he said. "Miss Isabel, we've got a new—"

Miss Mapp was very much puzzled at this slight confusion in his speech, for her utterance was usually remarkably distinct. There might be some little joke made at her expense on the effect of Grandmamma Mapp's invention if this lovely spoonerism was published. But if she who had only just tasted the red-currant fool tripped in her speech, how amply were Major Flint's good nature and Captain Puffin's incessant laugh accounted for. She herself felt very good-natured, too. How pleasant it all was!

"Oh, naughty!" she said to the Major. "Pray, hush! You're disturbing them at their rubber. And here's the Padre back again!"

The new rubber had only just begun (indeed, it was lucky that they cut their cards without any delay) when Mrs. Poppit appeared on her return from her expedition to London. Miss Mapp begged her to take her hand, and instantly began playing.

"It would really be a kindness to me, Mrs. Poppit," she said; "(No diamonds at all, partner?) but of course, if you won't— You've been missing such a lovely party. So much enjoyment!"

Suddenly she saw that Mrs. Poppit was wearing on her ample breast a small piece of riband with a little cross attached to it. Her entire stock of good humor vanished, and she smiled her widest.

"We needn't ask what took you to London," she said. "Congratulations! How was the dear King?"

This rubber was soon over, and even as they were adding up the score, there arose a shrill outcry from the next table, where Mrs. Plaistow, as usual, had made the tale of her winnings sixpence in excess of what anybody else considered was due to her. The sound of that was so familiar that nobody looked up or asked what was going on.

"Darling Diva and her bawbees, Padre," said Miss Mapp in an aside. "So modest in her demands. Oh, she's stopped! Somebody has given her sixpence. Not another rubber? Well, perhaps it is rather late, and I must say good night to my flowers before they close up for the night. All those shillings mine? Fancy!"

Miss Mapp was seething with excitement, curiosity, and rage, as with Major Flint on one side of her and Captain Puffin on the other, she was escorted home. The excitement was due to her winnings, the rage to Mrs. Poppit's Order, the curiosity to the clue she believed she had found to those inexplicable lights that burned so late in the houses of her companions. Certainly it seemed that Major Flint was trying not to step on the joints of the paving stones, and succeeding very imperfectly, while Captain Puffin, on her left, was walking very unevenly on the cobbles. Even making due allowance for the difficulty of walking evenly there at any time, Miss Mapp could not help thinking that a teetotaller would have made a better job of it than that. Both gentlemen talked at once, very agreeably but rather carefully, Major Flint promising himself a studious evening over some very interesting entries in his Indian Diary, while Captain Puffin anticipated the speedy solution of that problem

about the Roman road which had puzzled him so
long. As they said their "Au reservoirs" to her on her
doorstep, they took off their hats more often than politeness really demanded.

Once in her house Miss Mapp postponed her good
nights to her sweet flowers, and hurried with the utmost speed of which she was capable to her garden
room, in order to see what her companions were doing. They were standing in the middle of the street,
and Major Flint, with gesticulating forefinger, was
being very impressive over something. . . .

Interesting as was Miss Mapp's walk home, and
painful as was the light which it had conceivably
thrown on the problem that had baffled her so long,
she might have been even more acutely disgusted had
she lingered on with the rest of the bridge party in
Mrs. Poppit's garden, so revolting was the sycophantic
loyalty of the newly decorated Member of the British
Empire. . . . She described minutely her arrival at
the Palace, her momentary nervousness as she entered
the throne room, the instantaneousness with which
that all vanished when she came face to face with her
Sovereign.

"I assure you, he gave the most gracious smile," she
said, "just as if we had known each other all our lives,
and I felt at home at once. And he said a few words
to me—such a beautiful voice he has. Dear Isabel, I
wish you had been there to hear it, and then—"

"Oh, Mamma, what did he say?" asked Isabel, to
the great relief of Mrs. Plaistow and the Bartletts, for
while they were bursting with eagerness to know with
the utmost detail all that had taken place, the correct
attitude in Tilling was profound indifference to anybody of whatever degree who did not live at Tilling
and to anything that did not happen there. In particu-

lar, any manifestation of interest in kings or other distinguished people was held to be a very miserable failing. . . . So they all pretended to look about them, and take no notice of what Mrs. Poppit was saying, and you might have heard a pin drop. Diva silently and hastily unwound her cloud from over her ears, risking catching cold in the hole where her tooth had been, so terrified was she of missing a single syllable.

"Well, it was very gratifying," said Mrs. Poppit; "he whispered to some gentleman standing near him, who I think was the Lord Chamberlain, and then told me how interested he had been in the good work of the Tilling hospital, and how especially glad he was to be able—and just then he began to pin my Order on—to be able to recognize it. Now I call that wonderful to know all about the Tilling hospital! And such neat, quick fingers he has: I am sure it would take me double the time to make a safety-pin hold, and then he gave me another smile, and passed me on, so to speak, to the Queen, who stood next him, and who had been listening to all he had said."

"And did she speak to you, too?" asked Diva, quite unable to maintain the right indifference.

"Indeed she did; she said, 'So pleased,' and what she put into those two words I'm sure I can never convey to you. I could hear how sincere they were; it was no set form of words, as if she meant nothing by it. She *was* pleased; she was just as interested in what I had done for the Tilling hospital as the King was. And the crowds outside; they lined the Mall for at least fifty yards. I was bowing and smiling on this side and that till I felt quite dizzy."

"And was the Prince of Wales there?" asked Diva,

beginning to wind her head up again. She did not care about the crowds.

"No, he wasn't there," said Mrs. Poppit, determined to have no embroidery in her story, however much other people, especially Miss Mapp, decorated remarkable incidents till you hardly recognized them. "He wasn't there. I daresay something had unexpectedly detained him, though I shouldn't wonder if before long we all saw him. For I noticed in the evening paper which I was reading on the way down here, after I had seen the King, that he was going to stay with Lord Ardingly for this very next weekend. And what's the station for Ardingly Park if it isn't Tilling? Though it's quite a private visit, I feel convinced that the right and proper thing for me to do is to be at the station, or at any rate, just outside, with my Order on. I shall not claim acquaintance with him, or anything of that kind," said Mrs. Poppit, fingering her Order; "but after my reception today at the Palace, nothing can be more likely than that His Majesty might mention—quite casually, of course—to the Prince that he had just given a decoration to Mrs. Poppit of Tilling. And it would make me feel very awkward to think that that had happened, and I was not somewhere about to make my curtsy."

"Oh, Mamma, may I stand by you, or behind you?" asked Isabel, completely dazzled by the splendor of this prospect and prancing about the lawn. . . .

This was quite awful: it was as bad as, if not worse than, the historically disastrous remark about supertax, and a general rigidity, as of some partial cataleptic seizure, froze Mrs. Poppit's guests, rendering them, like incomplete Marconi installations, capable of receiving, but not of transmitting. They received these impressions; they also continued (mechani-

cally) to receive more chocolates and sandwiches,
and such refreshments as remained on the buffet; but
no one could intervene and stop Mrs. Poppit from exposing herself further. One reason for this, of course,
as already indicated, was that they all longed for her
to expose herself as much as she possibly could, for if
there was a quality—and, indeed, there were many—
on which Tilling prided itself, it was on its immunity
from snobbishness: there were, no doubt, in the great
world with which Tilling concerned itself so little
kings and queens and dukes and Members of the Order of the British Empire; but every Tillingite knew
that he or she (particularly she) was just as good as
any of them, and indeed better, being more fortunate
than they in living in Tilling. . . . And if there was a
process in the world which Tilling detested, it was
being patronized, and there was this woman telling
them all what she felt it right and proper for her, as
Mrs. Poppit of Tilling (M.B.E.), to do, when the Heir
Apparent should pass through the town on Saturday.
The rest of them, Mrs. Poppit implied, might do what
they liked, for they did not matter: but she—she must
put on her Order and make her curtsy. And Isabel, by
her expressed desire to stand beside, or even behind,
her mother for this degrading moment had showed of
what stock she came.

Mrs. Poppit had nothing more to say on this subject; indeed, as Diva reflected, there was really nothing more that could be said, unless she suggested that
they should all bow and curtsy to her for the future,
and their hostess proceeded, as they all took their
leave. to hope that they had enjoyed the bridge party
which she had been unavoidably prevented from attending.

"But my absence made it possible to include Miss

Mapp," she said. "I should not have liked poor Miss
Mapp to feel left out; I am always glad to give Miss
Mapp pleasure. I hope she won her rubber; she does
not like losing. Will no one have a little more red-cur-
rant fool? Boon has made it very tolerably today. A
Scotch recipe of my great-grandmother's."

Diva gave a little cackle of laughter as she enfolded
herself in her cloud again. She had heard Miss
Mapp's ironical inquiry as to how the dear King was,
and had thought at the time that it was probably a
pity that Miss Mapp had said that.

Though abhorrence of snobbery and immunity
from any taint of it was so fine a characteristic of
public social life at Tilling, the expected passage of
this distinguished visitor through the town on Saturday next became very speedily known, and before the
wicker baskets of the ladies in their morning marketing next day were half full, there was no quarter
which the news had failed to reach. Major Flint had
it from Mrs. Plaistow, as he went down to the 11:20
tram out to the golf links, and though he had not
much time to spare (for his work last night on his old
diaries had caused him to breakfast unusually late
that morning to the accompaniment of a dismal
headache from overapplication), he had stopped to
converse with Miss Mapp immediately afterwards,
with one eye on the time, for naturally he could not
fire off that sort of news point-blank at her, as if it
was a matter of any interest or importance.

"Good morning, dear lady," he said. "By Jove!
What a picture of health and freshness you are!"

Miss Mapp cast one glance at her basket to see that
the paper quite concealed that article of clothing
which the perfidious laundry had found. (Probably

the laundry knew where it was all the time, and—in a figurative sense, of course—was "trying it on.")

"Early to bed and early to rise, Major," she said. "I saw my sweet flowers open their eyes this morning! Such a beautiful dew!"

"Well, my diaries kept me up late last night," he said. "When all you fascinating ladies have withdrawn is the only time at which I can bring myself to sit down to them."

"Let me recommend six to eight in the morning, Major," said Miss Mapp earnestly. "Such a freshness of brain then."

That seemed to be a cul-de-sac in the way of leading up to the important subject, and the Major tried another turning.

"Good, well-fought game of bridge we had yesterday," he said. "Just met Mrs. Plaistow; she stopped on for a chat after we had gone."

"Dear Diva; she loves a good gossip," said Miss Mapp effusively. "Such an interest she has in other people's affairs. So human and sympathetic. I'm sure our dear hostess told her all about her adventures at the Palace."

There was only seven minutes left before the tram started, and though this was not a perfect opening, it would have to do. Besides, the Major saw Mrs. Plaistow coming energetically along the High Street with whirling feet.

"Yes, and we haven't finished with—ha—royalty yet," he said, getting the odious word out with difficulty. "The Prince of Wales will be passing through the town on Saturday, on his way to Ardingly Park, where he is spending the Sunday."

Miss Mapp was not betrayed into the smallest expression of interest.

"That will be nice for him," she said. "He will catch a glimpse of our beautiful Tilling."

"So he will! Well, I'm off for my game of golf. Perhaps the Navy will be a bit more efficient today."

"I'm sure you will both play perfectly!" said Miss Mapp.

Diva had "popped" into the grocer's. She always popped everywhere just now; she popped across to see a friend, and she popped home again; she popped into church on Sunday, and occasionally popped up to town; and Miss Mapp was beginning to feel that somebody ought to let her know, directly or by insinuation, that she popped too much. So, thinking that an opportunity might present itself now, Miss Mapp read the newsboard outside the stationer's till Diva popped out of the grocer's again. The headlines of news, even the largest of them, hardly reached her brain, because it was entirely absorbed in another subject. Of course, the first thing was to find out by what train . . .

Diva trundled swiftly across the street.

"Good morning, Elizabeth," she said. "You left the party too early yesterday. Missed a lot. How the King smiled! How the Queen said, 'So pleased.'"

"Our dear hostess would like that," said Miss Mapp pensively. "She would be so pleased, too. She and the Queen would both be pleased. Quite a pair of them."

"By the way, on Saturday next—" began Diva.

"I know, dear," said Miss Mapp. "Major Flint told me. It seemed quite to interest him. Now I must pop into the stationer's—"

Diva was really very obtuse.

"I'm popping in there too," she said. "Want a time-table of the trains."

Wild horses would not have dragged from Miss Mapp that this was precisely what she wanted.

"I only wanted a little ruled paper," she said. "Why, here's dear Evie popping out just as we pop in! Good morning, sweet Evie. Lovely day again."

Mrs. Bartlett thrust something into her basket which very much resembled a railway timetable. She spoke in a low, quick voice, as if afraid of being overheard, and was otherwise rather like a mouse. When she was excited she squeaked.

"So good for the harvest," she said. "Such an important thing to have a good harvest. I hope next Saturday will be fine; it would be a pity if we had a wet day. We were wondering, Kenneth and I, what would be the proper thing to do, if he came over for service—oh, here is Kenneth!"

She stopped abruptly, as if afraid that she had betrayed too much interest in next Saturday and Sunday. Kenneth would manage it much better.

"Ha! Lady fair," he exclaimed. "Having a bit crack with wee wifey? Any news this bright morning?"

"No, dear Padre," said Miss Mapp, showing her guns. "At least, I've heard nothing of any interest. I can only give you the news of my garden. Such lovely new roses in bloom today, bless them!"

Mrs. Plaistow had popped into the stationer's, so this perjury was undetected.

The Padre was noted for his diplomacy. Just now he wanted to convey the impression that nothing which could happen next Saturday or Sunday could be of the smallest interest to him; whereas he had spent an almost sleepless night in wondering whether it would, in certain circumstances, be proper to make a bow at the beginning of his sermon and another at the end; whether he ought to meet the visitor at the west door; whether the mayor ought to be told, and whether there ought to be special psalms. . . .

"Well, lady fair," he said. "Gossip will have it that ye Prince of Wales is staying at Ardingly for the Sunday; indeed, he will, I suppose, pass through Tilling on Saturday afternoon—"

Miss Mapp put her forefinger to her forehead, as if trying to recollect something.

"Yes, now somebody did tell me that," she said. "Major Flint, I believe. But when you asked for news, I thought you meant something that really interested me. Yes, Padre?"

"Aweel, if he comes to service on Sunday—?"

"Dear Padre, I'm sure he'll hear a very good sermon. Oh, I see what you mean! Whether you ought to have any special hymn? Don't ask poor little me! Mrs. Poppit, I'm sure, would tell you. She knows all about courts and etiquette."

Diva popped out of the stationer's at this moment.

"Sold out," she announced. "Everybody wanted timetables this morning. Evie got the last. Have to go to the station."

"I'll walk with you, Diva, dear," said Miss Mapp. "There's a parcel that—Good-by, dear Evie; au reservoir."

She kissed her hand to Mrs. Bartlett, leaving a smile behind it, as it fluttered away from her face, for the Padre.

Miss Mapp was so impenetrably wrapped in thought as she worked among her sweet flowers that afternoon, that she merely stared at a love-in-a-mist, which she had absently rooted up instead of a piece of groundsel, without any bleeding of the heart for one of her sweet flowers. There were two trains by which He might arrive—one at 4:15, which would get

him to Ardingly for tea, the other at 6:45. She was
quite determined to see him, but more inflexible than
that resolve was the Euclidean postulate that no one
in Tilling should think that she had taken any deliberate step to do so. For the present she had disarmed
suspicion by the blankness of her indifference as to
what might happen on Saturday or Sunday; but she
herself strongly suspected that everybody else, in
spite of the public attitude of Tilling to such subjects,
was determined to see him, too. How to see and not
be seen was the question which engrossed her, and
though she might possibly happen to be at that sharp
corner outside the station where every motor had to
go slow, on the arrival of the 4:15, it would never do
to risk being seen there again precisely at 6:45. Mrs.
Poppit, shameless in her snobbery, would no doubt be
at the station with her Order on at both these hours,
if the arrival did not take place by the first train, and
Isabel would be prancing by or behind her, and, in
fact, dreadful though it was to contemplate, all Tilling, she reluctantly believed, would be hanging
about. . . . Then an idea struck her, so glorious, that
she put the uprooted love-in-a-mist in the weed basket, instead of planting it again, and went quickly indoors, up to the attics, and from there popped—really
popped, so tight was the fit—through a trapdoor on to
the roof. Yes: the station was plainly visible, and if
the 4:15 was the favored train, there would certainly
be a motor from Ardingly Park waiting there in good
time for its arrival. From the house roof she could ascertain that, and she would then have time to trip
down the hill and get to her coal merchant's at that
sharp corner outside the station, and ask, rather
peremptorily, when the coke for her central heating
might be expected. It was due now, and though it

would be unfortunate if it arrived before Saturday, it was quite easy to smile away her peremptory manner, and say that Withers had not told her. Miss Mapp hated prevarication, but a major force sometimes came along. . . . But if no motors from Ardingly Park were in waiting for the 4:15 (as spied from her house roof), she need not risk being seen in the neighborhood of the station, but would again make observations some few minutes before the 6:45 was due. There was positively no other train by which He could come. . . .

The next day or two saw no traceable developments in the situation, but Miss Mapp's trained sense told her that there was underground work of some kind going on; she seemed to hear faint hollow taps and muffled knockings, and so to speak, the silence of some unusual pregnancy. Up and down the High Street she observed short whispered conversations going on between her friends, which broke off on her approach. This only confirmed her view that these secret colloquies were connected with Saturday afternoon, for it was not to be expected that, after her freezing reception of the news, any projected snobbishness should be confided to her, and though she would have liked to know what Diva and Irene and darling Evie were meaning to do, the fact that they none of them told her, showed that they were aware that she, at any rate, was utterly indifferent to and above that sort of thing. She suspected, too, that Major Flint had fallen victim to this un-Tillinglike mania, for on Friday afternoon, when passing his door, which happened to be standing open, she quite distinctly saw him in front of his glass in the hall (standing on the head of one of the tigers to secure a better view of himself), trying on a silk top hat. Her own errand at this moment was to the draper's, where she bought a quantity of pretty pale blue braid, for a little domestic dressmaking which was in arrears, and some riband of the same tint. At this clever and unusual hour for shopping, the High Street was naturally empty, and after a little hesitation and many anxious glances to right and left, she plunged into the toy shop and bought a pleasant little Union Jack with a short stick attached to it. She told Mr. Dabnet very distinctly that it was a present for her nephew, and concealed it inside her parasol, where it lay quite flat and made no perceptible bulge. . . .

At four o'clock on Saturday afternoon, she remembered that the damp had come in through her bedroom ceiling in a storm last winter, and told Withers she was going to have a look to see if any tiles were loose. In order to ascertain this for certain, she took up through the trapdoor a pair of binocular glasses, through which it was also easy to identify anybody who might be in the open yard outside the station. Even as she looked, Mrs. Poppit and Isabel crossed the yard into the waiting room and ticket office. It was a little surprising that there were not more friends in the station yard, but at the moment she heard a loud "Qui-hi" in the street below, and cautiously peering over the parapet, she got an admirable view of the Major in a frock coat and tall hat. A "Coo-ee" answered him, and Captain Puffin, in a new suit (Miss Mapp was certain of it) and a Panama hat, joined him. They went down the street and turned the corner. . . . Across the opening to the High Street, then shot the figure of darling Diva.

While waiting for them to appear again in the station yard, Miss Mapp looked to see what vehicles were standing there. It was already ten minutes past

four, and the Ardingly motors must have been there
by this time, if there was anything "doing" by the
4:15. But positively the only vehicle there was an
open trolley laden with a piano in a sack. Apart from
knowing all about that piano, for Mrs. Poppit had
talked about little else than her new upright Bluthner
before her visit to Buckingham Palace, a moment's reflection convinced Miss Mapp that this was a very unlikely mode of conveyance for any guest. . . . She
watched for a few moments more, but as no other
friends appeared in the station yard, she concluded
that they were hanging about the street somewhere,
poor things, and decided not to make inquiries about
her coke just yet.

She had tea while she arranged flowers, in the very
front of the window in her garden room, and
presently had the satisfaction of seeing many of the
baffled loyalists trudging home. There was no need to
do more than smile and tap the window and kiss her
hand: they all knew that she had been busy with her
flowers, and that she knew what they had been busy
about. . . . Out again they all came towards half past
six, and when she had watched the last of them down
the hill, she hurried back to the roof again, to make a
final inspection of the loose tiles through her binocu-
lars. Brief but exciting was that inspection, for opposite the entrance to the station was drawn up a
motor. So clear was the air and so serviceable her bin-
oculars that she could distinguish the vulgar coronet
on the panels, and as she looked Mrs. Poppit and Isabel hurried across the station yard. It was then but
the work of a moment to slip on the dust cloak
trimmed with blue braid, adjust the hat with the blue
riband, and take up the parasol with its furled Union

Jack inside it. The stick of the flag was uppermost; she could whip it out in a moment.

Miss Mapp had calculated her appearance to a nicety. Just as she got to the sharp corner opposite the station, where all cars slowed down and her coal merchant's office was situated, the train drew up. By the gates into the yard were standing the Major in his top hat, the Captain in his Panama, Irene in a civilized skirt, Diva in a brand-new walking dress, and the Padre and wee wifey. They were all looking in the direction of the station, and Miss Mapp stepped into the coal merchant's unobserved. Oddly enough the coke had been sent three days before, and there was no need for peremptoriness.

"So good of you, Mr. Wootten!" she said. "And why is everyone standing about this afternoon?"

Mr. Wootten explained the reason of this, and Miss Mapp, grasping her parasol, went out again as the car left the station. There were too many dear friends about, she decided, to use the Union Jack, and having seen what she wanted to, she determined to slip quietly away again. Already the Major's hat was in his hands, and he was bowing low, so too were Captain Puffin and the Padre, while Irene, Diva and Evie were making little ducking movements. . . . Miss Mapp was determined, when it came her turn, to show them, as she happened to be on the spot, what a proper curtsy was.

The car came opposite her, and she curtsied so low that recovery was impossible, and she sat down in the road. Her parasol flew out of her hands, and out of her parasol flew the Union Jack. She saw a young man looking out of the window, dressed in khaki, grinning broadly, but not, so she thought, graciously, and it suddenly struck her that there was something,

besides her own part in the affair, which was not as it
should be. As he put his head in again, there was
loud laughter from the inside of the car.

Mr. Wootten helped her up, and the entire assem-
bly of her friends crowded round her, hoping she was
not hurt.

"No, dear Major, dear Padre, not at all, thanks," she
said. "So stupid: my ankle turned. Oh, yes, the Union
Jack I bought for my nephew; it's his birthday tomorrow. Thank you. I just came to see about my coke; of
course, I thought the Prince had arrived when you all
went down to meet the 4:15. Fancy my running
straight into it all! How well he looked."

This was all rather lame, and Miss Mapp hailed
Mrs. Poppit's appearance from the station as a welcome diversion. . . . Mrs. Poppit was looking vexed.

"I hope you saw him well, Mrs. Poppit," said Miss
Mapp, "after meeting two trains, and taking all that
trouble."

"Saw who?" said Mrs. Poppit with a deplorable lack
both of manner and grammar. "Why"—light seemed
to break on her odious countenance—"why, you don't
think that was the Prince, do you, Miss Mapp? He arrived here at one, so the stationmaster has just told
me, and has been playing golf all afternoon."

The Major looked at the Captain, and the Captain
at the Major. It was months and months since they
had missed their Sunday afternoon's golf.

"It was the Prince of Wales who looked out of that
car window," said Miss Mapp firmly. "Such a pleasant
smile. I should know it anywhere."

"The young man who got into the car at the station
was no more the Prince of Wales than you are," said
Mrs. Poppit shrilly. "I was close to him as he came
out; I curtsied to him before I saw."

Miss Mapp instantly changed her attack; she could hardly hold her smile on her face for rage.

"How very awkward for you," she said. "What a laugh they will all have over it this evening. Delicious!"

Mrs. Poppit's face suddenly took on an expression of the tenderest solicitude.

"I hope, Miss Mapp, you didn't jar yourself when you sat down in the road just now," she said.

"Not at all, thank you so much," said Miss Mapp, hearing her heart beat in her throat. . . . If she had had a naval fifteen-inch gun handy, and had known how to fire it, she would, with a sense of duty accomplished, have discharged it point-blank at the Member of the Order of the British Empire, and at anybody else who might be within range.

Sunday, of course, with all the opportunities of that day, still remained, and the seats of the auxiliary choir, which were advantageously situated, had never been so full, but as it was all of no use, the Major and Captain Puffin left during the sermon to catch the 12:20 tram out to the links. On this delightful day it was but natural that the pleasant walk there across the marsh was very popular, and golfers that afternoon had a very trying and nervous time, for the ladies of Tilling kept bobbing up from behind sand dunes and bunkers, as, regardless of the players, they executed swift flank marches in all directions. Miss Mapp returned exhausted about tea time to hear from Withers that the Prince had spent an hour or more rambling about the town, and had stopped quite five minutes at the corner by the garden room. He had actually sat down on Miss Mapp's steps and smoked a cigarette. She wondered if the end of the cigarette was there still: it was hateful to have cigarette ends

defiling the steps to her front door, and often before
now, when sketchers were numerous, she had sent her
housemaid out to remove these untidy relics. She
searched for it, but was obliged to come to the reluc-
tant conclusion that there was nothing to remove. . . .

3

Diva was sitting at the open drawing-room window
of her house in the High Street, cutting with a pair of
sharp nail scissors into the old chintz curtains which
her maid had told her no longer "paid for the mending." So, since they refused to pay for their mending
any more, she was preparing to make them pay,
pretty smartly, too, in other ways. The pattern was of
little bunches of pink roses peeping out through trellis
work, and it was these which she had just begun to
cut out. Though Tilling was noted for the ingenuity
with which its more fashionable ladies devised novel
and quaint effects in their dress in an economical
manner, Diva felt sure, ransack her memory though
she might, that nobody had thought of *this* before.

The hot weather had continued late into September
and showed no signs of breaking yet, and it would be
agreeable to her and acutely painful to others that
just at the end of the summer she should appear in a
perfectly new costume, before the days of jumpers

and heavy skirts and large woolen scarves came in. She was preparing, therefore, to take the light white jacket which she wore over her blouse, and cover the broad collar and cuffs of it with these pretty roses. The belt of the skirt would be similarly decorated, and so would the edge of it, if there were enough clean ones. The jacket and skirt had already gone to the dyer's, and would be back in a day or two, white no longer, but of a rich purple hue, and by that time she would have hundreds of these little pink roses ready to be tacked on. Perhaps a piece of the chintz, trellis and all, could be sewn over the belt, but she was determined to have single little bunches of roses peppered all over the collar and cuffs of the jacket and, if possible, round the edge of the skirt. She had already tried the effect, and was of the opinion that nobody could possibly guess what the origin of these roses was. When carefully sewn on they looked as if they were a design in the stuff.

She let the circumcised roses fall on to the window seat, and from time to time, when they grew numerous, swept them into a cardboard box. Though she worked with zealous diligence, she had an eye to the movements in the street outside, for it was shopping hour, and there were many observations to be made. She had not anything like Miss Mapp's genius for conjecture, but her memory was appallingly good, and this was the third morning running on which Elizabeth had gone into the grocer's. It was odd to go to your grocer's every day like that: groceries twice a week was sufficient for most people. From here, on the floor above the street, she could easily look into Elizabeth's basket, and she certainly was carrying nothing away with her from the grocer's, for the only thing there was a small bottle done up in white paper with sealing wax, which, Diva had no need to be told, certainly came from the chemist's, and was no doubt connected with too many plums.

Miss Mapp crossed the street to the pavement below Diva's house, and precisely as she reached it, Diva's maid opened the door into the drawing room, bringing in the second post, or rather not bringing in the second post, but the announcement that there wasn't any second post. This opening of the door caused a draught, and the bunches of roses which littered the window seat rose brightly in the air. Diva managed to beat most of them down again, but two fluttered out of the window. Precisely then, and at no other time, Miss Mapp looked up, and one settled on her face, the other fell into her basket. Her trained faculties were all on the alert, and she thrust them both inside her glove for future consideration, without stopping to examine them just then. She only knew that they were little pink roses, and that they had fluttered out of Diva's window. . . .

She paused on the pavement, and remembered that Diva had not yet expressed regret about the worsted, and that she still "popped" as much as ever. Then Diva deserved a punishment of some sort, and happily, at that very moment, she thought of a subject on which she might be able to make her uncomfortable. The street was full, and it would be pretty to call up to her, instead of ringing her bell, in order to save trouble to poor overworked Janet. (Diva only kept two servants, though of course poverty was no crime.)

"Diva darling!" she cooed.

Diva's head looked out like a cuckoo in a clock preparing to chime the hour.

"Hullo!" she said. "Want me?"

"May I pop up for a moment, dear?" said Miss Mapp. "That's to say if you're not very busy."

"Pop away," said Diva. She was quite aware that Miss Mapp said "pop" in crude inverted commas, so to speak, for purposes of mockery, and so she said it herself more than ever. "I'll tell my maid to pop down and open the door."

While this was being done, Diva bundled her chintz curtains together and stored them and the roses she had cut out into her work cupboard, for secrecy was an essential to the construction of these decorations. But in order to appear naturally employed, she pulled out the woolen scarf she was knitting for the autumn and winter, forgetting for the moment that the rose-madder stripe at the end on which she was now engaged was made of that fatal worsted which Miss Mapp considered to have been feloniously appropriated. That was the sort of thing Miss Mapp never forgot. Even among her sweet flowers. Her eye fell on it the moment she entered the room, and she tucked the two chintz roses more securely into her glove.

"I thought I would just pop across from the grocer's," she said. "What a pretty scarf, dear! That's a lovely shade of rose madder. Where can I have seen something like it before?"

This was clearly ironical, and had best be answered by irony. Diva was no coward.

"Couldn't say, I'm sure," she said.

Miss Mapp appeared to recollect, and smiled as far back as her wisdom teeth. (Diva couldn't do that.)

"I have it," she said. "It was the wool I ordered at Heynes's, and then he sold it to you, and I couldn't get any more."

"So it was," said Diva. "Upset you a bit. There was the wool in the shop. I bought it."

"Yes, dear; I see you did. But that wasn't what I popped in about. This coal strike, you know."

"Got a cellar full," said Diva.

"Diva, you've not been hoarding, have you?" asked Miss Mapp with great anxiety. "They can take away every atom of coal you've got, if so, and fine you I don't know what for every hundredweight of it."

"Pooh!" said Diva, rather forcing the indifference of this rude interjection.

"Yes, love, pooh by all means, if you like poohing!" said Miss Mapp. "But I should have felt very unfriendly if one morning I found you were fined— found you were fined—quite a play upon words—and I hadn't warned you."

Diva felt a little less poohish.

"But how much do they allow you to have?" she asked.

"Oh, quite a little: enough to go on with. But I daresay they won't discover you. I just took the trouble to come and warn you."

Diva did remember something about hoarding; there had surely been dreadful exposures of prudent housekeepers in the papers which were very uncomfortable reading.

"But all these orders were only for the period of the war," she said.

"No doubt you're right, dear," said Miss Mapp brightly. "I'm sure I hope you are. Only if the coal strike comes on, I think you'll find that the regulations against hoarding are quite as severe as they ever were. Food hoarding, too. Twenlow—such a civil man—tells me he thinks we shall have plenty of food, or anyhow sufficient for everybody for quite a long time, provided that there's no hoarding. Not been hoarding food, too, dear Diva? You naughty thing: I believe that great cupboard is full of sardines and biscuits and bovril."

"Nothing of the kind," said Diva indignantly. "You shall see for yourself"—and then she suddenly remembered that the cupboard was full of chintz curtains and little bunches of pink roses, neatly cut out of them, and a pair of nail scissors.

There was a perfectly perceptible pause, during which Miss Mapp noticed that there were no curtains over the window. There certainly used to be, and they matched the chintz cover of the window seat, which was decorated with little bunches of pink roses peeping through trellis. This was in the nature of a bonus: she had not up till then connected the chintz curtains with the little things that had fluttered down upon her and were now safe in her glove; her only real object in this call had been to instill a general uneasiness into Diva's mind about the coal strike and the danger of being well provided with fuel. That she humbly hoped that she had accomplished. She got up.

"Must be going," she said. "Such a lovely little chat! But what has happened to your pretty curtains?"

"Gone to the wash," said Diva firmly.

"Liar," thought Miss Mapp, as she tripped downstairs. "Diva would have sent the cover of the window seat, too, if that was the case. Liar," she thought again as she kissed her hand to Diva, who was looking gloomily out of the window.

As soon as Miss Mapp had gained her garden room, she examined the mysterious treasures in her left-hand glove. Without the smallest doubt Diva had taken down her curtains (and high time, too, for they

were sadly shabby), and was cutting the roses out of
them. But what on earth was she doing that for? For
what garish purpose could she want to use bunches of
roses cut out of chintz curtains?

Miss Mapp had put the two specimens of which
she had so providentially become possessed in her
lap, and they looked very pretty against the navy
blue of her skirt (not kingfisher blue yet). Diva was
very ingenious; she used up all sorts of odds and ends
in a way that did credit to her undoubtedly parsimoni-
ous qualities. She could trim a hat with a tooth brush
and a banana in such a way that it looked quite Par-
isian till you firmly analysed its component parts, and
most of her ingenuity was devoted to dress: the more
was the pity that she had such a round-about figure
that her waistband always reminded you of the equa-
tor. . . .

"Eureka!" said Miss Mapp aloud, and though the
telephone bell was ringing, and the postulant might
be one of the servants' friends ringing them up at an
hour when their mistress was usually in the High
Street, she glided swiftly to the large cupboard underneath the stairs which was full of the things which no
right-minded person could bear to throw away: broken basket-chairs, pieces of brown paper, cardboard
boxes without lids, and cardboard lids without boxes,
old bags with holes in them, keys without locks and
locks without keys and worn chintz covers. There was
one—it had once adorned the sofa in the garden
room—covered with red poppies (very easy to cut
out), and Miss Mapp dragged it dustily from its corner, setting in motion a perfect cascade of cardboard
lids and some door handles.

Withers had answered the telephone, and came to

announce that Twenlow the grocer regretted he had only two large tins of corned beef, but—

"Then say I will have the tongue as well, Withers," said Miss Mapp. "Just a tongue—and then I shall want you and Mary to do some cutting out for me."

The three went to work with feverish energy, for Diva had got a start, and by four o'clock that afternoon there were enough poppies cut out to furnish, when in seed, a whole street of opium dens. The dress selected for decoration was, apart from a few mildew spots, the color of ripe corn, which was superbly appropriate for September. "Poppies in the corn," said Miss Mapp over and over to herself, remembering some sweet verses she had once read by Bernard Shaw or Clement Shorter or somebody like that about a garden of sleep somewhere in Norfolk. . . .

"No one can work as neatly as you, Withers," she said gaily, "and I shall ask you to do the most difficult part. I want you to sew my lovely poppies over the collar and facings of the jacket, just spacing them a little and making a dainty irregularity. And then Mary—won't you, Mary?—will do the same with the waistband while I put a border of them round the skirt, and my dear old dress will look quite new and lovely. I shall be at home to nobody, Withers, this afternoon, even if the Prince of Wales came and sat on my doorstep again. We'll all work together in the garden, shall we, and you and Mary must scold me if you think I'm not working hard enough. It will be delicious in the garden."

Thanks to this pleasant plan, there was not much opportunity for Withers and Mary to be idle. . . .

Just about the time that this harmonious party began their work, a far from harmonious couple were being just as industrious in the grand spacious bunker in front of the tee to the last hole on the golf links. It was a beautiful bunker, consisting of a great slope of loose, steep sand against the face of the hill, and solidly shored up with timber. The Navy had been in better form today, and after a decisive victory over the Army in the morning and an indemnity of half a crown, its match in the afternoon, with just the last hole to play, was all square. So Captain Puffin, having the honor, hit a low, nervous drive that tapped loudly at the timbered wall of the bunker, and cuddled down below it, well protected from any future assault.

"Phew! That about settles it," said Major Flint boisterously. "Bad place to top a ball! Give me the hole?"

This insolent question needed no answer, and Major Flint drove, skying the ball to a prodigious height. But it had to come to earth sometime, and it fell like Lucifer, son of the morning, in the middle of the same bunker. . . . So the Army played three more, and, sweating profusely, got out. Then it was the Navy's turn, and the Navy had to lie on its keel above the boards of the bunker, in order to reach its ball at all, and missed it twice.

"Better give it up, old chap," said Major Flint. "Unplayable."

"Then see me play it," said Captain Puffin with a chewing motion of his jaws.

"We shall miss the tram," said the Major, and, with the intention of giving annoyance, he sat down in the bunker with his back to Captain Puffin, and lit a cigarette. At his third attempt nothing happened; at the fourth the ball flew against the boards, rebounded briskly again into the bunker, trickled down the steep, sandy slope and hit the Major's boot.

"Hit you, I think," said Captain Puffin. "Ha! So it's my hole, Major!"

Major Flint had a short fit of aphasia. He opened and shut his mouth and foamed. Then he took a half-crown from his pocket.

"Give that to the Captain," he said to his caddie, and without looking round, walked away in the direction of the tram. He had not gone a hundred yards when the whistle sounded, and it puffed away homewards with ever-increasing velocity.

Weak and trembling from passion, Major Flint found that after a few tottering steps in the direction of Tilling he would be totally unable to get there unless fortified by some strong stimulant, and turned back to the clubhouse to obtain it. He always went dead-lame when beaten at golf, while Captain Puffin was lame in any circumstances, and the two, no longer on speaking terms, hobbled into the clubhouse, one after the other, each unconscious of the other's presence. Summoning his last remaining strength Major Flint roared for whisky, and was told that, according to regulation, he could not be served until six. There was lemonade and stone ginger-beer. . . . You might as well have offered a man-eating tiger bread and milk. Even the threat that he would instantly resign his membership unless provided with drink produced no effect on a polite steward, and he sat down to recover as best he might with an old volume of *Punch*. This seemed to do him little good. His forced abstemiousness was rendered the more intolerable by the fact that Captain Puffin, hobbling in immediately afterwards, fetched from his locker a large flask full of the required elixir, and proceeded to mix himself a long, strong tumblerful. After the Major's rudeness in the matter of the half-crown, it was impossible for any sailor of spirit to take the first step towards reconciliation.

Thirst is a great leveller. By the time the refreshed Puffin had penetrated halfway down his glass, the Major found it impossible to be proud and proper any longer. He hated saying he was sorry (no man more), and he wouldn't have been sorry if he had been able to get a drink. He twirled his moustache a great many times and cleared his throat—it wanted more than that to clear it—and capitulated.

"Upon my word, Puffin, I'm ashamed of myself for—ha!—for not taking my defeat better," he said. "A man's no business to let a game ruffle him."

Puffin gave his alto cackling laugh.

"Oh, that's all right, Major," he said. "I know it's awfully hard to lose like a gentleman."

He let this sink in, then added:

"Have a drink, old chap?"

Major Flint flew to his feet.

"Well, thank ye, thank ye," he said. "Now where's that soda water you offered me just now?" he shouted to the steward.

The speed and completeness of the reconciliation was in no way remarkable, for when two men quarrel whenever they meet, it follows that they make it up again with corresponding frequency, else there could be no fresh quarrels at all. This one had been a shade more acute than most, and the drop into amity again was a shade more precipitous.

Major Flint in his eagerness had put most of his moustache into the life-giving tumbler and dried it on his handkerchief.

"After all, it was a most amusing incident," he said. "There was I with my back turned, waiting for you to give it up, when your bl— wretched little ball hit my foot. I must remember that. I'll serve you with the same spoon some day; at least I would if I thought it sportsmanlike. Well, well, enough said. Astonishing good whisky, that of yours."

Captain Puffin helped himself to rather more than half of what now remained in the flask.

"Help yourself, Major," he said.

"Well, thank ye, I don't mind if I do," he said, reversing the flask over the tumbler. "There's a good tramp in front of us now that the last tram has gone. Tram and tramp! Upon my word, I've half a mind to telephone for a taxi."

This, of course, was a direct hint. Puffin ought clearly to pay for a taxi, having won two half-crowns today. This casual drink did not constitute the usual drink stood by the winner, and paid for with cash over the counter. A drink (or two) from a flask was not the same thing. . . . Puffin naturally saw it in another light. He had paid for the whisky which Major Flint had drunk (or owed for it) in his wine-merchant's bill. That was money just as much as a florin pushed across the counter. But he was so excessively pleased with himself over the adroitness with which he had claimed the last hole, that he quite overstepped the bounds of his habitual parsimony.

"Well, you trot along to the telephone and order a taxi," he said, "and I'll pay for it."

"Done with you," said the other.

Their comradeship was now on its most felicitous level again, and they sat on the bench outside the clubhouse till the arrival of their unusual conveyance.

"Lunching at the Poppits' tomorrow?" asked Major Flint.

"Yes. Meet you there? Good. Bridge afterwards, I suppose."

"Sure to be. Wish there was a chance of more red-currant fool. That was a decent tipple, all but the red currants. If I had had all the old brandy that was served for my ration in one glass, and all the champagne in another, I should have been better content."

Captain Puffin was a great cynic in his own misogynistic way.

"Camouflage for the fair sex," he said. "A woman will lick up half a bottle of brandy if it's called plum pudding, and ask for more, whereas if you offered her a small brandy and soda, she would think you were insulting her."

"Bless them, the funny little fairies," said the Major.

"Well, what I tell you is true, Major," said Puffin. "There's old Mapp. Teetotaller she calls herself, but she played a bo'sun's part in that red-currant fool. Bit rosy, I thought her, as we escorted her home."

"So she was," said the Major. "So she was. Said good-by to us on her doorstep as if she thought she was a perfect Venus Ana—Ana something."

"Ano Domini," giggled Puffin.

"Well, well, we all get long in the tooth in time," said Major Flint charitably. "Fine figure of a woman, though."

"Eh?" said Puffin archly.

"Now none of your sailor talk ashore, Captain," said the Major, in high good humor. "I'm not a marrying man any more than you are. Better if I had been perhaps, more years ago than I care to think about. Dear me, my wound's going to trouble me tonight."

"What do you do for it, Major?" asked Puffin.

"Do for it? Think of old times a bit over my diaries."

"Going to let the world have a look at them some day?" asked Puffin.

"No, sir, I am not," said Major Flint. "Perhaps a hundred years hence—the date I have named in my will for their publication—someone may think them not so uninteresting. But all this toasting and buttering and grilling and frying your friends, and serving them up hot for all the old cats at a teatable to mew over—Pah!"

Puffin was silent a moment in appreciation of these noble sentiments.

"But you put in a lot of work over them," he said at length. "Often when I'm going up to bed, I see the light still burning in your sitting-room window."

"And if it comes to that," rejoined the Major, "I'm sure I've often dozed off when I'm in bed and woken again, and pulled up my blind, and what not, and there's your light still burning. Powerful long roads those old Romans must have made, Captain."

The ice was not broken, but it was cracking in all directions under this unexampled thaw. The two had clearly indicated a mutual suspicion of each other's industrious habits after dinner. . . . They had never got quite so far as this before: some quarrel had congealed the surface again. But now, with a desperate disagreement just behind them, and the unusual luxury of a taxi just in front, the vernal airs continued blowing in the most springlike manner.

"Yes, that's true enough," said Puffin. "Long roads they were, and dry roads at that, and if I stuck to them from my supper every evening till midnight or more, I should be smothered in dust."

"Unless you washed the dust down just once in a while," said Major Flint.

"Just so. Brainwork's an exhausting process; requires a little stimulant now and again," said Puffin. "I sit in my chair, you understand, and perhaps doze for a bit after my supper, and then I'll get my maps out, and have them handy beside me. And then, if there's something interesting in the evening paper, perhaps I'll have a look at it, and bless me, if by that time it isn't already half-past ten or eleven, and it seems useless to tackle archaeology then. And I just—just while away the time till I'm sleepy. But there seems to be a sort of legend among the ladies here, that I'm a great student of local topography and Roman roads, and all sorts of truck, and I find it better to leave it at that. Tiresome to go into long explanations. In fact," added Puffin in a burst of confidence, "the study I've done on Roman roads these last six months wouldn't cover a threepenny piece."

Major Flint gave a loud, choking guffaw and beat his fat leg.

"Well, if that's not the best joke I've heard for many a long day," he said. "There I've been in the house opposite you these last two years, seeing your light burning late night after night, and thinking to myself, 'There's my friend Puffin still at it! Fine thing to be an enthusiastic archaeologist like that. That makes short work of a lonely evening for him if he's so buried in his books or his maps—Mapps, ha! ha!—that he doesn't seem to notice whether it's twelve o'clock or one or two, maybe!' And all the time you've been sitting snoozing and boozing in your chair, with your glass handy to wash the dust down."

Puffin added his falsetto cackle to this merriment.

"And, often I've thought to myself," he said, "'There's my friend the Major in his study opposite, with all his diaries round him, making a note here, and copying an extract there, and conferring with the Viceroy one day, and reprimanding the Maharaja of Bom-be-boo another. He's spending the evening on

India's coral strand, he is having tiffin and shooting tigers and Gawd knows what—' "

The Major's laughter boomed out again.

"And I never kept a diary in my life!" he cried. "Why there's enough cream in this situation to make a dishful of meringues. You and I, you know, the students of Tilling! The serious-minded students who do a hard day's work when all the pretty ladies have gone to bed. Often and often has old—I mean has that fine woman, Miss Mapp, told me that I work too hard at night! Recommended to me to get earlier to bed, and do my work between six and eight in the morning! Six and eight in the morning! That's a queer time of day to recommend an old campaigner to be awake at! Often she's talked to you, too, I bet my hat, about sitting up late and exhausting the nervous faculties."

Major Flint choked and laughed and inhaled tobacco smoke till he got purple in the face.

"And you sitting up one side of the street," he gasped, "pretending to be interested in Roman roads, and me on the other pulling a long face over my diaries, and neither of us with a Roman road or a diary to our names. Let's have an end to such unsociable arrangements, old friend; you bring your Roman roads and the bottle to lay the dust over to me one night, and I'll bring my diaries and my peg over to you the next. Never drink alone—one of my maxims in life—if you can find someone to drink with you. And there were you within a few yards of me all the time sitting by your old solitary self, and there was I sitting by my old solitary self, and we each thought the other a serious-minded old buffer, busy on his life-work. I'm blessed if I ever heard of two such pompous old frauds as you and I, Captain! What a sight of hypocrisy there is in the world, to be sure! No offence—

mind: I'm as bad as you, and you're as bad as me, and we're both as bad as each other. But no more solitary confinement of an evening for Benjamin Flint, as long as you're agreeable."

The advent of the taxi was announced, and arm in arm they limped down the steep path together to the road. A little way off to the left was the great bunker which, primarily, was the cause of their present amity. As they drove by it, the Major waggled his red hand at it.

"Au reservoir," he said. "Back again soon."

It was late that night when Miss Mapp felt that she was physically incapable of tacking on a single poppy more to the edge of her skirt, and went to the window of the garden room where she had been working to close it. She glanced up at the top story of her own house, and saw that the lights in the servants' rooms were out: she glanced to the right and concluded that her gardener had gone to bed: finally, she glanced down the street and saw with a pang of pleasure that the windows of the Major's house showed no sign of midnight labor. This was intensely gratifying: it indicated that her influence was at work in him, for in response to her wish, so often and so tactfully urged on him, that he would go to bed earlier and not work so hard at night, here was the darkened window, and she dismissed as unworthy the suspicion which had been aroused by the red-currant fool. The window of his bedroom was dark, too: he must have already put out his light, and Miss Mapp made haste over her little tidyings so that she might not be found a transgressor to her own precepts. But there was a light in Captain Puffin's house: he had a less impressionable nature than the Major and was in so many ways far

inferior. And did he really find Roman roads so wonderfully exhilarating? Miss Mapp sincerely hoped that
he did, and that it was nothing else of less pure and
innocent allurement that kept him up. . . . As she
closed the window very gently, it did just seem to her
that there had been something equally baffling in Major Flint's egoistical vigils over his diaries; that she
had wondered whether there was not something else
(she had hardly formulated what) which kept his
lights burning so late. But she would now cross him—
dear man—and his late habits, out of the list of riddles
about Tilling which awaited solution. Whatever it
had been (diaries or what not) that used to keep him
up, he had broken the habit now, whereas Captain
Puffin had not. She took her poppy-bordered skirt
over her arm, and smiled her thankful way to bed.
She could allow herself to wonder with a little more
definiteness, now that the Major's lights were out and
he was abed, what it could be which rendered Captain Puffin so oblivious to the passage of time, when
he was investigating Roman roads. How glad she was
that the Major was not with him . . . "Benjamin
Flint!" she said to herself as, having put her window
open, she trod softly (so as not to disturb the slum-
berer next door) across her room on her fat white feet
to her big white bed. "Good night, Major Benjy," she
whispered as she put her light out.

It was not to be supposed that Diva would act on
Miss Mapp's alarming hints that morning as to the
fate of coal hoarders, and give, say, a ton of fuel to
the hospital at once, in lieu of her usual smaller
Christmas contribution, without making further inquiries in the proper quarters as to the legal liabilities
of having, so she ascertained, three tons in her cellar,

and as soon as her visitor had left her this morning, she popped out to see Mr. Wootten, her coal merchant. She returned in a state of fury, for there were no regulations whatever in existence with regard to the amount of coal that any householder might choose to amass, and Mr. Wootten complimented her on her prudence in having got in a reasonable supply, for he thought it quite probable that, if the coal strike took place, there would be some difficulty in a month's time from now in replenishing cellars. "But we've had a good supply all summer," added agreeable Mr. Wootten, "and all my customers have got their cellars well stocked."

Diva rapidly recollected that the perfidious Elizabeth was among them.

"Oh, but, Mr. Wootten," she said, "Miss Mapp popped—dropped in to see me just now. Told me she had hardly got any."

Mr. Wootten turned up his ledger. It was not etiquette to disclose the affairs of one client to another, but if there was a cantankerous customer, one who was never satisfied with prices and quality, that client was Miss Mapp. . . . He allowed a broad grin to overspread his agreeable face.

"Well, ma'am, if in a month's time I'm short of coal, there are friends of yours in Tilling who can let you have plenty," he permitted himself to say. . . .

It was idle to attempt to cut out bunches of roses while her hand was so feverish, and she trundled up and down the High Street to cool off. Had she not been so prudent as to make inquiries, as likely as not she would have sent a ton of coal that very day to the hospital, so strongly had Elizabeth's perfidious warning inflamed her imagination as to the fate of hoarders, and all the time Elizabeth's own cellars were glutted, though she had asserted that she was almost fuelless. Why, she must have in her possession more coal than Diva herself, since Mr. Wootten had clearly implied that it was Elizabeth who could be borrowed from! And all because of a wretched piece of rose-madder worsted. . . .

By degrees she calmed down, for it was no use attempting to plan revenge with a brain at fever heat. She must be calm and icily ingenious. As the cooling process went on, she began to wonder whether it was worsted alone that had prompted her friend's diabolical suggestion. It seemed more likely that another motive (one strangely Elizabethan) was the cause of it. Elizabeth might be taken for certain as being a coal hoarder herself, and it was ever so like her to divert suspicion by pretending her cellar was next to empty. She had been equally severe on any who might happen to be hoarding food, in case transport was disarranged and supplies fell short, and with a sudden flare of authentic intuition, Diva's mind blazed with the conjecture that Elizabeth was hoarding food as well.

Luck ever attends the bold and constructive thinker: the apple, for instance, fell from the tree precisely when Newton's mind was groping after the law of gravity, and as Diva stepped into her grocer's to begin her morning's shopping (for she had been occupied with roses ever since breakfast), the attendant was at the telephone at the back of the shop. He spoke in a lucid telephone voice.

"We've only two of the big tins of corned beef," he said, and there was a pause, during which, to a psychic, Diva's ears might have seemed to grow as pointed with attention as a satyr's. But she could only hear little hollow quacks from the other end.

"Tongue as well. Very good. I'll send them up at once," he added, and came forward into the shop.

"Good morning," said Diva. Her voice was tremulous with anxiety and investigation. "Got any big tins of corned beef? The ones that contain six pounds."

"Very sorry, ma'am. We've only got two, and they've just been ordered."

"A small pot of ginger then, please," said Diva recklessly. "Will you send it round immediately?"

"Yes, ma'am. The boy's just going out."

That was luck. Diva hurried into the street, and was absorbed by the headlines of the news outside the stationer's. This was a favorite place for observation, for you appeared to be quite taken up by the topics of the day, and kept an oblique eye on the true object of your scrutiny. . . . She had not got to wait long, for almost immediately the grocer's boy came out of the shop with a heavy basket on his arm, delivered the small pot of ginger at her own door, and proceeded along the street. He was, unfortunately, a popular and a conversational youth, who had a great deal to say to his friends, and the period of waiting to see if he would turn up the steep street that led to Miss Mapp's house was very protracted. At the corner he deliberately put down the basket altogether and lit a cigarette, and never had Diva so acutely deplored the spread of the tobacco habit among the juvenile population.

Having refreshed himself he turned up the steep street.

He passed the fishmonger's and the fruiterer's; he did not take the turn down to the dentist's and Mr. Wyse's. He had no errand to the Major's house or to the Captain's. Then, oh, then, he rang the bell at Miss Mapp's back door. All the time Diva had been follow-

ing him, keeping her head well down, so as to avert
the possibility of observation from the window of the
garden room, and walking so slowly that the motion
of her feet seemed not circular at all. . . . Then the
bell was answered, and he delivered into Withers'
hands one, two tins of corned beef and a round ox
tongue. He put the basket on his head and came
down the street again, shrilly whistling. If Diva had
had any reasonably small change in her pocket, she
would assuredly have given him some small share in
it. Lacking this, she trundled home with all speed,
and began cutting out roses with swift and certain
strokes of the nail scissors.

Now she had already noticed that Elizabeth had
paid visits to the grocer's on three consecutive days
(three consecutive days: think of it!), and given that
her purchases on other occasions had been on the
same substantial scale as today, it became a matter of
thrilling interest as to where she kept these stores.
She could not keep them in the coal cellar, for that
was already bursting with coal, and Diva, who had
assisted her (the base one) in making a prodigious
quantity of jam that year from her well-stocked
garden, was aware that the kitchen cupboards were
like to be as replete as the coal cellar, before those
hoardings of dead oxen began. Then there was the
big cupboard under the stairs, but that could scarcely
be the site of this prodigious cache, for it was full of
cardboard and curtains and carpets and all the rub-
bishly accumulations which Elizabeth could not bear
to part with. Then she had large cupboards in her
bedroom and spare rooms full to overflowing of
moldy clothes, but there was positively not another
cupboard in the house that Diva knew of, and she

crushed her temples in her hands in the attempt to lo-
cate the hiding place of the hoard.

Diva suddenly jumped up with a happy squeal of
discovery, and in her excitement snapped her scissors
with so random a stroke that she completely cut in
half the bunch of roses that she was engaged on.
There was another cupboard, the best and biggest of
all and the most secret and most discreet. It lay
embedded in the wall of the garden room, cloaked
and concealed behind the shelves of a false bookcase,
which contained no more than the simulacra of books,
just books with titles that had never yet appeared on
any honest book. There were twelve volumes of "The
Beauties of Nature," a shelf full of "Elegant Extracts";
there were volumes simply called "Poems"; there were
"Commentaries"; there were "Travels" and "Astronomy," and the lowest and tallest shelf was full of
"Music." A card table habitually stood in front of this
false repository of learning, and it was only last week
that Diva, prying casually round the room while Elizabeth had gone to take off her gardening gloves, had
noticed a modest catch let into the woodwork. Without doubt, then, the bookcase was the door of the
cupboard, and with a stroke of intuition, too sure to
be called a guess, Diva was aware that she had cor-
rectly inferred the storage of this nefarious hoard. It
only remained to verify her conclusion, and, if possible, expose it with every circumstance of public ig-
nominy. She was in no hurry: she could bide her
time, aware that, in all probability, every day that
passed would see an addition to its damning contents.
Some day, when she was playing bridge and the card
table had been moved out, in some rubber when she
herself was dummy and Elizabeth greedily playing
the hand, she would secretly and accidentally press

the catch which her acute vision had so providentially revealed to her. . . .

She attacked her chintz curtains again with her appetite for the pink roses agreeably whetted. Another hour's work would give her sufficient bunches for her purpose, and unless the dyer was as perfidious as Elizabeth, her now purple jacket and skirt would arrive that afternoon. Two days' hard work would be sufficient for so accomplished a needlewoman as herself to make these original decorations.

In the meantime, for Diva was never idle, and was chiefly occupied with dress, she got out a certain American fashion paper. There was in it the description of a tea gown worn by Mrs. Titus W. Trout which she believed was within her dressmaking capacity. She would attempt it anyhow, and if it proved to be beyond her, she could entrust the more difficult parts to that little dressmaker whom Elizabeth employed, and who was certainly very capable. But the costume was of so daring and splendid a nature that she feared to take anyone into her confidence about it, lest some hint or gossip—for Tilling was a gossipy place—might leak out. Kingfisher blue! It made her mouth water to dwell on the sumptuous syllables!

Miss Mapp was so feverishly occupied all next morning with the application of poppies to the corn-colored skirt that she paid very little attention to the opening gambits of the day, either as regards the world in general, or, more particularly, Major Benjy. After his early retirement last night, he was probably up with the lark this morning, and when between ten and eleven his sonorous "Qui-hi!" sounded through her open window, the shock she experienced interrupted for a moment her floral industry. It was certainly

very odd that, having gone to bed at so respectable
an hour last night, he should be calling for his porridge only now, but with an impulse of unusual optimism, she figured him as having been at work on his
diaries before breakfast, and in that absorbing occupation having forgotten how late it was growing.
That, no doubt, was the explanation, though it would
be nice to know for certain, if the information positively forced itself on her notice. . . . As she worked
(framing her lips with elaborate motions to the syllables), she dumbly practised the phrase "Major
Benjy." Sometimes in moments of gallantry he called
her "Miss Elizabeth," and she meant, when she had
got accustomed to it by practice, to say "Major Benjy"
to him by accident, and he would, no doubt, beg her
to make a habit of that friendly slip of the
tongue. . . . "Tongue" led to a new train of thought,
and presently she paused in her work, and pulling the
card-table away from the deceptive bookcase, she
pressed the concealed catch of the door and peeped
in.

There was still room for further small precautions
against starvation owing to the impending coal strike,
and she took stock of her provisions. Even if the
strike lasted quite a long time, there would now be no
immediate lack of the necessaries of life, for the cupboard glistened with tinned meats, and the flour merchant had sent a very sensible sack. This with
considerable exertion she transferred to a high shelf
in the cupboard, instead of allowing it to remain
standing on the floor, for Withers had informed her of
an unpleasant rumor about a mouse, which Mary had
observed, lost in thought in front of the cupboard. "So
mousie shall only find tins on the floor now," thought
Miss Mapp. "Mousie shall try his teeth on tins." . . .

There were tea and coffee in abundance, jars of jam filled the kitchen shelves, and if this morning she laid in a moderate supply of dried fruits, there was no reason to face the future with anything but fortitude. She would see about that now, for, busy though she was, she could not miss the shopping parade. Would Diva, she wondered, be at her window, snipping roses out of chintz curtains? The careful, thrifty soul. Perhaps this time tomorrow, Diva, looking out of her window, would see that somebody else had been quicker about being thrifty than she. That would be fun!

The Major's dining-room window was open, and as Miss Mapp passed it, she could not help hearing loud, angry remarks about eggs coming from inside. That made it clear that he was still at breakfast, and that if he had been working at his diaries in the fresh morning hours and forgetting the time, early rising, in spite of his early retirement last night, could not be supposed to suit his Oriental temper. But a change of habits was invariably known to be upsetting, and Miss Mapp was hopeful that in a day or two he would feel quite a different man. Further down the street was quaint Irene lounging at the door of her new studio (a converted coach house), smoking a cigarette and dressed like a jockey.

"Hullo, Mapp," she said. "Come and have a look round my new studio. You haven't seen it yet. I shall give a housewarming next week. Bridge party!"

Miss Mapp tried to steel herself for the hundredth time to appear quite unconscious that she was being addressed when Irene said, "Mapp," in that odious manner. But she never could summon up sufficient nerve to be rude to so awful a mimic. . . .

"Good morning, dear one," she said sycophantically.
"Shall I peep in for a moment?"

The decoration of the studio was even more appalling than might have been expected. There was a German stove in the corner made of pink porcelain; the rafters and roof were painted scarlet; the walls were of magenta distemper; and the floor was blue. In the corner was a very large orange-colored screen. The walls were hung with specimens of Irene's art; there was a stout female with no clothes on at all, whom it was impossible not to recognize as being Lucy; there were studies of fat legs and ample bosoms; and on the easel was a picture, evidently in process of completion, which represented a man. From this Miss Mapp instantly averted her eyes.

"Eve," said Irene, pointing to Lucy.

Miss Mapp naturally guessed that the gentleman who was almost in the same costume was Adam, and turned completely away from him.

"And what a lovely idea to have a blue floor, dear," she said. "How original you are. And that pretty scarlet ceiling. But don't you find when you're painting that all these bright colors disturb you?"

"Not a bit: they stimulate your sense of color."

Miss Mapp moved towards the screen.

"What a delicious big screen," she said.

"Yes, but don't go behind it, Mapp," said Irene, "or you'll see my model undressing."

Miss Mapp retreated from it precipitately, as from a wasp's nest, and examined some of the studies on the wall, for it was more than probable from the unfinished picture on the easel that Adam lurked behind the delicious screen. Terrible though it all was, she was conscious of an unbridled curiosity to know who Adam was. It was dreadful to think there could be any man in Tilling so depraved as to stand to be looked at with so little on. . . .

Irene strolled round the walls with her.

"Studies of Lucy," she said.

"I see, dear," said Miss Mapp. "How clever! Legs and things! But when you have your bridge party, won't you perhaps cover some of them up, or turn them to the wall? We should all be looking at your pictures instead of attending to our cards. And if you were thinking of asking the Padre, you know. . . ."

They were approaching the corner of the room where the screen stood, when a movement there as if Adam had hit it with his elbow made Miss Mapp turn around. The screen fell flat on the ground and within a yard of her stood Mr. Hopkins, the proprietor of the fish shop just up the street. Often and often had Miss Mapp had pleasant little conversations with him, with a view to bringing down the price of flounders. He had little bathing drawers on. . . .

"Hullo, Hopkins, are you ready?" said Irene. "You know Miss Mapp, don't you?"

Miss Mapp had not imagined that Time and Eternity combined could hold so embarrassing a moment. She did not know where to look, but wherever she looked, it should not be at Hopkins. But (wherever she looked) she could not be unaware that Hopkins raised his large bare arm and touched the place where his cap would have been, if he had had one.

"Good morning, Hopkins," she said. "Well, Irene darling, I must be trotting, and leave you to your"— she hardly knew what to call it—"to your work."

She tripped from the room, which seemed to be entirely full of unclothed limbs, and redder than one of Mr. Hopkins's boiled lobsters hurried down the street. She felt that she could never face him again, but would be obliged to go to the establishment in the High Street where Irene dealt, when it was fish she wanted from a fish shop. . . . Her head was in a whirl at the brazenness of mankind, especially woman-kind. How had Irene started the overtures that led to this? Had she just said to Hopkins one morning: "Will you come to my studio and take off all your clothes?" If Irene had not been such a wonderful mimic, she would certainly have felt it her duty to go straight to the Padre, and, pulling down her veil, confide to him the whole sad story. But as that was out of the question, she went into Twenlow's and ordered four pounds of dried apricots.

4

THE DYER, as Diva had feared, proved perfidious, and it was not till the next morning that her maid brought her the parcel containing the coat and skirt of the projected costume. Diva had already done her marketing, so that she might have no other calls on her time to interfere with the tacking on of the bunches of pink roses, and she hoped to have the dress finished in time for Elizabeth's afternoon bridge party next day, an invitation to which had just reached her. She had also settled to have a cold lunch today, so that her cook as well as her parlormaid could devote themselves to the job.

She herself had taken the jacket for decoration, and was just tacking the first rose on to the collar, when she looked out of the window, and what she saw caused her needle to fall from her nerveless hand. Tripping along the opposite pavement was Elizabeth. She had on a dress, the material of which, after a moment's gaze, Diva identified: it was that corn-colored coat and skirt which she had worn so much last spring. But the collar, the cuffs, the waistband and the hem of the skirt were covered with staring red poppies. Next moment she called to remembrance the chintz that had covered Elizabeth's sofa in the garden room.

Diva wasted no time, but rang the bell. She had to make certain.

"Janet," she said, "go straight out into the High Street, and walk close behind Miss Mapp. Look very carefully at her dress; see if the poppies on it are of chintz."

Janet's face fell.

"Why, ma'am, she's never gone and—" she began.

"Quick!" said Diva in a strangled voice.

Diva watched from her window. Janet went out, looked this way and that, spied the quarry, and skimmed up the High Street on feet that twinkled as fast as her mistress's. She came back much out of breath with speed and indignation.

"Yes, ma'am," she said. "They're chintz sure enough. Tacked on, too, just as you were meaning to do. Oh, ma'am—"

Janet quite appreciated the magnitude of the calamity, and her voice failed.

"What are we to do, ma'am?" she added.

Diva did not reply for a moment, but sat with eyes closed in profound and concentrated thought. It re-

quired no reflection to decide how impossible it was
to appear herself tomorrow in a dress which seemed
to ape the costume which all Tilling had seen Elizabeth wearing today, and at first it looked as if there
was nothing to be done with all those laboriously acquired bunches of rosebuds; for it was clearly out of
the question to use them as the decoration for any
costume, and idle to think of sewing them back into
the snipped and gashed curtains. She looked at the
purple skirt and coat that hungered for their flowers,
and then she looked at Janet. Janet was a short,
roundabout person; it was ill-naturedly supposed that
she had much the same figure as her mistress. . . .

Then the light broke. dazzling and diabolical, and
Diva bounced to her feet, blinded by its splendor.

"My coat and skirt are yours, Janet," she said. "Get
on with the work both of you. Bustle. Cover it with
roses. Have it finished tonight. Wear it tomorrow.
Wear it always."

She gave a loud cackle of laughter and threaded
her needle.

"Lor, ma'am!" said Janet, admiringly. "That's a
teaser! And thank you, ma'am!"

"It was roses, roses all the way." Diva had quite
miscalculated the number required, and there were
sufficient not only to cover collar, cuffs and border of
the skirt with them but to make another line of them
six inches above the hem. Original and gorgeous as
the dress would be, it was yet a sort of parody on
Elizabeth's costume which was attracting so much interest and attention as she popped in and out of the
shops today. Tomorrow that would be worn by Janet,
and Janet (or Diva was much mistaken) should encourage her friends to get permission to use up old
bits of chintz. Very likely chintz decoration would be-

come quite a vogue among the servant maids of Tilling. . . . How Elizabeth had got hold of the idea mattered nothing, but anyhow she would be surfeited with the idea before Diva had finished with her. It was possible, of course (anything was possible), that it had occurred to her independently, but Diva was loath to give so innocent an ancestry to her adoption of it. It was far more sensible to take for granted that she had got wind of Diva's invention by some odious, underhand piece of spying. What that might be must be investigated (and probably determined) later, but at present the business of Janet's roses eclipsed every other interest.

Miss Mapp's shopping that morning was unusually prolonged, for it was important that every woman in Tilling should see the poppies on the corn-colored ground, and know that she had worn that dress before Diva appeared in some mean adaptation of it. Though the total cost of her entire purchases hardly amounted to a shilling, she went in and out of an amazing number of shops, and made a prodigious series of inquiries into the price of commodities that ranged from motor cars to sealing wax, and often entered a shop twice because (wreathed in smiling apologies for her stupidity) she had forgotten what she was told the first time. By twelve o'clock she was satisfied that practically everybody, with one exception, had seen her, and that her costume had aroused a deep sense of jealousy and angry admiration. So cunning was the handiwork of herself, Withers, and Mary that she felt fairly sure that no one had the slightest notion of how this decoration of poppies was accomplished, for Evie had run round her in small mouse-like circles, murmuring to herself, "Very effective idea; is it woven into the cloth, Elizabeth? Dear me, I

wonder where I could get some like it," and Mrs.
Poppit had followed her all up the street, with eyes
glued to the hem of her skirt, and a completely
puzzled face. "But then," so thought Elizabeth
sweetly, "even members of the Order of the British
Empire can't have everything their own way." As for
the Major, he had simply come to a dead stop when
he bounced out of his house as she passed, and said
something very gallant and appropriate. Even the absence of the one inhabitant of Tilling, dear Diva, did
not strike a jarring note in this paean of triumph, for
Miss Mapp was quite satisfied that Diva was busy indoors, working her fingers to the bone over the application of bunches of roses, and, as usual, she was
perfectly correct in her conjecture. But dear Diva
would have to see the new frock tomorrow afternoon,
at the latest, when she came to the bridge party. Perhaps she would then, for the first time, be wearing
the roses herself, and everybody would very
pleasantly pity her. This was so rapturous a thought,
that when Miss Mapp, after her prolonged shopping
and with her almost empty basket, passed Mr.
Hopkins standing outside his shop on her return home
again, she gave him her usual smile, though without
meeting his eye, and tried to forget how much of him
she had seen yesterday. Perhaps she might speak to
him tomorrow and gradually resume ordinary relations, for the prices at the other fish shop were as
high as the quality of the fish was low. . . . She told
herself that there was nothing actually immoral in the
human skin, however embarrassing it was.

Miss Mapp had experienced a cruel disappointment
last night, though the triumph of this morning had
done something to soothe it, for Major Benjy's win-

dow had certainly been lit up to a very late hour, and
so it was clear that he had not been able, twice in
succession, to tear himself away from his diaries, or
whatever else detained him, and go to bed at a
proper time. Captain Puffin, however, had not sat up
late; indeed he must have gone to bed quite unusually early, for his window was dark by half past nine.
Tonight, again the position was reversed, and it
seemed that Major Benjy was "good" and Captain
Puffin was "bad." On the whole, then, there was cause
for thankfulness, and as she added a tin of biscuits
and two jars of bovril to her prudent stores, she found
herself a conscious sceptic about those Roman roads.
Diaries (perhaps) were a little different, for egoism
was a more potent force than archaeology, and for
her part she now definitely believed that Roman
roads spelt some form of drink. She was sorry to believe it, but it was her duty to believe something of
the kind, and she really did not know what else to believe. She did not go so far as mentally to accuse him
of drunkenness, but considering the way he absorbed
red-currant fool, it was clear that he was no foe to al-
cohol and probably watered the Roman roads with it.
With her vivid imagination she pictured him—

Miss Mapp recalled herself from this melancholy
reflection and put up her hand just in time to save a
bottle of bovril, which she had put on the top shelf in
front of the sack of flour, from tumbling to the
ground. With the latest additions she had made to her
larder, it required considerable ingenuity to fit all the
tins and packages in, and for a while she diverted her
mind from Captain Puffin's drinking to her own
eating. But by careful packing and balancing, she
managed to stow everything away with sufficient
economy of space to allow her to shut the door, and

then put the card table in place again. It was then
late, and with a fond look at her sweet flowers sleeping in the moonlight, she went to bed. Captain Puffin's sitting room was still alight, and even as she
deplored this, his shadow in profile crossed the blind.
Shadows were queer things—she could make a beautiful shadow rabbit on the wall by a dexterous inter-
lacement of fingers and thumbs—and certainly this
shadow, in the momentary glance she had of it, appeared to have a large moustache. She could make
nothing whatever out of that, except to suppose that
just as fingers and thumbs became a rabbit, so his
nose became a moustache, for he could not have
grown one since he came back from golf. . . .

She was out early for her shopping next morning,
for there were some delicacies to be purchased for
her bridge party, more particularly some little chocolate cakes she had lately discovered which looked
very small and innocent, but were in reality of so
cloying and substantial a nature, that the partaker
thereof would probably not feel capable of making
any serious inroads into other provisions. Naturally
she was much on the alert today, for it was more than
possible that Diva's dress was finished and in evidence. What color it would be she did not know, but a
large quantity of rosebuds would, even at a distance,
make identification easy. Diva was certainly not at
her window this morning, so it seemed more than
probable that they would soon meet.

Far away, just crossing the High Street at the farther end, she caught sight of a bright patch of purple,
very much of the required shape. There was surely a
pink border round the skirt and a pink panel on the
collar, and just as surely Mrs. Bartlett, recognizable
for her gliding mouselike walk, was moving in its fas-

cinating wake. Then the purple patch vanished into a shop, and Miss Mapp, all smiles and poppies, went with her basket up the street. Presently she encountered Evie, who, also all smiles, seemed to have some communication to make, but only got as far as "Have you seen"—when she gave a little squeal of laughter, quite inexplicable, and glided into some dark entry. A minute afterwards, the purple patch suddenly appeared from a shop and almost collided with her. It was not Diva at all, but Diva's Janet.

The shock was so indescribably severe that Miss Mapp's smile was frozen, so to speak, as by some sudden congealment on to her face, and did not thaw off it till she had reached the sharp turn at the end of the street, where she leaned heavily on the railing and breathed through her nose. A light autumnal mist overlay the miles of marsh, but the sun was already drinking it up, promising the Tillingites another golden day. The tidal river was at the flood, and the bright water lapped the bases of the turf-covered banks that kept it within its course. Beyond that was the tram station towards which presently Major Benjy and Captain Puffin would be hurrying to catch the tram that would take them out to the golf links. The straight road across the marsh was visible, and the railway bridge. All these things were pitilessly unchanged, and Miss Mapp noted them blankly, until rage began to restore the numbed current of her mental processes.

If the records of history contained any similar instance of such treachery and low cunning as was involved in this plot of Diva's to dress Janet in the rosebud chintz, Miss Mapp would have liked to be told clearly and distinctly what it was. She could trace the workings of Diva's base mind with absolute accuracy, and if all the archangels in the hierarchy of heaven had assured her that Diva had originally intended the rosebuds for Janet, she would have scorned them for their clumsy perjury. Diva had designed and executed that dress for herself, and just because Miss Mapp's ingenuity (inspired by the two rosebuds that had fluttered out of the window) had forestalled her, she had taken this fiendish revenge. It was impossible to pervade the High Street covered with chintz poppies when a parlormaid was being equally pervasive in chintz rosebuds, and what was to be done with this frock executed with such mirth and malice by Withers, Mary and herself she had no idea. She might just as well give it to Withers, for she could no longer wear it herself, or tear the poppies from the hem and bestrew the High Street with them. . . . Miss Mapp's face froze into immobility again, for here, trundling swiftly towards her, was Diva herself.

Diva appeared not to see her till she got quite close.

"Morning, Elizabeth," she said. "Seen my Janet anywhere?"

"No," said Miss Mapp.

Janet (no doubt according to instructions received) popped out of a shop, and came towards her mistress.

"Here she is," said Diva. "All right, Janet. You can go home. I'll see to the other things."

"It's a lovely day," said Miss Mapp, beginning to lash her tail. "So bright."

"Yes. Pretty trimming of poppies," said Diva. "Janet's got rosebuds."

This was too much.

"Diva, I didn't think it of you," said Miss Mapp in a shaking voice. "You saw my new frock yesterday, and

you were filled with malice and envy, Diva, just because I had thought of using flowers off an old chintz
as well as you, and came out first with it. You had
meant to wear that purple frock yourself—though I
must say it fits Janet perfectly—and just because I was
first in the field you did this. You gave Janet that
frock, so that I should be dressed in the same style as
your parlormaid, and you've got a black heart, Diva!"

"That's nonsense," said Diva firmly. "Heart's as red
as anybody's, and talking of black hearts doesn't become *you*, Elizabeth. You knew I was cutting out
roses from my curtains—"

Miss Mapp laughed shrilly.

"Well, if I happen to notice that you've taken your
chintz curtains down," she said with an awful distinctness that showed the wisdom teeth of which
Diva had got three at the most, "and pink bunches of
roses come flying out of your window into the High
Street, even my poor wits, small as they are, are equal
to drawing the conclusion that you are cutting roses
out of curtains. Your well-known fondness for dress
did the rest. With your permission, Diva, I intend to
draw exactly what conclusions I please on every occasion, including this one."

"Ho! That's how you got the idea then," said Diva.
"I knew you had cribbed it from me."

"Cribbed?" asked Miss Mapp, in ironical ignorance
of what so vulgar and slangy an expression meant.

"Cribbed means taking what isn't yours," said Diva.
"Even then, if you had only acted in a straightforward manner—"

Miss Mapp, shaken as with palsy, regretted that she
had let slip, out of pure childlike joy, in irony, the
manner in which she had obtained the poppy notion,

but in a quarrel regrets are useless, and she went on again.

"And would you very kindly explain how or when I have acted in a manner that was not straightforward," she asked with laborious politeness. "Or do I understand that a monopoly of cutting up chintz curtains for personal adornment has been bestowed on you by Act of Parliament?"

"You knew I was meaning to make a frock with chintz roses on it," said Diva. "You stole my idea. Worked night and day to be first. Just like you. Mean behavior."

"It was meaner to give that frock to Janet," said Miss Mapp, getting her teeth into that good meat.

"You can give yours to Withers," snapped Diva.

"Much obliged, Mrs. Plaistow," said Miss Mapp.

Diva had been watching Janet's retreating figure, and feeling that though revenge was sweet, revenge was also strangely expensive, for she had sacrificed one of the most strikingly successful frocks she had ever made on that smoking altar. Now her revenge was gratified, and deeply she regretted the frock. Miss Mapp's heart was similarly wrung by torture: revenge too had been hers (general revenge on Diva for existing), but this dreadful counterstroke had made it quite impossible for her to enjoy the use of this frock any more, for she could not habit herself like a housemaid. Each, in fact, had, as matters at present stood, completely wrecked the other, like two express trains meeting in top-speed collision, and, since the quarrel had clearly risen to its utmost height, there was no farther joy of battle to be anticipated, but only the melancholy task of counting the corpses. So they paused, breathing very quickly and trembling, while both sought for some way out. Besides, Miss Mapp had a bridge party this afternoon, and if they parted now in this extreme state of tension, Diva might conceivably not come, thereby robbing herself of her bridge and spoiling her hostess's table. Naturally any permanent quarrel was not contemplated by either of them, for if quarrels were permanent in Tilling, nobody would be on speaking terms any more with anyone else in a day or two, and (hardly less disastrous) there could be no fresh quarrels with anybody, since you could not quarrel without words. There might be songs without words, as Mendelssohn had proved, but not rows without words. By what formula could this deadly antagonism be bridged without delay?

Diva gazed out over the marsh. She wanted desperately to regain her rosebud frock, and she knew that Elizabeth was starving for further wearing of her poppies. Perhaps the wide, serene plain below inspired her with a hatred of littleness. There would be no loss of dignity in making a proposal that her enemy, she felt sure, would accept: it merely showed a Christian spirit, and set an example to Elizabeth, to make the first move. Janet she did not consider.

"If you are in a fit state to listen to reason, Elizabeth," she began.

Miss Mapp heaved a sigh of relief. Diva had thought of something. She swallowed the insult at a gulp.

"Yes, dear," she said.

"Got an idea. Take away Janet's frock, and wear it myself. Then you can wear yours. Too pretty for parlormaids. Eh?"

A heavenly brightness spread over Miss Mapp's face.

"Oh, how wonderful of you to have thought of that, Diva," she said. "But how shall we explain it all to everybody?"

Diva clung to her rights. Though clearly Christian, she was human.

"Say I thought of tacking chintz on and told you," she said.

"Yes, darling," said Elizabeth. "That's beautiful. I agree. But poor Janet!"

"I'll give her some other old thing," said Diva. "Good sort, Janet. Wants me to win."

"And about her having been seen wearing it?"

"Say she hasn't ever worn it. Say they're mad," said Diva.

Miss Mapp felt it better to tear herself away before she began saying all sorts of acidities that welled up in her fruitful mind. She could, for instance, easily have agreed that nothing was more probable than that Janet had been mistaken for her mistress. . . .

"Au reservoir then, dear," she said tenderly. "See you at about four? And will you wear your pretty rosebud frock?"

This was agreed to, and Diva went home to take it away from Janet.

The reconciliation of course was strictly confined to matters relating to chintz and did not include such extraneous subjects as coal strike or food hoarding, and even in the first glowing moments of restored friendliness, Diva began wondering whether she would have the opportunity that afternoon of testing the truth of her conjecture about the cupboard in the garden room. Cudgel her brains as she might she could think of no other *cache* that could contain the immense amount of provisions that Elizabeth had probably accumulated, and she was all on fire to get to practical grips with the problem. As far as tins of corned beef and tongues went, Elizabeth might possibly have buried them in her garden in the manner of a dog, but it was not likely that a hoarder would limit herself to things in tins. No; there was a cupboard somewhere ready to burst with strong supporting foods. . . .

Diva intentionally arrived a full quarter of an hour on the hither side of punctuality, and was taken by Withers out into the garden room, where tea was laid, and two card tables were in readiness. She was, of course, the first of the guests, and the moment Withers withdrew to tell her mistress that she had come, Diva stealthily glided to the cupboard, from in front of which the bridge table had been removed, feeling the shrill joy of some romantic treasure hunter. She found the catch; she pressed it; she pulled open the door, and the whole of the damning profusion of provisions burst upon her delighted eyes. Shelf after shelf was crowded with eatables; there were tins of corned beef and tongues (that she knew already); there was a sack of flour; there were tubes of Bath Oliver biscuits, bottles of bovril, the yield of a thousand condensed Swiss cows, jars of prunes. . . . All these were in the front row, flush with the door, and who knew to what depth the cupboard extended? Even as she feasted her eyes on this incredible store, some package on the top shelf wavered and toppled, and she had only just time to shut the door to again, in order to prevent it falling out on to the floor. But this displacement prevented the door from wholly closing, and push and shove as Diva might, she could not get the catch to click home, and the only result of her energy and efforts was to give rise to a muffled explosion from within, just precisely as if something

made of cardboard had burst. That mental image was
so vivid that to her fevered imagination it seemed to be
real. This was followed by certain faint taps from
within against "Elegant Extracts" and "Astronomy."

Diva grew very red in the face, and said, "Drat it,"
under her breath. She did not dare open the door
again in order to push things back, for fear of an
uncontrollable stream of "things" pouring out. Some
nicely balanced equilibrium had clearly been upset in
those capacious shelves, and it was impossible to tell,
without looking, how deep and how extensive the disturbance was. And in order to look, she had to open
the bookcase again. . . . Luckily the pressure against
the door was not sufficiently heavy to cause it to
swing wide, so the best she could do was to leave it
just ajar with temporary quiescence inside. Simultaneously she heard Miss Mapp's step and had no more
than time to trundle at the utmost speed of her whirling feet across to the window, where she stood looking out, and appeared quite unconscious of her
hostess's entry.

"Diva darling, how sweet of you to come so early!"
she said. "A little cosy chat before the others arrive."

Diva turned round, much startled.

"Hullo!" she said. "Didn't hear you. Got Janet's
frock, you see."

("What makes Diva's face so red?" thought Miss
Mapp.)

"So I see, darling," she said. "Lovely rose garden.
How well it suits you, dear! Did Janet mind?"

"No. Promised her a new frock at Christmas."

"That will be nice for Janet," said Elizabeth enthusiastically. "Shall we pop into the garden, dear, till
my guests come?"

Diva was glad to pop into the garden and get away

from the immediate vicinity of the cupboard, for though she had planned and looked forward to the exposure of Elizabeth's hoarding, she had not meant it to come, as it now probably would, in crashes of tins and bursting of bovril bottles. Again she had intended to have opened that door quite casually and innocently while she was being dummy, so that everyone could see how accidental the exposure was, and to have gone poking about the cupboard in Elizabeth's absence was a shade too professional, so to speak, for the usual detective work of Tilling. But the fuse was set now. Sooner or later the explosion must come. She wondered as they went out to commune with Elizabeth's sweet flowers till the other guests arrived how great a torrent would be let loose. She did not repent her exploration—far from it—but her pleasurable anticipations were strongly diluted with suspense.

Miss Mapp had found such difficulty in getting eight players together today, that she had transgressed her principles and asked Mrs. Poppit as well as Isabel, and they, with Diva, the two Bartletts, and the Major and the Captain, formed the party. The moment Mrs. Poppit appeared, Elizabeth hated her more than ever, for she put up her glasses, and began to give her patronizing advice about her garden, which she had not been allowed to see before.

"You have quite a pretty little piece of garden, Miss Mapp," she said, "though to be sure, I fancied from what you said it was more expensive. Dear me, your roses do not seem to be doing very well. Probably they are old plants and want renewing. You must send your gardener round—you keep a gardener?—and I will let you have a dozen vigorous young bushes."

Miss Mapp licked her dry lips. She kept a kind of gardener; two days a week.

"Too good of you," she said, "but that rose bed is quite sacred, dear Mrs. Poppit. Not all the vigorous young bushes in the world would tempt me. It's my 'Friendship's Border'; some dear friend gave me each of my rose trees."

Mrs. Poppit transferred her gaze to the wistaria that grew over the steps up to the garden room. Some of the dear friends she thought must be centenarians.

"Your wistaria wants pruning sadly," she said. "Your gardener does not understand wistarias. That corner there was made, I may say, for fuchsias. You should get a dozen choice fuchsias."

Miss Mapp laughed.

"Oh, you must excuse me," she said with a glance at Mrs. Poppit's brocaded silk. "I can't bear fuchsias. They always remind me of overdressed women. Ah, there's Mr. Bartlett. How de do, Padre. And dear Evie!"

Dear Evie appeared fascinated by Diva's dress.

"Such beautiful rosebuds," she murmured. "And what a lovely shade of purple. And Elizabeth's poppies, too; quite a pair of you. But surely this morning, Diva, didn't I see your good Janet in just such another dress, and I thought at the time how odd it was that—"

"If you saw Janet this morning," said Diva quite firmly, "you saw her in her print dress."

"And here's Major Benjy," said Miss Mapp, who had made her slip about his Christian name yesterday, and had been duly entreated to continue slipping. "And Captain Puffin. Well, that is nice! Shall we go into my little garden shed, dear Mrs. Poppit, and have our tea?"

Major Flint was still a little lame, for his golf today had been of the nature of gardening, and he hobbled up the steps behind the ladies, with that little cock-sparrow sailor following him and telling the Padre how badly and yet how successfully he himself had played.

"Pleasantest room in Tilling, I always say, Miss Elizabeth," said he, diverting his mind from a mere game to the fairies.

"My dear little room," said Miss Mapp, knowing that it was much larger than anything in Mrs. Poppit's house. "So tiny!"

"Oh, not a bad-sized little room," said Mrs. Poppit encouragingly. "Much the same proportions, on a very small scale, as the throne room at Buckingham Palace."

"That beautiful throne room!" exclaimed Miss Mapp. "A cup of tea, dear Mrs. Poppit? None of that naughty red-currant fool, I am afraid. And a little chocolate cake?"

These substantial chocolate cakes soon did their fell work of producing the sense of surfeit, and presently Elizabeth's guests dropped off gorged from the tea table. Diva fortunately remembered their consistency in time, and nearly cleared a plate of jumbles instead, which the hostess had hoped would form a pleasant accompaniment to her dessert at her supper this evening, and was still crashingly engaged on them when the general drifting movement towards the two bridge tables set in. Mrs. Poppit, with her glasses up, followed by Isabel, was employed in making a tour of the room, in case, as Miss Mapp had already determined, she never saw it again, examining the quality of the carpet, the curtains, the chair backs, with the air of a doubtful purchaser.

"And quite a quantity of books, I see," she announced as she came opposite the fatal cupboard. "Look, Isabel, what a quantity of books. There is something strange about them, though, I do not believe they are real."

She put out her hand and pulled at the back of one of the volumes of "Elegant Extracts." The door swung open, and from behind it came a noise of rattling, bumping and clattering. Something soft and heavy thumped on to the floor, and a cloud of floury dust arose. A bottle of bovril embedded itself quietly there without damage, and a tin of Bath Oliver biscuits beat a fierce tattoo on one of the corned beef. Innumerable dried apricots from the burst package flew about like shrapnel, and tapped at the tins. A jar of prunes, breaking its fall on the floor, rolled merrily out into the middle of the floor.

The din was succeeded by complete silence. The Padre had said "What ho, i' fegs?" during the tumult, but his voice had been drowned by the rattling of the dried apricots. The Member of the Order of the British Empire stepped free of the provisions that bumped round her, and examined them through her glasses. Diva crammed the last jumble into her mouth and disposed of it with the utmost rapidity. The birthday of her life had come, as Miss Rossetti said.

"Dear Elizabeth!" she exclaimed. "What a disaster! All your little stores in case of the coal strike. Let me help you pick them up. I do not think anything is broken. Isn't that lucky?"

Evie hurried to the spot.

"Such a quantity of good things," she said rapidly under her breath. "Tinned meats and bovril and prunes, and ever so many apricots. Let me pick them all up, and with a little dusting . . . Why what a big cupboard, and such a quantity of good things."

Miss Mapp had certainly struck a streak of embarrassments. What with naked Mr. Hopkins, and Janet's frock and this unveiling of her hoard, life seemed at the moment really to consist of nothing else than beastly situations. How on earth that catch of the door had come undone, she had no idea, but much as she would have liked to suspect foul play from somebody, she was bound to conclude that Mrs. Poppit with her prying hands had accidentally pressed it. It was like Diva, of course, to break the silence with odious allusions to hoarding, and bitterly she wished that she had not started the topic the other day, but had been content to lay in her stores without so pointedly affirming that she was doing nothing of the kind. But this was no time for vain laments, and restraining a natural impulse to scratch and beat Mrs. Poppit, she exhibited an admirable inventiveness and composure. Though she knew it would deceive nobody, everybody had to pretend he was deceived.

"Oh, my poor little Christmas presents for your needy parishioners, Padre," she said. "You've seen them before you were meant to, and you must forget all about them. And so little hard done, just an apricot or two. Withers will pick them all up, so let us get to our bridge."

Withers entered the room at this moment to clear away tea, and Miss Mapp explained it all over again.

"All our little Christmas presents have come tumbling out, Withers," she said. "Will you put as many as you can back in the cupboard and take the rest indoors? Don't tread on the apricots."

It was difficult to avoid doing this, as the apricots were everywhere, and their color on the brown carpet was wonderfully protective. Miss Mapp herself had already stepped on two, and their adhesive stickiness was hard to get rid of. In fact, for the next few minutes the coal shovel was in strong request for their removal from the soles of shoes, and the fender was littered with their squashed remains. . . . The party generally was distinctly thoughtful as it sorted itself out into two tables, for every single member of it was trying to assimilate the amazing proposition that Miss Mapp had, halfway through September, loaded her cupboard with Christmas presents on a scale that staggered belief. The feat required thought: it required a faith so childlike as to verge on the imbecile. Conversation during deals had an awkward tendency towards discussion of the coal strike. As often as it drifted there, the subject was changed very abruptly, just as if there was some occult reason for not speaking of so natural a topic. It concerned everybody, but it was rightly felt to concern Miss Mapp the most. . . .

5

IT WAS THE MAJOR's turn to entertain his friend, and by half past nine, on a certain squally October evening, he and Puffin were seated by the fire in his "study," while the rain volleyed at the windows and occasional puffs of stinging smoke were driven down the chimney and into the room by the gale that squealed and buffeted around the house. Puffin, by way of keeping up the illusion of Roman roads, had brought a map of the district across from his house, but the more essential part of his equipment for this studious evening was a bottle of whisky. Originally the host had provided whisky for himself and his guest at these pleasant chats, but there were undeniable objections to this plan, because the guest always proved unusually thirsty, which tempted his host to keep pace with him, while if they both drank at their own expense, the causes of economy and abstemiousness had a better chance. Also, while the Major took his drinks short and strong in a small tumbler, Puffin enriched his with lemons and sugar in a large one, so that nobody could really tell if equality as well as fraternity was realised. But if each brought his own bottle. . . .

It had been a trying day, and the Major was very lame. A drenching storm had come up during their golf, while they were far from the clubhouse, and Puffin, being three up, had very naturally refused to accede to his opponent's suggestion to call the match off. He was perfectly willing to be paid his half crown and go home, but Major Flint, remembering that Puffin's game usually went to pieces if it rained, had rejected this proposal with the scorn that it deserved. There had been other disagreeable incidents as well. His driver, slippery from rain, had flown out of the Major's hands on the twelfth tee, and had "shot like a streamer of the northern morn," and landed in a pool of brackish water left by an unusually high tide. The ball had gone into another pool nearer the tee. The ground was greasy with moisture, and three holes further on. Puffin had fallen flat on his face instead of lashing his fifth shot home on to the green, as he had intended. They had given each other stimies, and each had holed his opponent's ball by mistake; they had wrangled over the correct procedure if you lay in a rabbit scrape or on the tram lines: the Major had lost a new ball; there was a mushroom on one of the greens between Puffin's ball and the hole. . . . All these untoward incidents had come crowding in together, and from the Major's point of view, the worst of them all had been the collective incident that Puffin, so far from being put off by the rain, had, in spite of the mushroom and falling down, played with a steadiness of which he was usually quite incapable. Consequently Major Flint was lame, and his wound troubled him, while Puffin, in spite of his obvious reasons for complacency, was growing irritated with his companion's ill-temper, and was half blinded by wood smoke.

He wiped his streaming eyes.

"You should get your chimney swept," he observed.

Major Flint had put his handkerchief over his face to keep the wood smoke out of his eyes. He blew it off with a loud, indignant puff.

"Oh! Ah! Indeed!" he said.

Puffin was rather taken aback by the violence of these interjections; they dripped with angry sarcasm.

"Oh, well! No offence," he said.

"A man," said the Major impersonally, "makes an offensive remark, and says 'No offence.' If your own fireside suits you better than mine, Captain Puffin, all I can say is that you're at liberty to enjoy it!"

This was all rather irregular: they had indulged in a good stiff breeze this afternoon, and it was too early to ruffle the calm again. Puffin plucked and proffered an olive branch.

"There's your handkerchief," he said, picking it up.

"Now let's have one of our comfortable talks. Hot glass of grog and a chat over the fire: that's the best thing after such a wetting as we got this afternoon. I'll take a slice of lemon, if you'll be so good as to give it me, and a lump of sugar."

The Major got up and limped to his cupboard. It struck him precisely at that moment that Puffin scored considerably over lemons and sugar, because he was supplied with them gratis every other night; whereas he himself, when Puffin's guest, took nothing of his host but hot water. He determined to ask for some biscuits, anyhow, tomorrow. . . .

"I hardly know whether there's a lemon left," he grumbled. "I must lay in a store of lemons. As for sugar—"

Puffin chose to disregard this suggestion.

"Amusing incident the other day," he said brightly, "when Miss Mapp's cupboard door flew open. The old lady didn't like it. Don't suppose the poor of the parish will see much of that corned beef."

The Major became dignified.

"Pardon me," he said. "When an esteemed friend like Miss Elizabeth tells me that certain provisions are destined for the poor of the parish, I take it that her statement is correct. I expect others of my friends, while they are in my presence, to do the same. I have the honor to give you a lemon, Captain Puffin, and a slice of sugar. I should say a lump of sugar. Pray make yourself comfortable."

This dignified and lofty mood was often one of the after effects of an unsuccessful game of golf. It generally yielded quite quickly to a little stimulant. Puffin filled his glass from the bottle and the kettle, while his friends put his handkerchief again over his face.

"Well, I shall just have my grog before I turn in,"

he observed, according to custom. "Aren't you going to join me, Major?"

"Presently, sir," said the Major.

Puffin knocked out the consumed cinders in his pipe against the edge of the fender. Major Flint apparently was waiting for this, for he withdrew his handkerchief and closely watched the process. A minute piece of ash fell from Puffin's pipe onto the hearthrug, and he jumped to his feet and removed it very carefully with the shovel.

"I have your permission, I hope?" he said witheringly.

"Certainly, certainly," said Puffin. "Now get your glass, Major. You'll feel better in a minute or two."

Major Flint would have liked to have kept up this magnificent attitude, but the smell of Puffin's steaming glass beat dignity down, and after glaring at him, he limped back to the cupboard for his whisky bottle. He gave a lamentable cry when he beheld it.

"But I got that bottle in only the day before yesterday," he shouted, "and there's hardly a drink left in it."

"Well, you did yourself pretty well last night," said Puffin. "Those small glasses of yours, if frequently filled up, empty a bottle quicker than you seem to realize."

Motives of policy prevented the Major from receiving this with the resentment that was proper to it, and his face cleared. He would get quits over these incessant lemons and lumps of sugar.

"Well, you'll have to let me borrow from you tonight," he said genially, as he poured the rest of the contents of his bottle into the glass. "Ah, that's more the ticket! A glass of whisky a day keeps the doctor away."

The prospect of sponging on Puffin was most exhilarating, and he put his large slippered feet onto the fender.

"Yes, indeed, that was a highly amusing incident about Miss Mapp's cupboard," he said. "And wasn't Mrs. Plaistow down on her like a knife about it? Our fair friends, you know, have a pretty sharp eye for each other's little failings. They've no sooner finished one squabble than they begin another, the pert little fairies. They can't sit and enjoy themselves like two old cronies I could tell you of, and feel at peace with all the world."

He finished his glass at a gulp, and seemed much surprised to find it empty.

"I'll be borrowing a drop from you, old friend," he said.

"Help yourself, Major," said Puffin, with a keen eye as to how much he took.

"Very obliging of you. I feel as if I caught a bit of a chill this afternoon. My wound."

"Be careful not to inflame it," said Puffin.

"Thank ye for the warning. It's this beastly climate that touches it up. A winter in England takes years off a man's life unless he takes care of himself. Take care of yourself, old boy. Have some more sugar."

Before long the Major's hand was moving slowly and instinctively towards Puffin's whisky bottle again.

"I reckon that big glass of yours, Puffin," he said, "holds between three and a half times and four times what my little tumbler holds. Between three and a half and four I should reckon. I may be wrong."

"Reckoning the water in, I daresay you're not far out, Major," said he. "And according to my estimate you mix your drink somewhere about three and a half times to four stronger than I mix mine."

"Oh, come, come!" said the Major.

"Three and a half to four times, *I* should say," repeated Puffin. "You won't find I'm far out."

He replenished his big tumbler, and instead of putting the bottle back on the table, absently deposited it on the floor on the far side of his chair. This second tumbler usually marked the most convivial period of the evening, for the first would have healed whatever unhappy discords had marred the harmony of the day, and those being disposed of, they very contentedly talked through their hats about past prowesses, and took a rosy view of the youth and energy which still beat in their vigorous pulses. They would begin, perhaps, by extolling each other; Puffin, when informed that his friend would be fifty-four next birthday, flatly refused (without offence) to believe it; and indeed, he was quite right in so doing, because the Major was in reality fifty-six. In turn, Major Flint would say that his friend had the figure of a boy of twenty, which caused Puffin presently to feel a little cramped and to wander negligently in front of the big looking glass between the windows, and find this compliment much easier to swallow than the Major's age. For the next half hour they would chiefly talk about themselves in a pleasant glow of self-satisfaction. Major Flint, looking at the various implements and trophies that adorned the room, would suggest putting a sporting challenge in the *Times*.

" 'Pon my word, Puffin," he would say, "I've half a mind to do it. Retired Major of His Majesty's Forces—the King, God bless him!" (and he took a substantial sip); " 'Retired Major, aged fifty-four, challenges any gentleman of fifty years or over.' "

"Forty," said Puffin sycophantically, as he thought over what he would say about himself when the old man had finished.

"Well, we'll halve it; we'll say forty-five, to please you, Puffin—let's see, where had I got to?—'Retired Major challenges any gentleman of forty-five years or over to—to a shooting match in the morning, followed by half a dozen rounds with four-ounce gloves, a game of golf, eighteen holes, in the afternoon, and a billiard match of two hundred up after tea.' Ha, ha! I shouldn't feel much anxiety as to the result."

"My confounded leg!" said Puffin. "But I know a retired captain from His Majesty's merchant service—the King, God bless him!—aged fifty—"

"Ho, ho! Fifty, indeed!" said the Major, thinking to himself that a dried-up little man like Puffin might be as old as an Egyptian mummy. Who can tell the age of a kipper?. . .

"Not a day less, Major. 'Retired Captain, aged fifty, who'll take on all comers of forty-two and over, at a steeplechase, round of golf, billiard match, hopping match, gymnastic competition, swinging Indian clubs—' No objection, gentlemen? Then, carried *nem. con.*"

This gaseous mood, athletic, amatory or otherwise (the amatory ones were the worst), usually faded slowly, like the light from the setting sun or an exhausted coal in the grate, about the end of Puffin's second tumbler, and the gentlemen after that were usually somnolent, but occasionally laid the foundation for some disagreement next day, which they were too sleepy to go into now. Major Flint by this time would have had some five small glasses of whisky (equivalent, as he bitterly observed, to one in pre-war days), and as he measured his next with extreme care and a slightly jerky movement, would announce it as being his nightcap, though you would have thought he had plenty of nightcaps on already. Puffin correspondingly took a thimbleful more (the thimble apparently belonging to some housewife of Anak), and after another half hour of sudden single snores and startings awake again, of pipes frequently lit and immediately going out, the guest, still perfectly capable of coherent speech and voluntary motion in the required direction, would stumble across the dark cobbles to his house, and doors would be very carefully closed for fear of attracting the attention of the lady who at this period of the evening was usually known as "Old Mappy." The two were perfectly well aware of the sympathetic interest Old Mappy took in all that concerned them, and that she had an eye on their evening séances was evidenced by the frequency with which the corner of her blind in the window of the garden room was raised between, say, half past nine and eleven at night. They had often watched with giggles the pencil of light that escaped, obscured at the lower end by the outline of Old Mappy's head, and occasionally drank to the "Guardian Angel." Guardian Angel, in answer to direct inquiries, had been told by Major Benjy during the last month that he worked at his diaries on three nights in the week and went to bed early on the others, to the vast improvement of his mental grasp.

"And on Sunday night, dear Major Benjy?" asked Old Mappy in the character of Guardian Angel.

"I don't think you knew my beloved, my revered mother, Miss Elizabeth," said Major Benjy. "I spend Sunday evening as—Well, well."

The very next Sunday evening, Guardian Angel had heard the sound of singing. She could not catch the words, and only fragments of the tune, which reminded her of "The roseate morn hath passed away." Brimming with emotion, she sang it softly to herself as she undressed, and blamed herself very much for ever having thought that dear Major Benjy—She peeped out of her window when she had extinguished her light, but fortunately the singing had ceased.

Tonight, however, the epoch of Puffin's second big tumbler was not accompanied by harmonious developments. Major Benjy was determined to make the most of this unique opportunity of drinking his friend's whisky, and whether Puffin put the bottle on the further side of him, or under his chair, or under the table, he came padding round in his slippers, and standing near the ambush while he tried to interest his friend in tales of love or tiger shooting so as to distract his attention. When he mistakenly thought he had done so, he hastily refilled his glass, taking unusually stiff doses for fear of not getting another opportunity, and altogether omitting to ask Puffin's leave for these maraudings. When this had happened four or five times, Puffin, acting on the instinct of the polar bear who eats her babies for fear anybody else should get them, surreptitiously poured the rest of his bottle into his glass, and filled it up to the top with hot water, making a mixture of extraordinary power.

Soon after this Major Flint came rambling round the table again. He was not sure whether Puffin had put the bottle by his chair or behind the coalscuttle, and was quite ignorant of the fact that wherever it was, it was empty. Amorous reminiscences tonight had been the accompaniment to Puffin's second tumbler.

"Devilish fine woman she was," he said, "and that was the last that Benjamin Flint ever saw of her. She went up to the hills next morning--"

"But the last you saw of her just now was on the deck of the P. and O. at Bombay," objected Puffin. "Or did she go up to the hills on the deck of the P. and O.? Wonderful line!"

"No, sir," said Benjamin Flint, "that was Helen, *la belle Hélène*. It was *la belle Hélène* whom I saw off at the Apollo Bunder. I don't know if I told you—By Gad, I've kicked the bottle over. No idea you'd put it there. Hope the cork's in."

"No harm if it isn't," said Puffin, beginning on his third, most fiery glass. The strength of it rather astonished him.

"You don't mean to say it's empty?" asked Major Flint. "Why just now there was close on a quarter of a bottle left."

"As much as that?" asked Puffin. "Glad to hear it."

"Not a drop less. You don't mean to say—Well, if you can drink that and can say hippopotamus afterwards, I should put that among your challenges, to men of four hundred and two; I should say forty-two. It's a fine thing to have a strong head, though if I drank what you've got in your glass, I should be tipsy, sir."

Puffin laughed in his irritating falsetto manner.

"Good thing that it's in my glass then, and not your glass," he said. "And lemme tell you, Major, in case you don't know it, that when I've drank every drop of this and sucked the lemon, you'll have had far more out of my bottle this evening than I have. My usual twice and—and my usual nightcap, as you say, is what's my ration, and I've had no more than my ration. Eight Bells."

"And a pretty good ration you've got there," said the baffled Major. "Without your usual twice."

Puffin was beginning to be aware of that as he

swallowed the fiery mixture, but nothing in the world would now have prevented his drinking every single drop of it. It was clear to him, among so much that was dim owing to the wood smoke, that the Major would miss a good many drives tomorrow morning.

"And whose whisky is it?" he said, gulping down the fiery stuff.

"I know whose it's going to be," said the other.

"And I know whose it is now," retorted Puffin, "and I know whose whisky it is that's filled you up ti' as a drum. Tight as a drum," he repeated very carefully.

Major Flint was conscious of an unusual activity of brain, and when he spoke, of a sort of congestion and entanglement of words. It pleased him to think that he had drunk so much of somebody's else whisky, but he felt that he ought to be angry.

"That's a very unmentionable sor' of thing to say," he remarked. "An' if it wasn't for the sacred claims of hospitality, I'd make you explain just what you mean by that, and make you eat your words. 'Pologize, in fact."

Puffin finished his glass at a gulp, and rose to his feet.

" 'Pologies be blowed," he said. "Hittopopamus!"

"And were you addressing that to me?" asked Major Flint with deadly calm.

"Of course, I was. Hippot—same animal as before. Pleasant old boy. And as for the lemon you lent me, well, I don't want it any more. Have a suck at it, ole fellow! I don't want it anymore."

The Major turned purple in the face, made a course for the door with a knight's move at chess (a long step in one direction and a short one at right angles to the first) and opened it. The door thus served as an aperture from the room and a support to himself. He

spoke no word of any sort or kind: his silence spoke
for him in a far more dignified manner than he could
have managed for himself.

Captain Puffin stood for a moment wreathed in
smiles, and fingering the slice of lemon, which he had
meant playfully to throw at his friend. But his smile
faded and by some sort of telepathic perception he
realized how much more decorous it was to say (or,
better, to indicate) good night in a dignified manner
than to throw lemons about. He walked in dots and
dashes like a Morse code out of the room, bestowing a
naval salute on the Major as he passed. The latter returned it with a military salute and a suppressed hic-
cup. Not a word passed.

Then Captain Puffin found his hat and coat without
much difficulty, and marched out of the house, slam-
ming the door behind him with a bang that echoed
down the street and made Miss Mapp dream about a
thunderstorm. He let himself into his own house, and
bent down before his expired fire, which he tried to
blow into life again. This was unsuccessful, and he
breathed in a quantity of wood ash.

He sat down by his table and began to think things
out. He told himself that he was not drunk at all, but
that he had taken an unusual quantity of whisky,
which seemed to produce much the same effect as intoxication. Allowing for that, he was conscious that he
was extremely angry about something, and had a firm
idea that the Major was very angry, too.

"But woz'it all been about?" he vainly asked himself. "Woz'it all been about?"

He was roused from his puzzling over this unan-
swerable conundrum by the clink of the flap in his letter box. Either this was the first post in the morning,
in which case it was much later than he thought, and

wonderfully dark still or it was the last post at night, in which case it was much earlier than he thought. But, whichever it was, a letter had been slipped into his box, and he brought it in. The gum on the envelope was still wet, which saved trouble in opening it. Inside was a half sheet containing but a few words. This curt epistle ran as follows:

SIR,
My seconds will wait on you in the course of tomorrow morning.
Your faithful obedient servant,
BENJAMIN FLINT

Captain Puffin.

Puffin felt as calm as a tropic night, and as courageous as a captain. Somewhere below his courage and his calm was an appalling sense of misgiving. That he successfully stifled.

"Very proper," he said aloud. "Qui' proper. Insults. Blood. Seconds won't have to wait a second. Better get a good sleep."

He went up to his room, fell on to his bed and instantly began to snore.

It was still dark when he awoke, but the square of his window was visible against the blackness, and he concluded that though it was not morning yet, it was getting on for morning, which seemed a pity. As he turned over onto his side, his hand came in contact with his coat, instead of a sheet, and he became aware that he had all his clothes on. Then, as with a crash of cymbals and the beating of a drum in his brain, the events of the evening before leaped into reality and significance. In a few hours now arrange-

ments would have been made for a deadly encounter.
His anger was gone; his whisky was gone; and in particular his courage was gone. He expressed all this
compendiously by moaning, "Oh, God!"

He struggled to a sitting position, and lit a match at
which he kindled his candle. He looked for his watch
beside it, but it was not there. What could have happened—then he remembered that it was in its accustomed place in his waistcoat pocket. A consultation of
it followed by holding it to his ear only revealed the
fact that it had stopped at half past five. With the lu-
cidity that was growing brighter in his brain, he concluded that this stoppage was due to the fact that he
had not wound it up. . . . It was after half past five
then, but how much later only the Lords of Time
knew—Time which bordered so close on Eternity.

He felt that he had no use whatever for Eternity
but that he must not waste Time. Just now, that was
far more precious.

From somewhere in the Cosmic Consciousness
there came to him a thought, namely, that the first
train to London started at half past six in the morning. It was a slow train, but it got there, and in any
case it went away from Tilling. He did not trouble to
consider how that thought came to him: the important point was that it had come. Coupled with that
was the knowledge that it was now an undiscoverable
number of minutes after half past five.

There was a Gladstone bag under his bed. He had
brought it back from the clubhouse only yesterday,
after that game of golf which had been so full of dis-
turbances and wet stockings, but which now wore the
shimmering security of peaceful, tranquil days long
past. How little, so he thought to himself, as he began

swiftly storing shirts, ties, collars and other useful things into his bag, had he appreciated the sweet amenities of life, its pleasant conversations and companionships, its topped drives, and mushrooms and incalculable incidents. Now they wore a glamor and a preciousness that was bound up with life itself. He starved for more of them, not knowing while they were his how sweet they were.

The house was not yet astir, when ten minutes later he came downstairs with his bag. He left on his sitting-room table, where it would catch the eye of his housemaid, a sheet of paper on which he wrote "Called away" (he shuddered as he traced the words), "Forward no letters. Will communicate . . ." (Somehow the telegraphic form seemed best to suit the urgency of the situation.) Then very quietly he let himself out of his house.

He could not help casting an apprehensive glance at the windows of his quondam friend and prospective murderer. To his horror he observed that there was a light behind the blind of the Major's bedroom, and pictured him writing to his seconds—he wondered who the "seconds" were going to be—or polishing up his pistols. All the rumors and hints of the Major's duels and affairs of honor, which he had rather scorned before, not wholly believing them, poured like a red torrent into his mind, and he found that now he believed them with a passionate sincerity. Why had he ever attempted (and with such small success) to call this fire-eater a hippopotamus?

The gale of the night before had abated, and thick chilly rain was falling from a sullen sky as he tiptoed down the hill. Once round the corner and out of sight of the duelist's house, he broke into a limping run which was accelerated by the sound of an engine

whistle from the station. It was mental suspense of
the most agonizing kind not to know how long it was
after his watch had stopped that he had awoke, and
the sound of that whistle, followed by several short
puffs of steam, might prove to be the six thirty bearing away to London, on business or pleasure, its secure and careless pilgrims. Splashing through
puddles, lopsidedly weighted by his bag, with his
mackintosh flapping against his legs, he gained the
sanctuary of the waiting room and booking office,
which was lighted by a dim expiring lamp, and scruti-
nized the face of the murky clock. . . .

With a sob of relief he saw that he was in time. He
was, indeed, in exceptionally good time, for he had a
quarter of an hour to wait. An anxious internal debate
followed as to whether or not he should take a return
ticket. Optimism, that is to say, the hope that he
would return to Tilling in peace and safety before the
six months for which the ticket was available inclined
him to the larger expense, but in these disquieting circumstances, it was difficult to be optimistic, and he
purchased a first-class single, for on such a morning,
and on such a journey, he must get what comfort he
could from looking glasses, padded seats and colored
photographs of places of interest on the line. He
formed no vision at all of the future: that was a dark
well into which it was dangerous to peer. There was
no bright speck in its unplumbable depths: unless Major Flint died suddenly without revealing the challenge he had sent last night, and the promptitude
with which its recipient had disappeared rather than
face his pistol, he could not frame any grouping of
events which would make it possible for him to come
back to Tilling again, for he would either have to
fight (and this he was quite determined not to do) or

be pointed at by the finger of scorn as the man who had refused to do so, and this was nearly as unthinkable as the other. Bitterly he blamed himself for having made a friend (and worse than that) an enemy of one so obsolete and old-fashioned as to bring duelling into modern life. . . . As far as he could be glad of anything, he was glad that he had taken a single, not a return ticket.

He turned his eyes away from the blackness of the future and let his mind dwell on the hardly less murky past. Then, throwing up his hands, he buried his face in them with a hollow groan. By some miserable forgetfulness he had left the challenge on his chimney piece, where his housemaid would undoubtedly find and read it. That would explain his absence far better than the telegraphic instructions he had left on his table. There was no time to go back for it now, even if he could have faced the risk of being seen by the Major, and in an hour or two the whole story, via Withers, Janet, etc., would be all over Tilling.

It was no use then thinking of the future nor of the past, and in order to anchor himself to the world at all and preserve his sanity, he had to confine himself to the present. The minutes, long though each tarried, were slipping away and provided his train was punctual, the passage of five more of these laggards would see him safe. The newsboy took down the shutters of his stall, a porter quenched the expiring lamp, and Puffin began to listen for the rumble of the approaching train. It stayed three minutes here; if up to time, it would be in before a couple more minutes had passed.

There came from the station yard outside the sound of heavy footsteps running. Some early traveller like himself was afraid of missing the train. The door burst open, and streaming with rain and panting for breath, Major Flint stood at the entry. Puffin looked wildly round to see whether he could escape, still perhaps unobserved, on to the platform, but it was too late, for their eyes met.

In that instant of abject terror, two things struck Puffin. One was that the Major looked at the open door behind him as if meditating retreat; the second, that he carried a Gladstone bag. Simultaneously Major Flint spoke, if indeed that reverberating thunder of scornful indignation can be called speech.

"Ha! I guessed right then," he roared. "I guessed, sir, that you might be meditating flight, and I—in fact, I came down to see whether you were running away. I was right. You are a coward, Captain Puffin! But relieve your mind, sir. Major Flint will not demean himself to fight with a coward."

Puffin gave one long sigh of relief, and then standing in front of his own Gladstone bag, in order to conceal it, burst into a cackling laugh.

"Indeed!" he said. "And why, Major, was it necessary for you to pack a Gladstone bag in order to stop me from running away? I'll tell you what has happened. You were running away, and you know it. I guessed you would. I came to stop you, you, you quaking runaway. Your wound troubled you, hey? Didn't want another, hey?"

There was an awful pause, broken by the entry from behind the Major of the outside porter, panting under the weight of a large portmanteau.

"You had to take your portmanteau, too," observed Puffin witheringly, "in order to stop me. That's a curious way of stopping me. You're a coward, sir! But go home. You're safe enough. This will be a fine story for tea parties."

Puffin turned from him in scorn, still concealing his own bag. Unfortunately the flap of his coat caught it, precariously perched on the bench, and it bumped to the ground.

"What's that?" said Major Flint.

They stared at each other for a moment and then simultaneously burst into peals of laughter. The train rumbled slowly into the station, but neither took the least notice of it, and only shook their heads and broke out again when the stationmaster urged them to take their seats. The only thing that had power to restore Captain Puffin to gravity was the difficulty of getting the money for his ticket refunded, while the departure of the train with his portmanteau in it did the same for the Major.

The events of that night and morning, as may easily be imagined, soon supplied Tilling with one of the most remarkable conundrums that had ever been forced upon its notice. Puffin's housemaid, during his absence at the station, found and read not only the notice intended for her eyes, but the challenge which he had left on the chimney piece. She conceived it to be her duty to take it down to Mrs. Gashly, his cook, and while they were putting the bloodiest construction on these inscriptions, their conference was interrupted by the return of Captain Puffin in the highest spirits, who, after a vain search for the challenge, was quite content, as its purport was no longer fraught with danger and death, to suppose that he had torn it up. Mrs. Gashly, therefore, after preparing breakfast at this unusually early hour, went across to the back door of the Major's house, with the challenge in her hand, to borrow a nutmeg grater, and gleaned the information that Mrs. Dominic's em-

ployer (for master he could not be called) had gone
off in a great hurry to the station early that morning
with a Gladstone bag and a portmanteau, the latter of
which had been seen no more, though the Major had
returned. So Mrs. Gashly produced the challenge, and
having watched Miss Mapp off to the High Street at
half past ten, Dominic and Gashly went together to
her house, to see if Withers could supply anything of
importance, or, if not, a nutmeg grater. They were
forced to be content with the grater, but pored over
the challenge with Withers, and she, having an errand to Diva's house, told Janet, who without further
ceremony bounded upstairs to tell her mistress.
Hardly had Diva heard than she plunged into the
High Street, and, with suitable additions, told Miss
Mapp, Evie, Irene and the Padre under promise in
each case, of the strictest secrecy. Ten minutes later
Irene had asked the defenceless Mr. Hopkins, who
was being Adam again, what he knew about it, and
Evie, with her mouselike gait that looked so rapid
and was so deliberate, had the mortification of seeing
Miss Mapp outdistance her and be admitted into the
Poppits' house, just as she came in view of the front
door. She rightly conjectured that after the affair of
the store-cupboard in the garden room, there could be
nothing of lesser importance than "the duel" which
could take that lady through those abhorred portals.
Finally, at ten minutes past eleven, Major Flint and
Captain Puffin were seen by one or two fortunate
people (the morning having cleared up) walking together to the tram, and without exception, everybody
knew that they were on their way to fight their duel
in some remote hollow of the sand dunes.

    Miss Mapp had gone straight home from her visit
to the Poppits just about eleven, and stationed herself

in the window where she could keep an eye on the
house of the duellists. In her anxiety to outstrip Evie
and be the first to tell the Poppits, she had not waited
to hear that they had both come back and knew only
of the challenge and that they had gone to the station. She had already formed a glorious idea of her
own as to what the history of the duel (past or future) was, and intoxicated with emotion had retired
from the wordy fray to think about it, and, as already
mentioned, to keep an eye on the two houses just below. Then there appeared in sight the Padre, walking
swiftly up the hill, and she had barely time under
cover of the curtain to regain the table where her
sweet chrysanthemums were pining for water when
Withers announced him. He wore a furrowed brow
and quite forgot to speak either Scotch or Elizabethan
English. A few rapid words made it clear that they
both had heard the main outlines.

"A terrible situation," said the Padre. "Duelling is in
direct contravention of all Christian principles, and, I
believe, of the civil law. The discharge of a pistol, in
unskillful hands, may lead to deplorable results. And
Major Flint, so one has heard, is an experienced duellist. . . . That, of course, makes it even more dangerous."

It was at this identical moment that Major Flint
came out of his house and Qui-hied cheerily to Puffin.
Miss Mapp and the Padre, deep in these bloody possibilities, neither saw nor heard them. They passed together down the road and into the High Street,
unconscious that their every look and action was
being more commented on than the Epistle to the He-
brews. Inside the garden room Miss Mapp sighed,
and bent her eyes on her chrysanthemums.

"Quite terrible!" she said. "And in our peaceful, tranquil Tilling!"

"Perhaps the duel has already taken place, and—and they've missed," said the Padre. "They were both seen to return to their houses early this morning."

"By whom?" asked Miss Mapp jealously. She had not heard that.

"By Hopkins," said he. "Hopkins saw them both return."

"I shouldn't trust that man too much," said Miss Mapp. "Hopkins may not be telling the truth. I have no great opinion of his moral standard."

"Why is that?"

This was no time to discuss the nudity of Hopkins, and Miss Mapp put the question aside.

"That does not matter now, dear Padre," she said. "I only wish I thought the duel had taken place without accident. But Major Benjy's—I mean Major Flint's—portmanteau has not come back to his house. Of that I'm sure. What if they have sent it away to some place where they are unknown, full of pistols and things?"

"Possibly—terribly possible," said the Padre. "I wish I could see my duty clear. I should not hesitate to—well, to do the best I could to induce them to abandon this murderous project. And what do you imagine was the root of the quarrel?"

"I couldn't say, I'm sure," said Miss Mapp. She bent her head over the chrysanthemums.

"Your distracting sex," said he with a moment's gallantry, "is usually the cause of quarrel. I've noticed that they both seemed to admire Miss Irene very much."

Miss Mapp raised her head and spoke with great animation.

"Dear, quaint Irene, I'm sure, has nothing whatever to do with it," she said with perfect truth. "Nothing whatever!"

There was no mistaking the sincerity of this, and the Padre, Tillingite to the marrow, instantly concluded that Miss Mapp knew what (or who) was the cause of all this unique disturbance. And as she bent her head again over the chrysanthemums, and quite distinctly grew brick-red in the face, he felt that delicacy prevented his inquiring any further.

"What are you going to do, dear Padre?" she asked in a low voice, choking with emotion. "Whatever you decide will be wise and Christian. Oh, these violent men! Such babies, too!"

The Padre was bursting with curiosity, but since his delicacy forbade him to ask any of the questions which effervesced like sherbet round his tongue, he propounded another plan.

"I think my duty is to go straight to the Major," he said, "who seems to be the principal in the affair, and tell him that I know all—and guess the rest," he added.

"Nothing that I have said," declared Miss Mapp in great confusion, "must have anything to do with your guesses. Promise me that, Padre."

This intimate and fruitful conversation was interrupted by the sound of two pairs of steps just outside, and before Withers had had time to say, "Mrs. Plaistow," Diva burst in.

"They have both taken the 11:20 tram," she said, and sank into the nearest chair.

"Together?" asked Miss Mapp, feeling a sudden chill of disappointment at the thought of a duel with pistols trailing off into one with golf clubs.

"Yes, but that's a blind," panted Diva. "They were

talking and laughing together. Sheer blind! Duel among the sand dunes!"

"Padre, it is your duty to stop it," said Miss Mapp faintly.

"But if the pistols are in a portmanteau—" he began.

"What portmanteau?" screamed Diva, who hadn't heard about that.

"Darling, I'll tell you presently," said Miss Mapp. "That was only a guess of mine, Padre. But there's no time to lose."

"But there's no tram to catch," said the Padre. "It has gone by this time."

"A taxi then, Padre! Oh, lose no time!"

"Are you coming with me?" he said in a low voice. "Your presence—"

"Better not," she said. "It might—Better not," she repeated.

He skipped down the steps and was observed running down the street.

"What about the portmanteau?" asked the greedy Diva.

It was with strong misgivings that the Padre started on his Christian errand, and had not the sense of adventure spiced it, he would probably have returned to his sermon instead, which was Christian, too. To begin with, there was the ruinous expense of taking a taxi out to the golf links, but by no other means could he hope to arrive in time to avert an encounter that might be fatal. It must be said to his credit that, though this was an errand distinctly due to his position as the spiritual head of Tilling, he rejected, as soon as it occurred to him, the idea of charging the hire of the taxi among Church Expenses, and as he whirled along the flat road across the marsh, the thing that chiefly buoyed up his drooping spirits and annealed his courage was the romantic nature of his mission. He no longer, thanks to what Miss Mapp had so clearly refrained from saying, had the slightest doubt that she, in some manner that scarcely needed conjecture, was the cause of the duel he was attempting to avert. For years it had been a matter of unwearied and confidential discussion as to whether and when she would marry either Major Flint or Captain Puffin, and it was superfluous to look for any other explanation. It was true that she, in popular parlance, was "getting on", but so, too, and at exactly the same rate, were the representatives of the United Services, and the sooner that two out of the three of them "got on" permanently, the better. No doubt some crisis had arisen, and inflamed with love. . . . He intended to confide all this to his wife on his return.

On his return! The unspoken words made his heart sink. What if he never did return? For he was about to place himself in a position of no common danger. His plan was to drive past the clubhouse, and then on foot, after discharging the taxi, to strike directly into the line of tumbled sand dunes which, remote and undisturbed and full of large convenient hollows, stretched along the coast above the flat beach. Any of those hollows, he knew, might prove to contain the duellists in the very act of firing, and over the rim of each he had to pop his unprotected head. He (if in time) would have to separate the combatants, and who knew whether, in their very natural chagrin at being interrupted, they might not turn their combined pistols on him first, and settle with each other afterwards? One murder the more made little difference to desperate men. Other shocks, less deadly but extremely unnerving, might await him. He might be too late, and pop his head over the edge of one of these

craters, only to discover it full of bleeding if not
mangled bodies. Or there might be only one mangled
body, and the other, unmangled, would pursue him
through the sand dunes and offer him life at the price
of silence. That, he painfully reflected, would be a
very difficult decision to make. Luckily Captain Puffin
(if he proved to be the survivor) was lame. . . .

With drawn face and agonized prayers on his lips,
he began a systematic search of the sand dunes. Often
his nerve nearly failed him, and he would sink panting among the prickly bents before he dared to peer
into the hollow up the sides of which he had climbed.
His ears shuddered at the anticipation of hearing
from near at hand the report of pistols, and once a
backfire from a motor passing along the road caused
him to leap high in the air. The sides of these dunes
were steep, and his shoes got so full of sand, that from
time to time, in spite of the urgency of his errand,
he was forced to pause in order to empty them out.
He stumbled in rabbit holes; he caught his foot and
once his trousers in strands of barbed wire, the rem-
nant of coast defenses in the German War; he crashed
among potsherds and abandoned kettles; but with a
thoroughness that did equal credit to his wind and his
Christian spirit, he searched a mile of perilous dunes
from end to end, and peered into every important
hollow. Two hours later, jaded and torn and streaming with perspiration, he came, in the vicinity of the
clubhouse, to the end of his fruitless search.

He staggered round the corner of it and came in
view of the eighteenth green. Two figures were occu-
pying it, and one of these was in the act of putting.
He missed. Then he saw who the figures were: it was
Captain Puffin who had just missed his putt; it was
Major Flint who now expressed elated sympathy.

"Bad luck, old boy," he said. "Well, a jolly good match, and we halve it. Why, there's the Padre. Been for a walk? Join us in a round this afternoon, Padre! Blow your sermon!"

6

THE SAME DELIGHTFUL prospect at the end of the High Street, over the marsh, which had witnessed not so long ago the final encounter in the Wars of the Roses and the subsequent armistice, was, of course, found to be peculiarly attractive that morning to those who knew (and who did not?) that the combatants had left by the 11:20 steam tram to fight among the sand dunes, and that the intrepid Padre had rushed after them in a taxi. The Padre's taxi had returned empty, and the driver seemed to know nothing whatever about anything, so the only thing for everybody to do was to put off lunch and wait for the arrival of the next tram, which occurred at 1:37. In consequence, all the doors in Tilling flew open like those of cuckoo clocks at ten minutes before that hour, and this pleasant promenade was full of those who so keenly admired autumn tints.

From here the progress of the tram across the plain was in full view; so, too, was the shedlike station across the river, which was the terminus of the line, and expectation, when the two-waggoned little train approached the end of its journey, was so tense that it was almost disagreeable. A couple of hours had elapsed since, like the fishers who sailed away into the West and were seen no more till the corpses lay out on the shining sand, the three had left for the sand dunes, and a couple of hours, so reasoned the Cosmic Consciousness of Tilling, gave ample time for a duel to be fought, if the Padre was not in time to stop it, and for him to stop it if he was. No surgical assistance, as far as was known, had been summoned, but the reason for that might easily be that a surgeon's skill was no longer, alas! of any avail for one, if not both, of the combatants. But if such was the case, it was nice to hope that the Padre had been in time to supply spiritual aid to anyone whom first-aid and probes were powerless to succour.

The variety of dénouements which the approaching tram, that had now cut off steam, was capable of providing was positively bewildering. They whirled through Miss Mapp's head like the autumn leaves which she admired so much, and she tried in vain to catch them all, and when caught, to tick them off on her fingers. Each, moreover, furnished diverse and legitimate conclusions. For instance (taking the thumb):

I. If nobody of the slightest importance arrived by the tram, that might be because

 a. Nothing had happened, and they were all playing golf.

 b. The worst had happened, and, as the Padre had feared, the duellists had first shot him and then each other.

 c. The next worst had happened, and the Padre was arranging for the reverent removal of the corpse of

  i. Major Benjy, or

> ii. Captain Puffin, or those of
> iii. Both.

Miss Mapp let go of her thumb and lightly touched her forefinger.

> II. The Padre might arrive alone.

In that case anything or nothing might have happened to either or both of the others, and the various contingencies hanging on this arrival were so numerous that there was not time to sort them out.

> III. The Padre might arrive with two limping figures whom he assisted.

Here it must not be forgotten that Captain Puffin always limped, and the Major occasionally. Miss Mapp did not forget it.

> IV. The Padre might arrive with a stretcher. Query—Whose?
> V. The Padre might arrive with two stretchers.
> VI. Three stretchers might arrive from the shining sands, at the town where the women were weeping and wringing their hands.

In that case Miss Mapp saw herself busily employed in strengthening poor Evie, who now was running about like a mouse from group to group picking up crumbs of Cosmic Consciousness.

Miss Mapp had got as far as sixthly, though she was aware she had not exhausted the possibilities, when the tram stopped. She furtively took out from her pocket (she had focussed them before she put them in) the opera glasses through which she had watched the station yard on a day which had been very much less exciting than this. After one glance she put them back again, feeling vexed and disappointed with herself, for the dénouement which they had so unerringly disclosed was one that had not entered her mind at all. In that moment she had seen that out of the tram there stepped three figures and no stretcher. One figure, it is true, limped, but in a manner so natural that she scorned to draw any deductions from that halting gait. They proceeded, side by side, across the bridge over the river towards the town.

It is no use denying that the Cosmic Consciousness of the ladies of Tilling was aware of a disagreeable anticlimax to so many hopes and fears. It had, of course, hoped for the best, but it had not expected that the best would be quite as bad as this. The best, to put it frankly, would have been a bandaged arm, or something of that kind. There was still room for the more hardened optimist to hope that something of some sort had occurred, or that something of some sort had been averted, and that the whole affair was not, in the delicious new slang phrase of the Padre's, which was spreading like wildfire through Tilling, a "wash-out." Pistols might have been innocuously discharged for all that was known to the contrary. But it looked bad.

Miss Mapp was the first to recover from the blow, and took Diva's pudgy hand.

"Diva, darling," she said, "I feel so deeply thankful. What a wonderful and beautiful end to all our anxiety!"

There was a subconscious regret with regard to the anxiety. The anxiety was, so to speak, a dear and beloved departed. . . . And Diva did not feel so sure that the end was so beautiful and wonderful. Her grandfather, Miss Mapp had reason to know, had been a butcher, and probably some inherited indifference to slaughter lurked in her tainted blood.

"There's the portmanteau still," she said hopefully. "Pistols in the portmanteau. Your idea, Elizabeth."

"Yes, dear," said Elizabeth; "but thank God I must have been very wrong about the portmanteau. The outside porter told me that he brought it up from the station to Major Benjy's house half an hour ago. Fancy your not knowing that! I feel sure it is true, for he attends the Padre's confirmation class. If there had been pistols in it, Major Benjy and Captain Puffin would have gone away, too. I am quite happy about that now. It went away, and it has come back. That's all about the portmanteau."

She paused a moment.

"But what does it contain, then?" she said quickly, more as if she was thinking aloud than talking to Diva. "Why did Major Benjy pack it and send it to the station this morning? Where has it come back from? Why did it go there?"

She felt that she was saying too much, and pressed her hand to her head.

"Has all this happened this morning?" she said. "What a full morning, dear! Lovely autumn leaves! I shall go home and have my lunch and rest. Au reservoir, Diva."

Miss Mapp's eternal reservoirs had begun to get on Diva's nerves, and as she lingered here a moment more a great idea occurred to her, which temporarily banished the disappointment about the duellists. Elizabeth, as all the world knew, had accumulated a great reservoir of provisions in the false bookcase in her garden room, and Diva determined that if she could think of a neat phrase, the very next time Eliza-

beth said, "Au reservoir," to her, she would work in
an allusion to Elizabeth's own reservoir of corned
beef, tongue, flour, bovril, dried apricots and condensed milk. She would have to frame some stinging
rejoinder which would "escape her" when next Elizabeth used that stale old phrase; it would have to be
short, swift and spontaneous, and therefore required
careful thought. It would be good to bring "pop" into
it also. "Your reservoir in the garden room hasn't gone
'pop' again, I hope, darling?" was the first draft that
occurred to her, but that was not sufficiently condensed. "Pop goes the reservoir," on the analogy of
the weasel, was better. And, better than either, was
there not some sort of corn called popcorn, which
Americans ate? . . . "Have you any popcorn in your
reservoir?" That would be a nasty one. . . .

But it all required thinking over, and the sight of
the Padre and the duellists crossing the field below, as
she still lingered on this escarpment of the hill,
brought the duel back to her mind. It would have
been considered inquisitive even at Tilling to put
direct questions to the combatants, and (still hoping
for the best) ask them point-blank, "Who won?" or
something of that sort; but until she arrived at some
sort of information, the excruciating pangs of curiosity that must be endured could be likened only to
some acute toothache of the mind with no dentist to
stop or remove the source of the trouble. Elizabeth
had already succumbed to these pangs of surmise and
excitement, and had frankly gone home to rest, and
her absence, the fact that for the next hour or two she
could not, except by some extraordinary feat on the
telephone, get hold of anything which would throw
light on the whole prodigious situation, inflamed
Diva's brain to the highest pitch of inventiveness. She

knew that she was Elizabeth's inferior in point of
reconstructive imagination, and the present moment,
while the other was recuperating her energies for
fresh assaults on the unknown, was Diva's opportunity. The one person who might be presumed to
know more than anybody else was the Padre, but
while he was with the duellists, it was as impossible
to ask him what had happened as to ask the duellists
who had won. She must, while Miss Mapp rested, get
hold of the Padre without the duellists.

Even as Athene sprang full grown and panoplied
from the brain of Zeus, so from Diva's brain there
sprang her plan complete. She even resisted the temp-
tation to go on admiring autumn tints, in order to see
how the interesting trio "looked" when, as they must
presently do, they passed close to where she stood,
and hurried home, pausing only to purchase, pay for,
and carry away with her from the provision shop a
large and expensively-dressed crab, a dainty of which
the Padre was inordinately fond. Ruinous as this was,
there was a note of triumph in her voice when, on arrival, she called loudly for Janet, and told her to lay
another place at the luncheon table. Then putting a
strong constraint on herself, she waited three minutes
by her watch, in order to give the Padre time to get
home, and then rang him up and reminded him that
he had promised to lunch with her that day. It was
no use asking him to lunch in such a way that he
might refuse; she employed without remorse this piti-
less *force majeure*.

The engagement was short and brisk. He pleaded
that not even now could he remember even having
asked (which was not surprising), and said that he
and wee wifie had begun lunch. On which Diva un-
masked her last gun, and told him that she had or-

dered a crab on purpose. That silenced further argument, and he said that he and wee wifie would be round in a jiffy, and rang off. She did not particularly want wee wifie, but there was enough crab.

Diva felt that she had never laid out four shillings to better purpose, when a quarter of an hour later, the Padre gave her the full account of his fruitless search among the sand dunes, so deeply impressive was his sense of being buoyed up to that incredibly fatiguing and perilous excursion by some Power outside himself. It never even occurred to her to think that it was an elaborate practical joke on the part of the Power outside himself, to spur him on to such immense exertions to no purpose at all. He had only got as far as this over his interrupted lunch with wee wifie, and though she, too, was in agonized suspense as to what happened next, she bore the repetition with great equanimity, only making small mouselike noises of impatience which nobody heard. He was quite forgetting to speak either Scotch or Elizabethan English, so obvious was the absorption of his hearers, without these added aids to command attention.

"And then I came round the corner of the clubhouse," he said, "and there was Captain Puffin and the Major finishing their match on the eighteenth hole."

"Then there's been no duel at all," said Diva, scraping the shell of the crab.

"I feel sure of it. There wouldn't have been time for a duel and a round of golf, in addition to the impossibility of playing golf immediately after a duel. No nerves could stand it. Besides, I asked one of their caddies. They had come straight from the train to the clubhouse, and from the clubhouse to the first tee. They had not been alone for a moment."

"Wash-out," said Diva, wondering whether this had been worth four shillings, so tame was the conclusion.

Mrs. Bartlett gave a little squeak which was her preliminary to speech.

"But I do not see why there may not be a duel yet, Kenneth," she said. "Because they did not fight this morning—excellent crab, dear Diva, so good of you to ask us—there's no reason why there shouldn't be a duel this afternoon. Oh, dear me, and cold beef as well; I shall be quite stuffed. Depend upon it, a man doesn't take the trouble to write a challenge and all that, unless he means business."

The Padre held up his hand. He felt that he was gradually growing to be the hero of the whole affair. He had certainly looked over the edge of numberless hollows in the sand dunes with vivid anticipations of having a bullet whiz by him on each separate occasion. It behooved him to take a sublime line.

"My dear," he said, "business is hardly a word to apply to murder. That within the last twenty-four hours there was the intention of fighting a duel, I don't deny. But something has decidedly happened which has averted that deplorable calamity. Peace and reconciliation is the result of it, and I have never seen two men so unaffectedly friendly."

Diva got up and whirled round the table to get the port for the Padre, so pleased was she at a fresh idea coming to her while still dear Elizabeth was resting. She attributed it to the crab.

"We've all been on a false scent," she said. "Peace and reconciliation happened before they went out to the sand dunes at all. It happened at the station. They met at the station, you know. It is proved that

Major Flint went there. Major wouldn't send port-manteau off alone. And it's proved that Captain Puffin went there, too, because the note which his house-maid found on the table before she saw the challenge from the Major, which was on the chimney piece, said that he had been called away very suddenly. No; they both went to catch the early train in order to go away before they could be stopped and kill each other. But why didn't they go? What happened? Don't suppose the outside porter showed them how wicked they were, confirmation class or no confirma-tion class. Stumps me. Almost wish Elizabeth was here. She's good at guessing."

The Padre's eyes brightened. Reaction after the perils of the morning, crab, and port combined to make a man of him.

"Eh, 'tis a bonny wee drappie of port whatever, Mistress Plaistow," he said. "And I dinna ken that ye're far wrang in jaloosing that Mistress Mapp might have a wee bitty word to say aboot it a', 'gin she had the mind."

"She was wrong about the portmanteau," said Diva. "Confessed she was wrong."

"Hoots! I'm not mindin' the bit pochmantie," said the Padre.

"What else does she know?" asked Diva feverishly.

There was no doubt that the Padre had the fullest attention of the two ladies again, and there was no need to talk Scotch any more.

"Begin at the beginning," he said. "What do we suppose was the cause of the quarrel?"

"Anything," said Diva. "Golf, tiger skins, coal strike, summer time."

He shook his head.

"I grant you words may pass on such subjects," he

said. "We feel keenly, I know, about summer time in Tilling, though we shall all be reconciled over that next Sunday, when real time, God's time, as I am venturing to call it in my sermon, comes in again."

Diva had to bite her tongue to prevent letting herself bolt off on this new scent. After all, she had invested in crab to learn about duelling, not about summer time.

"Well?" she said.

"We may have had words on that subject," said the Padre, booming as if he was in the pulpit already, "but we should, I hope, none of us go so far as to catch the earliest train with pistols, in defence of our conviction about summer time. No; Mrs. Plaistow, if you are right, and there is something to be said for your view, in thinking that they both went to such lengths as to be in time for the early train, in order to fight a duel undisturbed, you must look for a more solid cause than that."

Diva vainly racked her brains to think of anything more worthy of the highest pitches of emotion than this. If it had been she and Miss Mapp who had been embroiled, hoarding and dress would have occurred to her. But as it was, no one in his senses could dream that the Captain and the Major were sartorial rivals, unless they had quarrelled over the question as to which of them wore the snuffiest old clothes.

"Give it up," she said. "What did they quarrel about?"

"Passion!" said the Padre, in those full, deep tones in which next Sunday he would allude to God's time. "I do not mean anger, but the flame that exalts man to heaven or—or does exactly the opposite."

"But whomever for?" asked Diva, quite thrown off her bearings. Such a thing had never occurred to her, for as far as she was aware, passion, except in the sense of rage, did not exist in Tilling. Tilling was far too respectable.

The Padre considered this a moment.

"I am betraying no confidence," he said, "because no one has confided in me. But there certainly is a lady in this town—I do not allude to Miss Irene—who has long enjoyed the Major's particular esteem. May not some deprecating remark—"

Wee wifie gave a much louder squeal than usual.

"He means poor Elizabeth," she said in a high, tremulous voice. "Fancy, Kenneth!"

Diva, a few seconds before, had seen no reason why the Padre should drink the rest of her port, and was now in the act of drinking some of that unusual beverage herself. She tried to swallow it, but it was too late, and next moment all the openings in her face were fountains of that delicious wine. She choked and she gurgled, until the last drop had left her wind-pipe—under the persuasion of pattings on the back from the others—and then she gave herself up to the loud, hoarse laughter, through which there shrilled the staccato squeaks of wee wifie. Nothing, even if you are being laughed at yourself, is so infectious as prolonged laughter, and the Padre felt himself forced to join it. When one of them got a little better, a relapse ensued by reason of infection from the others, and it was not till exhaustion set in, that this triple volcano became quiescent again.

"Only fancy!" said Evie faintly. "How did such an idea get into your head, Kenneth?"

His voice shook as he answered.

"We, we were all a little worked up this morning," he said. "The idea—really, I don't know what we have all been laughing at—"

"I do," said Diva. "Go on. About the idea—"

A feminine, a diabolical inspiration flared within wee wifie's mind.

"Elizabeth suggested it herself," she squealed.

Naturally Diva could not help remembering that she had found Miss Mapp and the Padre in earnest conversation together when she forced her way in that morning with the news that the duellists had left by the 11:20 tram. Nobody could be expected to have so short a memory as to have forgotten *that*. Just now she forgave Elizabeth for anything she had ever done. That might have to be reconsidered afterwards, but at present it was valid enough.

"Did she suggest it?" she asked.

The Padre behaved like a man, and lied like Ananias.

"Most emphatically she did not," he said.

The disappointment would have been severe, had the two ladies believed this confident assertion, and Diva pictured a delightful interview with Elizabeth, in which she would suddenly tell her the wild surmise the Padre had made with regard to the cause of the duel, and see how she looked then. Just see how she looked then; that was all—self-consciousness and guilt would fly their colors. . . .

Miss Mapp had been tempted when she went home that morning, after enjoying the autumn tints, to ask Diva to lunch with her, but remembered in time that she had told her cook to broach one of the tins of corned beef which no human wizard could coax into the store-cupboard again, if he shut the door after it. Diva would have been sure to say something acid and allusive, to remark on its excellence being happily not wasted on the poor people in the hospital, or, if she

had not said anything at all about it, her silence as
she ate a great deal would have had a sharp flavor.
But Miss Mapp would have liked, especially when
she went to take her rest afterwards on the big sofa in
the garden room, to have had somebody to talk to, for
her brain seethed with conjectures as to what had
happened, was happening and would happen, and
discussion was the best method of simplifying a problem, of narrowing it down to the limits of probability,
whereas when she was alone now with her own imag-
inings, the most fantastic of them seemed plausible.
She had, however, handed a glorious suggestion to
the Padre, the one, that is, which concerned the cause
of the duel, and it had been highly satisfactory to observe the sympathy and respect with which he had
imbibed it. She had, too, been so discreet about it;
she had not come within measurable distance of as-
serting that the challenge had been in any way connected with her. She had only been very emphatic on
the point of its not being connected with poor dear
Irene, and then occupied herself with her sweet flowers. That had been sufficient, and she felt in her bones
and marrow that he inferred what she had meant him
to infer. . . .

The vulture of surmise ceased to peck at her for a
few moments as she considered this, and followed up
a thread of gold. . . . Though the Padre would
surely be discreet, she hoped that he would "let slip"
to dear Evie in the course of the vivid conversation
they would be sure to have over lunch, that he had a
good guess as to the cause which had led to that sav-
age challenge. Upon which dear Evie would be certain to ply him with direct squeaks and questions,
and when she "got hot" (as in animal, vegetable, and
mineral), his reticence would lead her to make a

good guess, too. She might be incredulous, but there
the idea would be in her mind, while if she felt that
these stirring days were no time for scepticism, she
could hardly fail to be interested and touched. Before
long (how soon Miss Mapp was happily not aware)
she would "pop in" to see Diva, or Diva would "pop
in" to see her, and Evie, observing a discretion similar
to that of the Padre and herself, would soon enable
dear Diva to make a good guess, too. After that, all
would be well, for dear Diva ("such a gossiping darling") would undoubtedly tell everybody in Tilling,
under vows of secrecy (so that she should have the
pleasure of telling everybody herself) just what her
good guess was. Thus, very presently, all Tilling
would know exactly that which Miss Mapp had not
said to the dear Padre, namely, that the duel which
had been fought (or which hadn't been fought) was
"all about" her. And the best of it was, that though
everybody knew, it would still be a great and beautiful secret, reposing inviolably in every breast or chest,
as the case might be. She had no anxiety about anybody asking direct questions of the duellists, for if duelling, for years past, had been a subject which no
delicately-minded person alluded to purposely in Major Benjy's presence, how much more now after this
critical morning would that subject be taboo? That
certainly was a good thing, for the duellists if closely
questioned might have a different explanation, and it
would be highly inconvenient to have two contradic-
tory stories going about. But, as it was, nothing could
be nicer: the whole of the rest of Tilling, under
promise of secrecy, would know, and even if under
further promises of secrecy they communicated their
secret to each other, there would be no harm
done. . . .

After this excursion into Elysian fields, poor Miss Mapp had to get back to her vulture again, and the hour's rest that she had felt was due to herself as the heroine of a duel became a period of extraordinary cerebral activity. Puzzle as she might, she could make nothing whatever of the portmanteau, and the excursion to the early train, and she got up long before her hour was over, since she found that the more she thought, the more invincible were the objections to any conclusion that she drowningly grasped at. Whatever attack she made on this mystery, the garrison failed to march out and surrender but kept their flag flying, and her conjectures were woefully blasted by the forces of the most elementary reasons. But as the agony of suspense, if no fresh topic of interest intervened, would be frankly unendurable, she determined to concentrate no more on it, but rather to commit it to the icehouse or safe of her subconscious mind, from which at will, when she felt refreshed and reinvigorated, she could unlock it and examine it again. The whole problem was more superlatively baffling than any that she could remember having encountered in all these inquisitive years, just as the subject of it was more majestic than any, for it concerned not hoarding, nor visits of the Prince of Wales, nor poppy-trimmed gowns, but life and death and firing of deadly pistols. And should love be added to this august list? Certainly not by her, though Tilling might do what it liked. In fact, Tilling always did.

She walked across to the bow window from which she had conducted so many exciting and successful investigations. But today the view seemed as stale and unprofitable as the world appeared to Hamlet, even though Mrs. Poppit at that moment went waddling down the street and disappeared round the cor-

ner where the dentist and Mr. Wyse lived. With a
sense of fatigue, Miss Mapp recalled the fact that she
had seen the housemaid cleaning Mr. Wyse's windows yesterday—"Children dear, was it yesterday?"—and had noted her industry, and drawn from it
the irresistible conclusion that Mr. Wyse was probably expected home. He usually came back about
mid-October, and let slip allusions to his enjoyable
visits in Scotland and his *villeggiatura* (so he was
pleased to express it) with his sister the Contessa di
Faraglione at Capri. That Contessa Faraglione was
rather a mythical personage to Miss Mapp's mind:
she was certainly not in a medieval copy of *Who's
Who* which was the only accessible handbook in matters relating to noble and notable personages, and
though Miss Mapp would not have taken an oath that
she did not exist, she saw no strong reason for supposing that she did. Certainly she had never been to Tilling, which was strange as her brother lived there, and
there was nothing but her brother's allusions to cer-
tify her. About Mrs. Poppit now: had she gone to see
Mr. Wyse or had she gone to the dentist? One or
other it must be, for apart from them that particular
street contained nobody who counted, and at the bottom it simply conducted you out into the uneventful
country. Mrs. Poppit was all dressed up, and she would
never walk in the country in such a costume. It would
do either for Mr. Wyse or the dentist, for she was
the sort of woman who would like to appear grand in
the dentist's chair, so that he might be shy of hurting
such a fine lady. Then again, Mrs. Poppit had wonderful teeth, almost too good to be true, and before
now she had asked who lived at that pretty little
house just round the corner, as if to show that she
didn't know where the dentist lived! Or had she

found out by some underhand means that Mr. Wyse
had come back, and had gone to call on him and give
him the first news of the duel, and talk to him about
Scotland? Very likely they had neither of them been
to Scotland at all: they conspired to say that they had
been to Scotland and stayed at shooting lodges
(keepers' lodges more likely) in order to impress Tilling with their magnificence. . . .

Miss Mapp sat down on the central-heating pipes
in her window, and fell into one of her reconstructive
musings. Partly, if Mr. Wyse was back, it was well
just to run over his record; partly she wanted to
divert her mind from the two houses just below, that
of Major Benjy on the one side and that of Captain
Puffin on the other, which contained the key to the
great, insoluble mystery, from conjecture as to which
she wanted to obtain relief. Mr. Wyse, anyhow,
would serve as a mild opiate, for she had never lost
an angry interest in him. Though he was for eight
months of the year, or thereabouts, in Tilling, he was
never, for a single hour, *of* Tilling. He did not exactly
invest himself with an air of condescension and su-
periority—Miss Mapp did him that justice—but he
made other people invest him with it, so that it came
to the same thing: he was invested. He did not drag
the fact of his sister being the Contessa Faraglione
into conversation, but if talk turned on sisters, and
he was asked about his, he confessed to her nobility.
The same phenomenon appeared when the innocent
county of Hampshire was mentioned, for it turned out
that he knew the county well, being one of the Wyses
of Whitchurch. You couldn't say he talked about it,
but he made other people talk about it. . . . He was
quite impervious to satire on such points, for when,
goaded to madness, Miss Mapp had once said that

she was one of the Mapps of Maidstone, he had
merely bowed and said: "A very old family, I believe," and when the conversation branched off on to
old families, he had rather pointedly said "we" to Miss
Mapp. So poor Miss Mapp was sorry she had been satirical. . . . But for some reason Tilling never ceased
to play up to Mr. Wyse, and there was not a tea party
or a bridge party given during the whole period of
his residence there to which he was not invited.
Hostesses always started with him, sending him round
a note with "To await answer," written in the top
left-hand corner, since he had clearly stated that he
considered the telephone an undignified instrument
only fit to be used for household purposes, and had
installed his in the kitchen, in the manner of the
Wyses of Whitchurch. That alone, apart from Mr.
Wyse's old-fashioned notions on the subject, made
telephoning impossible, for your summons was usually
answered by his cook, who instantly began scolding
the butcher irrespective and disrespectful of whom
you were. When her mistake was made known to her,
she never apologized, but grudgingly said she would
call Mr. Figgis, who was Mr. Wyse's valet. Mr. Figgis
always took a long time in coming, and when he
came he sneezed or did something disagreeable and
said: "Yes, yes, what is it?" in a very testy manner.
After explanations he would consent to tell his master,
which took another long time, and even then Mr.
Wyse did not come himself, and usually refused the
proffered invitation. Miss Mapp had tried the expedi-
ent of sending Withers to the telephone when she
wanted to get at Mr. Wyse, by way of taking them all
down a peg or two, but this had not succeeded, for
Withers and Mr. Wyse's cook quarrelled so violently
before they got to business that Mr. Figgis had to

calm the cook and Withers to complain to Miss
Mapp. . . . This, in brief, was the general reason why
Tilling sent notes to Mr. Wyse. As for chatting
through the telephone, which was the main use of
telephones, the thing was quite out of the question.

Miss Mapp revived a little as she made this piercing analysis of Mr. Wyse, and the warmth of the central-heating pipes, on this baffling day of autumn
tints, was comforting. . . . No one could say that Mr.
Wyse was not punctilious in matters of social etiquette, for though he refused three-quarters of the invitations which were showered on him, he invariably
returned the compliment by an autograph note
hoping that he might have the pleasure of entertaining you at lunch on Thursday next, for he always
gave a small luncheon party on Thursday. These invitations were couched in Chesterfield terms: Mr.
Wyse said that he had met a mutual friend just now
who had informed him that you were in residence,
and had encouraged him to hope that you might give
him the pleasure of your company, etc. This was al-
luring diction; it presented the image of Mr. Wyse
stepping briskly home again, quite heartened up by
this chance encounter, and no longer the prey to melancholy at the thought that you might not give him
the joy. He was encouraged to hope. . . . These polite expressions were traced in a neat upright hand on
paper which, when he had just come back from Italy,
often bore a coronet on the top with "Villa Faraglione, Capri" printed on the right-hand top corner
and "Amelia" (the name of his putative sister) in
sprawling gilt on the left, the whole being lightly
erased. Of course he was quite right to filch a few
sheets, but it threw rather a lurid light on his character that they should be such grand ones.

Last year only, in a fit of passion at Mr. Wyse having refused six invitations running on the plea of other engagements, Miss Mapp had headed a movement, the object of which was that Tilling should not accept any of Mr. Wyse's invitations unless he accepted its. This had met with theoretical sympathy; the Bartletts, Diva, Irene, and Poppits had all agreed—rather absently—that it would be a very proper thing to do, but the very next Thursday they had all, including the originator, met on Mr. Wyse's doorstep for a luncheon party, and the movement then and there collapsed. Though they all protested and rebelled against such a notion, the horrid fact remained that everybody basked in Mr. Wyse's effulgence whenever it was disposed to shed itself on them. Much as they distrusted the information they dragged out of him, they adored hearing about the Villa Faraglione, and dressed themselves in their very best clothes to do so. Then again there was the quality of the lunch itself; often there was caviar, and it was impossible (though the interrogator who asked whether it came from Twenlow's feared the worst) not to be mildly excited to know, when Mr. Wyse referred the question to Figgis, that the caviar had arrived from Odessa that morning. The haunch of roe deer came from Perthshire; the wine, on the subject of which the Major could not be silent, and which often made him extremely talkative, was from "my brother-in-law's vineyard." And Mr. Wyse would taste it with the air of a connoisseur and say: "Not quite as good as last year; I must tell the Cont—I mean my sister."

Again when Mr. Wyse did condescend to honor a tea party or a bridge party, Tilling writhed under the consciousness that their general deportment was quite

different from that which they ordinarily practiced
among themselves. There was never any squabbling
at Mr. Wyse's table, and such squabbling as took
place at the other tables was conducted in low hiss-
ings and whispers, so that Mr. Wyse should not hear.
Diva never haggled over her gains or losses when he
was there; the Padre never talked Scotch or Elizabethan English. Evie never squeaked like a mouse; no
shrill recriminations or stately sarcasms took place between partners; and if there happened to be a little
disagreement about the rules, Mr. Wyse's decision,
though he was not a better player than any of them,
was accepted without a murmur. At intervals for refreshment, in the same way, Diva no longer filled her
mouth and both hands with nougat chocolate; there
was no scrambling nor jostling, but the ladies were
waited on by the gentlemen, who then refreshed
themselves. And yet Mr. Wyse in no way asserted
himself, or reduced them all to politeness by talking
about the polished manners of Italians; it was Tilling
itself which chose to behave in this unusual manner
in his presence. Sometimes Diva might forget herself
for a moment, and address something withering to
her partner, but the partner never replied in suitable
terms, and Diva became honey-mouthed again. It
was, indeed, if Mr. Wyse had appeared at two or
three parties, rather a relief not to find him at the
next, and breathe freely in less rarified air. But
whether he came or not he always returned the invitation by one to a Thursday luncheon party, and thus
the high circles of Tilling met every week at his house.

Miss Mapp came to the end of this brief retrospect,
and determined, when once it was proved that Mr.
Wyse had arrived, to ask him to tea on Tuesday. That
would mean lunch with him on Thursday, and it was

unnecessary to ask anybody else unless Mr. Wyse accepted. If he refused, there would be no tea party. . . . But, after the events of the last twenty-four hours, there was no vividness in these plans and reminiscences, and her eye turned to the profile of the Major's house.

"The portmanteau," she said to herself. . . . No, she must take her mind off that subject. She would go for a walk, not into the High Street, but into the quiet level country, away from the turmoil of passion (in the Padre's sense) and quarrels (in her own), where she could cool her curiosity and her soul with contemplation of the swallows and the white butterflies (if they had not all been killed by the touch of frost last night) and the autumn tints of which there were none whatever in the treeless marsh. . . . Decidedly the shortest way out of the town was that which led past Mr. Wyse's house. But before leaving the garden room she practised several faces at the looking glass opposite the door, which should suitably express, if she met anybody to whom the cause of the challenge was likely to have spread, the bewildering emotion which the unwilling cause of it must feel. There must be a wistful wonder; there must be a certain pride; there must be the remains of romantic excitement, and there must be deep womanly anxiety. The carriage of the head "did" the pride; the wide-open eyes "did" the wistful wonder and the romance; the deep womanly anxiety lurked in the tremulous smile, and a violent rubbing of the cheeks produced the color of excitement. In answer to any impertinent questions, if she encountered such, she meant to give an absent answer, as if she had not understood. Thus equipped, she set forth.

It was rather disappointing to meet nobody, but as

she passed Mr. Wyse's bow window she adjusted the
chrysanthemums she wore, and she had a good sight
of his profile and the back of Mrs. Poppit's head. They
appeared deep in conversation, and Miss Mapp felt
that the tiresome woman was probably giving him a
very incomplete account of what had happened. She
returned late for tea, and broke off her apologies to
Withers for being such a trouble because she saw a
note on the hall table. There was a coronet on the
back of the envelope, and it was addressed in the
neat, punctilious hand which so well expressed its
writer. Villa Faraglione, Capri, a coronet and Amelia
all lightly crossed out headed the page, and she read:

DEAR MISS MAPP,
    It is such a pleasure to find myself in our little Till-
ing again, and our mutual friend Mrs. Poppit, M.B.E.,
tells me you are in residence, and encourages me to
hope that I may induce you to take *déjeuner* with me
on Thursday at one o'clock. May I assure you, with
all delicacy, that you will not meet here anyone whose
presence could cause you the slightest embarrassment?
    Pray excuse this hasty note. Figgis will wait for your
answer if you are in.
                                 Yours very sincerely,
                                     ALGERNON WYSE.

Had not Withers been present, who might have
misconstrued her action, Miss Mapp would have
kissed the note; failing that, she forgave Mrs. Poppit
for being an M.B.E.

"The dear woman!" she said. "She has heard, and
has told him."

Of course she need not ask Mr. Wyse to tea
now. . . .

7

A WHITE FROST on three nights running and a terrible blackening of dahlias, whose reputation was quite gone by morning, would probably have convinced the ladies of Tilling that it was time to put summer clothing in camphor and winter clothing in the back yard to get aired, even if the Padre had not preached that remarkable sermon on Sunday. It was so remarkable that Miss Mapp quite forgot to note grammatical lapses and listened entranced.

The text was, "He made summer and winter," and after repeating the words very impressively, so that there might be no mistake about the origin of the seasons, the Padre began to talk about something quite different—namely, the unhappy divisions which exist in Christian communities. That did not deceive Miss Mapp for a moment: she saw precisely what he was getting at over his oratorical fences. He got at it. . . .

Ever since summer time had been inaugurated a few years before, it had been one of the chronic dispensions of Tilling. Miss Mapp, Diva and the Padre flatly refused to recognize it, except when they were going by train or tram, when principle must necessarily go to the wall, or they would never have succeeded in getting anywhere, while Miss Mapp, with the halo of martyrdom round her head, had once

171

arrived at a summer-time party an hour late, in order
to bear witness to the truth, and in consequence, had
got only dregs of tea and the last faint strawberry. But
the Major and Captain Puffin used the tram so often,
that they had fallen into the degrading habit of dislocating their clocks and watches on the first of May,
and dislocating them again in the autumn, when they
were forced into uniformity with properly-minded
people. Irene was flippant on the subject, and said
that any old time would do for her. The Poppits followed convention, and Mrs. Poppit, in naming the
hour for a party to the stalwarts, wrote "4:30 (your
3:30)." The King, after all, had invited her to be decorated at a particular hour, summer time, and what
was good enough for the King was good enough for
Mrs. Poppit.

The sermon was quite uncompromising. There was
summer and winter, by Divine ordinance, but there
was nothing said about summer time and winter time.
There was but one Time, and even as Life only
stained the white radiance of eternity, as the gifted
but, alas! infidel poet remarked, so, too, did Time. But
ephemeral as Time was, noon in the Bible clearly
meant twelve o'clock, and not one o'clock: towards
even, meant towards even, and not the middle of a
broiling afternoon. The sixth hour similarly was the
Roman way of saying twelve. Winter time, in fact,
was God's time, and though there was nothing wicked
(far from it) in adopting strange measures, yet the
simple, the childlike, clung to the sacred tradition,
which they had received from their fathers and fore-
fathers at their mother's knee. Then followed a long
and eloquent passage, which recapitulated the opening about unhappy divisions, and contained several
phrases, regarding the lengths to which such divisions

might go, which were strikingly applicable to duelling. The peroration recapitulated the recapitulation,
in case anyone had missed it, and the coda, the close
itself, in the full noon of the winter sun, was full of
joy at the healing of all such unhappy divisions. And
now . . . The rain rattling against the windows
drowned the Doxology.

The doctrine was so much to her mind that Miss
Mapp gave a shilling to the offertory instead of her
usual sixpence, to be devoted to the organist and
choir fund. The Padre, it is true, had changed the
hour of services to suit the heresy of the majority, and
this for a moment made her hand falter. But the
hope, after this convincing sermon, that next year
morning service would be at the hour falsely called
twelve decided her not to withdraw this handsome
contribution.

Frosts and dead dahlias and sermons then were together overwhelmingly convincing, and when Miss
Mapp went out on Monday morning to do her shopping, she wore a tweed skirt and jacket, and round
her neck a long woollen scarf to mark the end of the
summer. Mrs. Poppit, alone in her disgusting ostentation, had seemed to think two days ago that it was
cold enough for furs, and she presented a truly ridiculous aspect in an enormous sable coat, under the
weight of which she could hardly stagger, and stood
rooted to the spot when she stepped out of the Royce.
Brisk walking and large woollen scarves saved the
others from feeling the cold and from being unable to
move, and this morning the High Street was dazzling
with the shifting play of bright colors. There was
quite a group of scarves at the corner, where Miss
Mapp's street debouched into the High Street: Irene
was there (for it was probably too cold for Mr.

Hopkins that morning), looking quainter than ever in
corduroys and mauve stockings with an immense
orange scarf bordered with pink. Diva was there,
wound up in so delicious a combination of rose madder and Cambridge blue, that Miss Mapp, remembering the history of the rose madder, had to remind
herself how many things there were in the world
more inportant than worsted. Evie was there in vivid
green with a purple border; the Padre had a knitted
magenta waistcoat; and Mrs. Poppit that great sable
coat which almost prevented movement. They were
all talking together in a very animated manner when
first Miss Mapp came in sight, and if, on her approach, conversation seemed to wither, they all wore,
besides their scarves, very broad, pleasant smiles.
Miss Mapp had a smile, too, as good as anybody's.

"Good morning, all you dear things," she said.
"How lovely you all look—just like a bed of delicious
flowers! Such nice colors! My poor dahlias are all
dead."

Quaint Irene uttered a hoarse laugh, and, swinging
her basket, went quickly away. She often did abrupt
things like that. Miss Mapp turned to the Padre.

"Dear Padre, what a delicious sermon!" she said.
"So glad you preached it! Such a warning against all
sorts of divisions!"

The Padre had to compose his face before he responded to these compliments.

"I'm reecht glad, fair lady," he replied, "that my bit
discourse was to your mind. Come, wee wifie, we
must be stepping."

Quite suddenly all the group, with the exception of
Mrs. Poppit, melted away. Wee wifie gave a loud
squeal, as if to say something, but her husband led
her firmly off, while Diva, with rapidly revolving feet,

sped like an arrow up the center of the High Street.

"Such a lovely morning!" said Miss Mapp to Mrs. Poppit, when there was no one else to talk to. "And everyone looks so pleased and happy, and all in such a hurry, busy as bees, to do their little businesses. Yes."

Mrs. Poppit began to move quietly away with the deliberate, tortoiselike progression necessitated by the fur coat. It struck Miss Mapp that she, too, had intended to take part in the general breaking up of the group, but had merely been unable to get under way as fast as the others.

"Such a lovely fur coat," said Miss Mapp sycophantically. "Such beautiful long fur! And what is the news this morning? Has a little bird been whispering anything?"

"Nothing," said Mrs. Poppit very decidedly, and having now sufficient way to turn, she went up the street down which Miss Mapp had just come. The latter was thus left all alone with her shopping basket and her scarf.

With the unerring divination which was the natural fruit of so many years of ceaseless conjecture, she instantly suspected the worst. All that busy conversation which her appearance had interrupted, all those smiles which her presence had seemed but to render broader and more hilarious, certainly concerned her. They could not still have been talking about that fatal explosion from the cupboard in the garden room, because the duel had completely silenced the last echoes of that, and she instantly put her finger on the spot. Somebody had been gossiping (and how she hated gossip); somebody had given voice to what she had been so studiously careful not to say. Until that moment, when she had seen the rapid breaking up of the group of her friends all radiant with merriment, she had longed to be aware that somebody had given voice to it, and that everybody (under seal of secrecy) knew the unique queenliness of her position, the overwhelmingly interesting role that the violent passions of men had cast her for. She had not believed in the truth of it herself, when that irresistible seizure of coquetry took possession of her as she bent over her sweet chrysanthemums; but the Padre's respectful reception of it had caused her to hope that everybody else might believe in it. The character of the smiles, however, that wreathed the faces of her friends did not quite seem to give fruition to that hope. There were smiles and smiles, respectful smiles, sympathetic smiles, envious and admiring smiles, but there were also smiles of hilarious and mocking incredulity. She concluded that she had to deal with the latter variety.

"Something," thought Miss Mapp, as she stood quite alone in the High Street, with Mrs. Poppit laboring up the hill, and Diva already a rose-madder speck in the distance, "has got to be done," and it only remained to settle what. Fury with the dear Padre for having hinted precisely what she meant, intended and designed that he should hint, was perhaps the paramount emotion in her mind, fury with everybody else for not respectfully believing what she did not believe herself made an important pendant.

"What am I to do?" said Miss Mapp aloud, and had to explain to Mr. Hopkins, who had all his clothes on, that she had not spoken to him. Then she caught sight again of Mrs. Poppit's sable coat hardly further off than it had been when first this thunderclap of an intuition deafened her, and still reeling from the shock, she remembered that it was almost certainly

Mrs. Poppit who was the cause of Mr. Wyse writing
her that exquisitely delicate note with regard to
Thursday. It was a herculean task, no doubt, to plug
up all the fountains of talk in Tilling which were spout-
ing so merrily at her expense, but a beginning must
be made before she could arrive at the end. A short
scurry of nimble steps brought her up to the sables.

"Dear Mrs. Poppit," she said, "if you are walking
by my little house, would you give me two minutes'
talk? And—so stupid of me to forget just now—will
you come in after dinner on Wednesday for a little
rubber? The days are closing in now; one wants to
make the most of the daylight, and I think it is time
to begin our pleasant little winter evenings."

This was a bribe, and Mrs. Poppit instantly pock-
eted it, with the effect that two minutes later she was
in the garden room, and had deposited her sable coat
on the sofa ("Quite shook the room with the weight
of it," said Miss Mapp to herself while she arranged
her plan).

She stood looking out of the window for a moment,
writhing with humiliation at having to be suppliant to
the Member of the British Empire. She tried to
remember Mrs. Poppit's Christian name, and was
even prepared to use that, but this crowning igno-
miny was saved her, as she could not recollect it.

"Such an annoying thing has happened," she said,
though the words seemed to blister her lips. "And
you, dear Mrs. Poppit, as a woman of the world, can
advise me what to do. The fact is that somehow or
other, and I can't think how, people are saying that
the duel last week, which was so happily averted, had
something to do with poor little me. So absurd! But
you know what gossips we have in our dear little Tilling."

Mrs. Poppit turned on her a fallen and disappointed face.

"But hadn't it?" she said. "Why, when they were all laughing about it just now" ("I was right, then," thought Miss Mapp, "and what a tactless woman!"), "I said I believed it. And I told Mr. Wyse."

Miss Mapp cursed herself for her frankness. But she could obliterate that again, and not lose a rare (goodness knew how rare!) believer.

"I am in such a difficult position," she said. "I think I ought to let it be understood that there is no truth whatever in such an idea, however much truth there may be. And did dear Mr. Wyse believe—in fact, I know he must have, for he wrote me—oh, such a delicate, understanding note. He, at any rate, takes no notice at all that is being said and hinted."

Miss Mapp was momentarily conscious that she meant precisely the opposite of this. Dear Mr. Wyse *did* take notice, most respectful notice, of all that was being said and hinted, thank goodness! But a glance at Mrs. Poppit's fat and interested face showed her that the verbal discrepancy had gone unnoticed, and that the luscious flavor of romance drowned the perception of anything else. She drew a handkerchief out, and buried her thoughtful eyes in it a moment, rubbing them with a stealthy motion, which Mrs. Poppit did not perceive, though Diva would have.

"My lips are sealed," she continued, opening them very wide, "and I can say nothing, except that I want this rumor to be contradicted. I daresay those who started it thought it was true, but, true or false, I must say nothing. I have always led a very quiet life in my little house, with my sweet flowers for my companions, and if there is one thing more than another that I dislike, it is that my private affairs should be made matters of public interest. I do no harm to anybody. I wish everybody well, and nothing—nothing will induce me to open my lips upon this subject. I will not," cried Miss Mapp, "say a word to defend or justify myself. What is true will prevail. It comes in the Bible."

Mrs. Poppit was too much interested in what she said to mind where it came from.

"What can I do?" she asked.

"Contradict, dear, the rumor that I have had anything to do with the terrible thing which might have happened last week. Say on my authority that it is so. I tremble to think"—here she trembled very much—"what might happen if the report reached Major Benjy's ears, and he found out who had started it. We must have no more duels in Tilling. I thought I should never survive that morning."

"I will go and tell Mr. Wyse instantly—dear," said Mrs. Poppit.

That would never do. True believers were so scarce that it was wicked to think of unsettling their faith.

"Poor Mr. Wyse!" said Miss Mapp with a magnanimous smile. "Do not think, dear, of troubling him with these little trumpery affairs. He will not take part in these little tittle-tattles. But if you could let dear Diva and quaint Irene and sweet Evie and the good Padre know that I laugh at all such nonsense—"

"But they laugh at it, too," said Mrs. Poppit.

That would have been baffling for anyone who allowed herself to be baffled, but that was not Miss Mapp's way.

"Oh, that bitter laughter!" she said. "It hurt me to hear it. It was envious laughter, dear, scoffing, bitter laughter. I heard! I cannot bear that the dear things should feel like that. Tell them that I say how silly

they are to believe anything of the sort. Trust me, I
am right about it. I wash my hands of such nonsense."

She made a vivid dumb show of this, and after dry-
ing them on an imaginary towel, let a sunny smile
peep out of the eyes which she had rubbed.

"All gone!" she said; "and we will have a dear little
party on Wednesday to show we are all friends again.
And we meet for lunch at dear Mr. Wyse's the next
day? Yes? He will get tired of poor little me if he sees
me two days running, so I shall not ask him. I will
just try to get two tables together, and nobody shall
contradict dear Diva, however many shillings she says
she has won. I would sooner pay them all myself
than have any more of our unhappy divisions. You
will have talked to them all before Wednesday, will
you not, dear?"

As there were only four to talk to, Mrs. Poppit
thought that she could manage it, and spent a most
interesting afternoon. For two years now she had
tried to unfreeze Miss Mapp, who, when all was said
and done, was the center of the Tilling circle and
who, if any attempt was made to shove her out
towards the circumference, always gravitated back
again. And now, on these important errands she was
Miss Mapp's accredited ambassador, and all the terrible business of the opening of the store-cupboard and
her decoration as M.B.E. was quite forgiven and forgotten. There would be so much walking to be done
from house to house, that it was impossible to wear
her sable coat unless she had the Royce to take her
about. . . .

The effect of her communications would have surprised anybody who did not know Tilling. A less
subtle society, when assured from a first-hand authori-
tative source that a report which it had entirely re-

fused to believe was false, would have prided itself on
its perspicacity, and said that it had laughed at such
an idea, as soon as ever it heard it, as being palpably
(look at Miss Mapp!) untrue. Not so Tilling. The
very fact that, by the mouth of her ambassador, she
so uncompromisingly denied it, was precisely why
Tilling began to wonder if there was not something in
it, and from wondering if there was not something in
it, surged to the conclusion that there certainly was.
Diva, for instance, the moment she was told that Elizabeth (for Mrs. Poppit remembered her Christian
name perfectly) utterly and scornfully denied the
truth of the report, became intensely thoughtful.

"Say there's nothing in it?" she observed. "Can't understand that."

At that moment Diva's telephone bell rang, and she
hurried out and in.

"Party at Elizabeth's on Wednesday," she said. "She
saw me laughing. Why ask me?"

Mrs. Poppit was full of her sacred mission.

"To show how little she minds your laughing," she
suggested.

"As if it wasn't true, then. Seems like that. Wants us
to think it's not true."

"She was very earnest about it," said the ambassador.

Diva got up, and tripped over the outlying skirts of
Mrs. Poppit's fur coat as she went to ring the bell.

"Sorry," she said. "Take it off and have a chat. Tea's
coming. Muffins!"

"Oh, no, thanks!" said Mrs. Poppit. "I've so many
calls to make."

"What? Similar calls?" asked Diva. "Wait ten
minutes. Tea, Janet. Quickly."

She whirled round the room once or twice, all corrugated with perplexity, beginning telegraphic sentences, and not finishing them: "Says it's not true—laughs at notion of—And Mr. Wyse believes—The Padre believed. After all, the Major—Little cock-sparrow Captain Puffin—Or t'other way round, do you think—No other explanation, you know—Might have been blood—"

She buried her teeth in a muffin.

"Believe there's something in it," she summed up.

She observed her guest had neither tea nor muffin.

"Help yourself," she said. "Want to worry this out."

"Elizabeth absolutely denies it," said Mrs. Poppit. "Her eyes were full of—"

"Oh, anything," said Diva. "Rubbed them. Or pepper if it was at lunch. That's no evidence."

"But her solemn assertion—" began Mrs. Poppit, thinking that she was being a complete failure as an ambassador. She was carrying no conviction at all.

"Saccharin!" observed Diva, handing her a small phial. "Haven't got more than enough sugar for myself. I expect Elizabeth's got plenty—well, never mind that. Don't you see? If it wasn't true she would try to convince us that it was. Seemed absurd on the face of it. But if she tries to convince us that it isn't true—well, something in it."

There was the gist of the matter, and Mrs. Poppit proceeding next to the Padre's house, found more muffins and incredulity. Nobody seemed to believe Elizabeth's assertion that there was "nothing in it." Evie ran round the room with excited squeaks; the Padre nodded his head, in confirmation of the opinion which, when he first delivered it, had been received with mocking incredulity over the crab. Quaint Irene, intent on Mr. Hopkins's left knee in the absence of the model, said, "Good old Mapp: better late than never."

Utter incredulity, in fact, was the ambassador's welcome . . . and all the incredulous were going to Elizabeth's party on Wednesday.

Mrs. Poppit had sent the Royce home for the last of her calls, and staggered up the hill past Elizabeth's house. Oddly enough, just as she passed the garden room, the window was thrown up.

"Cup of tea, dear Susan?" said Elizabeth. She had found an old note of Mrs. Poppit's among the waste paper for the firing of the kitchen oven fully signed.

"Just two minutes' talk, Elizabeth," she promptly responded.

The news that nobody in Tilling believed her left Miss Mapp more than calm: on the bright side of calm, that is to say. She had a few indulgent phrases that tripped readily off her tongue for the dear things who hated to be deprived of their gossip, but Susan certainly did not receive the impression that this playful magnanimity was attained with an effort. Elizabeth did not seem really to mind: she was very gay. Then, skillfully changing the subject, she mourned over her dead dahlias.

Though Tilling with all its perspicacity could not have known it, the intuitive reader will certainly have perceived that Miss Mapp's party for Wednesday night had, so to speak, further irons in its fire. It had originally been a bribe to Susan Poppit, in order to induce her to spread broadcast that that ridiculous rumor (whoever had launched it) had been promptly denied by the person whom it most immediately concerned. It served a second purpose in showing that Miss Mapp was too high above the mire of scandal, however interesting, to know or care who might happen to be wallowing in it, and for this reason she

asked everybody who had done so. Such loftiness of
soul had earned her an amazing bonus, for it had induced those who sat in the seat of the scoffers before
to come hastily off, and join the thin but unwavering
ranks of the true believers, who up till then had consisted only of Susan and Mr. Wyse. Frankly, so blest
a conclusion had never occurred to Miss Mapp: it
was one of those unexpected rewards that fall like
ripe plums into the lap of the upright. By denying a
rumor she had got everybody to believe it, and when
on Wednesday morning she went out to get the chocolate cakes which were so useful in allaying the appe-
tites of guests, she encountered no broken conversations and gleeful smiles, but sidelong glances of respectful envy.

But what Tilling did not and could not know was
that this, the first of the autumn after-dinner bridge
parties, was destined to look on the famous tea gown
of kingfisher blue, as designed for Mrs. Trout. No
doubt other ladies would have hurried up their new
gowns, or at least have camouflaged their old ones, in
honor of the annual inauguration of evening bridge,
but Miss Mapp had no misgivings about being outshone. And once again here she felt that luck waited
on merit, for though when she dressed that evening
she found she had not anticipated that artificial light
would cast a somewhat pale (though not ghastly) reflection from the vibrant blue on to her features, similar in effect to (but not so marked as) the light that
shines on the faces of those who lean over the burning brandy and raisins of "snapdragon," this interesting pallor seemed very aptly to bear witness to all
that she had gone through. She did not look ill—she
was satisfied as to that—she looked gorgeous and a
little wan.

The bridge tables were set out, not in the garden
room, which entailed a scurry over damp gravel on a
black, windy night, but in the little square parlor
above her dining room, where Withers, in the intervals of admitting her guests, was laying out plates of
sandwiches and the chocolate cakes, reinforced when
the interval for refreshments came with hot soup,
whisky and syphons, and a jog of "cup" prepared according to an ancestral and economical receipt, which
Miss Mapp had taken a great deal of trouble about. A
single bottle of white wine, with suitable additions of
ginger, nutmeg, herbs, and soda water, was the mother
of a gallon of a drink that seemed aflame with fiery and
probably spirituous ingredients. Guests were very careful how they partook of it, so stimulating it seemed.

Miss Mapp was reading a book on gardening up-
side down (she had taken it up rather hurriedly)
when the Poppits arrived, and sprang to her feet with
a pretty cry at being so unexpectedly but delightfully
disturbed.

"Susan! Isabel!" she said. "Lovely of you to have
come! I was reading about flowers, making plans for
next year."

She saw the four eyes riveted to her dress. Susan
looked quite shabby in comparison, and Isabel did
not look anything at all.

"My dear, too lovely!" said Mrs. Poppit slowly.

Miss Mapp looked brightly about, as if wondering
what was too lovely; at last she guessed.

"Oh, my new frock?" she said. "Do you like it,
dear? How sweet of you. It's just a little nothing that
I talked over with that nice Miss Greele in the High
Street. We put our heads together, and invented
something quite cheap and simple. And here's Evie
and the dear Padre. So kind of you to look in."

Four more eyes were riveted on it.

"Enticed you out just once, Padre," went on Miss Mapp. "So sweet of you to spare an evening. And here's Major Benjy and Captain Puffin. Well, that is nice!"

This was really tremendous of Miss Mapp. Here was she meeting without embarrassment or awkwardness the two, who if the duel had not been averted, would have risked their very lives over some dispute concerning her. Everybody else, naturally, was rather taken aback for the moment at this situation, so deeply dyed in the dramatic. Should either of the gladiators have heard that it was the Padre who undoubtedly had spread the rumor concerning their hostess, Mrs. Poppit was afraid that even his cloth might not protect him. But no such deplorable calamity occurred, and only four more eyes were riveted to the kingfisher blue.

"Upon my word," said the Major, "I never saw anything more beautiful than that gown, Miss Elizabeth. Straight from Paris, eh? Paris in every line of it."

"Oh, Major Benjy," said Elizabeth. "You're all making fun of me and my simple little frock. I'm getting quite shy. Just a bit of old stuff that I had. But so nice of you to like it. I wonder where Diva is? We shall have to scold her for being late. Ah—she shan't be scolded. Diva, darl—"

The endearing word froze on Miss Mapp's lips and she turned deadly white. In the doorway, in equal fury and dismay, stood Diva, dressed in precisely the same staggeringly lovely costume as her hostess. Had Diva and Miss Greele put their heads together too? Had Diva got a bit of old stuff?. . .

Miss Mapp pulled herself together first and moistened her dry lips.

"So sweet of you to look in, dear," she said. "Shall we cut?"

Naturally the malice of cards decreed that Miss Mapp and Diva should sit next each other as adversaries at the same table, and the combined effect of two lots of kingfisher blue was blinding. Complete silence on every subject connected, however remotely, with dress, was of course, the only line for correct diplomacy to pursue, but then Major Benjy was not diplomatic, only gallant.

"Never saw such stunning gowns, eh, Padre?" he said. "Dear me, they are very much alike, too, aren't they? Pair of exquisite sisters."

It would be hard to say which of the two found this speech the more provocative of rage, for while Diva was four years younger than Miss Mapp, Miss Mapp was four inches taller than Diva. She cut the cards to her sister with a hand that trembled so much that she had to do it again, and Diva could scarcely deal.

Mr. Wyse frankly confessed the next day when, at one o'clock, Elizabeth found herself the first arrival at his house, that he had been very self-indulgent.

"I have given myself a treat, dear Miss Mapp," he said. "I have asked three entrancing ladies to share my humble meal with me, and have provided—is it not shocking of me?—nobody else to meet them. Your pardon, dear lady, for my greediness."

Now this was admirably done. Elizabeth knew very well why two out of the three men in Tilling had not been asked (very gratifying, that reason was), and with the true refinement of which Mr. Wyse was so amply possessed, here he was taking all the blame on himself, and putting it so prettily. She bestowed her widest smile on him.

"Oh, Mr. Wyse," she said. "We shall all quarrel over you."

Not until Miss Mapp had spoken did she perceive how subtle her words were. They seemed to bracket herself and Mr. Wyse together: all the men (two out of the three, at any rate) had been quarreling over her, and now there seemed a very fair prospect of three of the women quarreling over Mr. Wyse. . . .

Without being in the least effeminate, Mr. Wyse this morning looked rather like a modern troubador. He had a velveteen coat on, a soft, fluffy, mushy tie which looked as if made of Shirley poppies, very neat knickerbockers, brown stockings with blobs, like the fruit of plane trees, dependent from elaborate "tops," and shoes with a cascade of leather frilling covering the laces. He might almost equally well be about to play golf over putting holes on the lawn as the guitar. He made a gesture of polished, polite dissent, not contradicting, yet hardly accepting this tribute, remitting it perhaps, just as the King when he enters the City of London touches the sword of the Lord Mayor and tells him to keep it. . . .

"So pleasant to be in Tilling again," he said. "We shall have a cosy, busy winter, I hope. You, I know, Miss Mapp, are always busy."

"The day is never long enough for me," said Elizabeth enthusiastically. "What with my household duties in the morning, and my garden, and our pleasant little gatherings, it is always bedtime too soon. I want to read a great deal this winter, too."

Diva (at the sight of whom Elizabeth had to make a strong effort of self-control) here came in, together with Mrs. Poppit, and the party was complete. Eliza-

beth would have been willing to bet that, in spite of
the warmness of the morning, Susan would have on
her sable coat, and though, technically, she would
have lost, she more than won morally, for Mr. Wyse's
repeated speeches about his greediness were hardly
out of his mouth when she discovered that she had
left her handkerchief in the pocket of her sable coat,
which she had put over the back of a conspicuous
chair in the hall. Figgis, however, came in at the moment to say that lunch was ready, and she delayed
them all very much by a long, ineffectual search for
it, during which Figgis, with a visible effort, held up
the sable coat, so that it was displayed to the utmost
advantage. And then, only fancy, Susan discovered
that it was in her sable muff all the time!

All three ladies were on tenterhooks of anxiety as to
who was to be placed on Mr. Wyse's right, who on
his left, and who would be given only the place between two other women. But his tact was equal to
anything.

"Miss Mapp," he said, "will you honor me by taking
the head of my table and be hostess for me? Only I
must have that vase of flowers removed, Figgis; I can
look at my flowers when Miss Mapp is not here. Now,
what have we got for breakfast—lunch, I should say?"

The macaroni which Mr. Wyse had brought back
with him from Naples naturally led on to Italian subjects, and the general scepticism about the Contessa
di Faraglione had a staggering blow dealt it.

"My sister," began Mr. Wyse (and by a swift sucking motion, Diva drew into her mouth several serpents of dependent macaroni in order to be able to
listen better without this agitating distraction), "my
sister, I hope, will come to England this winter, and
spend several weeks with me." (Sensation.)

"And the Count?" asked Diva, having swallowed the serpents.

"I fear not; Cecco—Francesco, you know—is a great stay-at-home. Amelia is looking forward very much to seeing Tilling. I shall insist on her making a long stay here, before she visits our relations at Whitchurch."

Elizabeth found herself reserving judgment. She would believe in the Contessa Faraglione—no one more firmly—when she saw her, and had reasonable proofs of her identity.

"Delightful!" she said, abandoning with regret the fruitless pursuit with a fork of the few last serpents that writhed on her plate. "What an addition to our society! We shall all do our best to spoil her, Mr. Wyse. When do you expect her?"

"Early in December. You must be very kind to her, dear ladies. She is an insatiable bridge player. She has heard much of the great players she will meet here."

That decided Mrs. Poppit. She would join the correspondence class conducted by "Little Slam," in "Cosy Corner." Little Slam, for the sum of two guineas, payable in advance, engaged to make first-class players of anyone with normal intelligence. Diva's mind flew off to the subject of dress, and the thought of the awful tragedy concerning the tea gown of kingfisher blue, combined with the endive salad, gave a wry twist to her mouth for a moment.

"I, as you know," continued Mr. Wyse, "am no hand at bridge."

"Oh, Mr. Wyse, you play beautifully," interpolated Elizabeth.

"Too flattering of you, Miss Mapp. But Amelia and Cecco do not agree with you. I am never allowed to play when I am at the Villa Faraglione, unless a table cannot be made up without me. But I shall look forward to seeing many well-contested games."

The quails and the figs had come from Capri, and Miss Mapp, greedily devouring each in turn, was so much incensed by the information that she had elicited about them, that, though she joined in the general *Lobgesang*, she was tempted to inquire whether the ice had not been brought from the South Pole by some Antarctic expedition. Her mind was not, like poor Diva's, taken up with obstinate questionings about the kingfisher-blue tea gown, for she had already determined what she was going to do about it. Naturally it was impossible to contemplate fresh encounters like that of last night, but another gown, crimson lake, the color of Mrs. Trout's toilet for the second evening of the Duke of Hampshire's visit, as *Vogue* informed her, had completely annihilated Newport with its splendor. She had already consulted Miss Greele about it, who said that if the kingfisher blue was bleached first the dye of crimson lake would be brilliant and pure. . . . The thought of that, and the fact that Miss Greele's lips were professionally sealed, made her able to take Diva's arm as they strolled about the garden afterwards. The way in which both Diva and Susan had made up to Mr. Wyse during lunch was really very shocking, though it did not surprise Miss Mapp, but she supposed their heads had been turned by the prospect of playing bridge with a countess. Luckily she expected nothing better of either of them, so their conduct was in no way a blow or a disappointment to her.

This companionship with Diva was rather prolonged, for the adhesive Susan, staggering about in her sables, clung close to their host and simulated a clumsy interest in chrysanthemums; and whatever the

other two did, maneuvered herself into a strong position between them and Mr. Wyse, from which, oper-
ating on interior lines, she could cut off either
assailant. More depressing yet (and throwing a sad
new light on his character), Mr. Wyse seemed to ap-
preciate rather than resent the appropriation of himself, and instead of making a sortie through the
beleaguering sables, would beg Diva and Elizabeth,
who were so fond of fuchsias and knew about them
so well, to put their heads together over an afflicted
bed of these flowers in quite another part of the
garden, and tell him what was the best treatment for
their anaemic condition. Pleasant and proper though
it was to each of them that Mr. Wyse should pay so
little attention to the other, it was bitter as the endive
salad to both that he should tolerate, if not enjoy, the
companionship which the forwardness of Susan
forced on him, and while they absently stared at the
fuchsias, the fire kindled, and Elizabeth spake with
her tongue.

"How very plain poor Susan looks today," she said.
"Such a color, though to be sure I attribute that more
to what she ate and drank than to anything else.
Crimson. Oh, those poor fuchsias! I think I should
throw them away."

The common antagonism, Diva felt, had drawn her
and Elizabeth into the most cordial of understand-
ings. For the moment she felt nothing but enthusiastic
sympathy with Elizabeth, in spite of her kingfisher-
blue gown. . . . What on earth, in parenthesis, was she
to do with hers? She could not give it to Janet: it was
impossible to contemplate the idea of Janet walking
about the High Street in a tea gown of kingfisher blue
just in order to thwart Elizabeth. . . .

"Mr. Wyse seems taken with her," said Diva. "How

he can! Rather a snob. M.B.E. She's always popping
in here. Saw her yesterday going round the corner of
the street."

"What time, dear?" asked Elizabeth, nosing the
scent.

"Middle of the morning."

"And I saw her in the afternoon," said Elizabeth.
"That great lumbering Rolls-Royce went tacking and
skidding round the corner below my garden room."

"Was she in it?" asked Diva.

This appeared rather a slur on Elizabeth's reli-
ability in observation.

"No, darling, she was sitting on the top," she said,
taking the edge off the sarcasm, in case Diva had not
intended to be critical, by a little laugh. Diva drew
the conclusion that Elizabeth had actually seen her
inside.

"Dentist lives here, too," she said. "May be him.
Can't tell."

"Very likely that's it," said Elizabeth. "Dear Susan's
teeth look very good. But such a clever dentist. You
often have teeth taken out by him, don't you, darling?" she added, remembering the wisdom tooth.

This was carrying the war into a friend's country,
and Diva was not slow to remember that Elizabeth's
teeth looked very good, too, which coupled with her
apparent anxiety that everybody else should be constantly having their teeth out, suggested very reasonable suspicions. But she reserved them to form the
basis for future observation. Certainly Elizabeth
smiled and laughed very openly: you could see her
uvula when she was much amused.

"Pooh!" she said. "Had two teeth out in my life.
Talking of Susan. Think it's serious? Think he'll marry
her?"

The idea of course, repellent and odious as it was, had occurred to Elizabeth, and so she instantly denied it.

"Oh, you busy little matchmaker," she said brightly to Diva. "Such an idea never entered my head. You shouldn't make such fun of dear Susan. Come, dear, I can't look at fuchsias any more. I must be getting home and must say goodby—au reservoir, rather—to Mr. Wyse, if Susan will allow me to get a word in edgeways."

Susan seemed delighted to let Miss Mapp get this particular word in edgewise, and after a little speech from Mr. Wyse, in which he said that he would not dream of allowing them to go yet, and immediately afterwards shook hands warmly with them both, and said that the reservoir must be a very small one (he included Diva in this hope), the two were forced to leave the artful Susan in possession of the field. . . .

It all looked rather black. Miss Mapp's vivid imagination altogether failed to picture what Tilling would be like if Susan succeeded in becoming Mrs. Wyse, and the sister-in-law of a countess, and she sat down in her garden room and closed her eyes for a moment, in order to concentrate her power of figuring the situation. What dreadful people these climbers were! How swiftly they swarmed up the social ladder with their Rolls-Royces and their red-currant fool, and their sables! A few weeks ago she herself had never asked Susan into her house, while the very first time she came she unloosed the sluices of the store-cupboard, and now, owing to the necessity of getting her aid in stopping that mischievous rumor, which she herself had been so careful to set on foot, regarding the cause of the duel, Miss Mapp had been positively obliged to flatter and to "Susan" her. And if Diva's

awful surmise proved to be well-founded, Susan
would be in a position to patronize them all, and talk
about counts and countesses with the same air of
unconcern as Mr. Wyse. She would be bidden to the
Villa Faraglione; she would play bridge with Cecco
and Amelia; she would visit the Wyses of
Whitchurch. . . .

What was to be done? She might head another
movement to put Mr. Wyse in his proper place; this,
if successful, would have the agreeable result of pulling down Susan a rung or two should she carry out
her design. But the failure of the last attempt and Mr.
Wyse's eminence did not argue well for any further
maneuver of the kind. Or should she poison Mr.
Wyse's mind with regard to Susan? . . . Or was she
herself causelessly agitated?

Or—

Curiosity rushed like a devastating tornado across
Miss Mapp's mind, rooting up all other growths, buf-
feting her with the necessity of knowing what the two
whom she had been forced to leave in the garden
were doing now, and snatching up her opera glasses
she glided upstairs, and let herself out through the
trapdoor onto the roof. She did not remember if it
was possible to see Mr. Wyse's garden or any part of
it from the watch tower, but there was a chance. . . .

Not a glimpse of it was visible. It lay quite hidden
behind the red-brick wall which bounded it, and not
a chrysanthemum or a fuchsia could she see. But her
blood froze as, without putting the glasses down, she
ran her eye over such part of the house wall as rose
above the obstruction. In his drawing-room window,
on the first floor, were seated two figures. Susan had
taken her sables off; it was as if she intended remaining there for ever, or at least for tea. . . .

8

THE HIPPOPOTAMUS QUARREL over their whisky between Major Flint and Captain Puffin, which culminated in the challenge and all the shining sequel, had had the excellent effect of making the United Services more united than ever. They both knew that had they not severally run away from the encounter and, so providentially, met at the station, very serious consequences might have ensued. Had not both but only one of them been averse from taking or risking life, that one would surely have remained in Tilling, and spread disastrous reports about the bravery of the other; while if neither of them had had scruples on the sacredness of human existence there might have been one if not two corpses lying on the shining sands. Naturally the fact that they both had taken the very earliest opportunity of averting an encounter by flight, made it improbable that any future quarrel would be proceeded with to violent extremes, but it was much safer to run no risks, and not let verbal disagreements rise to hippopotamus pitch again. Consequently when there was any real danger of such savagery as was implied in sending challenges, they hastened, by mutual concessions, to climb down from these perilous places, where loss of balance might possibly occur. For which of them could be absolutely certain that next time the other of them might not be more courageous? . . .

They were coming up from the tram station one November evening, both fizzing and fuming a good deal, and the Major was extremely lame, lamer than Puffin. The rattle of the tram had made argument impossible during the transit from the links, but they had both in this enforced silence thought of several smart repartees, supposing that the other made the requisite remarks to call them out, and on arrival at the Tilling station they went on at precisely the same point at which they had broken off on starting from the station by the links.

"Well, I hope I can take a beating in as English a spirit as anybody," said the Major.

This was lucky for Captain Puffin: he had thought it likely that he would say just that, and had got a stinger for him.

"And it worries you to find that your hopes are doomed to disappointment," he swiftly said.

Major Flint stepped in a puddle which cooled his foot but not his temper.

"Most offensive remark," he said. "I wasn't called Sporting Benjy in the regiment for nothing. But never mind that. A worm cast—"

"It wasn't a worm cast," said Puffin. "It was sheep's dung!"

Luck had veered here: the Major had felt sure that Puffin would reiterate that utterly untrue contention.

"I can't pretend to be such a specialist as you in those matters," he said, "but you must allow me sufficient power of observation to know a worm cast when I see it. It was a worm cast, sir, a cast of a worm, and you had no right to remove it. If you will do me the favor to consult the rules of golf—"

"Oh, I grant you that you are more a specialist in the rules of golf, Major, than in the practice of it," said Puffin brightly.

Suddenly it struck Sporting Benjy that the red signals of danger danced before his eyes, and though the odious Puffin had scored twice to his once, he called up all his powers of self-control, for if his friend was anything like as exasperated as himself, the breeze of disagreement might develop into a hurricane. At the moment he was passing through a swing gate which led to a short cut back to the town, but before he could take hold of himself he had slammed it back in his fury, hitting Puffin, who was following him, on the knee. Then he remembered he was a sporting Christian gentleman, and no duellist.

"I'm sure I beg your pardon, my dear fellow," he said with the utmost solicitude. "Uncommonly stupid of me. The gate flew out of my hand. I hope I didn't hurt you."

Puffin had just come to the same conclusion as Major Flint; magnanimity was better than early trains, and ever so much better than bullets. Indeed there was no comparison. . . .

"Not hurt a bit, thank you, Major," he said, wincing with the shrewdness of the blow, silently cursing his friend for what he felt sure was no accident, and limping with both legs. "It didn't touch me. Ha! What a brilliant sunset. The town looks amazingly picturesque."

"It does indeed," said the Major. "Fine subject for Miss Mapp."

Puffin shuffled alongside.

"There's still a lot of talk going on in the town," he said, "about that duel of ours. Those fairies of yours are all agog to know what it was about. I am sure they all think that there was a lady in the case. Just like the vanity of the sex. If two men have a quarrel, they think it must be because of their silly faces."

Ordinarily the Major's gallantry would have resented this view, but the reconciliation with Puffin was too recent to risk just at present.

"Poor little devils," he said. "It makes an excitement for them. I wonder who they think it is. It would puzzle me to name a woman in Tilling worth catching an early train for."

"There are several who'd be surprised to hear you say that, Major," said Puffin archly.

"Well, well," said the other, strutting and swelling and walking without a sign of lameness. . . .

They had come to where their houses stood opposite each other on the steep cobbled street, fronted at its top end by Miss Mapp's garden room. She happened to be standing in the window, and the Major made a great flourish of his cap, and laid his hand on his heart.

"And there's one of them," said Puffin, as Miss Mapp acknowledged these florid salutations with a wave of her hand and tripped away from the window.

"Poking your fun at me," said the Major. "Perhaps she was the cause of our quarrel, hey? Well, I'll step across, shall I, about half past nine, and bring my diaries with me?"

"I'll expect you. You'll find me at my Roman roads."

The humor of this joke never staled, and they parted with hoots and guffaws of laughter.

It must not be supposed that duelling, puzzles over the portmanteau, or the machinations of Susan had put out of Miss Mapp's head her amiable interest in the hour at which Major Benjy went to bed. For some time she had been content to believe, on direct in-

formation from him, that he went to bed early and
worked at his diaries on alternate evenings, but ma-
turer consideration had led her to wonder whether he
was being quite as truthful as a gallant soldier should
be. For though (on alternate evenings) his house
would be quite dark by half past nine, it was not for
twelve hours or more afterwards that he could be
heard Qui-hi-ing for his breakfast, and unless he was
in some incipient stage of sleeping sickness, such
hours provided more than ample slumber for a
growing child, and might be considered excessive for
a middle-aged man. She had a mass of evidence to
show that on the other set of alternate nights his diaries (which must, in parenthesis, be of extraordinary
fullness) occupied him into the small hours, and to go
to bed at half past nine on one night and after one
o'clock on the next implied a complicated kind of regularity which cried aloud for elucidation. If he had
only breakfasted early on the mornings after he had
gone to bed early, she might have allowed herself to
be weakly credulous, but he never Qui-hied earlier
than half-past nine, and she could not but think that
to believe blindly in such habits would be a triumph
not for faith but for foolishness. "People," said Miss
Mapp to herself, as her attention refused to concentrate on the evening paper, "don't do it. I never heard
of a similar case."

She had been spending the evening alone, and even
the conviction that her cold apple tart had suffered
diminution by at least a slice, since she had so much
enjoyed it hot at lunch, failed to occupy her mind for
long, for this matter had presented itself with a clam-
oring insistence that drowned all other voices. She
had tried, when, at the conclusion of her supper, she
had gone back to the garden room, to immerse herself

in a book, in an evening paper, in the portmanteau
problem, in a jig-saw puzzle, and in Patience, but
none of these supplied the stimulus to lead her mind
away from Major Benjy's evenings, or the narcotic
to dull her unslumbering desire to solve a problem
that was rapidly becoming one of the greater mys-
teries.

Her radiator made a seat in the window agreeably
warm, and a chink in the curtains gave her a view of
the Major's lighted window. Even as she looked, the
illumination was extinguished. She had expected this,
as he had been at his diaries late—quite naughtily
late—the evening before, so this would be a night of
infant slumber for twelve hours or so.

Even as she looked, a chink of light came from his
front door, which immediately enlarged itself into a
full oblong. Then it went completely out. "He has
opened the door, and has put out the hall light,"
whispered Miss Mapp to herself. . . . "He has gone
out and shut the door. . . . Perhaps he is going to
post a letter. . . . He has gone into Captain Puffin's
house without knocking. So he is expected."

Miss Mapp did not at once guess that she held in
her hand the key to the mystery. It was certainly Major Benjy's night for going to bed early. . . . Then a
fierce illumination beat on her brain. Had she not, so
providentially, actually observed the Major cross the
road, unmistakable in the lamplight, and had she only
looked out of her window after the light in his was
quenched, she would surely have told herself that
good Major Benjy had gone to bed. But good Major
Benjy, on ocular evidence, she now knew to have
done nothing of the kind: he had gone across to see
Captain Puffin. . . . He was not good.

She grasped the situation in its hideous entirety.

She had been deceived and hoodwinked. Major Benjy
never went to bed early at all; on alternate nights he
went and sat with Captain Puffin. And Captain Puffin,
she could not but tell herself, sat up on the other set
of alternate nights with the Major, for it had not escaped her observation that when the Major seemed to
be sitting up, the Captain seemed to have gone to
bed. Instantly, with strong conviction, she suspected
orgies. It remained to be seen (and she would remain
to see it) to what hour these orgies were kept up.

About eleven o'clock a little mist had begun to
form in the street, obscuring the complete clarity of
her view, but through it there still shone the light
from behind Captain Puffin's red blind, and the mist
was not so thick as to be able wholly to obscure the
figure of Major Flint when he should pass below the
gas lamp again into his house. But no such figure
passed. Did he then work at his diaries every evening? And what price, to put it vulgarly, Roman
roads?

Every moment her sense of being deceived grew
blacker, and every moment her curiosity as to what
they were doing became more unbearable. After a
spasm of tactical thought, she glided back into her
house from the garden room, and, taking an envelope
in her hand, so that she might, if detected, say that
she was going down to the letter box at the corner to
catch the early post, she unbolted her door and let
herself out. She crossed the street and tiptoed along
the pavement to where the red light from Captain
Puffin's window shone like a blurred danger signal
through the mist.

From inside came a loud duet of familiar voices:
sometimes they spoke singly, sometimes together. But
she could not catch the words: they sounded blurred

and indistinct, and she told herself that she was very glad that she could not hear what they said, for that would have seemed like eavesdropping. The voices sounded angry. Was there another duel pending? And what was it about this time?

Quite suddenly, from so close at hand that she positively leaped off the pavement into the middle of the road, the door was thrown open, and the duet, louder than ever, streamed out into the street. Major Benjy bounced out on to the threshold, and stumbled down the two steps that led from the door.

"Tell you it was a worm cast," he bellowed. "Think I don't know a worm cast when I see a worm cast?"

Suddenly his tone changed: this was getting too near a quarrel.

"Well, good night, old fellow," he said. "Jolly evening."

He turned and saw, veiled and indistinct in the mist, the female figure in the roadway. Undying coquetry, as Mr. Stevenson so finely remarked, awoke, for the topic preceding the worm cast was "the sex."

"Bless me," he crowed, "if there isn't an unprotected lady all 'lone here in the dark, and lost in the fog. 'Llow me to 'scort you home, madam. Lemme introduce myself and friend—Major Flint, that's me, and my friend Captain Puffin."

He put up his hand and whispered an aside to Miss Mapp: "Revolutionized the theory of navigation."

Major Benjy was certainly rather gay and rather indistinct, but his polite gallantry could not fail to be attractive. It was naughty of him to have said that he went to bed early on alternate nights, but really. . . . Still, it might be better to slip away unrecognized, and, thinking it would be nice to scriggle by him and disappear in the mist, she made a tactical er-

ror in her scriggling, for she scriggled full into the
light that streamed from the open door where Captain Puffin was standing.

He gave a shrill laugh.

"Why, it's Miss Mapp," he said in his high falsetto.
"Blow me, if it isn't our mutual friend Miss Mapp.
What a 'strordinary coincidence."

Miss Mapp put on her most winning smile. To be
dignified and at the same time pleasant was the
proper way to deal with this situation. Gentlemen often had a glass of grog when they thought the ladies
had gone upstairs. That was how, for the moment, she
summed things up.

"Good evening," she said. "I was just going down to
the pillar box to post a letter," and she exhibited her
envelope. But it dropped out of her hand, and the
Major picked it up for her.

"I'll post it for you," he said very pleasantly. "Save
you the trouble. Insist on it. Why, there's no stamp on
it! Why, there's no address on it. I say, Puffie, here's a
letter with no address on it. Forgotten the address,
Miss Mapp? Think they'll remember it at the post office? Well, that's one of the mos' comic things I ever
came across. An, an, anonymous letter, eh?"

The night air began to have a most unfortunate effect on Puffin. When he came out, it would have been
quite unfair to have described him as drunk. He was
no more than gay and ready to go to bed. Now he became portentously solemn, as the cold mist began to
do its deadly work.

"A letter," he said impressively, "without an address
is an uncommonly dangerous thing. Hic! Can't tell
into whose hands it may fall. I would sooner go 'bout
with a loaded pistol than with a letter without any
address. Send it to the bank for safety. Send for the

police. Follow my advice and send for the p'lice. Police!"

Miss Mapp's penetrating mind instantly perceived that that dreadful Captain Puffin was drunk, and she promised herself that Tilling should ring with the tale of his excesses tomorrow. But Major Benjy, whom, if she mistook not, Captain Puffin had been trying, with perhaps some small success, to lead astray, was a gallant gentleman still, and she conceived the brilliant but madly mistaken idea of throwing herself on his protection.

"Major Benjy," she said, "I will ask you to take me home. Captain Puffin has had too much to drink—"

"Woz' that?" asked Captain Puffin, with an air of great interest.

Miss Mapp abandoned dignity and pleasantness, and lost her temper.

"I said you were drunk," she said with great distinctness. "Major Benjy, will you—"

Captain Puffin came carefully down the two steps from the door onto the pavement.

"Look here," he said, "this all needs 'splanation. You say I'm drunk, do you? Well, I say you're drunk, going out like this in mill' of the night to post letter with no 'dress on it. Shamed of yourself, mill'aged woman going out in the mill' of the night in the mill' of Tilling. Very shocking thing. What do you say, Major?"

Major Benjy drew himself up to his full height, and put on his hat in order to take it off to Miss Mapp.

"My frien' Cap'n Puffin," he said, "is a man of strictly 'stemious habits. Boys together. Very serious thing to call a man of my frien's character drunk. If you call him drunk, why shouldn't he call you drunk? Can't take away a man's character like that."

"Abso—" began Captain Puffin. Then he stopped and pulled himself together.

"Absolooly," he said without a hitch.

"Tilling shall hear of this tomorrow," said Miss Mapp, shivering with rage and sea mist.

Captain Puffin came a step closer.

"Now I'll tell you what it is, Miss Mapp," he said. "If you dare to say that I was drunk, Major and I, my frien' the Major and I will say you were drunk. Perhaps you think my frien' the Major's drunk, too. But sure's I live, I'll say we were taking lil' walk in the moonlight and found you trying to post a letter with no 'dress on it, and couldn't find the slit to put it in. But 'slong as you say nothing, I say nothing. Can't say fairer than that. Liberal terms. Mutual Protection Society. Your lips sealed; our lips sealed. Strictly private. All trespassers will be prosecuted. By order. Hic!"

Miss Mapp felt that Major Benjy ought instantly to have challenged his ignoble friend to another duel for this insolent suggestion, but he did nothing of the kind, and his silence, which had some awful quality of consent about it, chilled her mind, even as the sea mist, now thick and cold, made her certain that her nose was turning red. She still boiled with rage, but her mind grew cold with odious apprehensions: she was like an ice pudding with scalding sauce. . . . There they all stood, veiled in vapors, and outlined by the red light that streamed from the still open door of the intoxicated Puffin, getting colder every moment.

"Yessorno," said Puffin with chattering teeth.

Bitter as it was to accept those outrageous terms, there really seemed, without the Major's support, to be no way out of it.

"Yes," said Miss Mapp.

Puffin gave a loud crow.

"The ayes have it, Major," he said. "So we're all friens' again. Goonight everybody."

Miss Mapp let herself into her house in an agony of mortification. She could scarcely realize that her little expedition, undertaken with so much ardent and earnest curiosity only a quarter of an hour ago had ended in so deplorable a surfeit of sensation. She had gone out in obedience to an innocent and, indeed, laudable desire to ascertain how Major Benjy spent those evenings on which he had deceived her into imagining that, owing to her influence, he had gone ever so early to bed, only to find that he sat up ever so late and that she was fettered by a promise not to breathe to a soul a single word about the depravity of Captain Puffin, on pain of being herself accused out of the mouth of two witnesses of being equally depraved herself. More wounding yet was the part played by her Major Benjy in these odious transactions, and it was only possible to conclude that he put a higher value on his fellowship with his degraded friend than on chivalry itself. . . . And what did his silence imply? Probably it was a defensive one; he imagined that he, too, would be included in the stories that Miss Mapp proposed to sow broadcast upon the fruitful fields of Tilling, and, indeed when she called to mind his bellowing about worm casts, his general instability of speech and equilibrium, she told herself that he had ample cause for such a supposition. He, when his lights were out, was abetting, assisting and perhaps joining Captain Puffin. When his window was alight on alternate nights, she made no doubt now that Captain Puffin was performing a simi-

lar rôle. This had been going on for weeks under her
very nose, without her having the smallest suspicion
of it.

Humiliated by all that had happened, and flattened
in her own estimation by the sense of her blindness,
she penetrated to the kitchen and lit a gas ring to
make herself some hot cocoa, which would at least
comfort her physical chatterings. There was a letter
for Withers, slipped sideways into its envelope, on the
kitchen table, and mechanically she opened and read
it by the bluish flame of the burner. She had always
suspected Withers of having a young man, and here
was proof of it. But that he should be Mr. Hopkins of
the fish shop!

There is known to medical science a pleasant
device known as a counterirritant. If the patient has
an aching and rheumatic joint, he is counselled to put
some hot burning application on the skin, which
smarts so agonizingly that the ache is quite extinguished. Metaphorically, Mr. Hopkins was thermo-
gene to Miss Mapp's outraged and aching
consciousness, and the smart occasioned by the
knowledge that Withers must have encouraged Mr.
Hopkins (else he could scarcely have written a letter
so familiar and amorous), and thus be contemplating
matrimony, relieved the aching humiliation of all that
had happened in the sea mist. It shed a new and lurid
light on Withers; it made her mistress feel that she
had nourished a serpent in her bosom, to think that
Withers was contemplating committing so odious an
act of selfishness as matrimony. It would be necessary
to find a new parlormaid, and all the trouble connected with that would not nearly be compensated for by
being able to buy fish at a lower rate. That was the
least that Withers could do for her, to insist that Mr.

Hopkins should let her have dabs and plaice exceptionally cheap. And ought she to tell Withers that she had seen Mr. Hopkins? . . . No, that was impossible: she must write it, if she decided (for Withers' sake) to make this fell communication.

Miss Mapp turned and tossed on her uneasy bed, and her mind went back to the Major and the Captain and that fiasco in the fog. Of course she was perfectly at liberty (having made her promise under practical compulsion) to tell everybody in Tilling what had occurred, trusting to the chivalry of the men not to carry out their counterthreat, but looking at the matter quite dispassionately, she did not think it would be wise to trust too much to chivalry. Still, even if they did carry out their unmanly menace, nobody would seriously believe that she had been drunk. But they might make a very disagreeable joke of pretending to do so, and, in a word, the prospect frightened her. Whatever Tilling did or did not believe, a residuum of ridicule would assuredly cling to her, and her reputation of having perhaps been the cause of the quarrel which, so happily did not end in a duel, would be lost for ever. Evie would squeak; quaint Irene would certainly burst into hoarse laughter when she heard the story. It was very inconvenient that honesty should be the best policy.

Her brain still violently active switched off for a moment on to the eternal problem of the portmanteau. Why, so she asked herself for the hundredth time, if the portmanteau contained the fatal apparatus of duelling, did not the combatants accompany it? And if (the only other alternative) it did not—?

An idea so luminous flashed across her brain that she almost thought the room had leaped into light.

The challenge distinctly said that Major Benjy's seconds would wait upon Captain Puffin in the course of the morning. With what object then could the former have gone down to the station to catch the early train? There could be but one object, namely to get away as quickly as possible from the dangerous vicinity of the challenged Captain. And why did Captain Puffin leave that note on his table to say that he was suddenly called away, except in order to escape from the ferocious neighborhood of his challenger?

"The cowards!" ejaculated Miss Mapp. "They both ran away from each other! How blind I've been!"

The veil was rent. She perceived how, carried away with the notion that a duel was to be fought among the sand dunes, Tilling had quite overlooked the significance of the early train. She felt sure that she had solved everything now, and gave herself up to a rapturous consideration of what use she would make of the precious solution. All regrets for the impossibility of ruining the character of Captain Puffin with regard to intoxicants were gone, for she had an even deadlier blacking to hand. No faintest hesitation at ruining the reputation of Major Benjy as well crossed her mind; she gloried in it, for he had not only caused her to deceive herself about the early hours on alternate nights, but by his infamous willingness to back up Captain Puffin's bargain, he had shown himself imperviously waterproof to all chivalrous impulses. For weeks now the sorry pair of them had enjoyed the spurious splendors of being men of blood and valor, when all the time they had put themselves to all sorts of inconvenience in catching early trains and packing bags by candlelight in order to escape the hot impulses of quarrel that, as she saw now, was probably derived from drained whisky bottles. That mysterious holloaing about worm casts was just such another disagreement. And, crowning rapture of all, her own position as cause of the projected duel was quite unassailed. Owing to her silence about drink, no one would suspect a mere drunken brawl: she would still figure as heroine, though the heroes were terribly dismantled. To be sure, it would have been better if their ardor about her had been such that one of them, at least, had been prepared to face the ordeal, that they had not both preferred flight, but even without that, she had much to be thankful for. "It will serve them both," said Miss Mapp (interrupted by a sneeze, for she had been sitting up in bed for quite a considerable time), "right."

To one of Miss Mapp's experience, the first step of her new and delightful strategic campaign was obvious, and she spent hardly any time at all in the window of her garden room after breakfast next morning, but set out with her shopping basket at an unusually early hour. She shuddered as she passed between the front doors of her miscreant neighbors, for the chill of last night's mist and its dreadful memories still lingered there, but her present errand warmed her soul even as the tepid November day comforted her body. No sign of life was at present evident in those bibulous abodes, no Qui-his had indicated breakfast, and she put her utmost irony into the reflection that the United Services slept late after their protracted industry last night over diaries and Roman roads. By a natural revulsion, violent in proportion to the depth of her previous regard for Major Benjy, she hugged herself more closely on the prospect of exposing him than on that of exposing the other. She had had daydreams about Major Benjy, and the conversion of these into nightmares annealed her softness into the semblance of some red-hot stone, giving vengeance a concentrated sweetness as of saccharine contrasted with ordinary lump sugar. This sweetness was of so powerful a quality that she momentarily forgot all about the contents of Withers's letter on the kitchen table, and tripped across to Mr. Hopkins's with an oblivious smile for him.

"Good morning, Mr. Hopkins," she said. "I wonder if you've got a nice little dab for my dinner today? Yes? Will you send it up then, please? What a mild morning, like May!"

The opening move, of course, was to tell Diva about the revelation that had burst on her the night before. Diva was incomparably the best disseminator of news: she walked so fast, and her telegraphic style was so brisk and lucid. Her terse tongue, her revolving feet! Such a gossip!

"Diva darling, I had to look in a moment," said Elizabeth, pecking her affectionately on both cheeks. "Such a bit of news!"

"Oh, Contessa di Faradiddleony," said Diva sarcastically. "I heard yesterday. Journey put off."

Miss Mapp just managed to stifle the excitement which would have betrayed that this was news to her.

"No, dear, not that," she said. "I didn't suspect you of not knowing that. Unfortunate though, isn't it, just when we were all beginning to believe that there was a Contessa di Faradiddleony! What a sweet name! For my part I shall believe in her when I see her. Poor Mr. Wyse!"

"What's the news then?" asked Diva.

"My dear, it all came upon me in a flash," said Elizabeth. "It explains the portmanteau and the early train and the duel."

Diva looked disappointed. She thought this was to

be some solid piece of news, not one of Elizabeth's ideas only.

"Drive ahead," she said.

"They ran away from each other," said Elizabeth, mouthing her words as if speaking to a totally deaf person who understood lip-reading. "Never mind the cause of the duel: that's another affair. But whatever the cause"—here she dropped her eyes—"the Major having sent the challenge packed his portmanteau. He ran away, dear Diva, and met Captain Puffin at the station running away, too."

"But did—" began Diva.

"Yes, dear, the note on Captain Puffin's table to his housekeeper said he was called away suddenly. What called him away? Cowardice, dear! How ignoble it all is. And we've all been thinking how brave and wonderful they were. They fled from each other, and came back together and played golf. I never thought it was a game for men. The sand dunes where they were supposed to be fighting! They might lose a ball there, but that would be the utmost. Not a life. Poor Padre! Going out there to stop a duel, and only finding a game of golf. But I understand the nature of men better now. What an eye-opener!"

Diva by this time was trundling away round the room, and longing to be off in order to tell everybody. She could find no hole in Elizabeth's arguments; they were founded as solidly as a Euclidean proposition.

"Ever occurred to you that they drink?" she asked. "Believe in Roman roads and diaries? I don't."

Miss Mapp bounded from her chair. Danger flags flapped and crimsoned in her face. What if Diva went flying round Tilling, suggesting that in addition to being cowards the two men were drunkards? They would, as soon as any hint of the further exposure reached them, conclude that she had set the idea on foot, and then—

"No, Diva darling," she said, "don't dream of imagining such a thing. So dangerous to hint anything of the sort. Cowards they may be, and indeed are, but never have I seen anything that leads me to suppose that they drink. We must give them their due, and stick to what we know; we must not launch accusations wildly about other matters, just because we know they are cowards. A coward need not be a drunkard, thank God! It is all miserable enough as it is!"

Having averted this danger, Miss Mapp, with her radiant, excited face, seemed to be bearing all the misery very courageously, and as Diva could no longer be restrained from starting on her morning round, they plunged together into the maelstrom of the High Street, riding and whirling in its waters with the solution of the portmanteau and the early train for lifebuoy. Very little shopping was done that morning, for every permutation and combination of Tilling society (with the exception, of course, of the cowards) had to be formed on the pavement with a view to the amplest possible discussion. Diva, as might have been expected, gave proof of her accustomed perfidy before long, for she certainly gave the Padre to understand that the chain of inductive reasoning was of her own welding, and Elizabeth had to hurry after him to correct this grabbing impression; but the discovery in itself was so great, that small false notes like these could not spoil the glorious harmony. Even Mr. Wyse abandoned his usual neutrality with regard to social politics and left his tall malacca cane in the chemist's, so keen was his gusto, on seeing Miss Mapp on the pavement outside, to glean any fresh detail of evidence.

By eleven o'clock that morning, the two duellists were universally known as "the cowards," the Padre alone demurring, and being swampingly outvoted. He held (sticking up for his sex) that the Major had been brave enough to send a challenge (on whatever subject) to his friend, and had, though he subsequently failed to maintain that high level, shown courage of a high order, since, for all he knew, Captain Puffin might have accepted it. Miss Mapp was spokesman for the mind of Tilling on this too indulgent judgment.

"Dear Padre," she said, "you are too generous altogether. They both ran away: you can't get over that. Besides you must remember that, when the Major sent the challenge, he knew Captain Puffin, oh, so well, and quite expected he would run away—"

"Then why did he run away himself?" asked the Padre.

This was rather puzzling for a moment, but Miss Mapp soon thought of the explanation.

"Oh, just to make sure," she said, and Tilling applauded her ready irony.

And then came the climax of sensationalism, when at about ten minutes past eleven the two cowards emerged into the High Street on their way to catch the 11:20 tram out to the links. The day threatened rain, and they both carried bags which contained a change of clothes. Just round the corner of the High Street was the group which had applauded Miss Mapp's quickness, and the cowards were among the breakers. They glanced at each other, seeing that Miss Mapp was the most towering of the breakers, but it was too late to retreat, and they made the usual salutations.

"Good morning," said Diva, with her voice trembling. "Off to catch the early train together—I mean the tram."

"Good morning, Captain Puffin," said Miss Mapp with extreme sweetness. "What a nice little travelling bag! Oh, and the Major's got one too! H'm!"

A certain dismay looked from Major Flint's eyes; Captain Puffin's mouth fell open, and he forgot to shut it.

"Yes, change of clothes," said the Major. "It looks a threatening morning."

"Very threatening," said Miss Mapp. "Almost rash of you."

There was a moment's silence, and the two looked from one face to another of this fell group. They all wore fixed, inexplicable smiles.

"It will be pleasant among the sand dunes," said the Padre, and his wife gave a loud squeak.

"Well, we shall be missing our tram," said the Major. "Au—au reservoir, ladies."

Nobody responded at all, and they hurried off down the street, their bags bumping together very inconveniently.

"Something's up, Major," said Puffin, with true Tilling perspicacity, as soon as they had got out of hearing. . . .

Precisely at the same moment Miss Mapp gave a little cooing laugh.

"Now I must run and do my bittie shopping, Padre," she said, and kissed her hand all round. . . . The curtain had to come down for a little while on so dramatic a situation. Any discussion, just then, would be an anticlimax.

9

CAPTAIN PUFFIN found but a somber diarist when he came over to study his Roman roads with Major Flint that evening, and indeed he was a somber antiquarian himself. They had pondered a good deal during the day over their strange reception in the High Street that morning, and the recondite allusions to bags, sand dunes and early trains, and the more they pondered, the more probable it became that not only was something up, but, as regards the duel, everything was up. For weeks now they had been regarded by the ladies of Tilling with something approaching veneration, but there seemed singularly little veneration at the back of the comments this morning. Following so closely on the encounter with Miss Mapp last night, this irreverent attitude was probably due to some atheistical maneuver of hers. Such, at least, was the Major's view, and when he held a view he usually stated it, did Sporting Benjy.

"We've got you to thank for this, Puffin," he said. "Upon my soul, I was ashamed of you for saying what you did to Miss Mapp last night. Utter absence of any chivalrous feeling, hinting that if she said you were drunk, you would say she was. She was as sober and lucid last night as she was this morning. And she was devilish lucid, to my mind, this morning."

"Pity you didn't take her part last night," said Puffin. "You thought that was a very ingenious idea of mine to make her hold her tongue."

"There are finer things in this world, sir, than ingenuity," said the Major. "What your ingenuity has led to is this public ridicule. You may not mind that yourself—you may be used to it—but a man should regard the consequences of his act on others. . . . My status in Tilling is completely changed. Changed for the worse, sir."

Puffin emitted his fluty, disagreeable laugh.

"If your status in Tilling depended on a reputation for bloodthirsty bravery," he said, "the sooner it was changed the better. We're in the same boat; I don't say I like the boat, but there we are. Have a drink, and you'll feel better. Never mind your status."

"I've a good mind never to have a drink again," said the Major, pouring himself out one of his stiff little glasses, "if a drink leads to this sort of thing."

"But it didn't," said Puffin. "How it all got out, I can't say, nor for that matter can you. If it hadn't been for me last night, it would have been all over Tilling that you and I were tipsy as well. That wouldn't have improved our status that I can see."

"It was in consequence of what you said to Mapp—" began the Major.

"But, good Lord, where's the connection?" asked Puffin. "Produce the connection! Let's have a look at the connection! There ain't any connection! Duelling wasn't as much as mentioned last night."

Major Flint pondered this in gloomy, sipping silence.

"Bridge party at Mrs. Poppit's the day after tomorrow," he said. "I don't feel as if I could face it. Suppose they all go on making allusions to duelling and early trains and that? I shan't be able to keep my mind on the cards for fear of it. More than a sensitive man ought to be asked to bear."

Puffin made a noise that sounded rather like "Fudge!"

"Your pardon?" said the Major, haughtily.

"Granted by all means," said Puffin. "But I don't see what you're in such a taking about. We're no worse off than we were before we got a reputation for being such fire-eaters. Being fire-eaters is a wash-out, that's all. Pleasant while it lasted, and now we're as we were."

"But we're not," said the Major. "We're detected frauds! That's not the same as being a fraud; far from it. And who's going to rub it in, my friend? Who's been rubbing away for all she's worth? Miss Mapp, to whom, if I may say so without offense, you behaved like a cur last night."

"And another cur stood by and wagged his tail," retorted Puffin.

This was about as far as it was safe to go, and Puffin hastened to say something pleasant about the hearthrug, to which his friend had a suitable rejoinder. But after the affair last night, and the dark sayings in the High Street this morning, there was little content or cosiness about the session. Puffin's brazen optimism was but a tinkling cymbal, and the Major did not feel like tinkling at all. He but snorted and glowered, revolving in his mind how to square Miss Mapp. Allied with her, if she could but be won over, he felt he could face the rest of Tilling with indifference, for hers would be the most penetrating shafts, the most stinging pleasantries. He had more, too, so he reflected, to lose than Puffin, for till the affair of the duel the other had never been suspected of deeds of blood-thirsty gallantry, whereas he had enjoyed no end of a reputation in amorous and honorable affairs. Marriage, no doubt, would settle it satisfactorily, but this bachelor life, with plenty of golf and diaries, was not to be lightly exchanged for the unknown. Short of that. . . .

A light broke, and he got to his feet, following the gleam and walking very lame out of general discomfiture.

"Tell you what it is, Puffin," he said. "You and I, particularly you, owe that estimable lady a very profound apology for what happened last night. You ought to withdraw every word you said, and I every word that I didn't say."

"Can't be done," said Puffin. "That would be giving up my hold over your lady friend. We should be known as drunkards all over the shop before you could say winkie. Worse off than before."

"Not a bit of it. If it's Miss Mapp, and I'm sure it is, who has been spreading these—these damaging rumors about our duel, it's because she's outraged and offended, quite rightly, at your conduct to her last night. Mine, too, if you like. Ample apology, sir, that's the ticket."

"Dog ticket," said Puffin. "No thanks."

"Very objectionable expression," said Major Flint. "But you shall do as you like. And so, with your permission, shall I. I shall apologize for my share in that sorry performance, in which, thank God, I only played a minor role. That's my view, and if you don't like it, you may dislike it."

Puffin yawned.

"Mapp's a cat," he said. "Stroke a cat and you'll get scratched. Shy a brick at a cat, and she'll spit at you and skedaddle. You're poor company tonight, Major, with all these qualms."

"Then, sir, you can relieve yourself of my company," said the Major, "by going home."

"Just what I was about to do. Good night, old boy. Same time tomorrow for the tram, if you're not too badly mauled."

Miss Mapp, sitting by the hot-water pipes in the garden room, looked out not long after to see what the night was like. Though it was not yet half past ten the cowards' sitting rooms were both dark, and she wondered what precisely that meant. There was no bridge party anywhere that night, and apparently there were no diaries or Roman roads either. Why this sober and chastened darkness? . . .

The Major Qui-hied for his breakfast at an unusually early hour next morning, for the courage of this resolve to placate, if possible, the hostility of Miss Mapp had not, like that of the challenge, oozed out during the night. He had dressed himself in his frock coat, seen last on the occasion when the Prince of Wales proved not to have come by the 6:37, and no female breast however furious could fail to recognize the compliment of such a formality. Dressed thus, with top hat and patent-leather boots, he was clearly observed from the garden room to emerge into the street just when Captain Puffin's hand thrust the sponge on to the window sill of his bathroom. Probably he, too, had observed this apparition, for his fingers prematurely loosed hold of the sponge, and it bounded into the street. Wild surmises flashed into Miss Mapp's active brain, the most likely of which was that Major Benjy was going to propose to Mrs. Poppit, for if he had been going up to London for some ceremonial occasion, he would be walking down the street instead of up it. And then she saw his agitated finger press the electric bell of her own door. So he was not on his way to propose to Mrs. Poppit. . . .

She slid from the room and hurried across the few steps of garden to the house just in time to intercept Withers though not with any idea of saying that she was out. Then Withers, according to instructions, waited till Miss Mapp had tiptoed upstairs, and conducted the Major to the garden room, promising that she would "tell" her mistress. This was unnecessary, as her mistress knew. The Major pressed a half-crown into her astonished hand, thinking it was a florin. He couldn't precisely account for that impulse, but general propitiation was at the bottom of it.

Miss Mapp meantime had sat down on her bed, and firmly rejected the idea that his call had anything to do with marriage. During all these years of friendliness he had not got so far as that, and, whatever the future might hold, it was not likely that he would begin now at this moment when she was so properly punishing him for his unchivalrous behavior. But what could the frock coat mean? (There was Captain Puffin's servant picking up the sponge. She hoped it was covered with mud.) It would be a very just continuation of his punishment to tell Withers she would not see him, but the punishment which that would entail on herself would be more than she could bear, for she would not know a moment's peace while she was ignorant of the nature of his errand. Could he be on his way to the Padre's to challenge him for that very stinging allusion to sand dunes yesterday, and was he come to give her fair warning, so that she might stop a duel? It did not seem likely. Unable to bear the suspense any longer, she adjusted her face in the glass to an expression of frozen dignity and threw over her shoulders the cloak trimmed with blue in which, on the occasion of the Prince's visit, she had sat down in the middle of the road. That matched the Major's frock coat.

She hummed a little song as she mounted the few steps to the garden room, and stopped just after she had opened the door. She did not offer to shake hands.

"You wish to see me, Major Flint?" she said in such a voice as icebergs might be supposed to speak to each other when passing each other by night in the Arctic seas.

Major Flint certainly looked as if he hated seeing her, instead of wishing it, for he backed into a corner of the room and dropped his hat.

"Good morning, Miss Mapp," he said. "Very good of you. "I—I called."

He clearly had a difficulty in saying what he had come to say, but if he thought that she was proposing to give him the smallest assistance, he was in error.

"Yes, you called," said she. "Pray be seated."

He did so; she stood; he got up again.

"I called," said the Major, "I called to express my very deep regret at my share, or, rather, that I did not take a more active share—I allowed, in fact, a friend of mine to speak to you in a manner that did equal discredit—"

Miss Mapp put her head on one side, as if trying to recollect some trivial and unimportant occurrence.

"Yes?" she said. "What was that?"

"Captain Puffin," began the Major.

Then Miss Mapp remembered it all.

"I hope, Major Flint," she said, "that you will not find it necessary to mention Captain Puffin's name to me. I wish him nothing but well, but he and his are no concern of mine. I have the charity to suppose that he was quite drunk on the occasion to which I imagine you allude. Intoxication alone could excuse what he said. Let us leave Captain Puffin out of whatever you have come to say to me."

This was adroit; it compelled the Major to begin all over again.

"I come entirely on my own account," he began.

"I understand," said Miss Mapp, instantly bringing Captain Puffin in again, "Captain Puffin, now I presume sober, has no regret for what he said when drunk. I quite see, and I expected no more and no less from him. Yes. I am afraid I interrupted you."

Major Flint threw his friend overboard like ballast from a bumping balloon.

"I speak for myself," he said. "I behaved, Miss Mapp, like a—ha—worm. Defenceless lady, insolent fellow drunk—I allude to Captain P—. I'm very sorry for my part in it."

Up till this moment Miss Mapp had not made up her mind whether she intended to forgive him or not; but here she saw how crushing a penalty she might be able to inflict on Puffin if she forgave the erring and possibly truly repentant Major. He had already spoken strongly about his friend's offence, and she could render life supremely nasty for them both—particularly Puffin—if she made the Major agree that he could not, if truly sorry, hold further intercourse with him. There would be no more golf, no more diaries. Besides, if she was observed to be friendly with the Major again and to cut Captain Puffin, a very natural interpretation would be that she had learned that in the original quarrel the Major had been defending her from some odious tongue to the extent of a challenge, even though he subsequently ran away. Tilling was quite clever enough to make that inference without any suggestion from her. . . . But if she forgave neither of them, they would probably go on boozing and golfing together, and saying quite dreadful things about her, and not care very much whether she forgave them or not. Her mind was made up, and she gave a wan smile.

"Oh, Major Flint," she said, "it hurt me so dreadfully that you should have stood by and heard that man—if he is a man—say those awful things to me and not take my side. It made me feel so lonely. I had always been such good friends with you, and then you turned your back on me like that. I didn't know what I had done to deserve it. I lay awake ever so long."

This was affecting, and he violently rubbed the nap of his hat the wrong way. . . . Then Miss Mapp broke into her sunniest smile.

"Oh, I'm so glad you came to say you were sorry!" she said. "Dear Major Benjy, we're quite friends again."

She dabbed her handkerchief on her eyes.

"So foolish of me!" she said. "Now sit down in my most comfortable chair and have a cigarette."

Major Flint made a peck at the hand she extended to him, and cleared his throat to indicate emotion. It really was a great relief to think that she would not make awful allusions to duels in the middle of bridge parties.

"And since you feel as you do about Captain Puffin," she said, "of course, you won't see anything more of him. You and I are quite one, aren't we, about that? You have dissociated yourself from him completely. The fact of your being sorry does that."

It was quite clear to the Major that this condition was involved in his forgiveness, though that fact, so obvious to Miss Mapp, had not occurred to him before. Still, he had to accept it, or go unhoused again. He could explain to Puffin, under cover of night, or perhaps in deaf-and-dumb alphabet from his window. . . .

"Infamous, unforgivable behavior!" he said. "Pah!"

"So glad you feel that," said Miss Mapp, smiling till he saw the entire row of her fine teeth. "And oh, may I say one little thing more? I feel this: I feel that the dreadful shock to me of being insulted like that was quite a lovely little blessing in disguise, now that the effect has been to put an end to your intimacy with him. I never liked it, and I liked it less than ever the other night. He's not a fit friend for you. Oh, I'm so thankful!"

Major Flint saw that for the present he was irrevocably committed to this clause in the treaty of peace. He could not face seeing it torn up again, as it certainly would be, if he failed to accept it in its entirety, nor could he imagine himself leaving the room with a renewal of hostilities. He would lose his game of golf today as it was, for apart from the fact that he would scarcely have time to change his clothes (the idea of playing golf in a frock coat and top hat was inconceivable) and catch the 11:20 tram, he could not be seen in Puffin's company at all. And, indeed, in the future, unless Puffin could be induced to apologize and Miss Mapp to forgive, he saw, if he was to play golf at all with his friend, that endless deceptions and subterfuges were necessary in order to escape detection. One of them would have to set out ten minutes before the other, and walk to the tram by some unusual and circuitous route; they would have to play in a clandestine and furtive manner, parting company before they got to the clubhouse; disguises might be needful; there was a peck of difficulties ahead. But he would have to go into these later; at present he must be immersed in the rapture of his forgiveness.

"Most generous of you, Miss Elizabeth," he said. "As for that—well, I won't allude to him again."

Miss Mapp gave a happy little laugh, and having made a further plan, switched away from the subject of captains and insults with alacrity.

"Look!" she said. "I found these little rosebuds in flower still, though it is the end of November. Such brave little darlings, aren't they? One for your button-hole, Major Benjy? And then I must do my little shopping, or Withers will scold me—Withers is so severe with me, keeps me in such order! If you are going into town, will you take me with you? I will put on my hat."

Requests for the present were certainly commands, and two minutes later they set forth. Luck, as usual, befriended ability, for there was Puffin at his door, itching for the Major's return (else they would miss the tram); and lo! there came stepping along Miss Mapp in her blue-trimmed cloak, and the Major attired as for marriage—top hat, frock coat and button-hole. She did not look at Puffin and cut him; she did not seem (with the deceptiveness of appearances) to see him at all, so eager and agreeable was her conversation with her companion. The Major, so Puffin thought, attempted to give him some sort of dazed and hunted glance; but he could not be certain even of that, so swiftly had it to be transformed into a genial interest in what Miss Mapp was saying, and Puffin stared open-mouthed after them, for they were terrible as an army with banners. Then Diva, trundling swiftly out of the fish shop, came, as well she might, to a dead halt, observing this absolutely inexplicable phenomenon.

"Good morning, Diva darling," said Miss Mapp. "Major Benjy and I are doing our little shopping to-

gether. So kind of him, isn't it? and very naughty of
me to take up his time. I told him he ought to be
playing golf. Such a lovely day! Au reservoir, sweet!
Oh, and there's the Padre, Major Benjy! How quickly
he walks! Yes, he sees us! And there's Mrs. Poppit; everybody is enjoying the sunshine. What a beautiful
fur coat, though I should think she found it very
heavy and warm. Good morning, dear Susan! You
shopping too, like Major Benjy and me? How is your
dear Isabel?"

Miss Mapp made the most of that morning; the
magnanimity of her forgiveness earned her incredible
dividends. Up and down the High Street she went,
with Major Benjy in attendance, buying grocery, sta-
tionery, gloves, eau-de-Cologne, boot laces, the "Liter-
ary Supplement" of *The Times*, dried camomile
flowers, and every conceivable thing that she might
possibly need in the next week, so that her shopping
might be as protracted as possible. She allowed him
(such was her firmness in "spoiling" him) to carry her
shopping basket, and when that was full, she decked
him like a sacrificial ram with little parcels hung by
loops of string. Sometimes she took him into a shop in
case there might be someone there who had not seen
him yet on her leash; sometimes she left him on the
pavement in a prominent position, marking, all the
time, just as if she had been a clinical thermometer,
the feverish curiosity that was burning in Tilling's
veins. Only yesterday she had spread the news of his
cowardice broadcast; today their comradeship was of
the chattiest and most genial kind. There he was, carrying her basket, and wearing frock coat and top hat
and hung with parcels like a Christmas tree, spending
the entire morning with her instead of golfing with
Puffin. Miss Mapp positively shuddered as she tried to

realize what her state of mind would have been if she
had seen him thus coupled with Diva. She would
have suspected (rightly in all probability) some
loathsome intrigue against herself. And the cream of
it was that until she chose, nobody could possibly find
out what had caused this metamorphosis so paralys-
ing to inquiring intellects, for Major Benjy would assuredly never tell anyone that there was a
reconciliation, due to his apology for his rudeness,
when he had stood by and permitted an intoxicated
Puffin to suggest disgraceful bargains. Tilling—poor
Tilling—would go crazy with suspense as to what it
all meant.

Never had there been such a shopping! It was
nearly lunch-time when, at her front door, Major
Flint finally stripped himself of her parcels and her
companionship and hobbled home, profusely perspir-
ing, and lame from so much walking on pavements in
tight patent-leather shoes. He was weary and foot-
sore; he had had no golf, and, though forgiven, was
but a wreck. She had made him ridiculous all the
morning with his frock coat and top hat and his por-
terages, and if forgiveness entailed any more of these
nightmare sacraments of friendliness, he felt that he
would be unable to endure the fatiguing accessories
of the regenerate state. He hung up his top hat
and wiped his wet and throbbing head; he kicked off
his shoes and shed his frock coat, and furiously Qui-
hied for a whisky and soda and lunch.

His physical restoration was accompanied by a
quickening of dismay at the general prospect. What
(to put it succinctly) was life worth, even when un-
harassed by allusions to duels, without the solace of
golf, quarrels and diaries in the companionship of
Puffin? He hated Puffin—no one more so—but he could

not possibly get on without him, and it was entirely
due to Puffin that he had spent so outrageous a morning, for Puffin, seeking to silence Miss Mapp by his
intoxicated bargain, had been the prime cause of all
this misery. He could not even, for fear of that all-
seeing eye in Miss Mapp's garden room, go across to
the house of the unforgiven sea captain, and by a
judicious recital of his woes induce him to beg Miss
Mapp's forgiveness instantly. He would have to wait
till the kindly darkness fell. . . . "Mere slavery!" he
exclaimed with passion.

A tap at his sitting-room door interrupted the chain
of these melancholy reflections, and his permission to
enter was responded to by Puffin himself. The Major
bounced from his seat.

"You mustn't stop here," he said in a low voice, as if
afraid that he might be overheard. "Miss Mapp may
have seen you come in."

Puffin laughed shrilly.

"Why, of course she did," he gaily assented. "She
was at her window all right. Ancient lights, I shall
call her. What's this all about now?"

"You must go back," said Major Flint agitatedly.
"She must see you go back. I can't explain now. But I'll
come across after dinner when it's dark. Go; don't wait."

He positively hustled the mystified Puffin out of the
house, and Miss Mapp's face, which had grown sharp
and pointed with doubts and suspicions when she observed him enter Major Benjy's house, dimpled, as she
saw him return, into her sunniest smiles. "Dear Major
Benjy," she said, "he has refused to see him," and she
cut the string of the large cardboard box which had
just arrived from the dyer's with the most pleasurable
anticipations. . . .

Well, it was certainly very magnificent, and Miss

Greele was quite right, for there was not the faintest
tinge to show that it had originally been kingfisher
blue. She had not quite realized how brilliant crimson
lake was in the piece; it seemed almost to cast a rich
ruddy glow on the very ceiling, and the fact that she
had caused the orange chiffon with which the neck
and sleeves were trimmed to be dyed black (following the exquisite taste of Mrs. Titus Trout) only
threw the splendor of the rest into more dazzling radiance. Kingfisher blue would appear quite ghostly
and corpselike in its neighborhood; and painful
though that would be for Diva, it would, as all her
well-wishers might hope, be a lesson to her not to indulge in such garishness. She should be taught her
lesson (D. V.), thought Miss Mapp, at Susan's bridge
party tomorrow evening. Captain Puffin was being
taught a lesson, too, for we are never too old to learn,
or for that matter, to teach.

Though the night was dark and moonless, there
was an inconveniently brilliant gas lamp close to the
Major's door, and that strategist, carrying his round
roll of diaries, much the shape of a bottle, under his
coat, went about half past nine that evening to look at
the rain gutter which had been weeping into his yard,
and let himself out of the back door round the corner.
From there he went down past the fishmonger's,
crossed the road, and doubled back again up Puffin's
side of the street, which was not so vividly illuminated, though he took the precaution of making himself little with bent knees, and of limping. Puffin was
already warming himself over the fire and imbibing
Roman roads, and was disposed to be hilarious over
the Major's shopping.

"But why top hat and frock coat, Major?" he asked.
"Another visit of the Prince of Wales, I asked myself,

or the Voice that breathed o'er Eden? Have a drink—
one of mine, I mean? I owe you a drink for the good
laugh you gave me."

Had it not been for this generosity and the need of
getting on the right side of Puffin, Major Flint would
certainly have resented such clumsy levity, but this
double consideration caused him to take it with unwonted good humor. His attempt to laugh, indeed,
sounded a little hollow, but that is the habit of self-di-
rected merriment.

"Well, I allow it must have seemed amusing," he
said. "The fact was that I thought she would appreci-
ate my putting a little ceremony into my errand of
apology, and then she whisked me off shopping before I could go and change."

"Kiss and friends again, then?" asked Puffin.

The Major grew a little stately over this.

"No such familiarity passed," he said. "But she accepted my regrets with—ha—the most gracious generosity. A fine-spirited woman, sir; you'll find the same."

"I might if I looked for it," said Puffin. "But why
should I want to make it up? You've done that, and
that prevents her talking about duelling and early
trains. She can't mock at me because of you. You
might pass me back my bottle, if you've taken your
drink."

The Major reluctantly did so.

"You must please yourself, old boy," he said. "It's
your business, and no one's ever said that Benjy Flint
has interfered in another man's affairs. But I trust you
will do what good feeling indicates. I hope you value
our jolly games of golf and our pleasant evenings sufficiently highly."

"Eh! how's that?" asked Puffin. "You going to cut
me, too?"

The Major sat down and put his large feet on the fender. "Tact and diplomacy, Benjy, my boy," he reminded himself.

"Ha! That's what I like," he said, "a good fire and a friend, and the rest of the world may go hang. There's no question of cutting, old man; I needn't tell you that—but we must have one of our good talks. For instance, I very unceremoniously turned you out of my house this afternoon, and I owe you an explanation of that. I'll give it you in one word: Miss Mapp saw you come in. She didn't see me come in here this evening—ha! ha!—and that's why I can sit at my ease. But if she knew—"

Puffin guessed.

"What has happened, Major, is that you've thrown me over for Miss Mapp," he observed.

"No, sir, I have not," said the Major with emphasis. "Should I be sitting here and drinking your whisky if I had? But this morning, after that lady had accepted my regret for my share in what occurred the other night, she assumed that since I condemned my own conduct unreservedly, I must equally condemn yours. It really was like a conjuring trick; the thing was done before I knew anything about it. And before I'd had time to say, 'Hold on a bit,' I was being led up and down the High Street, carrying as much merchandise as a drove of camels. God, sir, I suffered this morning; you don't seem to realize that I suffered; I couldn't stand any more mornings like that: I haven't the stamina."

"A powerful woman," said Puffin reflectively.

"You may well say that," observed Major Flint. "That is finely said. A powerful woman she is, with a powerful tongue, and able to be powerful nasty, and if she sees you and me on friendly terms again, she'll

turn the full hose on to us both unless you make it up
with her."

"H'm, yes. But as likely as not she'll tell me and my
apologies to go hang."

"Have a try, old man," said the Major encouragingly.

Puffin looked at his whisky bottle.

"Help yourself, Major," he said. "I think you'll have
to help me out, you know. Go and interview her: see
if there's a chance of my favorable reception."

"No, sir," said the Major firmly, "I will not run the
risk of another morning's shopping in the High
Street."

"You needn't. Watch till she comes back from her
shopping tomorrow."

Major Benjy clearly did not like the prospect at all,
but Puffin grew firmer and firmer in his absolute re-
fusal to lay himself open to rebuff, and presently they
came to an agreement that the Major was to go on his
ambassadorial errand next morning. That being
settled, the still undecided point about the worm cast
gave rise to a good deal of heat, until, it being discovered that the window was open, and that their voices
might easily carry as far as the garden room, they
made malignant rejoinders to each other in whispers.
But it was impossible to go on quarrelling for long in
so confidential a manner, and the disagreement was
deferred to a more convenient occasion. It was late
when the Major left, and after putting out the light in
Puffin's hall, so that he should not be silhouetted
against it, he slid into the darkness, and reached his
own door by a subtle detour.

Miss Mapp had a good deal of division of her swift
mind, when, next morning, she learned the nature of
Major Benjy's second errand. If she, like Mr. Wyse,

was to encourage Puffin to hope that she would accept his apologies, she would be obliged to remit all further punishment of him, and allow him to consort with his friend again. It was difficult to forego the pleasure of his chastisement, but, on the other hand, it was just possible that the Major might break away, and whether she liked it or not (and she would not), refuse permanently to give up Puffin's society. That would be awkward since she had publicly paraded her reconciliation with him, and for the sake only of the now flourishing legend that the challenge for the duel which had not been fought about her was Major Benjy's way of silencing a disrespectful remark. . . . Not for a moment did she believe that herself, but it was sweet to think that Tilling did. What further inclined her to clemency was that this very evening the crimson-lake tea gown would shed its effulgence over Mrs. Poppit's bridge party, and Diva would never want to hear the word "kingfisher" again. That was enough to put anybody in a good temper. So the diplomatist returned to the miscreant with the glad tidings that Miss Mapp would hear his supplication with a favorable ear, and she took up a stately position in the garden room, which she selected as audience chamber, near the bell so that she could ring for Withers if necessary.

Miss Mapp's mercy was largely tempered with justice, and she proposed, in spite of the leniency which she would eventually exhibit, to give Puffin "what for" first. She had not for him, as for Major Benjy, that feminine weakness which had made it a positive luxury to forgive him: she never even thought of Puffin as Captain Dicky, far less let the pretty endearment slip off her tongue accidentally, and the luxury which she anticipated from the interview was that of administering a quantity of hard slaps. She had appointed half past twelve as the hour for his suffering, so that he must go without his golf again.

She put down the book she was reading when he appeared, and gazed at him stonily without speech. He limped into the middle of the room. This might be forgiveness, but it did not look like it, and he wondered whether she had got him here on false pretences.

"Good morning," said he.

Miss Mapp inclined her head. Silence was gold.

"I understood from Major Flint—" began Puffin.

Speech could be gold, too.

"If," said Miss Mapp, "you have come to speak about Major Flint you have wasted your time. And mine!"

(How different from Major Benjy, she thought. What a shrimp!)

The shrimp gave a slight gasp. The thing had got to be done, and the sooner he was out of range of this powerful woman the better.

"I am extremely sorry for what I said to you the other night," he said.

"I am glad you are sorry," said Miss Mapp.

"I offer you my apologies for what I said," continued Puffin.

The whip whistled.

"When you spoke to me on the occasion to which you refer," said Miss Mapp, "I saw of course at once that you were not in a condition to speak to anybody. I instantly did you that justice, for I am just to everybody. I paid no more attention to what you said than I should have paid to any tipsy vagabond in the slums. I daresay you hardly remember what you said, so that before I hear your expression of regret, I will remind you of what you said. You threatened, unless I promised to tell nobody in what a disgusting condition you were, to say that I was tipsy. Elizabeth Mapp tipsy! That was what you said, Captain Puffin."

Captain Puffin turned extremely red. ("Now the shrimp's being boiled," thought Miss Mapp.)

"I can't do more than apologize, " said he. He did not know whether he was angrier with his ambassador or her.

"Did you say you couldn't do 'more,'" said Miss Mapp with an air of great interest. "How curious! I should have thought you couldn't have done less."

"Well, what more can I do?" asked he.

"If you think," said Miss Mapp, "that you hurt me by your conduct that night, you are vastly mistaken. And if you think you can do no more than apologize, I will teach you better. You can make an effort, Captain Puffin, to break with your deplorable habits, to try to get back a little of the self-respect, if you ever had any, which you have lost. You can cease trying, oh, so unsuccessfully, to drag Major Benjy down to your level. That's what you can do."

She let these withering observations blight him.

"I accept your apologies," she said. "I hope you will do better in the future, Captain Puffin, and I shall look anxiously for signs of improvement. We will meet with politeness and friendliness when we are brought together and I will do my best to wipe all remembrance of your tipsy impertinence from my mind. And you must do your best, too. You are not young, and ingrained habits are difficult to get rid of. But do not despair, Captain Puffin. And now I will ring for Withers, and she will show you out."

She rang the bell, and gave a sample of her generous oblivion.

"And we meet, do we not, this evening at Mrs. Poppit's?" she said, looking not at him, but about a foot above his head. "Such pleasant evenings one always has there, I hope it will not be a wet evening, but the glass is sadly down. Oh, Withers, Captain Puffin is going. Good morning, Captain Puffin. Such a pleasure!"

Miss Mapp hummed a rollicking little tune as she observed him totter down the street.

"There!" she said, and had a glass of Burgundy for lunch as a treat.

10

THE NEWS THAT Mr. Wyse was to be of the party that evening at Mrs. Poppit's and was to dine there first, *en famille* (as he casually let slip in order to air his French), created a disagreeable impression that afternoon in Tilling. It was not usual to do anything more than "have a tray" for your evening meal, if one of these winter bridge parties followed, and there was, to Miss Mapp's mind, a deplorable tendency to ostentation in this dinner giving before a party. Still, if Susan was determined to be extravagant, she might have asked Miss Mapp as well, who resented this want of hospitality. She did not like, either, this hole-and-corner *en famille* work with Mr. Wyse; it indicated a pushing familiarity to which, it was hoped, Mr. Wyse's eyes were open.

There was another point: the party, it had been ascertained, would in all number ten, and if, as was certain, there would be two bridge tables, that seemed to imply that two people would have to cut out. There were often nine at Mrs. Poppit's bridge parties (she appeared to be unable to count), but on those occasions Isabel was generally told by her mother that she did not care for bridge, and so there was no cutting out, but only a pleasant book for Isabel. But what would be done with ten? It was idle to hope that Susan would sit out: as hostess she always considered it part of her duties to play solidly the entire evening. Still, if the cutting of cards malignantly ordained that Miss Mapp was ejected, it was only reasonable to expect that after her magnanimity to the United Services, either Major Benjy or Captain Puffin would be so obdurate in his insistence that she must play instead of him, that it would be only ladylike to yield.

She did not, therefore, allow this possibility to dim the pleasure she anticipated from the discomfiture of darling Diva, who would be certain to appear in the kingfisher-blue tea gown, and find herself ghastly and outshone by the crimson lake which was the color of Mrs. Trout's second toilet, and Miss Mapp, after prolonged thought as to her most dramatic moment of entrance in the crimson lake, determined to arrive when she might expect the rest of the guests to have already assembled. She would risk, it is true, being out of a rubber for a little, since bridge might have already begun, but play would have to stop for a minute of greetings when she came in, and she would beg everybody not to stir, and would seat herself quite, quite close to Diva, and openly admire her pretty frock, "like one I used to have. . . . !"

It was, therefore, not much lacking of ten o'clock

when, after she had waited a considerable time on
Mrs. Poppit's threshold, Boon sulkily allowed her to
enter, but gave no answer to her timid inquiry of "Am
I very late, Boon?" The drawing-room door was a
little ajar, and as she took off the cloak that masked
the splendor of the crimson lake, her acute ears heard
the murmur of talk going on, which indicated that
bridge had not yet begun, while her acute nostrils detected the faint but certain smell of roast grouse,
which showed what Susan had given Mr. Wyse for
dinner, probably telling him that the birds were a
present to her from the shooting lodge where she had
stayed in the summer. Then, after she had thrown
herself a glance in the mirror, and put on her smile,
Boon preceded her, slightly shrugging his shoulders,
to the drawing-room door, which he pushed open,
and grunted loudly, which was his manner of announcing a guest. Miss Mapp went tripping in, almost
at a run, to indicate how vexed she was at herself for
being late, and there, just in front of her, stood Diva,
dressed not in kingfisher blue at all, but in the crimson lake of Mrs. Trout's second toilet, which had rendered Newport like the Queen of Sheba, with no
spirit left in it. There is a fatality about great beauty,
and Mrs. Trout's second toilet had caused devastation
again, this time in Tilling.

Miss Mapp's courage rose to the occasion. Other
people, Majors and tipsy Captains, might be cowards,
but not she. Twice now (omitting the matter of the
Wars of the Roses) had Diva by some cunning, which
it was impossible not to suspect of a diabolical origin,
clad her odious little roundabout form in splendors
identical with Miss Mapp's, but now, without falter-
ing even when she heard Evie's loud squeak, she
turned to her hostess, who wore the Order of M.B.E.

on her ample breast, and made her salutations in a perfectly calm voice.

"Dear Susan, don't scold me for being so late," she said, "though I know I deserve it. So sweet of you! Isabel darling and dear Evie! Oh, and Mr. Wyse! Sweet Irene! Major Benjy and Captain Puffin! Had a nice game of golf? And the Padre!"

She hesitated a moment wondering, if she could, without screaming or scratching, seem aware of Diva's presence. Then she soared, lambent as flame.

"Diva darling!" she said, and bent and kissed her even as St. Stephen in the moment of martyrdom prayed for those who stoned him. Flesh and blood could not manage more, and she turned to Mr. Wyse, remembering that Diva had told her that the Contessa Faradiddleony's arrival was postponed.

"And your dear sister has put off her journey, I understand," she said. "Such a disappointment! Shall we see her at Tilling at all, do you think?"

Mr. Wyse looked surprised.

"Dear lady," he said, "you're the second person who has said that to me. Mrs. Plaistow asked me just now—"

"Yes, it was she who told me," said Miss Mapp in case there was a mistake. "Isn't it true?"

"Certainly not. I told my housekeeper that the Contessa's maid was ill, and would follow her, but that's the only foundation I know of for this rumor. Amelia encourages me to hope that she will be here early next week."

"Oh, no doubt, that's it!" said Miss Mapp in an aside so that Diva could hear. "Darling Diva's always getting hold of the most erroneous information. She must have been listening to servants' gossip. So glad she's wrong about it."

Mr. Wyse made one of his stately inclinations of the head.

"Amelia will regret very much not being here tonight," he said, "for I see all the great bridge players are present."

"Oh, Mr. Wyse!" she said. "We shall all be humble learners compared with the Contessa, I expect."

"Not at all!" said Mr. Wyse. "But what a delightful idea of yours and Mrs. Plaistow's to dress alike in such lovely gowns. Quite like sisters."

Miss Mapp could not trust herself to speak on this subject, and showed all her teeth, not snarling but amazingly smiling. She had no occasion to reply, however, for Captain Puffin joined them eagerly deferential.

"What a charming surprise you and Mrs. Plaistow have given us, Miss Mapp," he said, "in appearing again in the same beautiful dresses. Quite like—"

Miss Mapp could not bear to hear what she and Diva were like, and wheeled about, passionately regretting that she had forgiven Puffin. This maneuver brought her face to face with the Major.

"Upon my word, Miss Elizabeth," he said, "you look magnificent tonight."

He saw the light of fury in her eyes, and guessed, mere man as he was, what it was about. He bent to her and spoke low.

"But by Jove!" he said with supreme diplomacy, "somebody ought to tell our good Mrs. Plaistow that some women can wear a wonderful gown and others—ha!"

"Dear Major Benjy," said she. "Cruel of you to poor Diva."

But instantly her happiness was clouded again, for the Padre had a very ill-inspired notion.

"What, ho! Fair Madame Plaistow," he humorously observed to Miss Mapp. "Ah! *Peccavi!* I am in error. It is Mistress Mapp. But let us to the cards! Our hostess craves thy presence at yon table."

Contrary to custom, Mrs. Poppit did not sit firmly down at a table, nor was Isabel told that she had an invincible objection to playing bridge. Instead she bade everybody else take their seats, and said that she and Mr. Wyse had settled at dinner that they much preferred looking on and learning to playing. With a view to enjoying this incredible treat as fully as possible, they at once seated themselves on a low sofa at the far end of the room where they could not look or learn at all, and engaged in conversation. Diva and Elizabeth, as might have been expected from the malignant influence which watched over their attire, cut in at the same table and were partners, so that they had, in spite of the deadly antagonism of identical tea gowns, a financial interest in common, while a further bond between them was the eagerness with which they strained their ears to overhear anything that their hostess and Mr. Wyse were saying to each other.

Miss Mapp and Diva alike were perhaps busier when they were being dummy than when they were playing the cards. Over the background of each mind was spread a hatred of the other, red as their tea gowns, and shot with black despair as to what on earth they should do now with those ill-fated pieces of pride. Miss Mapp was prepared to make a perfect chameleon of hers, if only she could get away from Diva's hue, but what if, having changed, say, to purple, Diva became purple, too? She could not stand a third coincidence, and besides, she much doubted whether any gown that had once been of so pronounced a crimson lake, could successfully attempt to

appear of any other hue except perhaps black. If
Diva died, she might perhaps consult Miss Greele as
to whether black would be possible, but then if Diva
died, there was no reason for not wearing crimson
lake forever, since it would be an insincerity of which
Miss Mapp humbly hoped she was incapable, of going into mourning for Diva just because she died.

In front of this lurid background of rage and
despair moved the figures which would have commanded all her attention, have aroused all the
feelings of disgust and pity of which she was capable, had only Diva stuck to kingfisher blue. There
they sat on the sofa, talking in voices which it was
impossible to overhear, and if ever a woman made
up to a man, and if ever a man was taken in by shallow artifices, "they," thought Miss Mapp, "are the
ones." There was no longer any question that Susan
was doing her utmost to inveigle Mr. Wyse into matrimony, for no other motive, not politeness, not the
charm of conversation, not the low, comfortable seat
by the fire could possibly have had force enough to
keep her for a whole evening from the bridge table.
That dinner *en famille,* so Miss Mapp sarcastically reflected—what if it was the first of hundreds of similar
dinners *en famille?* Perhaps, when safely married,
Susan would ask her to one of the family dinners,
with a glassful of foam which she called champagne,
and the leg of a crow which she called game from the
shooting lodge. . . . There was no use in denying
that Mr. Wyse seemed to be swallowing flattery and
any other form of bait as fast as they were supplied
him; never had he been so made up to since the day,
now two years ago, when Miss Mapp herself wrote
him down as uncapturable. But now, on this awful
evening of crimson lake, it seemed only prudent to

face the prospect of his falling into the nets which were spread for him. . . . Susan the sister-in-law of a Contessa! Susan the wife of the man whose urbanity made all Tilling polite to each other, Susan a Wyse of Whitchurch! It made Miss Mapp feel positively weary of earth. . . .

Nor was this the sum of Miss Mapp's mental activities, as she sat being dummy to Diva, for, in addition to the rage, despair and disgust with which these various topics filled her, she had narrowly to watch Diva's play, in order, at the end, to point out to her with lucid firmness all the mistakes she had made, while with snorts and sniffs and muttered exclamations and jerks of the head and pullings out of cards and puttings of them back with amazing assertions that she had not quitted them, she wrestled with the task she had set herself of getting two no-trumps. It was impossible to count the tricks that Diva made, for she had a habit of putting her elbow on them after she had raked them in, as if in fear that her adversaries would filch them when she was not looking, and Miss Mapp, distracted with other interests, forgot that no-trumps had been declared and thought it was hearts, of which Diva played several after their adversaries' hands were quite denuded of them. She often did that "to make sure."

"Three tricks," she said triumphantly at the conclusion, counting the cards in the cache below her elbow.

Miss Mapp gave a long sigh, but remembered that Mr. Wyse was present.

"You could have got two more," she said, "if you hadn't played those hearts, dear. You would have been able to trump Major Benjy's club and the Padre's diamond, and we should have gone out. Never mind, you played it beautifully otherwise."

"Can't trump when it's no-trumps," said Diva, forgetting that Mr. Wyse was there. "That's nonsense. Got three tricks. Did go out. Did you think it was hearts? Wasn't."

Miss Mapp naturally could not demean herself to take any notice of this.

"Your deal, is it, Major Benjy?" she asked. "Me to cut?"

Diva had remembered just after her sharp speech to her partner that Mr. Wyse was present, and looked towards the sofa to see if there were any indications of pained surprise on his face which might indicate that he had heard. But what she saw there—or, to be more accurate, what she failed to see there—forced her to give an exclamation which caused Miss Mapp to look round in the direction where Diva's bulging eyes were glued. . . . There was no doubt whatever about it: Mrs. Poppit and Mr. Wyse were no longer there. Unless they were under the sofa, they had certainly left the room together and altogether. Had she gone to put on her sable coat on this hot night? Was Mr. Wyse staggering under its weight as he fitted her into it? Miss Mapp rejected the supposition; they had gone to another room to converse more privately. This looked very black indeed, and she noted the time on the clock in order to ascertain, when they came back, how long they had been absent.

The rubber went on its wild way, relieved from the restraining influence of Mr. Wyse, and when, thirty-nine minutes afterwards, it came to its conclusion and neither the hostess nor Mr. Wyse had returned, Miss Mapp was content to let Diva muddle herself madly, adding up the score with the assistance of her fingers, and went across to the other table till she could be called back to check her partner's figures. They would be certain to need checking.

"Has Mr. Wyse gone away already, dear Isabel?" she said. "How early!"

("And four makes nine," muttered Diva, getting to her little finger.)

Isabel was dummy, and had time for conversation.

"I think he has only gone with Mamma into the conservatory," she said, "—no more diamonds, partner?—to advise her about the orchids."

Now the conservatory was what Miss Mapp considered a potting shed with a glass room, and the orchids were one anaemic odontoglossum, and there would scarcely be room besides that for Mrs. Poppit and Mr. Wyse. The potting shed was visible from the drawing-room window, over which curtains were drawn.

"Such a lovely night," said Miss Mapp. "And while Diva is checking the score, may I have a peep at the stars, dear? So fond of the sweet stars."

She glided to the window (conscious that Diva was longing to glide, too, but was preparing to quarrel with the Major's score) and took her peep at the sweet stars. The light from the hall shone full into the potting shed, but there was nobody there. She made quite sure of that.

Diva had heard about the sweet stars, and for the first time in her life made no objection to her adversaries' total.

"You're right, Major Flint, eighteen pence," she said. "Stupid of me: I've left my handkerchief in the pocket of my cloak. I'll pop and get it. Back in a minute. Cut again for partners."

She trundled to the door and popped out of it before Miss Mapp had the slightest chance of intercept-

ing her progress. This was bitter, because the dining
room opened out of the hall, and so did the book cupboard with a window which dear Susan called her
boudoir. Diva was quite capable of popping into both
of these apartments. In fact, if the truants were there,
it was no use bothering about the sweet stars any
more, and Diva would already have won. . . .

There was a sweet moon as well, and just as baffled
Miss Mapp was turning away from the window, she
saw that which made her positively glue her nose to
the cold window pane, and tuck the curtain in, so
that her silhouette should not be visible from outside.
Down the middle of the garden path came the two
truants, Susan in her sables and Mr. Wyse close
beside her with his coat collar turned up. Her ample
form with the small round head on the top looked like
a short-funnelled locomotive engine, and he like the
driver on the footplate. The perfidious things had said
they were going to consult over the orchid. Did orchids grow on the lawn? It was news to Miss Mapp if
they did.

They stopped, and Mr. Wyse quite clearly pointed
to some celestial object, moon or star, and they both
gazed at it. The sight of two such middle-aged people
behaving like this made Miss Mapp feel quite sick,
but she heroically continued a moment more at her
post. Her heroism was rewarded, for immediately after the inspection of the celestial object, they turned
and inspected each other. And Mr. Wyse kissed her.

Miss Mapp "scriggled" from behind the curtain into
the room again.

"Aldebaran!" she said. "So lovely!"

Simultaneously Diva re-entered with her handkerchief, thwarted and disappointed, for she had certainly found nobody either in the boudoir or in the

dining room. But there was going to be a sit-down supper, and as Boon was not there, she had taken a *marron glacé*.

Miss Mapp was flushed with excitement and disgust, and almost forgot about Diva's gown.

"Found your hanky, dear?" she said. "Then shall we cut for partners again? You and me, Major Benjy. Don't scold me if I play wrong."

She managed to get a seat that commanded a full-face view of the door, for the next thing was to see how "the young couple" (as she had already labelled them in her sarcastic mind) "looked" when they returned from their amorous excursion to the orchid that grew on the lawn. They entered, most unfortunately, while she was in the middle of playing a complicated hand, and her brain was so switched off from the play by their entrance that she completely lost the thread of what she was doing, and threw away two tricks that simply required to be gathered up by her, but now lurked below Diva's elbow. What made it worse was that no trace of emotion, no heightened color, no coy and downcast eye, betrayed a hint of what had happened on the lawn. With brazen effrontery Susan informed her daughter that Mr. Wyse thought a little leaf mold . . .

"What a liar!" thought Miss Mapp, and triumphantly put her remaining trump on to her dummy's best card. Then she prepared to make the best of it.

"We've lost three, I'm afraid, Major Benjy," she said. "Don't you think you overbid your hand just a little wee bit?"

"I don't know about that, Miss Elizabeth," said the Major. "If you hadn't let those two spades go, and hadn't trumped my best heart—"

Miss Mapp interrupted with her famous patter.

"Oh, but if I had taken the spades," she said quickly, "I should have had to lead up to Diva's clubs, and then they would have got the ruff in diamonds, and I should have never been able to get back into your hand again. Then at the end if I hadn't trumped your heart, I should have had to lead the losing spade and Diva would have overtrumped, and brought in her club, and we should have gone down two more. If you follow me, I think you'll agree that I was right to do that. But all good players overbid their hands sometimes, Major Benjy. Such fun!"

The supper was unusually ostentatious, but Miss Mapp saw the reason for that; it was clear that Susan wanted to impress poor Mr. Wyse with her wealth, and probably when it came to settlements, he would learn some very unpleasant news. But there were agreeable little circumstances to temper her dislike of this extravagant display, for she was hungry, and Diva, always a gross feeder, spilt some hot chocolate sauce on the crimson lake, which, if indelible, might supply a solution to the problem of what was to be done now about her own frock. She kept an eye, too, on Captain Puffin, to see if he showed any signs of improvement in the direction she had indicated to him in her interview, and was rejoiced to see that one of these glances was clearly the cause of his refusing a second glass of port. He had already taken the stopper out of the decanter when their eyes met . . . and then he put it back again. Improvement already!

Everything else (pending the discovery as to whether chocolate on crimson lake spelt ruin) now faded into a middle distance, while the affairs of Susan and poor Mr. Wyse occupied the entire foreground of Miss Mapp's consciousness. Mean and cun-

ning as Susan's conduct must have been in entrapping
Mr. Wyse when others had failed to gain his affec-
tion, Miss Mapp felt that it would be only prudent to
continue on the most amicable of terms with her, for
as future sister-in-law to a countess, and wife to the
man who by the mere exercise of his presence could
make Tilling sit up and behave, she would doubtless
not hesitate about giving Miss Mapp some nasty ones
back if retaliation demanded. It was dreadful to think
that this audacious climber was so soon to belong to
the Wyses of Whitchurch, but since the moonlight
had revealed that such was Mr. Wyse's intention, it
was best to be friends with the Mammon of the
British Empire. Poppit-cum-Wyse was likely to be a
very important center of social life in Tilling, when
not in Scotland or Whitchurch or Capri, and Miss
Mapp wisely determined that even the announcement
of the engagement should not induce her to give
voice to the very proper sentiments which it could not
help inspiring.

After all she had done for Susan, in letting the door
of high life in Tilling swing open for her when she
could not possibly keep it shut any longer, it seemed
only natural that, if she only kept on good terms with
her now, Susan would insist that her dear Elizabeth
must be the first to be told of the engagement. This
made her pause before adopting the obvious course of
setting off immediately after breakfast next morning,
and telling all her friends, under promise of secrecy,
just what she had seen in the moonlight last night.
Thrilling to the narrator as such an announcement
would be, it would be even more thrilling provided
only that Susan had sufficient sense of decency to tell
her of the engagement before anybody else, to hurry
off to all the others and inform them that she had

known of it ever since the night of the bridge party.

It was important, therefore, to be at home whenever there was the slightest chance of Susan coming round with her news, and Miss Mapp sat at her window the whole of that first morning, so as not to miss her, and hardly attended at all to the rest of the pageant of life that moved within the radius of her observation. Her heart beat fast when, about the middle of the morning, Mr. Wyse came round the dentist's corner, for it might be that the bashful Susan had sent him to make the announcement, but if so, he was bashful, too, for he walked by her house without pause. He looked rather worried, she thought (as well he might), and passing on he disappeared round the church corner, clearly on his way to his betrothed. He carried a square parcel in his hand, about as big as some jewel case that might contain a tiara. Half an hour afterwards, however, he came back, still carrying the tiara. It occurred to her that the engagement might have been broken off. . . . A little later, again with a quickened pulse, Miss Mapp saw the Royce lumber down from the church corner. It stopped at her house, and she caught a glimpse of sables within. This time she felt certain that Susan had come with her interesting news, and waited till Withers, having answered the door, came to inquire, no doubt, whether she would see Mrs. Poppit. But, alas, a minute later the Royce lumbered on, carrying the additional weight of the Christmas number of *Punch*, which Miss Mapp had borrowed last night and had not, of course, had time to glance at yet.

Anticipation is supposed to be pleasanter than any fulfillment, however agreeable, and if that is the case, Miss Mapp during the next day or two had more enjoyment than the announcement of fifty engagements

could have given her, so constantly (when from the
garden room she heard the sound of the knocker on
her front door) did she spring up in certainty that
this was Susan, which it never was. But however enjoyable it all might be, she appeared to herself at
least to be suffering tortures of suspense, through
which by degrees an idea, painful and revolting in
the extreme, yet strangely exhilarating, began to in-
sinuate itself into her mind. There seemed a deadly
probability of the correctness of the conjecture, as the
week went by without further confirmation of that
kiss, for, after all, who knew anything about the character and antecedents of Susan? As for Mr. Wyse was
he not a constant visitor to the fierce and fickle South,
where, as everyone knew, morality was wholly ex-
tinct? And how, if it was all too true, should Tilling
treat this hitherto unprecedented situation? It was terrible to contemplate this moral upheaval, which
might prove to be a social upheaval also. Time and
again, as Miss Mapp vainly waited for news, she was
within an ace of communicating her suspicions to the
Padre. He ought to know, for Christmas (as was
usual in December) was daily drawing nearer. . . .

There came some halfway through that month a
dark and ominous afternoon, the rain falling sad and
thick, and so unusual a density of cloud dwelling in
the upper air that by three o'clock Miss Mapp was
quite unable, until the street lamp at the corner was
lit, to carry out the minor duty of keeping an eye on
the houses of Captain Puffin and Major Benjy. The
Royce had already lumbered by her door since
lunch-time, but so dark was it that, peer as she might,
it was lost in the gloom before it came to the dentist's
corner, and Miss Mapp had to face the fact that she
really did not know whether it had turned into the

street where Susan's lover lived or had gone straight
on. It was easier to imagine the worst, and she had already pictured to herself a clandestine meeting between those passionate ones, who under cover of this
darkness were imperviously concealed from any observation (beneath an umbrella) from her house roof.
Nothing but a powerful searchlight could reveal what
was going on in the drawing-room window of Mr.
Wyse's house, and apart from the fact that she had
not got a powerful searchlight, it was strongly improbable that anything of a very intimate nature was
going on there . . . it was not likely that they would
choose the drawing-room window. She thought of
calling on Mr. Wyse and asking for the loan of a
book, so that she would see whether the sables were
in the hall, but even then she would not really be
much further on. Even as she considered this a sea
mist began to creep through the street outside, and in
a few minutes it was blotted from view. Nothing was
visible, and nothing audible but the hissing of the
shrouded rain.

Suddenly from close outside came the sound of a
door knocker imperiously plied, which could be no
other than her own. Only a telegram or some urgent
errand could bring anyone out on such a day, and unable to bear the suspense of waiting till Withers had
answered it, she hurried into the house to open the
door herself. Was the news of the engagement coming
to her at last? Late though it was, she would welcome
it even now, for it would atone, in part at any rate. . . .
It was Diva.

"Diva dear!" said Miss Mapp enthusiastically, for
Withers was already in the hall. "How sweet of you
to come round. Anything special?"

"Yes," said Diva, opening her eyes very wide and

spreading a shower of moisture as she whisked off her mackintosh. "She's come."

This could not refer to Susan. . . .

"Who?" asked Miss Mapp.

"Faradiddleony," said Diva.

"No!" said Miss Mapp very loud, so much interested that she quite forgot to resent Diva's being the first to have the news. "Let's have a comfortable cup of tea in the garden room. Tea, Withers."

Miss Mapp lit the candles there, for, lost in meditation, she had been sitting in the dark, and with reckless hospitality poked the fire to make it blaze.

"Tell me all about it," she said. That would be a treat for Diva, who was such a gossip.

"Went to the station just now," said Diva. "Wanted a new timetable. Besides the Royce had just gone down. Mr. Wyse and Susan on the platform."

"Sables?" asked Miss Mapp parenthetically, to complete the picture.

"Swaddled. Talked to them. Train came in. Woman got out. Kissed Mr. Wyse. Shook hands with Susan. Both hands. While luggage was got out."

"Much?" asked Miss Mapp quickly.

"Hundreds. Covered with coronets and F's. Two cabs."

Miss Mapp's mind, on a hot scent, went back to the previous telegraphic utterance.

"Both hands did you say, dear?" she asked. "Perhaps that's the Italian fashion."

"Maybe. Then what else do you think? Faradiddleony kissed Susan! Mr. Wyse and she must be engaged. I can't account for it any other way. He must have written to tell his sister. Couldn't have told her then at the station. Must have been engaged some

days and we never knew. They went to look at the
orchid. Remember? That was when."

It was bitter, no doubt, but the bitterness could be
transmuted into an amazing sweetness.

"Then now I can speak," said Miss Mapp with a
sigh of great relief. "Oh, it has been so hard keeping
silence, but I felt I ought to. I knew all along, Diva
dear, all, all along."

"How?" asked Diva with a fallen crest.

Miss Mapp laughed merrily.

"I looked out of the window, dear, while you went
for your hanky and peeped into dining room and
boudoir, didn't you? There they were on the lawn,
and they kissed each other. So I said to myself, 'Dear
Susan has got him! Perseverance rewarded!' "

"H'm. Only a guess of yours. Or did Susan tell
you?"

"No, dear, she said nothing. But Susan was always
secretive."

"But they might not have been engaged at all," said
Diva with a brightened eye. "Man doesn't always
marry a woman he kisses!"

Diva had betrayed the lowness of her mind now by
hazarding that which had for days dwelt in Miss
Mapp's mind as almost certain. She drew in her
breath with a hissing noise as if in pain.

"Darling, what a dreadful suggestion," she said.
"No such idea ever occurred to me. Secretive I
thought Susan might be, but immoral, never. I must
forget you ever thought that. Let's talk about something less painful. Perhaps you would like to tell me
more about the Contessa."

Diva had the grace to look ashamed of herself, and
to take refuge in the new topic so thoughtfully suggested.

"Couldn't see clearly," she said. "So dark. But tall and lean. Sneezed."

"That might happen to anybody, dear," said Miss Mapp, "whether tall or short. Nothing more?"

"An eyeglass," said Diva after thought.

"A single one?" asked Miss Mapp. "On a string? How strange for a woman."

That seemed positively the last atom of Diva's knowledge, and though Miss Mapp tried on the principles of psychoanalysis to disinter something she had forgotten, the catechism led to no results whatever. But Diva had evidently something else to say, for after finishing her tea she whizzed backwards and forwards from window to fireplace with little grunts and whistles, as was her habit when she was struggling with utterance. Long before it came out, Miss Mapp had, of course, guessed what it was. No wonder Diva found difficulty in speaking of a matter in which she had behaved so deplorably. . . .

"About that wretched dress," she said at length. "Got it stained with chocolate first time I wore it, and neither I nor Janet can get it out."

("Hurrah," thought Miss Mapp.)

"Must have it dyed again," continued Diva. "Thought I'd better tell you. Else you might have yours dyed the same color as mine again. Kingfisher blue to crimson lake. All came out of *Vogue* and Mrs. Trout. Rather funny, you know, but expensive. You should have seen your face, Elizabeth, when you came in to Susan's the other night."

"Should I, dearest?" said Miss Mapp, trembling violently.

"Yes. Wouldn't have gone home with you in the dark for anything. Murder."

"Diva dear," said Miss Mapp anxiously, "you've got

a mind which likes to put the worst construction on
everything. If Mr. Wyse kisses his intended, you think
things too terrible for words; if I look surprised, you
think I'm full of hatred and malice. Be more generous, dear. Don't put evil constructions on all you see."

"Ho!" said Diva with a world of meaning.

"I don't know what you intend to convey by 'Ho!' "
said Miss Mapp, "and I shan't try to guess. But be
kinder, darling, and it will make you happier. Think-
eth no evil, you know! Charity!"

Diva felt that the limit of what was tolerable was
reached when Elizabeth lectured her on the need for
Charity, and she would no doubt have explained terse-
ly and unmistakably exactly what she meant by
"Ho!" had not Withers opportunely entered to clear
away tea. She brought a note with her, which Miss
Mapp opened. "Encourage me to hope" were the first
words that met her eye: Mrs. Poppit had been encour-
aging him to hope again.

"To dine at Mr. Wyse's tomorrow," she said. "No
doubt the announcement will be made then. He probably wrote it before he went to the station. Yes, a few
friends. You going, dear?"

Diva instantly got up.

"Think I'll run home and see," she said. "By the
by, Elizabeth, what about the—the tea gown, if I go?
You or I?"

"If yours is all covered with chocolate, I shouldn't
think you'd like to wear it," said Miss Mapp.

"Could tuck it away," said Diva, "just for once. Put
flowers. Then send it to dyer's. You won't see it again.
Not crimson lake, I mean."

Miss Mapp summoned the whole of her magnanimity. It had been put to a great strain already and was
tired out, but it was capable of one more effort.

"Wear it then," she said. "It'll be a treat to you. But let me know if you're not asked. I daresay Mr. Wyse will want to keep it very small. Good-by, dear; I'm afraid you'll get very wet going home."

11

THE SEA MIST and the rain continued without intermission next morning, but shopping with umbrellas and mackintoshes was unusually brisk, for there was naturally a universally felt desire to catch sight of a Contessa with as little delay as possible. The foggy conditions perhaps added to the excitement, for it was not possible to see more than a few yards, and thus at any moment anybody might almost run into her. Diva's impressions, meager though they were, had been thoroughly circulated, but the morning passed, and the ladies of Tilling went home to change their wet things and take a little ammoniated quinine as a precaution after so long and chilly an exposure, without a single one of them having caught sight of the single eyeglass. It was disappointing, but the disappointment was bearable since Mr. Wyse, so far from wanting his party to be very small, had been encouraged by Mrs. Poppit to hope that it would include all his world of Tilling with one exception. He had hopes with regard to the Major and the Captain, and the Mapp, and of course, Isabel. But apparently he despaired of Diva.

She alone therefore was absent from this long, wet shopping, for she waited indoors, almost pen in hand, to answer in the affirmative the invitation which had at present not arrived. Owing to the thickness of the fog, her absence from the street passed unnoticed, for everybody supposed that everybody else had seen her, while she, biting her nails at home, waited and waited and waited. Then she waited. About a quarter past one she gave it up, and duly telephoned, according to promise, via Janet and Withers, to Miss Mapp to say that Mr. Wyse had not yet been encouraged to hope. It was very unpleasant to let them know, but if she had herself rung up and been answered by Elizabeth, who usually rushed to the telephone, she felt that she would sooner have choked than have delivered this message. So Janet telephoned, and Withers said she would tell her mistress. And did.

Miss Mapp was steeped in pleasant conjectures. The most likely of all was that the Contessa had seen that roundabout little busybody in the station, and taken an instant dislike to her through her single eyeglass. Or she might have seen poor Diva inquisitively inspecting the luggage with the coronets and the F's on it, and have learned with pain that this was one of the ladies of Tilling. "Algernon," she would have said (so said Miss Mapp to herself), "Who is that queer little woman? Is she going to steal some of my luggage?" And then Algernon would have told her that this was poor Diva, quite a decent sort of little body. But when it came to Algernon asking his guests for the dinner party in honor of his betrothal and her arrival at Tilling, no doubt the Contessa would have

said, "Algernon, I beg . . ." Or if Diva—poor Diva—
was right in her conjectures that the notes had been
written before the arrival of the train, it was evident
that Algernon had torn up the one addressed to Diva,
when the Contessa heard whom she was to meet the
next evening. . . . Or Susan might easily have insinu-
ated that they would have two very pleasant tables of
bridge after dinner without including Diva, who was
so wrong and quarrelsome over the score. Any of
these explanations were quite satisfactory, and since
Diva would not be present, Miss Mapp would
naturally don the crimson lake. They would all see
what crimson lake looked like when it decked a
suitable wearer and was not parodied on the other
side of a card table. How true, as dear Major Benjy
had said, that one woman could wear what another
could not. . . . And if there was a woman who could
not wear crimson lake it was Diva. . . . Or was Mr.
Wyse really ashamed to let his sister see Diva in the
crimson lake? It would be just like him to be con-
siderate of Diva, and not permit her to make a guy of
herself before the Italian aristocracy. No doubt he
would ask her to lunch some day, quite quietly. Or
had . . . Miss Mapp bloomed with pretty conjectures,
like some Alpine meadow when smitten into flower
by the spring, and enjoyed her lunch very much
indeed.

The anxiety and suspense of the morning, which,
instead of being relieved, had ended in utter gloom,
gave Diva a headache, and she adopted her usual
strenuous methods of getting rid of it. So, instead of
lying down and taking aspirin and dozing, she set out
after lunch to walk it off. She sprinted and splashed
along the miry roads, indifferent as to whether she
stepped in puddles or not, and careless how wet she

got. She bit on the bullet of her omission from the
dinner party this evening, determining not to mind
one atom about it, but to look forward to a pleasant
evening at home instead of going out (like this) in
the wet. And never—never under any circumstances
would she ask any of the guests what sort of an evening had been spent, how Mr. Wyse announced the
news, and how the Faradiddleony played bridge.
(She said that satirical word aloud, mouthing it to the
puddles and the dripping hedgerows.) She would not
evince the slightest interest in it all; she would cover
it with spadefuls of oblivion, and when next she met
Mr. Wyse she would, whatever she might feel, behave exactly as usual. She plumed herself on this dignified resolution, and walked so fast that the
hedgerows became quite transparent. That was the
proper thing to do; she had been grossly slighted, and
like a true lady, would be unaware of that slight;
whereas poor Elizabeth, under such circumstances,
would have devised a hundred petty schemes for rendering Mr. Wyse's life a burden to him. But if—if
(she only said "if") she found any reason to believe
that Susan was at the bottom of this, then probably
she would think of something worthy not so much of
a true lady but of a true woman. Without asking any
questions, she might easily arrive at information
which would enable her to identify Susan as the cul-
prit, and she would then act in some way which
would astonish Susan. What that was she need not
think yet, and so she devoted her entire mind to the
question all the way home.

Feeling better and with her headache quite gone,
she arrived in Tilling again drenched to the skin. It
was already after teatime, and she abandoned tea altogether, and prepared to console herself for her ex-

clusion from gaiety with a "good blow-out" in the shape of regular dinner, instead of the usual muffin now and a tray later. To add dignity to her feast, she put on the crimson lake (though the same tea gown still), since tomorrow it would be sent to the dyer's to go into perpetual mourning for its vanished glories. She had meant to send it today, but all this misery and anxiety had put it out of her head.

Having dressed thus, to the great astonishment of Janet, she sat down to divert her mind from trouble by Patience. As if to reward her for her stubborn fortitude, the malignity of the cards relented, and she brought out an intricate matter three times running. The clock on her mantelpiece chiming a quarter to eight, surprised her with the lateness of the hour, and recalled to her with a stab of pain that it was dinnertime at Mr. Wyse's, and at this moment some seven pairs of eager feet were approaching the dentist's corner. Well, she was dining at a quarter to eight, too; Janet would enter presently to tell her that her own banquet was ready, and gathering up her cards, she spent a pleasant though regretful minute in looking at herself and the crimson lake for the last time in her long glass. The tremendous walk in the rain had given her an almost equally high color. Janet's foot was heard on the stairs, and she turned away from the glass. Janet entered.

"Dinner?" she said.

"No, ma'am, the telephone," said Janet. "Mr. Wyse is on the telephone, and wants to speak to you very particularly."

"Mr. Wyse himself?" asked Diva, hardly believing her ears, for she knew Mr. Wyse's opinion of the telephone.

"Yes, ma'am."

Diva walked slowly, but reflected rapidly. What must have happened was that somebody had been taken ill at the last moment—was it Elizabeth?—and that he now wanted her to fill the gap. . . .

She was torn in two. Passionately as she longed to dine at Mr. Wyse's, she did not see how such a course was compatible with dignity. He had only asked her to suit his own convenience; it was not out of encouragement to hope that he invited her now. No; Mr. Wyse should want. She would say that she had friends dining with her; that was what the true lady would do.

She took up the earpiece and said, "Hullo!"

It was certainly Mr. Wyse's voice that spoke to her, and it seemed to tremble with anxiety.

"Dear lady," he began, "a most terrible thing has happened—"

(Wonder if Elizabeth's very ill, thought Diva.)

"Quite terrible," said Mr. Wyse. "Can you hear?"

"Yes," said Diva, hardening her heart.

"By the most calamitous mistake the note which I wrote you yesterday was never delivered. Figgis has just found it in the pocket of his overcoat. I shall certainly dismiss him unless you plead for him. Can you hear?"

"Yes," said Diva excitedly.

"In it I told you that I had been encouraged to hope that you would dine with me tonight. There was such a gratifying response to my other invitations that I most culpably and carelessly, dear lady, thought that everybody had accepted. Can you hear?"

"Of course I can!" shouted Diva.

"Well, I come on my knees to you. Can you possibly forgive the joint stupidity of Figgis and me, and honor me after all? We will put dinner off, of course.

At what time, in case you are ever so kind and indulgent as to come, shall we have it? Do not break my heart by refusing. Su—Mrs. Poppit will send her car for you."

"I have already dressed for dinner," said Diva proudly. "Very pleased to come at once."

"You are too kind; you are angelic," said Mr. Wyse. "The car shall start at once; it is at my door now."

"Right," said Diva.

"Too good—too kind," murmured Mr. Wyse. "Figgis, what do I do next?"

Diva clapped the instrument into place.

"Powder," she said to herself, remembering what she had seen in the glass, and whizzed upstairs. Her fish would have to be degraded into kedgeree, though plaice would have done just as well as sole for that; the cutlets could be heated up again, and perhaps the whisking for the apple meringue had not begun yet, and could still be stopped.

"Janet!" she shouted. "Going out to dinner! Stop the meringue."

She dashed an interesting pallor on to her face as she heard the hooting of the Royce, and coming downstairs, stepped into its warm luxuriousness, for the electric lamp was burning. There were Susan's sables there—it was thoughtful of Susan to put them in, but ostentatious—and there was a carriage rug, which she was convinced was new, and was very likely a present from Mr. Wyse. And soon there was the light streaming out from Mr. Wyse's open door, and Mr. Wyse himself in the hall to meet and greet and thank and bless her. She pleaded for the contrite Figgis, and was conducted in a blaze of triumph into the drawing room, where all Tilling was awaiting her. She was led up to the Contessa, with whom Miss

Mapp, wreathed in sycophantic smiles, was eagerly conversing.

The crimson lakes. . . .

There were embarrassing moments during dinner; the Contessa confused by having so many people introduced to her in a lump, got all their names wrong, and addressed her neighbors as Captain Flint and Major Puffin, and thought that Diva was Mrs. Mapp. She seemed vivacious and good-humored, dropped her eyeglass into her soup, talked with her mouth full, and drank a good deal of wine, which was a very bad example for Major Puffin. Then there were many sudden and complete pauses in the talk, for Diva's news of the kissing of Mrs. Poppit by the Contessa had spread like wildfire through the fog this morning, owing to Miss Mapp's dissemination of it, and now whenever Mr. Wyse raised his voice ever so little, everybody else stopped talking, in the expectation that the news was about to be announced. Occasionally, also, the Contessa addressed some remark to her brother in shrill and voluble Italian, which rather confirmed the gloomy estimate of her table manners in the matter of talking with her mouth full, for to speak in Italian was equivalent to whispering, since the purport of what she said could not be understood by anybody except him. . . . Then also, the sensation of dining with a countess produced a slight feeling of strain, which, in addition to the correct behavior which Mr. Wyse's presence always induced, almost congealed correctness into stiffness. But as dinner went on, her evident enjoyment of herself made itself felt, and her eccentricities, though carefully observed and noted by Miss Mapp, were not succeeded by silence and hurried bursts of conversation.

"And is your ladyship making a long stay in Tilling?" asked the (real) Major, to cover the pause which had been caused by Mr. Wyse saying something across the table to Isabel.

She dropped her eyeglass with quite a splash into her gravy, pulled it out again by the string as if landing a fish, and sucked it.

"That depends on you gentlemen," she said with greater audacity than was usual in Tilling. "If you and Major Puffin and that sweet little Scotch clergyman all fall in love with me, and fight duels about me, I will stop for ever. . . ."

The Major recovered himself before anybody else.

"Your ladyship may take that for granted," he said gallantly, and a perfect hubbub of conversation rose to cover this awful topic.

She laid her hand on his arm.

"You must not call me ladyship, Captain Flint," she said. "Only servants say that. Contessa, if you like. And you must blow away this fog for me. I have seen nothing but bales of cotton wool out of the window. Tell me this, too: why are those ladies dressed alike? Are they sisters? Mrs. Mapp, the little round one, and her sister, the big round one?"

The Major cast an apprehensive eye on Miss Mapp seated just opposite, whose acuteness of hearing was one of the terrors of Tilling. . . . His apprehensions were perfectly well founded, and Miss Mapp hated and despised the Contessa from that hour.

"No, not sisters," said he, "and your la—you've made a little error about the names. The one opposite is Miss Mapp; the other, Mrs. Plaistow."

The Contessa moderated her voice.

"I see. She looks vexed, your Miss Mapp. I think she must have heard, and I will be very nice to her afterwards. Why does not one of you gentlemen marry her? I see I shall have to arrange that. The sweet little Scotch clergyman now; little men like big wives. Ah! Married already is he to the mouse? Then it must be you, Captain Flint. We must have more marriages in Tilling."

Miss Mapp could not help glancing at the Contessa, as she made this remarkable observation. It must be the cue, she thought for the announcement of that which she had known so long. . . . In the space of a wink the clever Contessa saw that she had her attention, and spoke rather loudly to the Major.

"I have lost my heart to your Miss Mapp," she said. "I am jealous of you, Captain Flint. She will be my great friend in Tilling, and if you marry her, I shall hate you, for that will mean that she likes you best."

Miss Mapp hated nobody at that moment, not even Diva, off whose face the hastily-applied powder was crumbling, leaving little red marks peeping out like the stars on a fine evening. Dinner came to an end with roasted chestnuts brought by the Contessa from Capri.

"I always scold Amelia for the luggage she takes with her," said Mr. Wyse to Diva. "Amelia dear, you are my hostess tonight"—everybody saw him look at Mrs. Poppit—"you must catch somebody's eye."

"I will catch Miss Mapp's," said Amelia, and all the ladies rose as if connected with some hidden mechanism which moved them simultaneously. . . .

There was a great deal of pretty diffidence at the door, but the Contessa put an end to that.

"Eldest first," she said, and marched out, making Miss Mapp, Diva, and the mouse feel remarkably young. She might drop her eyeglass and talk with her mouth full, but really such tact. . . . They all deter-

mined to adopt this pleasing device in the future. The
disappointment about the announcement of the engagement was sensibly assuaged, and Miss Mapp and
Susan, in their eagerness to be younger than the Contessa, and yet take precedence of all the rest, almost
stuck in the doorway. They rebounded from each
other, and Diva whizzed out between them. Quaint
Irene went in her right place—last. However quaint
Irene was, there was no use in pretending that she
was not the youngest.

However hopelessly Amelia had lost her heart to
Miss Mapp, she did not devote her undivided attention to her in the drawing room, but swiftly es-
tablished herself at the card table, where she
proceeded, with a most complicated sort of Patience
and a series of cigarettes, to while away the time till
the gentlemen joined them. Though the ladies of Tilling had plenty to say to each other, it was all about
her, and such comments could not conveniently be
made in her presence. Unless, like her, they talked
some language unknown to the subject of their conversation, they could not talk at all, and so they
gathered round her table, and watched the lightning
rapidity with which she piled black knaves on red
queens in some packs and red knaves on black queens
in others. She had taken off all her rings in order to
procure a greater freedom of finger, and her eyeglass
continued to crash onto a glittering mass of magnificent gems. The rapidity of her motions was only
equalled by the swift and surprising monologue that
poured from her mouth.

"There, that odious king gets in my way," she said.
"So like a man to poke himself in where he isn't
wanted. *Bacco!* No, not that: I have a cigarette. I
hear all you ladies are terrific bridge players: we will

have a game presently, and I shall sink into the earth
with terror at your Camorra! *Dio!* there's another
king, and that's his own queen whom he doesn't want
at all. He is *amoroso* for that black queen, who is
quite covered up, and he would like to be covered up
with her. Susan, my dear" (that was interesting, but
they all knew it already), "kindly ring the bell for
coffee. I expire if I do not get my coffee at once, and
a toothpick. Tell me all the scandal of Tilling, Miss
Mapp, while I play—all the dreadful histories of that
Major and that Captain. Such a grand air has the
Captain—no, it is the Major, the one who does not limp.
Which of all you ladies do they love most? It is Miss
Mapp, I believe: that is why she does not answer me.
Ah! here is the coffee, and the other king: three lumps
of sugar, dear Susan, and then stir it up well, and hold
it to my mouth, so that I can drink without interrup-
tion. Ah, the ace! He is the intervener, or is it the
King's proctor? It would be nice to have a proctor who
told you all the love affairs that were going on. Susan,
you must get me a proctor; you shall be my proctor.
And here are the men—the wretches, they have been
preferring wine to women—and we will have our
bridge, and if anybody scolds me, I shall cry, Miss
Mapp, and Captain Flint will hold my hand and comfort me."

She gathered up a heap of cards and rings, dropped
them on the floor, and cut with the remainder.

Miss Mapp was very lenient with the Contessa,
who was her partner, and pointed out the mistakes of
her and their adversaries with the most winning smile
and eagerness to explain things clearly. Then she
revoked heavily herself, and the Contessa, so far from
being angry with her, burst into peals of unquencha-
ble merriment. This way of taking a revoke was new

to Tilling, for the right thing was for the revoker's partner to sulk and be sarcastic for at least twenty minutes after. The Contessa's laughter continued to spurt out at intervals during the rest of the rubber, and it was all very pleasant; but at the end she said she was not up to Tilling standards at all, and refused to play any more. Miss Mapp, in her highest good humor, urged her not to despair.

"Indeed, dear Contessa," she said, "you play very well. A little overbidding of your hand, perhaps, do you think? But that is a tendency we are all subject to; I often overbid my hand myself. Not a little wee rubber more? I'm sure I should like to be your partner again. You must come and play at my house some afternoon. We will have tea early, and get a good two hours. Nothing like practice."

The evening came to an end without the great announcement being made, but Miss Mapp, as she reviewed the events of the party, sitting next morning in her observation window, found the whole evidence so overwhelming that it was no longer worth while to form conjectures, however fruitful, on the subject, and she diverted her mind to pleasing reminiscences and projects for the future. She had certainly been distinguished by the Contessa's marked regard, and her opinion of her charm and ability was of the very highest. . . . No doubt her strange remark about duelling at dinner had been humorous in intention, but many a true word is spoken in jest, and the Contessa—perspicacious woman—had seen at once that Major Benjy and Captain Puffin were just the sort of men who might get to duelling (or, at any rate, challenging) about a woman. And her asking which of the ladies the men were most in love with, and her saying that she believed it was Miss Mapp! Miss

Mapp had turned nearly as red as poor Diva when
that came out, so lightly and yet so acutely. . . .

Diva! It had, of course, been a horrid blow to find
that Diva had been asked to Mr. Wyse's party in the
first instance, and an even shrewder one when Diva
entered (with such unnecessary fussing and apology
on the part of Mr. Wyse) in the crimson lake. Luckily, it would be seen no more, for Diva had
promised—if you could trust Diva—to send it to the
dyer's; but it was a great puzzle to know why Diva
had it on at all, if she was preparing to spend a solitary evening at home. By eight o'clock she ought by
rights to have already had her tray, dressed in some
old thing; but within three minutes of her being telephoned for, she had appeared in the crimson lake and
eaten so heartily that it was impossible to imagine,
greedy though she was, that she had already consumed her tray. . . . But in spite of Diva's adventi-
tious triumph, the main feeling in Miss Mapp's mind
was pity for her. She looked so ridiculous in that
dress with the powder peeling off her red face. No
wonder the dear Contessa stared when she came in.

There was her bridge party for the Contessa to consider. The Contessa would be less nervous, perhaps, if
there was only one table: that would be more homey
and cosy, and it would at the same time give rise to
great heartburnings and indignation in the breasts of
those who were left out. Diva would certainly be one
of the spurned, and the Contessa would not play with
Mr. Wyse. . . . Then there was Major Benjy; he must
certainly be asked, for it was evident that the Contessa delighted in him. . . .

Suddenly Miss Mapp began to feel less sure that
Major Benjy must be of the party. The Contessa,
charming though she was, had said several very tropi-

cal, Italian things to him. She had told him that she
would stop here for ever if the men fought duels
about her. She had said "you dear darling" to him at
bridge when, as adversary, he failed to trump her losing card, and she had asked him to ask her to tea
("with no one else, for I have a great deal to say to
you"), when the general macédoine of sables, au reservoirs, and thanks for such a nice evening took
place in the hall. Miss Mapp was not, in fact, sure,
when she thought it over, that the Contessa was a
nice friend for Major Benjy. She did not do him the
injustice of imagining that he would ask her to tea
alone; the very suggestion proved that it must be a
piece of the Contessa's southern extravagance of expression. But, after all, thought Miss Mapp to herself,
as she writhed at the idea, her other extravagant expressions were proved to cover a good deal of truth.
In fact, the Major's chance of being asked to the select bridge party diminished swiftly towards vanish-
ing point.

It was time (and indeed late) to set forth on morning marketings, and Miss Mapp had already determined not to carry her capacious basket with her
today, in case of meeting the Contessa in the High
Street. It would be grander and Wysier and more
magnificent to go basketless, and direct that the goods
should be sent up, rather than run the risk of encoun-
tering the Contessa with a basket containing a couple
of mutton cutlets, a ball of wool and some tooth powder. So she put on her Prince of Wales's cloak, and,
postponing further reflection over the bridge party till
a less busy occasion, set forth in unencumbered gen-
tility for the morning gossip. At the corner of the
High Street, she ran into Diva.

"News," said Diva. "Met Mr. Wyse just now. Engaged to Susan. All over the town by now. Everybody knows. Oh, there's the Padre for the first time."

She shot across the street, and Miss Mapp, shaking the dust of Diva off her feet, proceeded on her chagrined way. Annoyed as she was with Diva, she was almost more annoyed with Susan. After all she had done for Susan, Susan ought to have told her long ago, pledging her to secrecy. But to be told like this by that common Diva, without any secrecy at all, was an affront that she would find it hard to forgive Susan for. She mentally reduced by a half the sum that she had determined to squander on Susan's wedding present. It should be plated, not silver, and if Susan was not careful, it shouldn't be plated at all.

She had just come out of the chemist's, after an indignant interview about precipitated chalk. He had deposited the small packet on the counter when she asked to have it sent up to her house. He could not undertake to deliver small packages. She left the precipitated chalk lying there. Emerging, she heard a loud, foreign sort of scream from close at hand. There was the Contessa, all by herself, carrying a marketing basket of unusual size and newness. It contained a bloody steak and a crab.

"But where is your basket, Miss Mapp?" she exclaimed. "Algernon told me that all the great ladies of Tilling went marketing in the morning with big baskets, and that if I aspired to be *du monde*, I must have my basket, too. It is the greatest fun, and I have already written to Cecco to say I am just going marketing with my basket. Look, the steak is for Figgis, and the crab is for Algernon and me, if Figgis does not get it. But why are you not *du monde?* Are you *du demimonde*, Miss Mapp?"

She gave a croak of laughter and tickled the crab. . . .

"Will he eat the steak, do you think?" she went on. "Is he not lively? I went to the shop of Mr. Hopkins, who was not there, because he was engaged with Miss Coles. And was that not Miss Coles last night at my brother's? The one who spat in the fire when nobody but I was looking? You are enchanting at Tilling. What is Mr. Hopkins doing with Miss Coles? Do they kiss? But your market basket: that disappoints me, for Algernon said you had the biggest market basket of all. I bought the biggest I could find. Is it as big as yours?"

Miss Mapp's head was in a whirl. The Contessa said in the loudest possible voice all that everybody else only whispered; she displayed (in her basket) all that everybody else covered up with thick layers of paper. If Miss Mapp had only guessed that the Contessa would have a market basket, she would have paraded the High Street with a leg of mutton protruding from one end and a pair of Wellington boots from the other. . . . But who could have suspected that a Contessa. . . .

Black thoughts succeeded. Was it possible that Mr. Wyse had been satirical about the affairs of Tilling? If so, she wished him nothing worse than to be married to Susan. But a playful face must be put, for the moment, on the situation.

"Too lovely of you, dear Contessa," she said. "May we go marketing together tomorrow, and we will measure the size of our baskets? Such fun I have, too, laughing at the dear people in Tilling. But what thrilling news this morning about our sweet Susan and your dear brother, though of course I knew it long ago."

"Indeed! How was that?" asked the Contessa quite sharply.

Miss Mapp was "nettled" at her tone.

"Oh, you must allow me two eyes," she said, since it was merely tedious to explain how she had seen them from behind a curtain kissing in the garden. "Just two eyes."

"And a nose for scent," remarked the Contessa very genially.

This was certainly coarse, though probably Italian. Miss Mapp's opinion of the Contessa fluctuated violently like a barometer before a storm and indicated "Changeable."

"Dear Susan is such an intimate friend," she said.

The Contessa looked at her very fixedly for a moment, and then appeared to dismiss the matter.

"My crab, my steak," she said. "And where does your nice Captain, no, Major Flint live? I have a note to leave for him, for he has asked me to tea all alone, to see his tiger skins. He is going to be my flirt while I am in Tilling, and when I go, he will break his heart, but I will have told him who can mend it again."

"Dear Major Benjy!" said Miss Mapp, at her wits' end to know how to deal with so feather-tongued a lady. "What a treat it will be to him to have you to tea. Today, is it?"

The Contessa quite distinctly winked behind her eyeglass, which she had put up to look at Diva, who whirled by on the other side of the street.

"And if I said 'Today,'" she remarked, "you would—what is it that that one says?"—and she indicated Diva—"yes, you would pop in, and the good Major would pay no attention to me. So I tell you I shall go today and you will know that is a lie, you clever Miss Mapp, and so you will go to tea with him tomorrow and find me there. *Bene!* Now where is his house?"

This was a sort of scheming that had never entered into Miss Mapp's life, and she saw with pain how shallow she had been all these years. Often and often she had, when inquisitive questions were put her, answered them without any strict subservience to truth, but never had she thought of confusing the issues like this. If she told Diva a lie, Diva probably guessed it was a lie, and acted accordingly, but she had never thought of making it practically impossible to tell whether it was a lie or not. She had no more idea when she walked back along the High Street with the Contessa swinging her basket by her side, whether that lady was going to tea with Major Benjy today or tomorrow or when, than she knew whether the crab was going to eat the beefsteak.

"There's his house," she said, as they paused at the dentist's corner, "and there's mine next it, with the little bow window of my garden room looking out on to the street. I hope to welcome you there, dear Contessa, for a tiny game of bridge and some tea one of these days very soon. What day do you think? Tomorrow?"

(Then she would know if the Contessa was going to tea with Major Benjy tomorrow . . . unfortunately the Contessa appeared to know that she would know it, too.)

"My flirt!" she said. "Perhaps I may be having tea with my flirt tomorrow."

Better anything than that.

"I will ask him, too, to meet you," said Miss Mapp, feeling in some awful and helpless way that she was playing her adversary's game. "Adversary" did she say

to herself? She did. The inscrutable Contessa was "up
to" that, too.

"I will not amalgamate my threats," she said. "So
that is his house! What a charming house! How my
heart flutters as I ring the bell!"

Miss Mapp was now quite distraught. There was
the possibility that the Contessa might tell Major
Benjy that it was time he married, but on the other
hand she was making arrangements to go to tea with
him on an unknown date, and the hero of amorous
adventures in India and elsewhere might lose his
heart again to somebody quite different from one
whom he could hope to marry. By daylight the dear
Contessa was undeniably plain. That was something,
but in these short days, tea would be conducted by
artificial light, and by artificial light she was not so
like a rabbit. What was worse was that by any light
she had a liveliness which might be mistaken for wit,
and a flattering manner which might be taken for sincerity. She hoped men were not so easily duped as
that, and was sadly afraid that they were. Blind fools!

The number of visits that Miss Mapp made about
teatime in this week before Christmas to the postbox
at the corner of the High Street, with an envelope in
her hand containing Mr. Hopkins's bill for fish (and a
postal order enclosed), baffles computation. Naturally, she did not intend, either by day or night,
to risk being found again with a blank unstamped envelope in her hand by anybody, and the one enclos-
ing Mr. Hopkins's bill and the postal order would
have passed scrutiny for correctness anywhere. But
fair and calm as was the exterior of that envelope,
none could tell how agitated was the hand that carried it backwards and forwards until the edges got
crumpled and the inscription clouded with much fin-

gering. Indeed, all of the tricks that Miss Mapp had
compassed for others, none was so sumptuously con-
trived as that which she had now made for herself.

For these December days were dark, and in consequence not only would the Contessa be looking her
best (such as it was) at teatime, but from Miss
Mapp's window, darkness having fallen, it was impossible to tell whether she had gone to tea with him on
any particular afternoon, for there had been a strike
at the gas works, and the lamp at the corner, which,
in happier days, would have told all, told nothing
whatever. Miss Mapp must therefore trudge to the
letter box with Mr. Hopkins's bill in her hand as she
went out, and (after a feint of posting it) with it in
her pocket as she came back, in order to gather by
such indications as could be seen from the street,
from the light in the windows, from the sound of conversation that would be audible as she passed close
beneath them, whether he was having tea there or
not, and with whom. Should she hear that ringing
laugh which was so pleasant when she revoked, but
now was so sinister, she had quite determined to go
in and borrow a book or a tiger skin—anything. The
Major could scarcely fail to ask her to tea, and once
there, wild horses should not drag her away until she
had outstayed the other visitor. Then, as her malady
of jealousy grew more feverish, she began to perceive,
as by the ray of some dreadful dawn, that lights in
the Major's room and sounds of elfin laughter were
not completely trustworthy as proofs that the Contessa
was there. It was possible, awfully possible, that the
two might be sitting in the firelight, that voices might
be hushed to amorous whisperings, that pregnant
smiles might be taking the place of laughter. On one
such afternoon, as she came back from the letter box

with patient Mr. Hopkins's overdue bill in her pocket, a wild certainty seized her, when she saw how closely the curtains were drawn, and how still it seemed inside his room, that firelight dalliance was going on.

She rang the bell, and imagined she heard whisperings inside while it was being answered. Presently the light went up in the hall, and the Major's Mrs. Dominic opened the door.

"The Major is in, I think. Isn't he, Mrs. Dominic?" said Miss Mapp, in her most insinuating tones.

"No, miss. Out," said Dominic uncompromisingly. (Miss Mapp wondered if Dominic drank.)

"Dear me! How tiresome, when he told me—" said she with playful annoyance. "Would you be very kind, Mrs. Dominic, and just see for certain that he is not in his room? He may have come in."

"No, miss, he's out," said Dominic, with the parrot-like utterance of the determined liar. "Any message?"

Miss Mapp turned away, more certain than ever that he was in and immersed in dalliance. She would have continued to be quite certain about it, had she not, glancing distractedly down the street, caught sight of him coming up with Captain Puffin.

Meantime she had twice attempted to get up a cosy little party of four (so as not to frighten the Contessa) to play bridge from tea till dinner, and on both occasions the Faradiddleony (for so she had become) was most unfortunately engaged. But the second of these disappointing replies contained the hope that they would meet at their marketings tomorrow morning, and though poor Miss Mapp was really getting very tired with these innumerable visits to the post-box, whether wet or fine, she set forth next morning with the hopes anyhow of finding out whether the Contessa had been to tea with Major Flint, or on

what day she was going. . . . There she was, just opposite the post office, and there—oh, shame!—was Major Benjy on his way to the tram, in light-hearted
conversation with her. It was a slight consolation that
Captain Puffin was there, too.

Miss Mapp quickened her steps to a little tripping
run.

"Dear Contessa, so sorry I am late," she said. "Such
a lot of little things to do this morning. (Major Benjy!
Captain Puffin!) Oh, how naughty of you to have begun your shopping without me!"

"Only been to the grocer's," said the Contessa. "Major Benjy has been so amusing that I haven't got on
with my shopping at all. I have written to Cecco to
say that there is no one so witty."

(Major Benjy! thought Miss Mapp bitterly, remembering how long it had taken her to arrive at that.
"And witty"; she had not yet arrived at that.)

"No, indeed!" said the Major. "It was the Contessa,
Miss Mapp, who has been so entertaining."

"I'm sure she would be," said Miss Mapp with an
enormous smile. "And, oh, Major Benjy, you'll miss
your train unless you hurry, and get no golf at all,
and then be vexed with us for keeping you. You men
always blame us poor women."

"Well, upon my word, what's a game of golf compared with the pleasure of being with the ladies?"
asked the Major with a great fat bow.

"I want to catch that tram," said Puffin quite distinctly, and Miss Mapp found herself more nearly forgetting his inebriated insults than ever before.

"You poor Captain Puffin," said the Contessa, "you
shall catch it. Be off, both of you, at once. I will not
say another word to either of you. I will never forgive

you if you miss it. But tomorrow afternoon, Major Benjy."

He turned round to bow again, and a bicycle, luckily for the rider going very slowly, butted softly into him behind.

"Not hurt?" called the Contessa. "Good! Ah, Miss Mapp, let us get to our shopping! How well you manage those men! How right you are about them! They want their golf more than they want us, whatever they may say. They would hate me, if we kept them from their golf. So sorry not to have been able to play bridge with you yesterday, but an engagement. What a busy place Tilling is. Let me see! Where is the list of things that Figgis told me to buy? That Figgis! A roller towel for his pantry, and some blacking for his boots, and some flannel I suppose for his fat stomach. It is all for Figgis. And there is that swift Mrs. Plaistow. She comes like a train with a red light in her face and wheels and whistlings. She talks like a telegram—Good morning, Mrs. Plaistow."

"Enjoyed my game of bridge, Contessa," panted Diva. "Delightful game of bridge yesterday."

The Contessa seemed in rather a hurry to reply. But long before she could get a word out, Miss Mapp felt she knew what had happened. . . .

"So pleased," said the Contessa quickly. "And now for Figgis's towels, Miss Mapp. Ten and sixpence apiece, he says. What a price to give for a towel! But I learn housekeeping like this, and Cecco will delight in all the economies I shall make. Quick, to the draper's, lest there should be no towels left."

In spite of Figgis's list, the Contessa's shopping was soon over, and Miss Mapp, having seen her as far as the dentist's corner, walked on as if to her own house, in order to give her time to get to Mr. Wyse's, and

then fled back to the High Street. The suspense was
unbearable: she had to know without delay when and
where Diva and the Contessa had played bridge yesterday. Never had her eyes so rapidly scanned the
movement of passengers in that entrancing thorough-
fare in order to pick Diva out and learn from her precisely what had happened. . . . There she was,
coming out of the dyer's with her basket completely
filled by a bulky package, which it needed no ingenuity to identify as the late crimson lake. She would
have to be pleasant with Diva, for much as that perfidious woman might enjoy telling her where this furtive bridge party had taken place, she might enjoy
even more torturing her with uncertainty. Diva could,
if put to it, give no answer whatever to a direct question, but, skillfully changing the subject, talk about
something utterly different.

"The crimson lake," said Miss Mapp, pointing to
the basket. "Hope it will turn out well, dear."

There was rather a wicked light in Diva's eyes.

"Not crimson lake," she said. "Jet black."

"Sweet of you to have it dyed again, dear Diva,"
said Miss Mapp. "Not very expensive, I trust?"

"Send the bill in to you, if you like," said Diva.

Miss Mapp laughed very pleasantly.

"That would be a good joke," she said. "How nice it
is that the dear Contessa takes so warmly to our Tilling ways. So amusing she was about the commissions
Figgis had given her. But a wee bit satirical, do you
think?"

This ought to put Diva in a good temper, for there
was nothing she liked so much as a few little dabs at
somebody else. (Diva was not very good-natured.)

"She is rather satirical," said Diva.

"Oh, tell me some of her amusing little speeches!"

said Miss Mapp enthusiastically. "I can't always follow her, but you are so quick! A little coarse, too, at times, isn't she? What she said the other night when she was playing Patience, about the queens and kings, wasn't quite?—was it? And the toothpick."

"Yes. Toothpick," said Diva.

"Perhaps she has bad teeth," said Miss Mapp; "it runs in families, and Mr. Wyse's, you know—We're lucky, you and I."

Diva maintained a complete silence, and they had now come nearly as far as her door. If she would not give the information that she knew Miss Mapp longed for, she must be asked for it, with the uncertain hope that she would give it then.

"Been playing bridge lately, dear?" asked Miss Mapp.

"Quite lately," said Diva.

"I thought I heard you say something about it to the Contessa. Yesterday, was it? Whom did you play with?"

Diva paused, and, when they had come quite to her door, made up her mind.

"Contessa, Susan, Mr. Wyse, me," she said.

"But I thought she never played with Mr. Wyse," said Miss Mapp.

"Had to get a four," said Diva. "Rather satirical. Nobody else."

She popped into her house.

There is no use in describing Miss Mapp's state of mind, except by saying that for the moment she quite forgot that the Contessa was almost certainly going to tea with Major Benjy tomorrow.

12

"PEACE ON EARTH and mercy mild," sang Miss Mapp, holding her head back with her uvula clearly visible. She sat in her usual seat close below the pulpit, and the sun streaming in through a stained-glass window opposite made her face of all colors, like Joseph's coat. Not knowing how it looked from outside, she pictured to herself a sort of celestial radiance coming from within, though Diva, sitting opposite, was reminded of the iridescent hues observable on cold boiled beef. But then, Miss Mapp had registered the fact that Diva's notion of singing alto was to follow the trebles at the uniform distance of a minor third below, so that matters were about square between them. She wondered between the verses if she could say something very tactful to Diva, which might before next Christmas induce her not to make that noise. . . .

Major Flint came in just before the first hymn was over, and held his top hat before his face by way of praying in secret, before he opened his hymnbook. A piece of loose holly fell down from the window ledge above him on the exact middle of his head, and the jump that he gave was, considering his baldness, quite justifiable. Captain Puffin, Miss Mapp was sorry to see, was not there at all. But he had been unwell lately with attacks of dizziness, one of which had

caused him, in the last game of golf that he had
played, to fall down on the eleventh green and groan.
If these attacks were not due to his lack of perseverance, no right-minded person could fail to be very
sorry for him.

There was a good deal more peace on earth as regards Tilling than might have been expected considering what the week immediately before Christmas
had been like. A picture by Miss Coles (who had
greatly dropped out of society lately, owing to her
odd ways) called "Adam," which was certainly Mr.
Hopkins (though no one could have guessed) had appeared for sale in the window of a dealer in pictures
and curios, but had been withdrawn from public view
at Miss Mapp's personal intercession and her revelation of whom, unlikely as it sounded, the picture
represented. The unchivalrous dealer had told the artist the history of its withdrawal, and it had come to
Miss Mapp's ears (among many other things) that
quaint Irene had imitated the scene of intercession
with such piercing fidelity that her servant, Lucy-Eve,
had nearly died of laughing. Then there had been
clandestine bridge at Mr. Wyse's house on three consecutive days, and on none of these occasions was
Miss Mapp asked to continue the instruction which
she had professed herself perfectly willing to give to
the Contessa. The Contessa, in fact—and there seemed
to be no doubt about it—had declared that she would
sooner not play bridge at all than play with Miss
Mapp, because the effort of not laughing would put
an unwarrantable strain on those muscles which prevented you from doing so. . . . Then the Contessa had
gone to tea quite alone with Major Benjy, and though
her shrill and senseless monologue was clearly audible
in the street as Miss Mapp went by to post her letter

again, the Major's Dominic had stoutly denied that he was in, and the notion that the Contessa was haranguing all by herself in his drawing room was too ridiculous to be entertained for a moment. . . . And Diva's dyed dress had turned out so well that Miss Mapp gnashed her teeth at the thought that she had not had hers dyed instead. With some green chiffon round the neck, even Diva looked quite distinguished—for Diva.

Then, quite suddenly, an angel of peace had descended on the distracted garden room, for the Poppits, the Contessa, and Mr. Wyse all went away to spend Christmas and the New Year with the Wyses of Whitchurch. It was probable that the Contessa would then continue a round of visits with all that coroneted luggage, and leave for Italy again without revisiting Tilling. She had behaved as if that was the case, for taking advantage of a fine afternoon, she had borrowed the Royce and whirled round the town on a series of calls, leaving P.P.C. cards everywhere, and saying only (so Miss Mapp gathered from Withers), "Your mistress not in? So sorry," and had driven away before Withers could get out the information that her mistress was very much in, for she had a bad cold.

But there were the P.P.C. cards, and the Wyses with their future connections were going to Whitchurch, and after a few hours of rage against all that had been going on, without revenge being now possible, and of reaction after the excitement of it, a different reaction set in. Odd and unlikely as it would have appeared a month or two earlier, when Tilling was seething with duels, it was a fact that it was possible to have too much excitement. Ever since the Contessa had arrived, she had been like an active volcano planted down among elements which were suffi-

ciently volcanic already, and the removal of the
volcano was, especially if it was a satirical one, a matter of relief. Miss Mapp felt that she would be
dealing again with materials whose properties she
knew, and since, no doubt, the strain of Susan's marriage would soon follow, it was a merciful dis-
pensation that the removal of these elements granted
Tilling a short restorative pause. The young couple
would be back before long, and with Susan's approaching elevation certainly going to her head, and
making her talk in a manner wholly intolerable about
the grandeur of the Wyses of Whitchurch, it was a
boon to be allowed to recuperate for a little, before
settling to work afresh to combat Susan's pretensions.
There was no fear of being dull, for plenty of things
had been going on in Tilling before the Contessa
flared on the High Street, and plenty of things would
continue to go on after she had taken her explosions
elsewhere. Everyone was capable of being satirical
enough as it was; extraneous satire was not wanted.

By the time that the second lesson was being read,
the sun had shifted from Miss Mapp's face, and en-
abled her to see how ghastly dear Evie looked when
focussed, so to speak, under the blue robe of Jonah
who was leaving the whale. She had had her disap-
pointments to contend with, for the Contessa had
never really grasped at all who she was. Sometimes
she mistook her for Irene; sometimes she did not seem
to see her; but never had she appeared fully to identify her as Mr. Bartlett's wee wifey. But then, dear
Evie was very insignificant even when she squeaked
her loudest. Her best friends, among whom was Miss
Mapp, would not deny that. She had been wilted by
nonrecognition; she would recover again, now that
they were all left to themselves.

The sermon contained many repetitions and a quantity of split infinitives. The Padre had once openly stated that Shakespeare was good enough for him, and that Shakespeare was guilty of many split infinitives. On that occasion there had nearly been a breach between him and Mistress Mapp, for Mistress Mapp had said, "But then you are not Shakespeare, dear Padre." And he could find nothing better to reply than "Hoots!" . . . There was nothing more of interest about the sermon.

At the end of the service Miss Mapp lingered in the church looking at the lovely decorations of holly and laurel, for which she was so largely responsible, until her instinct assured her that everybody else had shaken hands and was wondering what to say next about Christmas. Then, just then, she hurried out.

They were all there, and she came like the late and honored guest (poor Diva).

"Diva, darling," she said. "Merry Christmas! And Evie! And the Padre. Padre dear, thank you for your sermon! And Major Benjy! Merry Christmas, Major Benjy. What a small company we are, but not the less Christmassy. No Mr. Wyse, no Susan, no Isabel. Oh, and no Captain Puffin. Not quite well again, Major Benjy? Tell me about him. Those dreadful fits of dizziness. So hard to understand."

She beautifully succeeded in detaching the Major from the rest. With the peace that had descended on Tilling, she had forgiven him for being made a fool of by the Contessa.

"I'm anxious about my friend Puffin," he said. "Not at all up to the mark. Most depressed. I told him he had no business to be depressed. It's selfish to be depressed, I said. If we were all depressed it would be a dreary world, Miss Elizabeth. He's sent for the doctor. I was to have had a round of golf with Puffin this afternoon, but he doesn't feel up to it. It would have done him much more good than a host of doctors."

"Oh, I wish I could play golf, and not disappoint you of your round, Major Benjy," said she.

Major Benjy seemed rather to recoil from the thought. He did not profess, at any rate, any sympathetic regret.

"And we were going to have had our Christmas dinner together tonight," he said, "and spend a jolly evening afterwards."

"I'm sure quiet is the best thing for Captain Puffin with his dizziness," said Miss Mapp firmly.

A sudden audacity seized her. Here was the Major feeling lonely as regards his Christmas evening: here was she delighted that he should not spend it "jollily" with Captain Puffin . . . and there was plenty of plum pudding.

"Come and have your dinner with me," she said. "I'm alone, too."

He shook his head.

"Very kind of you, I'm sure, Miss Elizabeth," he said, "but I think I'll hold myself in readiness to go across to poor old Puffin, if he feels up to it. I feel lost without my friend Puffin."

"But you must have no jolly evening, Major Benjy," she said. "So bad for him. A little soup and a good night's rest. That's the best thing. Perhaps he would like me to go in and read to him. I will gladly. Tell him so from me. And if you find he doesn't want anybody, not even you, well, there's a slice of plum pudding at your neighbor's, and such a warm welcome."

She stood on the steps of her house, which in summer were so crowded with sketches, and would have kissed her hand to him had not Diva been following

close behind, for even on Christmas Day poor Diva
was capable of finding something ill-natured to say
about the most tender and womanly action . . . and
Miss Mapp let herself into her house with only a little
wave of her hand. . . .

Somehow the idea that Major Benjy was feeling
lonely and missing the quarrelsome society of his de-
bauched friend was not entirely unpleasing to her. It
was odd that there should be anybody who missed
Captain Puffin. Who would not sooner play golf all
alone (if that was possible) than with him, or spend
an evening alone rather than with his companionship?
But if Captain Puffin had to be missed, she would
certainly have chosen Major Benjy to be the person
who missed him. Without wishing Captain Puffin any
unpleasant experience, she would have borne with
equanimity the news of his settled melancholia, or his
permanent dizziness, for Major Benjy with his bright
robustness was not the sort of man to prove a willing
comrade to a chronically dizzy or melancholic friend.
Nor would it be right that he should be so. Men in
the prime of life were not meant for that. Nor were
they meant to be the victims of designing women,
even though Wyses of Whitchurch. . . . He was
saved from that by their most opportune departure.

It spite of her readiness to be interrupted at any
moment, Miss Mapp spent a solitary evening. She had
pulled a cracker with Withers, and severely jarred a
tooth over a threepenny piece in the plum pudding,
but there had been no other events. Once or twice, in
order to see what the night was like, she had gone to
the window of the garden room, and been aware that
there was a light in Major Benjy's house, but when
half past ten struck, she had despaired of company
and gone to bed. A little carol singing in the streets

gave her a Christmas feeling, and she hoped that the singers got a nice supper somewhere.

Miss Mapp did not feel as genial as usual when she came down to breakfast next day, and omitted to say good morning to her rainbow of piggies. She had run short of wool for her knitting, and Boxing Day appeared to her a very ill-advised institution. You would have imagined, thought Miss Mapp, as she began cracking her egg, that the trades people had had enough relaxation on Christmas Day, especially when, as on this occasion, it was immediately preceded by Sunday, and would have been all the better for getting to work again. She never relaxed her efforts for a single day in the year, and why—

An overpowering knocking on her front door caused her to stop cracking her egg. That imperious summons was succeeded by but a moment of silence, and then it began again. She heard the hurried step of Withers across the hall, and almost before she could have been supposed to reach the front door, Diva burst into the room.

"Dead!" she said. "In his soup. Captain Puffin. Can't wait!"

She whirled out again and the front door banged.

Miss Mapp ate her egg in three mouthfuls, had no marmalade at all, and putting on the Prince of Wales's cloak, tripped down into the High Street. Though all shops were shut, Evie was there with her market basket, eagerly listening to what Mrs. Brace, the doctor's wife, was communicating. Though Mrs. Brace was not, strictly speaking, "in society," Miss Mapp waived all social distinctions, and pressed her hand with a mournful smile.

"Is it all too terribly true?" she asked.

Mrs. Brace did not take the smallest notice of her,

and dropping her voice spoke to Evie in tones so low that Miss Mapp could not catch a single syllable except the word soup, which seemed to imply that Diva had got hold of some correct news at last. Evie gave a shrill little scream at the concluding words, whatever they were, as Mrs. Brace hurried away.

Miss Mapp firmly cornered Evie and heard what had happened. Captain Puffin had gone up to bed last night, not feeling well, without having any dinner. But he had told Mrs. Gashly to make him some soup, and he would not want anything else. His parlormaid had brought it to him, and had soon afterwards opened the door to Major Flint, who, learning that his friend had gone to bed, went away. She called her master in the morning, and found him sitting, still dressed, with his face in the soup which he had poured out into a deep soup plate. This was very odd, and she had called Mrs. Gashly. They settled that he was dead, and rang up the doctor who agreed with them. It was clear that Captain Puffin had had a stroke of some sort, and had fallen forward into the soup which he had just poured out.

"But he didn't die of his stroke," said Evie in a strangled whisper. "He was drowned."

"Drowned, dear?" said Miss Mapp.

"Yes. Lungs were full of oxtail. Oh, dear me! A stroke first, and he fell forward with his face in his soup plate and got his nose and mouth quite covered with the soup. He was drowned. All on dry land and in his bedroom. Too terrible. What dangers we are all in!"

She gave a loud squeak and escaped, to tell her husband.

Diva had finished calling on everybody, and approached rapidly.

"He must have died of a stroke," said Diva. "Very

much depressed lately. That precedes a stroke."

"Oh, then, haven't you heard, dear?" said Miss Mapp. "It is all too terrible! On Christmas Day, too!"

"Suicide?" asked Diva. "Oh, how shocking!"

"No, dear. It was like this. . . ."

Miss Mapp got back to her house long before she usually left it. Her cook came up with the proposed bill of fare for the day.

"That will do for lunch," said Miss Mapp. "But not soup in the evening. A little fish from what was left over yesterday, and some toasted cheese. That will be plenty. Just a tray."

Miss Mapp went to the garden room and sat at her window.

"All so sudden," she said to herself.

She sighed.

"I daresay there may have been much that was good in Captain Puffin," she thought, "that we knew nothing about."

She wore a wintry smile.

"Major Benjy will feel very lonely," she said.

Epilogue

Miss Mapp went to the garden room and sat at her window. . . .

It was a warm, bright day of February, and a butterfly was enjoying itself in the pale sunshine on the other window, and perhaps (so Miss Mapp sympathetically interpreted its feelings) was rather annoyed that it could not fly away through the pane. It was not a white butterfly, but a tortoiseshell, very pretty, and in order to let it enjoy itself more, she opened the window, and it fluttered out into the garden. Before it had flown many yards, a starling ate most of it up, so the starling enjoyed itself, too.

Miss Mapp fully shared in the pleasure first of the tortoiseshell and then of the starling, for she was enjoying herself very much, too, though her left wrist was terribly stiff. But Major Benjy was so cruel; he insisted on her learning that turn of the wrist which was so important in golf.

"Upon my word, you've got it now, Miss Elizabeth," he had said to her yesterday, and then made her do it all over again fifty times more. ("Such a bully!") Sometimes she struck the ground; sometimes she struck the ball; sometimes she struck the air. But he had been very much pleased with her. And she was very much pleased with him. She forgot about the butterfly and remembered the starling.

It was idle to deny that the last six weeks had been a terrific strain, and the strain on her left wrist was nothing to them. The worst tension of all, perhaps, was when Diva had bounced in with the news that the Contessa was coming back. That was so like Diva; the only foundation for the report proved to be that Figgis had said to her Janet that Mr. Wyse was coming back, and either Janet had misunderstood Figgis, or Diva (far more probably) had misunderstood Janet, and Miss Mapp only hoped that Diva had not done so on purpose, though it looked like it. Stupid as poor Diva undoubtedly was, it was hard for Charity itself to believe that she had thought that Janet really

said that. But when this report proved to be totally
unfounded, Miss Mapp rose to the occasion, and said
that Diva had spoken out of stupidity and not out of
malice towards her. . . .

Then in due course Mr. Wyse had come back and
the two Poppits had come back, and only three days
ago one Poppit had become a Wyse, and they had all
three gone for a motor tour on the Continent in the
Royce. Very likely they would go as far south as
Capri, and Susan would stay with her new grand Italian connections. What she would be like when she
got back, Miss Mapp forbore to conjecture since it
was no use anticipating trouble; but Susan had been
so grandiose about the Wyses, multiplying their incomes and their acreage by fifteen or twenty, so Miss
Mapp conjectured, and talking so much about county
families, that the liveliest imagination failed to picture what she would make of the Faragliones. She already alluded to the Count as, "My brother-in-law
Cecco Faraglione," but had luckily heard Diva say,
"Faradiddleony," in a loud aside, which had made her
a little more reticent. Susan had taken the insignia of
the Member of the British Empire with her, as she at
once conceived the idea of being presented to the
Queen of Italy by Amelia, and going to a court ball,
and Isabel had taken her manuscript book of
malapropisms and spoonerisms. If she put down all
the Italian malapropisms, that Mrs. Wyse would commit, it was likely that she would bring back two
volumes instead of one.

Though all these grandeurs were so rightly irritating, the departure of the "young couple" and Isabel
had left Tilling, already shocked and shattered by the
death of Captain Puffin, rather flat and purposeless.
Miss Mapp alone refused to be flat, and had never

been so full of purpose. She felt that it would be unpardonably selfish of her if she regarded for a moment her own loss, when there was one in Tilling who suffered so much more keenly, and she set herself with admirable singleness of purpose to restore Major Benjy's zest in life, and fill the gap. She wanted no assistance from others in this; Diva, for instance, with her jerky ways would be only too apt to jar on him, and her black dress might remind him of his loss if Miss Mapp had asked her to go shares in the task of making the Major's evenings less lonely. Also the weather, during the whole of January, was particularly inclement, and it would have been too much to expect of Diva to come all the way up the hill in the wet, while it was but a step from the Major's door to her own. So there was little or nothing in the way of winter bridge as far as Miss Mapp and the Major were concerned. Piquet with a single sympathetic companion who did not mind being rubiconned at threepence a hundred were as much as he was up to at present.

With the end of the month, a balmy foretaste of spring (such as had encouraged the tortoiseshell butterfly to hope) set in, and the Major used to drop in after breakfast and stroll round Miss Mapp's garden with her, smoking his pipe. The sweet snowdrops had begun to appear, and green spikes of crocuses pricked the black earth, and the sparrows were having such fun in the creepers. Then one day the Major, who was going out to catch the 11:20 tram, had a "golf stick," as Miss Mapp so foolishly called it, with him, and a golf ball, and after making a dreadful hole in her lawn, she had hit the ball so hard that it rebounded from the brick wall, which was quite a long way off, and came back to her very feet, as if asking to be

hit again by the golf stick—no, golf club. She learned
to keep her wonderfully observant eye on the ball
and bought one of her own. The Major lent her a
mashie, and before anyone would have thought it
possible, she had learned to propel her ball right over
the bed where the snowdrops grew, without behead-
ing any of them in its passage. It was the turn of the
wrist that did that, and Withers cleaned the dear
little mashie afterwards, and put it safely in the corner of the garden room.

Today was to be epoch-making. They were to go
out to the real links by the 11:20 tram (consecrated
by so many memories), and he was to call for her at
eleven. He had Qui-hied for porridge fully an hour ago.

After letting out the tortoiseshell butterfly from the
window looking into the garden, she moved across to
the post of observation on the street, and arranged
snowdrops in a little glass vase. There were a few
over when that was full, and she saw that a reel of
cotton was close at hand, in case she had an idea of
what to do with the remainder. Eleven o'clock chimed
from the church, and on the stroke she saw him coming up the few yards of street that separated his doors
from hers. So punctual! So manly!

Diva was careering about the High Street as they
walked along it, and Miss Mapp kissed her hand to
her.

"Off to play golf, darling," she said. "Is that not
grand? Au reservoir."

Diva had not missed seeing the snowdrops in the
Major's buttonhole, and stood stupefied for a moment
at this news. Then she caught sight of Evie, and shot
across the street to communicate her suspicions.
Quaint Irene joined them and the Padre.

"Snowdrops, i'fegs!" said he. . . .

The Male Impersonator

*This short story was published by Elkin Mathews &
Marrot, London, 1929, in an edition limited to five
hundred and thirty copies. The rest of the details of
its publication are, to quote the English agent, "lost in
the dim mist of history."*

*Thanks are due to Edward Gorey, America's chief
Luciaphile, for bringing it to our attention.*

1

Miss Elizabeth Mapp was sitting, on this warm September morning, in the little public garden at Tilling, busy as a bee with her water-color sketch. She had taken immense pains with the drawing of the dykes that intersected the marsh, of the tidal river which ran across it from the coast, and of the shipyard in the foreground: indeed she had procured a photograph of this particular view and, by the judicious use of tracing-paper, had succeeded in seeing the difficult panorama precisely as the camera saw it: now the rewarding moment was come to use her paint box. She was intending to be very bold over this, following the method which Mr. Sargent practised with such satisfactory results, namely of painting not what she knew was there but what her eye beheld, and there was no doubt whatever that the broad waters of the high tide, though actually grey and muddy, appeared to be as blue as the sky which they reflected. So, with a fierce glow of courage she filled her broad brush with the same strong solution of cobalt as she had used for the sky, and unhesitatingly applied it.

"There!" she said to herself. "That's what he would have done. And now I must wait till it dries."

The anxiety of waiting to see the effect of so reckless a proceeding by no means paralysed the

natural activity of Miss Mapp's mind, and there was
plenty to occupy it. She had returned only yesterday
afternoon from a month's holiday in Switzerland, and
there was much to plan and look forward to. Already
she had made a minute inspection of her house and
garden, satisfying herself that the rooms had been
kept well-aired, that no dusters or dishcloths were
missing, that there was a good crop of winter lettuces,
and that all her gardener's implements were there except one trowel, which she might possibly have overlooked; she did not therefore at present entertain any
dark suspicions on the subject. She had also done her
marketing in the High Street, where she had met
several friends, of whom Godiva Plaistow was coming
to tea to give her all the news, and thus while the cobalt dried, she could project her mind into the future.
The little circle of friends, who made life so pleasant
and busy (and sometimes so agitating) an affair in
Tilling would all have returned now for the winter,
and the days would scurry by in a round of housekeeping, bridge, weekly visits to the workhouse, and
intense curiosity as to anything of domestic interest
which took place in the strenuous world of this little
country town.

The thought of bridge caused a slight frown to
gather on her forehead. Bridge was the chief intellectual pursuit of her circle, and, shortly before she went
away, that circle had been convulsed by the most
acute divergences of opinion with regard to majority
calling. Miss Mapp had originally been strongly
against it.

"I'm sure I don't know by what right the Portland
Club tells us how to play bridge," she witheringly remarked. "Tilling might just as well tell the Portland

Club to eat salt with gooseberry tart, and for my part I shall continue to play the game I prefer."

But then one evening Miss Mapp held no less than nine clubs in her hand, and this profusion caused her to see certain advantages in majority calling to which she had hitherto been blind, and she warmly espoused it. Unfortunately, of the eight players who spent so many exciting evenings together, there were thus left five who rejected majority (which was a very inconvenient number since one must always be sitting out) and three who preferred it. This was even more inconvenient, for they could not play bridge at all.

"We really must make a compromise," thought Miss Mapp, meaning that everybody must come round to her way of thinking, "or our dear little cosy bridge evenings won't be possible."

The warm sun had now dried her solution of cobalt, and holding her sketch at arm's length, she was astonished to observe how blue she had made the river, and wondered if she had seen it quite as brilliant as that. But the cowardly notion of toning it down a little was put out of her head by the sound of the church clock striking one, and it was time to go home to lunch.

The garden where she had been sketching was on the southward slope of the hill below the Church square, and having packed her artistic implements, she climbed the steep little rise. As she skirted along one side of this square, which led into Curfew Street, she saw a large pantechnicon van lumbering along its cobbled way. It instantly occurred to her that the house at the far end of the street, which had stood empty so long, had been taken at last, and since this was one of the best residences in Tilling, it was

naturally a matter of urgent importance to ascertain if
this surmise was true. Sure enough the van stopped at
the door, and Miss Mapp noticed that the bills in the
windows of "Suntrap," which announced that it was
for sale, had been taken down. That was extremely
interesting, and she wondered why Diva Plaistow,
who, in the brief interview they had held in the High
Street this morning, had been in spate with a torrent
of miscellaneous gossip, had not mentioned a fact of
such primary importance. Could it be that dear Diva
was unaware of it? It was pleasant to think that after
a few hours in Tilling she knew more local news than
poor Diva who had been here all August.

She retraced her steps and hurried home. Just as
she opened the door she heard the telephone bell
ringing, and was met by the exciting intelligence that
this was a trunk call. Trunk calls were always thrilling; no one trunked over trivialities. She applied ear
and mouth to the proper places.

"Tilling 76?" asked a distant insectlike voice.

Now, Miss Mapp's real number was Tilling 67, but
she had a marvellous memory, and it instantly flashed
through her mind that the number of Suntrap was 76.
The next process was merely automatic, and she said,
"Yes." If a trunk call was coming for Suntrap and a
pantechnicon van had arrived at Suntrap, there was
no question of choice: the necessity of hearing what
was destined for Suntrap knew no law.

"Her ladyship will come down by motor this afternoon," said the insect, "and she—"

"Who will come down?" asked Miss Mapp with her
mouth watering.

"Lady Deal, I tell you. Has the first van arrived?"

"Yes," said Miss Mapp.

"Very well. Fix up a room for her ladyship. She'll

get her food at some hotel, but she'll stop for a night or two settling in. How are you getting on, Susie?"

Miss Mapp did not feel equal to saying how Susie was getting on, and she slid the receiver quietly into its place.

She sat for a moment considering the immensity of her trove, feeling perfectly certain that Diva knew nothing about it all, or the fact that Lady Deal had taken Suntrap must have been her very first item of news. Then she reflected that a trunk call had been expended on Susie, and that she could do no less than pass the message on. A less scrupulous woman might have let Susie languish in ignorance, but her fine nature dictated the more honorable course. So she rang up Tilling 76, and in a hollow voice passed on the news. Susie asked if it was Jane speaking, and Miss Mapp again felt she did not know enough about Jane to continue the conversation.

"It's only at Tilling that such interesting things happen," she thought as she munched her winter lettuce. . . . She had enjoyed her holiday at the Riffel Alp, and had had long talks to a Bishop about the revised prayer book, and to a Russian exile about Bolshevism and to a member of the Alpine Club about Mount Everest, but these remote cosmic subjects really mattered far less than the tenant of Suntrap, for the new prayer book was only optional, and Russia and Mount Everest were very far away and had no bearing on daily life, as she had not the smallest intention of exploring either of them. But she had a consuming desire to know who Susie was, and since it would be a pleasant little stroll after lunch to go down Curfew Street, and admire the wide view at the end of it, she soon set out again. The pantechnicon van was in process of unlading, and as she lingered, a

big bustling woman came to the door of Suntrap, and
told the men where to put the piano. It was a slight
disappointment to see that it was only an upright:
Miss Mapp would have preferred a concert grand for
so territorially-sounding a mistress. When the piano
had bumped its way into the rather narrow entrance,
she put on her most winning smile, and stepped up to
Susie with a calling card in her hand, of which she
had turned down the right-hand corner to show by
this mystic convention that she had delivered it in
person.

"Has her ladyship arrived yet?" she asked. "No?
Then would you kindly give her my card when she
gets here? *Thank* you!"

Miss Mapp had a passion for indirect procedure: it
was so much more amusing, when in pursuit of any
object, however trivial and innocent, to advance with
stealth under cover rather than march up to it in the
open and grab it, and impersonating Susie and Jane,
though only for a moment at the end of a wire, supplied that particular sauce which rendered her life at
Tilling so justly palatable. But she concealed her
stalkings under the brushwood, so to speak, of a frank
and open demeanor, and though she was sure she had
a noble quarry within shot, did not propose to disclose herself just yet. Probably Lady Deal would return her card next day, and in the interval she would
be able to look her up in the *Peerage,* of which she
knew she had somewhere an antique and venerable
copy, and she would thus be in a position to deluge
Diva with a flood of information: she might even
have ascertained Lady Deal's views on majority calling at bridge. She made search for this volume but
without success, in the bookshelves of her big garden
room, which had been the scene of so much of Til-

ling's social life, and of which the bow window, looking both towards the church and down the cobbled
way which ran down to the High Street, was so admirable a post for observing the activities of the town.
But she knew this book was somewhere in the house,
and she could find it at leisure when she had finished
picking Diva's brains of all the little trifles and shreds
of news which had happened in Tilling during her
holiday.

Though it was still only four o'clock, Miss Mapp
gazing attentively out of her window suddenly observed Diva's round squat little figure trundling down
the street from the church in the direction of her
house, with those short twinkling steps of hers which
so much resembled those of a thrush scudding over
the lawn in search of worms. She hopped briskly into
Miss Mapp's door, and presently scuttled into the
garden room, and began to speak before the door was
more than ajar.

"I know I'm very early, Elizabeth," she said, "but I
felt I must tell you what has happened without losing
a moment. I was going up Curfew Street just now,
and what do you think! Guess!"

Elizabeth gave a half yawn and dexterously transformed it into an indulgent little laugh.

"I suppose you mean that the new tenant is settling
into Suntrap," she said.

Diva's face fell: all the joy of the herald of great
news died out of it.

"What? You know?" she said.

"Oh, dear me, yes," replied Elizabeth. "But thank
you, Diva, for coming to tell me. That was a kind intention."

This was rather irritating: it savored of condescension.

"Perhaps you know who the tenant is," said Diva with an unmistakable ring of sarcasm in her voice.

Miss Mapp gave up the idea of any further secrecy, for she could never find a better opportunity for making Diva's sarcasm look silly.

"Oh, yes, it's Lady Deal," she said. "She is coming down—let me see, Thursday isn't it?—she is coming down today."

"But how did you know?" asked Diva.

Miss Mapp put a meditative finger to her forehead. She did not mean to lie, but she certainly did not mean to tell the truth.

"Now, who was it who told me?" she said. "Was it someone at the Riffel Alp? No, I don't think so. Someone in London, perhaps: yes, I feel sure that was it. But that doesn't matter: it's Lady Deal anyhow who has taken the house. In fact, I was just glancing round to see if I could find a *Peerage*: it might be useful just to ascertain who she was. But here's tea. Now it's your turn, dear: you shall tell me all the news of Tilling, and then we'll see about Lady Deal."

After this great piece of intelligence, all that poor Diva had to impart of course fell very flat: the forth-coming harvest festival, the mistake (if it was a mistake) that Mrs. Poppit* had made in travelling first class with a third-class ticket, the double revoke made by Miss Terling at bridge, were all very small beer compared to this noble vintage, and presently the two ladies were engaged in a systematic search for the *Peerage*. It was found eventually in a cupboard in the spare bedroom, and Miss Mapp eagerly turned up "Deal."

---

*Mrs. Poppit became Mrs. Wyse in *Miss Mapp*, which was originally published six years before this story.

"Viscount," she said. "Born, succeeded, and so on. Ah, married—"

She gave a cry of dismay and disgust.

"Oh, how shocking!" she said. "Lady Deal was Helena Herman. I remember seeing her at a music hall."

"No!" said Diva.

"Yes," said Miss Mapp firmly. "And she was a male impersonator. That's the end of her; naturally we can have nothing to do with her, and I think everybody ought to know at once. To think that a male impersonator should come to Tilling and take one of the best houses in the place! Why, it might as well have remained empty."

"Awful!" said Diva. "But what an escape I've had, Elizabeth. I very nearly left my card at Suntrap, and then I should have had this dreadful woman calling on me. What a mercy I didn't."

Miss Mapp found bitter food for thought in this, but that had to be consumed in private, for it would be too humiliating to tell Diva that she had been caught in the trap which Diva had avoided. Diva must not know that, and when she had gone, Miss Mapp would see about getting out.

At present Diva showed no sign of going.

"How odd that your informant in London didn't tell you what sort of a woman Lady Deal was," she said, "and how lucky we've found her out in time. I am going to the choir practice this evening, and I shall be able to tell several people. All the same, Elizabeth, it would be thrilling to know a male impersonator, and she may be a very decent woman."

"Then you can go and leave your card, dear," said Miss Mapp, "and I should think you would know her at once."

"Well, I suppose it wouldn't do," said Diva regretfully. As Elizabeth had often observed with pain, she had a touch of Bohemianism about her.

Though Diva prattled endlessly on, it was never necessary to attend closely to what she was saying, and long before she left, Miss Mapp had quite made up her mind as to what to do about that card. She only waited to see Diva twinkle safely down the street and then set off in the opposite direction for Suntrap. She explained to Susie with many apologies that she had left a card here by mistake, intending to bestow it next door, and thus triumphantly recovered it. That she had directed that the card should be given to Lady Deal was one of those trumpery little inconsistencies which never troubled her.

The news of the titled male impersonator spread like influenza through Tilling, and though many ladies secretly thirsted to know her, public opinion felt that such moral proletarianism was impossible. Classes, it was true, in these democratic days were being sadly levelled, but there was a great gulf between male impersonators and select society which even viscountesses could not bridge. So the ladies of Tilling looked eagerly but furtively at any likely stranger they met in their shopping, but their eyes assumed a glazed expression when they got close. Curfew Street, however, became a very favorite route for strolls before lunch when shopping was over, for the terrace at the end of it not only commanded a lovely view of the marsh but also of Suntrap. Miss Mapp, indeed, abandoned her Sargentesque sketch of the river, and began a new one here. But for a couple of days there were no great developments in the matter of the male impersonator.

Then one morning the wheels of fate began to

whizz. Miss Mapp saw emerging from the door of Suntrap a Bath chair, and presently, heavily leaning on two sticks, there came out an elderly lady who got into it, and was propelled up Curfew Street by Miss Mapp's part-time gardener. Curiosity was a quality she abhorred, and with a strong effort but a trembling hand she went on with her sketch without following the Bath chair, or even getting a decent view of its occupant. But in ten minutes she found it was quite hopeless to pursue her artistic efforts when so overwhelming a human interest beckoned, and bundling her painting materials into her satchel, she hurried down towards the High Street, where the Bath chair had presumably gone. But before she reached it, she met Diva scudding up towards her house. As soon as they got within speaking distance, they broke into telegraphic phrases, being both rather out of breath.

"Bath chair came out of Suntrap," began Miss Mapp.

"Thought so," panted Diva. "Saw it through the open door yesterday."

"Went down towards the High Street," said Miss Mapp.

"I passed it twice," said Diva proudly.

"What's she like?" asked Miss Mapp. "Only got glimpse."

"Quite old," said Diva. "Should think between fifty and sixty. How long ago did you see her at the music hall?"

"Ten years. But she seemed quite young then. . . . Come into the garden room, Diva. We shall see in both directions from there, and we can talk quietly."

The two ladies hurried into the bow window of the garden room, and having now recovered their breath, went on less spasmodically.

"That's very puzzling, you know," said Miss Mapp. "I'm sure it wasn't more than ten years ago, and as I say, she seemed quite young. But of course make-up can do a great deal, and also I should think impersonation was a very ageing life. Ten years of it might easily have made her an old woman."

"But hardly as old as this," said Diva. "And she's quite lame: two sticks, and even then great difficulty in walking. Was she lame when you saw her on the stage?"

"I can't remember that," said Miss Mapp. "Indeed, she could have been lame, for she was Romeo, and swarmed up to a high balcony. What was her face like?"

"Kind and nice," said Diva, "but much wrinkled and a good deal of moustache."

Miss Mapp laughed in a rather unkind manner.

"That would make the male impersonation easier," she said. "Go on, Diva. What else?"

"She stopped at the grocer's, and Cannick came hurrying out in the most sycophantic manner. And she ordered something—I couldn't hear what—to be sent up to Suntrap. Also she said some name, which I couldn't hear, but I'm sure it wasn't Lady Deal. That would have caught my ear at once."

Miss Mapp suddenly pointed down the street.

"Look! there's Cannick's boy coming up now," she said. "They have been quick. I suppose that's because she's a viscountess. I'm sure I wait hours sometimes for what I order. Such a snob! I've got an idea!"

She flew out into the street.

"Good morning, Thomas," she said. "I was wanting to order—let me see now, what was it? What a heavy basket you've got. Put it down on my steps, while I recollect."

The basket may have been heavy, but its contents were not, for it contained but two small parcels. The direction on them was clearly visible, and having ascertained that, Miss Mapp ordered a pound of apples and hurried back to the garden room.

"To Miss Mackintosh, Suntrap," she said. "What do you make of that, Diva?"

"Nothing," said Diva.

"Then I'll tell you. Lady Deal wants to live down her past, and she has changed her name. I call that very deceitful, and I think worse of her than ever. Lucky that I could see through it."

"That's far-fetched," said Diva, "and it doesn't explain the rest. She's much older than she could possibly be if she was on the stage ten years ago, and she says she isn't Lady Deal at all. She may be right, you know."

Miss Mapp was justly exasperated, the more so because some faint doubt of the sort had come into her own mind, and it would be most humiliating if all her early and superior information proved false. But her vigorous nature rejected such an idea and she withered Diva.

"Considering I know that Lady Deal has taken Suntrap," she said, "and that she was a male impersonator, and that she did come down here some few days ago, and that this woman and her Bath chair came out of Suntrap, I don't think there can be much question about it. So that, Diva, is that."

Diva got up in a huff.

"As you always know you're right, dear," she said, "I won't stop to discuss it."

"So wise, darling," said Elizabeth.

Now Miss Mapp's social dictatorship among the ladies of Tilling had long been paramount, but every

now and then signs of rebellious upheavals showed
themselves. By virtue of her commanding personality
these had never assumed really serious proportions,
for Diva, who was generally the leader in these upris-
ings, had not the same moral massiveness. But now
when Elizabeth was so exceedingly superior, the
fumes of Bolshevism mounted swiftly to Diva's head.
Moreover, the sight of this puzzling male impersonator, old, wrinkled, and moustached, had kindled to a
greater heat her desire to know her and learn what it
felt like to be Romeo on the music-hall stage and, after years of that delirious existence, to subside into a
Bath chair and Suntrap and Tilling. What a wonderful life! . . . And behind all this there was a vague
notion that Elizabeth had got her information in some
clandestine manner and had muddled it. For all her
clear-headedness and force Elizabeth did sometimes
make a muddle, and it would be sweeter than honey
and the honeycomb to catch her out. So in a state of
brooding resentment Diva went home to lunch and
concentrated on how to get even with Elizabeth.

Now it had struck her that Mrs. Bartlett, the wife
of the Vicar of Tilling, had not been so staggered
when she was informed at the choir practice of the
identity and of the lurid past of the new parishioner
as might have been expected: indeed, Mrs. Bartlett
had whispered, "Oh, dear me, how exciting—I mean,
how shocking," and Diva suspected that she did not
mean "shocking." So that afternoon she dropped in at
the Vicarage with a pair of socks which she had
knitted for the Christmas tree at the workhouse,
though that event was still more than three months
away. After a cursory allusion to her charitable errand, she introduced the true topic.

"Poor woman!" she said. "She was being wheeled

about the High Street this morning and looked so lonely. However many males she has impersonated, that's all over for her. She'll never be Romeo again."

"No indeed, poor thing!" said Mrs. Bartlett: "and, dear me, how she must miss the excitement of it. I wonder if she'll write her memoirs: most people do if they've had a past. Of course, if they haven't, there's nothing to write about. Shouldn't I like to read Lady Deal's memoirs! But how much more exciting to hear her talk about it all, if we only could!"

"I feel just the same," said Diva, "and besides, the whole thing is mysterious. What if you and I went to call? Indeed I think it's almost your duty to do so, as the clergyman's wife. Her settling in Tilling looks very like repentance, in which case you ought to set the example, Evie, of being friendly."

"But what would Elizabeth Mapp say?" asked Mrs. Bartlett. "She thought nobody ought to know her."

"Pooh," said Diva. "If you'll come and call, Evie, I'll come with you. And is it really quite certain that she is Lady Deal?"

"Oh, I hope so," said Evie.

"Yes, so do I, I'm sure, but all the authority we have for it at present is that Elizabeth said that Lady Deal had taken Suntrap. And who told Elizabeth that? There's too much Elizabeth in it. Let's go and call there, Evie: now, at once."

"Oh, but dare we?" said the timorous Evie. "Elizabeth will see us. She's sketching at the corner there."

"No, that's her morning sketch," said Diva. "Besides, who cares if she does?"

The socks for the Christmas tree were now quite forgotten, and with this parcel still unopened, the two ladies set forth, with Mrs. Bartlett giving fearful side-long glances this way and that. But there were no signs of Elizabeth, and they arrived undetected at Suntrap, and enquired if Lady Deal was in.

"No, ma'am," said Susie, "Her ladyship was only here for two nights settling Miss Mackintosh in, but she may be down again tomorrow. Miss Mackintosh is in."

Susie led the way to the drawing room, and there, apparently, was Miss Mackintosh.

"How good of you to come and call on me," she said. "And will you excuse my getting up? I am so dreadfully lame. Tea, Susie, please!"

Of course it was a disappointment to know that the lady in the Bath chair was not the repentant male impersonator, but the chill of that was tempered by the knowledge that Elizabeth had been completely at sea, and how far from land, no one yet could conjecture. Their hostess seemed an extremely pleasant woman, and under the friendly stimulus of tea even brighter prospects disclosed themselves.

"I love Tilling already," said Miss Mackintosh, "and Lady Deal adores it. It's her house, not mine, you know—but I think I had better explain it all, and then I've got some questions to ask. You see, I'm Florence's old governess, and Susie is her old nurse, and Florence wanted to make us comfortable, and at the same time to have some little house to pop down to herself when she was utterly tired out with her work."

Diva's head began to whirl. It sounded as if Florence was Lady Deal, but then, according to the *Peerage*, Lady Deal was Helena Herman. Perhaps she was Helena Florence Herman.

"It may get clearer soon," she thought to herself, "and, anyhow, we're coming to Lady Deal's work."

"Her work must be very tiring indeed," said Evie.

"Yes, she's very naughty about it," said Miss Mackintosh. "Girl guides, mothers' meetings, Primrose League, and now she's standing for Parliament. And it was so like her; she came down here last week, before I arrived, in order to pull furniture about and make the house comfortable for me when I got here. And she's coming back tomorrow to spend a week here, I hope. Won't you both come in and see her? She longs to know Tilling. Do you play bridge by any chance? Florence adores bridge."

"Yes, we play a great deal in Tilling," said Diva. "We're devoted to it too."

"That's capital. Now, I'm going to insist that you should both dine with us tomorrow, and we'll have a rubber and a talk. I hope you both hate majority calling as much as we do."

"Loathe it," said Diva.

"Splendid. You'll come, then. And now I long to know something. Who was the mysterious lady who called here in the afternoon when Florence came down to move furniture, and returned an hour or two afterwards and asked for the card she had left with instructions that it should be given to Lady Deal? Florence is thrilled about her. Some short name, Tap or Rap. Susie couldn't remember it."

Evie suddenly gave vent to a shrill cascade of squeaky laughter.

"Oh, dear me," she said. "That would be Miss Mapp. Miss Mapp is a great figure in Tilling. And she called! Fancy!"

"But why did she come back and take her card away?" asked Miss Mackintosh. "I told Florence that Miss Mapp had heard something dreadful about her. And how did she know that Lady Deal was coming here at all? The house was taken in my name."

"That's just what we all long to find out," said Diva eagerly. "She said that somebody in London told her."

"But who?" asked Miss Mackintosh. "Florence only settled to come at lunchtime that day, and she told her butler to ring up Susie and say she would be arriving."

Diva's eyes grew round and bright with inductive reasoning.

"I believe we're on the right tack," she said. "Could she have received Lady Deal's butler's message, do you think? What's your number?"

"Tilling 76," said Miss Mackintosh.

Evie gave three ecstatic little squeaks.

"Oh, that's it; that's it!" she said. "Elizabeth Mapp is Tilling 67. So careless of them, but all quite plain. And she did hear it from somebody in London. Quite true, and so dreadfully false and misleading, and so like her. Isn't it, Diva? Well, it does serve her right to be found out."

Miss Mackintosh was evidently a true Tillingite.

"How marvellous!" she said. "Tell me much more about Miss Mapp. But let's go back. Why did she take that card away?"

Diva looked at Evie, and Evie looked at Diva.

"You tell her," said Evie.

"Well, it was like this," said Diva. "Let us suppose that she heard the butler say that Lady Deal was coming—"

"And passed it on," interrupted Miss Mackintosh. "Because Susie got the message and said it was wonderfully clear for a trunk call. That explains it. Please go on."

"And so Elizabeth Mapp called," said Diva, "and left her card. I didn't know that until you told me just now. And now I come in. I met her that very afternoon, and she told me that Lady Deal, so she had heard in London, had taken this house. So we looked up Lady Deal in a very old *Peerage* of hers—"

Miss Mackintosh waved her arms wildly.

"Oh, please stop, and let me guess," she cried. "I shall go crazy with joy if I'm right. It was an old *Peerage*, and so she found that Lady Deal was Helena Herman—"

"Whom she had seen ten years ago at a music hall as a male impersonator," cried Diva.

"And didn't want to know her," interrupted Miss Mackintosh.

"Yes, that's it, but that is not all. I hope you won't mind, but it's too rich. She saw you this morning coming out of your house in your Bath chair, and was quite sure that you were *that* Lady Deal."

The three ladies rocked with laughter. Sometimes one recovered, and sometimes two, but they were re-infected by the third, and so they went on, solo and chorus, and duet and chorus, till exhaustion set in.

"But there's still a mystery," said Diva at length, wiping her eyes. "Why did the *Peerage* say that Lady Deal was Helena Herman?"

"Oh, that's the last Lady Deal," said Miss Mackintosh. "Helena Herman's Lord Deal died without children, and Florence's Lord Deal, my Lady Deal, succeeded. Cousins."

"If that isn't a lesson for Elizabeth Mapp," said Diva. "Better go to the expense of a new *Peerage* than make such a muddle. But what a long call we've made. We must go."

"Florence shall hear every word of it tomorrow night," said Miss Mackintosh. "I promise not to tell her till then. We'll all tell her."

"Oh, that is kind of you," said Diva.

"It's only fair. And what about Miss Mapp being told?"

"She'll find it out by degrees," said the ruthless Diva. "It will hurt more in bits."

"Oh, but she mustn't be hurt," said Miss Mackintosh. "She's too precious, I adore her."

"So do we," said Diva. "But we like her to be found out occasionally. You will, too, when you know her."